ALSO BY KIERAN KRAMER

Sweet Talk Me

THE HOUSE OF BRADY SERIES
Loving Lady Marcia
The Earl Is Mine
Say Yes to the Duke

THE IMPOSSIBLE BACHELOR SERIES
When Harry Met Molly
Dukes to the Left of Me, Princes to the Right
Cloudy with a Chance of Marriage
If You Give a Girl a Viscount

YOU'RE SO
Fine

KIERAN KRAMER

St. Martin's Paperbacks

This is a work of fiction. All of the characters, organizations, and events portrayed in this novel are either products of the author's imagination or are used fictitiously.

YOU'RE SO FINE

Copyright © 2015 by Kieran Kramer.
Excerpt from *Trouble When You Walked In* copyright © 2015 by Kieran Kramer.

All rights reserved.

For information address St. Martin's Press, 175 Fifth Avenue, New York, NY 10010.

ISBN: 978-1-250-00992-0

Printed in the United States of America

St. Martin's Paperbacks edition / January 2015

St. Martin's Paperbacks are published by St. Martin's Press, 175 Fifth Avenue, New York, NY 10010.

To all mothers,
especially my cousin Patrice Morris and my late cousin
Lizzie Brinkman Larson

"My mother taught me to walk proud and tall
as if the world was mine."
—Sophia Loren

ACKNOWLEDGMENTS

Every book is a labor of love, and that caring and effort extend well beyond my own office walls. I have to thank the loving, smart, absolutely fun family at St. Martin's Press for always believing in me, especially my brilliant editor Jennifer Enderlin. I'm also tremendously grateful to Annelise Robey and the Jane Rotrosen Agency for their unflagging support. I'd like to hug every writer friend of mine—the old and the new, the beginners and the experts—and tell them that they've kept me going through thick and thin. We are a community bonded beyond measure in a way that only we understand. But we're so willing to share our knowledge, aren't we? And we're always ready to lift each other up, including those storytellers among us who haven't dared put pen to paper yet. We get you, so join a writers' group. Meet other writers! We all started from the beginning, with an empty page. I highly recommend joining Romance Writers of America, an organization I'm proud to belong to (rwa.org). Finally, I'd like to thank my family, all of whom have given so much of themselves to help me reach my dreams. I can never repay any of you for your selflessness, but know that I love you to the moon and back times infinity.

CHAPTER ONE

Lacey Clark was one of those GRITS women—a Girl Raised In The South—and knew all about Scarlett O'Hara and Tara and how to hang on during rough times. Out in LA she thought she'd escaped a bottom-of-the-barrel existence, but now she was right back where she started, home again—the same way she'd left it, too, with only a few dollars in her pocket.

Still, she did have Henry, her five-year-old son.

In his tiny cubby of a room, she dutifully got him into bed and tucked him in tight with a threadbare quilt, her heart squeezing with a love so strong she knew she could take whatever craziness life threw at her because she had something bigger and better—the love of this little man. His hand curled in hers, and his lips, puffy and dry from keeping the car window down for three thousand miles, curved like a slice of watermelon, sweet and pink.

"Tell me a story, Mama." Henry's husky boy voice sounded like snakes and snails and puppy dog tails— along with jellyfish and horseshoe crab carcasses, his new favorite things.

The rain came down something fierce, but the weatherman said it'd all clear out by morning, which was a good thing. Lacey had a life to build from scratch. "How about the story of the brave little boy who crossed the country in an old ambulance and survived on white powdered doughnuts and hot dogs?"

"Hey!" Henry grinned. "That's me!"

"Yeah, well"—she smoothed his hair back—"you'd think it was you. But this boy was named Frank. And he was a secret spy."

"He *was*?"

"Uh-huh." She wished *she'd* had spy skills in LA. She'd never have allowed herself to get caught up in the privileged life she'd lived the past five years. She should have known it was all a mirage, a silly game she'd been playing, too good to be true. What kind of mother let her life implode like that?

Never again.

"Where's *our* house, Mama?" Henry's clear brown eyes were worried. "You said we can't stay here very long. I wish we could."

"Home is wherever you and me are together, right?" She smiled at her boy. It was a miracle how her young, naive self had also apparently contained a deep well of wisdom that had guided her to the best decision of her life: to adopt the infant son of her first Hollywood boyfriend, a wannabe actor who'd cheated on her with a seventeen-year-old aspiring actress and become a father as a result.

But Henry still looked troubled.

"We'll have six weeks of fun here," she said, "but after that, we need to move on."

Here was Indigo Beach, South Carolina, in the ultimate of cool rentals, a lighthouse. Lacey's name wasn't on the lease. Nope, Callum, her most recent actor ex-boyfriend, had signed off on it. But she and Henry were staying anyway.

Hell, yes, they were staying. Callum—the loser—was

madly in love with her former boss Monique, the up-and-coming French actress who'd hired Lacey as her personal assistant. Both of them had roles in the movie being filmed on Indigo, but they'd followed their selfish Hollywood hearts and run off together to Italy instead, to a bigger and better movie, leaving their lawyers and agents to handle the fallout at work and Lacey to kick herself for being an extremely slow learner when it came to getting romantically involved with actors.

It wasn't her fault that Callum's agent—a twice-divorced woman—had pitied her, handed over the key to the lighthouse, and told her to "have the vacay of a lifetime."

But being here wasn't about escape for her. She didn't want to think of all she'd have to accomplish in six weeks: get a temporary job and make some money, enough to go somewhere less expensive where she and Henry could start over being—she had to face it—rootless again.

"I want to stay in this town," Henry said. "I like it."

"You've only seen the gas station." She chuckled.

Above the rain, she heard a car door slam shut.

"What was that?" Henry's brow creased, the same way it had when she'd first held him at the hospital, and he'd looked up at her with those dark brown infant eyes, a lost boy—a boy who had neither father nor mother who wanted him. *I want you*, she'd thought, shocking herself with the realization that she'd found her first starring role, and it was a doozie. "I thought no one was coming here for a while," he added, his voice scraping like a plastic kid's shovel over sand, his nighttime voice.

Lacey stood. "It's probably the pizza man delivering to the wrong address," she said smoothly, but no one came out this way and in this kind of weather unless they had a reason. Her heart pounded like the dance floor at a honky-tonk on a Saturday night. "Don't you worry a thing. Just close your eyes and I'll take care of this." She leaned down and blew out the candle in front of the solitary window. "'Night. I promise I'll finish Frank's story tomorrow."

"Yeah." Henry's eyelids drooped. "'Night, Mama."

She shut the door, walked briskly through her own connecting bedroom, then raced down the spiral stairs, glad for the loud downpour and her bare feet. *Dear God, let him sleep and dream, lulled by the rain. The sea.*

At the bottom of the stairs, a cozy brass lantern lamp on the kitchen counter glowed yellow behind its old paper shade. She strode past the plank table and heard a grunt, a clattering of metal against metal. Visions of ax murderers made her turn back and grab the flashlight lying on the counter. A second later she was at the thick wooden arched door. No window, no peephole. On the other side was a small portico, but it wouldn't provide much cover for whoever stood out there.

She felt very much like the Cowardly Lion until she thought of Henry. And then she was Dirty Harry and Indiana Jones, all rolled into one. "Who's there?" she called coolly.

"Can you give me a hand with this door?" a man shouted above the torrent.

The keyhole rattled, but the door stayed shut.

She knew that voice. She did. And she wasn't scared of it. Annoyed, yes. But . . .

How did she know that voice?

Adrenaline made her throat tight. "You're at the wrong place," she called. "This is a private residence."

"Yeah, I know. Hurry it up, please. The rain's coming down sideways, and this Louis Vuitton bag ain't cheap."

He said *ain't* with all the insouciance of a true Southern male. Whether gentleman or redneck, they knew a guy's worth had nothing to do with his grammar, how much money he had in the bank, or what his ancestors' names were. It was about how well he could hold a rifle, drink his bourbon, and tell a good story.

Her guard went up another notch. "I'm sorry you're miserable, but I'm not letting you in. Only a fool would open the door to a stranger these days."

Especially when you're a woman alone with a precious child upstairs.

She held the flashlight tightly. If he stormed the door, she'd clonk him on the head with it if she had to.

"You think a psycho killer would bother having this conversation? If you're the Molly Maid people, you're going to regret leaving me out here. I'll be tracking in sand and—"

"I'm not the cleaning service." Her heart hammered against her ribs. "I'm telling you again, sir. I'm not letting you in. I'm about to call the police. So you'd better skedaddle."

"Skedaddle, my ass!" He gave a good thunk on the door. "But hey, what's a little more water? And a little more humiliation? I've endured plenty the last couple of days. Oh, yes, indeedy."

She was the one with the sob story, so she wasn't going to feel sorry for him. But somehow she did. All Southern men could hold TED talks about how to charm the ladies.

Don't go soft on him.

"You should get back in your car," she said. "I don't care how wet you and your luggage are. When are you men gonna take responsibility for your own choices? I'm so sick of y'all expecting women to be your mothers. Honestly."

She was breathing a little hard, and her accent was coming back thicker than a Dagwood sandwich.

"Don't take your man woes out on me, girlfriend. And you can keep my mother out of this discussion, if you don't mind." There was a flash of lightning and an almost instantaneous clap of thunder. "Now, open the damned *door.*"

She swallowed hard and ignored her wobbly knees. Lightning didn't sit well with her. Neither did being responsible for a man getting fried on her doorstep. But she wouldn't panic. She couldn't afford to.

"Your key"—she said in her best no-nonsense voice—"doesn't work because you're at the wrong place. *I* have the lease here." It was a lie, but she was the double-crossed former employee and ex-girlfriend with no place to go. That had to count for something.

"That's it," the stranger said. "I'm calling Callum."

Lacey's eyes widened. "You know Callum?"

"Of course I know him. Why else would I be here? *You* know him?"

"Yes, but—" Callum lived on the West Coast. A local wouldn't know him. Unless—shoot. Unless he was somehow involved with the movie. Lacey's heart sank. She was hoping to steer clear of the movie and all the hoopla associated with it.

"Lady?"

"Yes?" She bit her thumbnail, wondering what he would say next to coax her to open the door.

"I'm telling you now." The man's tone was softer now, a little menacing. "I'm not going to drive to that crappy Beach Bum Inn and deal with this tomorrow. I have to get to work early in the morning, and I need my sleep. Callum said no one was here and to make myself at home. I intend to do that. With or without your permission. And with or without the proper key."

Lacey drew a breath. "I'm going to let you in," she said slowly. "But only for a minute."

"About damned time."

With shaking hands—but ready to do battle—she opened the door. A huge crack of thunder split the air.

"You're in my lighthouse," he said in toneless greeting and strode past her—*whoosh*—like a freight train without brakes heading downhill. He wore old jeans, Red Wing boots, and a brown quail jacket with the corduroy brim popped up, not for show, it appeared, but to keep off the rain. Beneath the coat was a ratty mustard brown sweater vest with braided leather buttons and underneath that, a faded red Henley open at the neck.

He was about her age, with hard cheekbones and a distinctly pissed-off demeanor that intensified when he turned to look directly at her, water streaming off his high-crowned, wide-brimmed sable fedora.

Her heart nearly stopped in her chest.

It was Beau Wilder. *The* Beau Wilder. Box-office superstar. He'd worked his way up through coming-of-age comedies and slasher flicks to gladiator dramas, legal thrillers, and action-adventures. Hollywood wasn't putting out many romantic comedies these days, but when they did, he was their go-to leading man.

"Holy bejeezus." Even as a Hollywood insider of sorts, she was gobsmacked.

"Uh-huh, I know," he said dismissively.

He hadn't shaved for days—typical behavior for your average macho male celebrity—but he was Ralph Lauren handsome, too, tall and broad-shouldered. A man's man, for sure, but distinguished—elegant, even—in the way that a sweaty, mud-laden horse with highly muscled flanks is when it wins the Kentucky Derby.

Shock—and, she had to admit it, *awe*—were quickly replaced by indignation. His eyes were bloodshot, and he reeked of alcohol. "I've got some bad news for you, Mr. Wilder." Her voice shook just a little, but he was only a man—and an actor at that. "This isn't your lighthouse."

"For the next two months it is," he shot back and dropped his bag with a thunk, managing to avoid the puddle forming at his feet. "I traded Callum four front-row seats to a Lakers game to get this place. That's a business transaction. I have rights."

"You don't really expect me to buy that." She laced her right arm over her left. "You're in a *light*house. Not a courthouse. I'm not your perp, and *you're* drunk."

She shifted on her feet, nervous again because suddenly he exuded unholy joy, his eyes glowing the same green golden-brown as the tips of marsh grass caught in a beam of sunlight.

"Well, I'll be," he said. "You're the hot tamale who starred in *Biker Aliens*."

Released online-only, five years ago. It had gone viral, too, but in a bad way. Which was why Lacey was no longer a natural blonde. She tossed her head. "Don't get sexist with me, Mr. Stud Muffin."

"Oh, for crying out loud. It was a compliment." He lofted a *very* suggestive brow. "Greta."

He might be a pain in her backside right now, but, Lord, he drew the eye. And he'd seen her movie. She couldn't believe it! Her whole body responded to the new energy he put out—at her expense, yes, but she'd always liked bad people. Really bad people. Not pretend ones who rebelled because they needed attention but people who bucked the system because they were too smart to stay bored—too selfish to sacrifice fun.

Like her.

But she was done. Done with bad people and the excitement they brought into her life. For Henry's sake, she was willing to learn bored. There had to be something to it.

"You look like *I Love Lucy* now," he said. "But you're still Greta Gildensturm. You can't hide those eyes, or that—that—"

Despite her warnings, he gazed at her as if she were

Cool Whip and he was the spoon—which, considering the source, she knew she should find flattering. But she was over all that malarkey and over all the men who did it, even one-in-a-billion men like Mr. Beau Hot Stuff Wilder. And because he must have valued his life, he didn't finish the sentence.

"Her name was Lucy Ricardo, not *I Love Lucy*." She made a *duh* face. "That was the name of the show." And she refused to acknowledge her character's name in *Biker Aliens*. She'd refuse to her dying day. She'd refuse even after death, if that were possible. She'd come and haunt anyone who tried to put her and Greta Gildensturm together.

"She'll always be I Love Lucy to me." He was smug. Still a little drunk. But damned cute. And bad clear through.

Oh, God. The worst kind of man.

And the best kind of movie star.

She crossed her arms over her ample breasts, which she'd declined to have reduced. Her back didn't hurt. So why should she? Was it her fault that God made her that way? And she was scared of doctors and knives and, oh, anything that had to do with medicine, including Band-Aids and Luden's cherry cough drops, which she'd choked on once when she was five.

So it would be a cold day in hell when she got a breast reduction.

"Let me get this straight," she said. "If you meet someone who looks like Theodore Cleaver, you're gonna say, you look like *Leave It to Beaver*? Does that make sense?"

He didn't seem to be listening. "And you were just in the news. You were a brunette when you did it, but you spilled a whole pitcher of margaritas over Callum's head at a West Hollywood restaurant with Monique Bonnay sitting right next to him. Don't tell me you wanted to break up those two lovebirds. They deserve each other." He lifted a wet cigar to his mouth and clamped down on it, grinning. "Yep, *Biker Aliens* and Greta Gildensturm both trended on Twitter that day."

But not Lacey Clark. No one knew her real name because she wasn't a memorable enough actress, was she? She wasn't even memorable enough to get on *Survivor* or any B-list Hollywood reality show. She was on the F list. F for failure. And there was a much worse F word to apply to her acting career, but she was a lady, and she wouldn't use it, much less think it.

Which might explain why she liked fudge so much. And they made a lot of it on Indigo Beach. That was one good thing about being here.

"You can go to hell." Lacey angled her chin at the open door. "And lose the cigar while you're at it."

His grin disappeared, and he threw the cigar outside. "Wow. You really *are* a buzzkill."

"Apparently guys like you have nothing better to do than point that out."

"Guys like me?"

He might think he was one of a kind. But he wasn't. There were plenty spoiled, rich, handsome, charming men—many of them *actors*, a word she could barely say anymore without seeing red—who'd been blessed with a confidence they hadn't earned. But she wouldn't bother to explain. His kind was too arrogant to get it.

"Callum may be a jackass," he said, "but I'm not Callum. So lay off the I-hate-men routine, please, until you see the guy—or guys—who've actually done you wrong. 'Kay?"

"Fine." She felt a small stab of guilt—but not on his behalf. Oh, no. He'd merely reminded her that she'd let Callum off too easy. "I'll overlook your general lack of sensitivity and make you a cup of coffee." Maybe she'd find out how he knew Callum. "But then you're leaving. If you're not sober enough to drive thirty minutes from now, I'll call the sheriff to pick you up. Now, that's a Tweet that would trend! Why don't you get on there right now and let everyone know you were driving under the influence?"

The rain fell steadily but with less force. It had wimped out, something she wasn't going to do anymore.

"I didn't drive," he said, "and I'm not going anywhere. Nor do I tweet. My assistant does." He went to the door. "Thanks, doll," he called to someone and blew a kiss.

There was the honk of a horn, and then the loud, sputtering sound of a car engine starting up.

"Wait!" Lacey pushed past him. "Was that your assistant?" From the light of the small sconce on the portico, she caught a glimpse of a silhouette of big pageant hair in the driver's seat of a white Ford pickup truck. It spun up some sand and took off, its oversized tires and raised chassis rocking like mad over the uneven surface of the drive as it sped away. Lacey recognized monster truck rally mania when she saw it.

Over her shoulder, Beau Wilder murmured, "You could call her that. For the past twenty-four hours."

"Ewww."

He shook his head, a ghost of a smile on his lips as he watched her go. "I love a woman who can drive like a bat outta hell. Cooks up a storm, too. Homemade biscuits and ham this morning, along with her mama's own peach jam. Suh-weet."

And he didn't mean about the jam, either. That much was obvious.

Lacey had had enough. "You'll have to walk or text your one-day assistant for a ride. If she's not here in half an hour, I'm calling the police."

He pulled out his phone. "I don't think so. *You're* trespassing. Not me." He dialed a number and held the phone to his ear.

"Who are you calling?" Her heart pounded.

"Sheriff's office." His face was serene.

"*No*." She swiped at his phone.

But he swiftly lifted his arm. "Why not? You're about to call them anyway."

"We can solve this," she said, realizing too late that he'd only pretended to dial, "without contacting the authorities." She stared him down like a viper hypnotizing its prey.

Mr. Wilder cocked his head. "Whoa."

To intensify the effect, she put her hand on her right hip and turned her left foot out.

But all he did was send her a searing look—he was good at that—and tuck the phone back in his pocket. "Were you ever an evil first-grade teacher in another life? Because I swear you're channeling Mrs. Biddle right now. She's why I hate naps and milk in little cartons to this day."

"You were the nonstop talker, weren't you? Or the sly boy who hid on the playground at the end of recess."

"Don't change the subject. I thought you were all about getting the police involved."

A flush of heat spread across her chest and up her neck. "Why should I? I've got a lease. You don't. Your consolation prize is that cup of coffee, and then you're outta here. Deal with it."

"Little lady"—he opened his jacket and pulled out a plastic grocery bag with an oblong shape inside—"since I'm actually where I'm supposed to be, and you might be kinda cute when you're not frowning—I'll try to be patient. I've got a steak, and I'm about to cook it. And then I'm going to sit back and enjoy my new place, me and Jim Beam, since the liquor store was all out of Jack." He tossed the steak on the table, pulled a silver flask out of another pocket, twisted off the cap, and took a swig.

"Sorry, but you're not invited, although I could be persuaded to change my mind." He arched that famous brow at her.

"Forget it."

"Are you sure?"

"Yes."

Their eyes met, and for a split second she thought he saw everything she'd been trying to hide.

He advanced toward her, his tread slow, careful. She wasn't in physical danger. That she knew. His was the careful walk of a man who was either still drunk or hungover—hardly aggressive. But it was more than that. He approached her the way he'd done that poor lame horse that had to be put down in the only Western he'd ever made.

She stuck her chin up. No need to feel sorry for her. She was A-okay. She had a head on her shoulders, and she'd been through the wringer in the craziest town on the West Coast and come out on the other side not totally crushed. And man, had she seen some people out in LA plowed over, innocents like her who'd gone out there to find themselves and lost themselves instead.

But Hollywood crazy had nothing on Southern crazy. *Therefore*, she told herself as she exhaled through her nose, *I can handle anything, including this man*.

When he was a mere foot away, he stopped. "If you're hoping Callum's gonna show," he said in that velvety-rough Southern drawl that had melted millions of women's hearts, "I hate to tell you this—he's not coming. But you can keep me company for a couple of hours instead. If your heart's broken, that is." He chucked her chin softly. "Maybe that accounts for your ornery attitude."

She pushed past him, her hands trembling, and straightened the place mats on one side of the table. Dancing blue crab and shrimp. Henry loved them. "I'm not heartbroken." She looked up. "And you're obviously a womanizer, a trait I find a complete turnoff. How do you know Callum anyway?"

"He accidentally on purpose runs into me all the time at the gym. He says he wants to lift weights with me, but he's too busy kissing my ass to be a good spotter. He's after my agent and wants an in."

"Is that why he gave you a key to this place?"

"Probably. I threw in the Lakers seats so I don't owe him a favor. No way am I referring him to my agent. What are *you* doing here?"

He had her there. "He owes me."

"Didn't you get your revenge at that restaurant?"

"You know what?" She sent him her best withering look. "I really don't need any actors around here."

Understatement of the century.

She needed sleep, salt air, wind, and Henry. She needed a job, too.

"It's a moot point," he replied. "You're not staying."

"Yes, I am." Her words might as well have been hammered into rock by a big, sweaty hand gripping a chisel, they were so solid. "You may be a big star, but I got here first. That counts for something under the law. You'll have to pry me outta here by my fingernails, you hear? Or spend weeks trying to evict me. Your publicist won't appreciate the news stories that'll come out of that."

The corner of his mouth crooked. "Here's your problem, Greta. You overact. All Southerners do. It's in our blood to live larger than life. Doesn't matter if we come from a trailer park or a mansion. It's our thing. But here's a secret: If you want to make it big in Hollywood, you gotta bury your own heart. It's easy for me. I don't have one."

"Look at you," she said, "throwing drama right back at me. Of course you have a heart. You couldn't have played all those roles without one."

"You saying I'm good?"

"*No*." She gave another short laugh. Was he kidding? She wasn't going to say that, not when he was trying to throw her out on her ear! "I'm just saying I see why maybe you make the big bucks. *Maybe*."

She winced. It was not intended to be a smile in any way, shape, or form, so it annoyed her when he chuckled.

He pulled down a frying pan hanging over the sink, released it with a quick twirling motion through the air, then caught it right above the stovetop and set it down on a burner. "I'm not used to sharing, Miz Greta."

Big baby. Which didn't jibe with his knowing his way around a kitchen, but that was probably a fluke.

He flicked on the gas, and a bright blue flame appeared beneath the pan. Over his shoulder, he said, "This lighthouse is out of the way, and it's big enough for just one person—me. Now in Casa Wilder, I fry up a steak the night before I start work on a movie set. I also give damsels in distress breaks if they cooperate, at least until morning. You'll be packed and ready to go."

He sprinkled salt in the pan. Then he unwrapped the steak—just held one end of the paper and let it roll out into the pan. It was probably the way women unwrapped themselves for him all the time.

The sizzling smell made Lacey hungry. She'd been going light lately to save her food money for Henry. Tonight she'd made him scrambled eggs, but there were only three left, so she'd saved them for tomorrow and had eaten a peanut-butter-and-jelly sandwich instead.

"Well," she huffed. "I can tell you think the sun comes up just to hear you crow, Mr. Wilder. But I've had enough of your talk. If you insist on staying, I'm going up. But don't you *dare* smoke inside, leave the stovetop on, abandon dirty dishes in the sink, or walk around naked. I'm armed with a Colt .45, and I'm not afraid to use it."

She turned on her heel, hoping he believed her lie about the gun. She wouldn't tell him about the Heinz 57 sauce she'd found in the cupboard yesterday, either. He could eat his dadblasted steak without it.

CHAPTER TWO

Beau was a little drunk, but he saw that Lacey Clark hadn't been acting in *Biker Aliens* when she'd taken on the role of Greta. She'd played herself—a Southern-fried version of Kate Upton with a little bit of Marilyn Monroe and Cher—yes, mouthy, offbeat Cher—thrown in. She was lush. Sexy as hell. The kind of woman every man wanted in his bed, with meat on her bones and a face that rocked the classic male fantasy, all pouty swagger one minute and fresh-off-the-farm country girl the next.

And the unaccountability of her slings and arrows kept a man waiting for it, waiting for it . . . What man didn't like a little danger?

She was some kind of woman. The kind he didn't need.

He was better off focusing on the steak. The smell of cooking beef reminded him of his dad, who insisted on having filets every Friday night. Beau remembered slicing through them with a sterling-silver knife, his fork clinking on Mom's fine bone china.

"You get the small room," Greta said, apparently an afterthought from near the stairs. "I earned the big one through years of hard work that went unappreciated. You're only here because you're rich enough to trade Lakers seats."

"Gotcha," he said nonchalantly without looking at her.

He could feel her resentment, the energy coming off her in big, invisible waves. Or maybe she was staring at his butt. Women tended to do that.

"Just so you know." He turned to face her.

She flushed pink. "What?"

"You're not going to boss me around. Maybe I've been a little liberal with the whiskey tonight. But I have just as much right to be here as you. In fact, I suspect more. Way more."

"First impressions don't lie, Mr. Wilder." Her breasts strained against a sexy wraparound top, and her hips, encased in dark-blue denim jeans, most certainly didn't lie, either. "Watch your step."

"I suggest you do the same."

He went back to his steak. But he could see her lingering out of the corner of his eye.

"I guess a limo will come pick you up in the morning to take you to the set, huh?" Her voice was chockful of bravado.

But he knew. She was wondering what time their next confrontation would be. "Nope. I'm running to the set."

"But it's miles down the beach."

"That's why I've got my running shoes."

"Movie people don't *run* to their sets."

"This one does." He flipped the steak. "You been hanging around the spoiled Hollywood crowd too long, Miz Gildensturm. Maybe it's rubbed off a little on *you*."

She advanced a few steps toward him. "But *you're* the spoiled Hollywood set. I read the papers, Mr. French Château."

"You got me there. I'm a real sumbitch when I'm in it, too. The servants have to call me *monsoor* and bring me

American-style french fries done up in truffle oil. They hate that."

"Hmmph" was all she said.

He smiled to himself. She was easy to rile.

Next second she was springing up the staircase, her feet making a hollow, *boing*-y noise on the metal steps. *Lithesome* and *light* were words that came to mind. Funny, because when he thought of Greta Gildensturm, he thought *voluptuous*, *dark*.

His dad used to go to his library and shut the door after steak night. The next morning, he and Beau would go off hunting or traipsing through the woods with Beau's best friend, Ricky.

Little rituals. They made you feel good. Safe.

But ultimately, they were a crock of shit.

Beau slid the medium-rare slab onto a plate, found some old tinfoil, wrapped it up, and put it in the fridge. Eff the steak. Eff everything but the new job, which was gonna suck.

No way around it.

He cleaned the pan, drank two glasses of water from the tap—surprisingly good—and walked around the kitchen for five minutes, opening and shutting cupboards, staring mindlessly at their contents, at the wallpaper, the table, and the old lamp, which he eventually switched off. And then he crossed the entryway, past the spiral stairs, and entered a darkened sitting room barely illuminated by a moonbeam peeking through the storm clouds.

He sat on a couch with questionable springs, put his head in his hands, and breathed deeply for a few minutes, his eyes shut, images jumbled in his mind: Imogene, an old friend who'd looked after him today in more ways than one; sloe-eyed Greta Gildensturm from the movie; this version of her tonight, pricklier than a guilty politician facing a Senate hearing; and the upcoming movie.

When the old contract intruded—full of legalese that had skewered him to the proverbial wall—he stood up. There was nothing to be done.

Or was there?

Maybe his agent could stay up all night with the attorneys and come up with a last-minute rescue plan.

"Susan," he said when she picked up.

"It's too late," she said right away. "We've gone over that contract with a fine-tooth comb. You're stuck, Beau."

He could hear her twin eleven-year-old girls shrieking in the background.

"If I break it—"

"Then you're in for a big legal mess. And you'll piss off some studio old-timers, including a few directors. They may not make movies anymore, but their opinions still hold sway with the younger movers-and-shakers. Just do it and get it behind you."

"I want to kill Randy."

"He's already dead."

"I know." He felt stupid hating on a dead man. But worse, he was an idiot for letting his old agent screw him over.

"Stop kicking yourself," Susan said. "You were young and ambitious and naive. There are growing pains in this business, like any other. You just happen to be hitting a big one."

"I should have read it line-by-line." His father had offered to pay for a lawyer to review that first contract for him—and Beau had said no. He hadn't wanted anything from his dad. And it had felt like a slap in the face, like Beau couldn't handle his own business.

"Suck it up," Susan said again. "It's only six weeks."

"Six weeks of hell. I don't like symbolism. And nuance. I like to speed to the airport to win the girl. Or blow things up. You know that."

"We can't always get what we want."

He thought of his new roommate. "Hey, one more thing. You ever heard of *Biker Aliens*? The character Greta Gildensturm?"

"Vaguely. I think I've heard a story about that actress, but I can't remember who she is or what the story was. Why?"

"Just wondering. She's here. We're sharing the lighthouse, at least for tonight. It was a big mix-up."

"You're sharing the lighthouse?" Susan was suddenly very alert. "Is she in the movie?"

"Oops, gotta go, Susan. Pot boiling over on the stove." He clicked off and shoved his phone in his jacket pocket. He didn't mind torturing her just a little.

He wished he'd tortured Randy a lot more, instead of buying everything he said at face value. He'd seemed so knowledgeable, so savvy. His agency passed all its contracts by an entertainment law firm in Los Angeles. He'd never said a word about the little codicil that demanded then-newbie-actor Beau make a short movie with an experimental little production company called Wilbur's Ears within eight years.

So when Beau got sent his umpteenth weird script from Wilbur's Ears this past week and sent it back, as usual, wondering why the heck they bothered with him— this time they wouldn't take no for an answer. He *would* be in the movie, called *Flowers from the Heart*.

The name alone made a man want to grab his gonads and go. But if he said no, he'd be in breach of that long-ago contract he'd signed.

And now Beau couldn't run anywhere but right off a cliff.

He picked up his bag near the door, and walked quietly up the spiral staircase and into the room with a wide-open door. The switch on the wall was stubborn. It turned on a ship-in-a-bottle lamp on the bedside table, casting an arc of light and shadow on the steep-sloped ceiling. Beneath it, a double bed covered in an old blue-and-yellow star quilt reminded him of long-ago camping days. *Remind me not to have crazy sex on it*, he thought. Not unless he wanted a concussion.

Another door outside his room was slightly ajar, so he went there next and tried to admire the cramped bathroom space for its vintage charm because he wasn't a snob, as much as he liked his luxuries. A vast bathroom space happened to be one of them, but the old house he grew up in never had big bathrooms. He could certainly make do.

A faded white claw-footed tub—deep and with a rust scratch on its curved lip—took up one wall. Above it, a chrome oval curtain rod suspended from the ceiling held a clean, clear plastic shower curtain—a dollar store buy, he was sure.

Greta naked in here flashed through his head.

No. Those kinds of thoughts weren't going to happen.

So he tried to think of the generations of hardy lighthouse keepers who'd lived here over the years. They'd had dangerous shoals and squalls to worry about, boats to keep safe. There wasn't time to think of women. They'd had jobs to do.

He'd be just the same.

But the last thought he had before he dropped off to sleep was *Hurricane Greta*.

Really, Lacey? she chided herself the next morning in her bedroom mirror as she put on her pink-peony-colored lipstick, lined her eyes Sophia Loren–style, and used up the last of her drugstore mascara. She brushed her hair back so it poufed on top—a retro look still popular in the South—and swept the rest up in a high ponytail cinched in a button band monogrammed with an *L*, a gift to herself from a kids' accessory store.

Next she put on some thick gold hoop earrings and slipped into her favorite yellow sundress—*yella*, as everyone said around these parts—along with flat open-toed gold-and-cream reptile-leather sandals, leftover Jack Rogers from Monique.

She did her own manis and pedis. She was a whiz, too, her hand steady and sure. Her fingernails were filed to graceful ovals, and they were polished the same pink-peony color as her toenails. Cheap dollar store lotion used to be her best friend, but now she was into coconut oil. A spoonful went a long way, so she measured it out carefully and used it in her hair, on her legs, and on her face.

Lacey loved dressing up and standing out. It was her thing. Always had been, and she wasn't vain. She did it because she liked color and fun and maybe occasionally, she did it for a little shock value. All the things Sheena steered clear of.

In the kitchen, she made another search through the cabinets for coffee. She tried to pretend she was only cranky because she needed caffeine, but the truth was she was disgusted with herself. She'd had a dream about Beau Wilder—not the real Beau Wilder, of course. It had been a mishmash of him in all his movie roles, an entirely implausible—*pleasurable*—dream in which they'd locked lips and made love.

She'd woken up with her pelvis pulsing with a legitimate mini orgasm, her brain flooded with crush feelings about the guy—the hot, powerful movie Beau who was sexy and protective and wanted only *her*—before she'd really come to and sat up, horrified at how sad and desperate she must be deep inside, beneath that layer of Cajun-Slim-Jim-and-Mountain-Dew sass she kept wrapped around herself for her own protection.

And Henry's.

Which reminded her, she needed to call Sheena and let her know they were there. Henry needed a grandmother, even if Lacey was doing just fine on her own. At the kitchen window, she watched the surf roll in a few seconds then dialed her mother on her text-only phone, bracing her stomach on the counter edge when someone picked up at the other end.

" 'Lo?" If the woman in the *American Gothic* painting could step out of the canvas wearing twenty-year-old floral-and-lace-collar thrift store dresses, she'd be Lacey's mom.

"Hey, Sheena. It's Lacey." For the millionth time, she wondered how her dreary mother could have been given the wildly extravagant name of Sheena and why she made her daughters call her by it.

There was a pause, a thunk, a pot against a sink. "Everything okay?"

That warmed a little piece of her. "Just fine." She kept her eye on the line where the sea met the sky. "I've got some news. Henry and I are back on this side of the country. For good."

"Really?"

"Yes, we're done with California."

"I'm glad." Not a hitch in her voice, nor a waver or inflection. "Where are you?"

Lacey hung on. She always did. "Indigo Beach for now." Maybe someday her mother would wake up. Sparkle. Lavish her with maternal adoration.

"That's right close to where we are." Sheena grew up in a holler in West Virginia. "How long will you be there?"

"Six weeks."

"Oh, my. What'll happen then?"

"I don't know, but it's a place to start looking at options."

There was a long sigh at the other end of the phone. "Oh, Lacey. I worry about you."

Really? It felt way more like judgment to her, which was why her gut was tighter than a sail cinched hard against the wind. "You don't need to worry. I'm smart. I can handle whatever comes." *You could, too*, she wanted to add, and wrapped her free arm round her middle. It didn't mean she wasn't scared. She was scared so often, she didn't remember what it was like not to be. "Where's Walt?"

"At the hardware."

She figured. Her mother was always slightly more animated when he wasn't around. "How is he?"

"Fine. His heart's not nearly as skippy as it used to be. The meds seem to work."

"I'm glad he's doing better." But the truth was, Lacey didn't give a hoot about Walt. Yes, he was the only one of five Thompson brothers who'd managed to get out of the coal mines before his twenty-fifth birthday. But he was an ass, and she hated how her mother was around him. "Where are y'all at the moment?"

"The Myrtle Beach Craft Expo."

"No kidding. You're really close." For all she knew, Sheena could have been as far away as Alabama or Tennessee. This was a sign. A good sign. "I remember that show well."

The RV park's playground equipment was always broken. Every year, a haughty woman wearing a magnificent black swan hat took tickets at the entrance. She'd hated the vendors' kids, who ran in and out squealing all the time.

"You and Devra loved the free hot chocolate," Sheena said.

Lacey heard a smile in her mother's voice and grinned. "We did, didn't we?" Truth be told, it had been a thrill to mix her own hot chocolate at the vendor's table. Watery. No more than lukewarm. But free. *Free* had been a big word in their household. She felt a tiny bit of hope. They were connecting, at least a little bit. "How's Devra?"

"Good. Kevin just bought the Rainbow vacuum dealership in Tuscaloosa. They traded in their little Hyundai for a yellow Pontiac Grand Am to impress the door-to-door clientele."

"Oh. Smart." She guessed. What did she know about vacuum buyers and their taste in cars?

"She's not pregnant yet, if that's what you're wondering."

"No, but I hope she will be soon." A seagull swooped in front of the window. "I know how much she wants a baby."

"In her own time." Sheena sighed. "She'll have a passel of 'em."

Cousins for Henry! Although Lacey and Devra weren't at all close. Lord knows, she'd tried winning her baby half sister over, but there was a disconnect there, and it went straight back to Walt, who was indifferent to any child who hadn't sprung from his loins and spoiled rotten the solitary one who had.

It made her sad, thinking of the thousands of hours she and Devra had spent together sleeping on the same pullout bed in the RV. But what could she do?

"Sold anything at the expo?" That was solid ground.

"Two bed quilts."

"Great!"

Sheena's bed quilts cost at least four hundred dollars. The really fancy ones—or the big ones—went for a thousand. She had a website now. Every once in a while, when Lacey could scrape together the money, she'd buy a $250 lap quilt with one of her LA friends' credit cards so Sheena wouldn't guess it was her. She had three in the back of the ambulance right now.

"Let's talk about *you*," Sheena said.

Uh-oh.

"Have you found a nice man yet?"

"*No.* I'd rather talk about the expo. Did you sell any kits?" Tying all those cut-out fabric squares into colorful little bundles was one of Lacey's main chores growing up. She'd do it while she listened to audiobooks on an old CD player.

"Lots of 'em. They're my most popular item. But you're not getting any younger, honey." Sheena's voice quivered with the nervous energy she usually suppressed when Walt was around.

"No one's getting any younger, and I'm doing just fine with that."

"And I know from experience"—Sheena wasn't listening *at all*—"that with a child in tow, it's gonna be that much harder to find someone."

"I don't *want* a man."

"Now, that's something you shouldn't say," Sheena said low, as if she was afraid the National Security Agency was listening in.

"Why not?" Lacey gave a little laugh. "I love 'em. But I love a lot of things that aren't good for me. A hot fudge sundae from Dairy Queen comes to mind. What has Walt done for you?"

"Besides be your stepfather, give me my second daughter—your sister—and support me all these years?"

"He hasn't supported you. Not in ways that matter outside the holler."

"I've told you that I don't want to hear that kind of talk." Sheena sounded starchy. "It's ungrateful. And I'm not a country bumpkin. Californians might be high-class folk, but that's no call to insult *me*."

"I'm sorry. I didn't mean to. All I meant was that you deserve more."

"More? What's wrong with being grateful for what you have? My values have stood the test of time, child. You could learn something from watching me."

Lacey had. And seen her mother's light dim with each passing year.

"Fine," she said softly. She hadn't meant for their conversation to take an ill turn. "Maybe I'll meet a man who'll wind up loving Henry and who sets my heart on fire, but if I don't, we'll be a fabulous twosome. And you'll be happy for me, no matter what."

"I don't understand you modern women."

"You should be glad I am one. And Sheena? I hope you sell more quilts at the expo." How would her mother's choices have been different if she hadn't tied her financial wagon to Walt's?

"I hope I do, too." Sheena sounded somewhat mollified. "But stop trying to change the subject. It would make me a lot happier to hear you're no longer floating around on your own. It's not right."

"You mean it embarrasses you to have a daughter who's a single mother."

Sheena didn't jump in to deny it.

Ask, Sheena. Ask about Henry!

But nothing happened.

"Your grandson's doing well," Lacey said, her jaw tight.

"I'm glad he is."

"His name is Henry. Remember?"

"Of course I do." There wasn't an ounce of embarrassment or remorse in Sheena's voice. "You tell Henry I said hello," she added, as if she actually had a relationship with him.

As if everything were normal.

Every year on his birthday, she sent him a flimsy card—the kind you get free in the mail from Save the

Whales—with her tight little scrawl: "To Henry, Happy Birthday from Sheena and Walt."

She couldn't even call herself *Grandma* or *Nana* or *Meemaw.* Or send him a lousy dollar.

Lacey's right foot beat a tattoo on the linoleum floor. "I expect you can tell him hello yourself. We're not more than a two hour's drive from y'all. Surely you can come over after the expo is over."

"We have to get to Birmingham and then down to Tuscaloosa for the Rainbow store's grand opening."

"One *day*, Sheena. That's all I ask."

"Why don't you come up here?" The old tightness in her voice was back, the tone she retreated to when you were asking too much of her. "We're busy. You know how it is, once we're done selling, we have to pack out."

Lacey's eyes stung. "I know you want to see him," she whispered. "You're my mother. He's my son. And I haven't seen you, either, in six years. Why are you making these excuses? You can pack up in an hour. I've seen you do it. *Tell Walt you want to come.*"

There was another clunking noise and water running. "I don't know if he'll agree."

It always came down to that.

"You tell him it would mean a lot to you to see your grandchild," Lacey said.

"You were *foolish* to adopt."

The words were like a whip. "Is that you talking? Or are you repeating what Walt says?"

"He's not here at the moment—"

"And you sound like a broken record. Talk to me, Sheena. I want to hear what *you* think."

There was silence on the line.

"Maybe Walt's jealous," Lacey said. "He's whiter than a fish belly, and he won't look too healthy standing next to

Henry. He always looks like he has a really good spray tan, and he's all boy. I've sent you pictures. Do you have them up somewhere? He's got sturdy little legs and a sparkle in his eye—"

"It's that you're unmarried and single, and it made no sense for you to adopt him."

Devra was the star. She was the one who was supposed to have children first.

Lacey swallowed hard. "Becoming Henry's mother is the only thing in my entire life that *does* make sense. I adopted him because I know exactly what it feels like to be alone at your very core. No one—*no one*—should have to experience that, least of all an innocent child. Now, you be happy for me, Sheena. You damned well better be happy, or—"

Or what? Lacey would never break off contact. Ever. Yet she was never more miserable than when she was talking to her mom.

"Why are you back East for good?" Sheena asked. "Is it because of what happened to you at that restaurant?"

"You saw it, huh?"

"Of course."

Lacey sank onto a chair. "I obviously broke up with Callum. I'm starting over. I'm going to try to get a job. A regular job like everyone else."

"You're finally done with Hollywood? That Monique—"

For years, Lacey had heard *That Monique*. "You were right. I shouldn't have trusted her."

"Any woman who'd throw out a brand-new pair of shoes—"

"She was wasteful. And spoiled. I know. I *knew*. I just thought I'd never be affected by her choices." But she'd thrown Lacey away without a backward glance. Lacey and Henry, both. At least she'd gotten the shoes.

"Do you have any money?"

"Not much. The sooner I get a job, the better. I really can't afford to come up and see y'all. Besides, you have to see where we are. It's beautiful. Take a little time to get to know Henry. Have a nice day at the beach."

"You know your father was born on Indigo Beach."

Everything stopped for a minute. Lacey remembered her father as a pair of kind gray eyes and very big hands that used to pick her up at the waist and hold her high above his head. "He was?"

"I think they were visiting friends, stopping through on their way to a job in Florida. He came six weeks early. Almost didn't make it."

Thank God he did. If he hadn't, Henry wouldn't have Lacey as his mother.

She was having a hard time speaking. Anytime the subject of her dad came up, all sorts of emotions bottled up inside her started jostling around, demanding attention.

Sheena sighed. "I'll talk to Walt about us coming down."

Lacey closed her eyes, relieved. "Thanks."

"I'm not making any promises."

She never had. Not even one. But wasn't that what parents were supposed to do? Make a pledge, as God was their witness? Show their children they could trust them to do whatever it took to fight for them?

She opened her eyes, looked at her worn-out sandals. "You've got my number."

Family was hard, she thought when she hung up. Family made no sense. But she had her own—hers and Henry's—and she'd focus on that.

When a door opened upstairs—Mr. Wilder's—her whole body went on alert. A few seconds later, the bathroom door shut, and the shower came on.

It should be pretty cool that one of the world's most famous men was probably stripping naked at this very moment in her lighthouse. But he was a man who wanted her gone.

That wasn't gonna happen.

In fact, she ought to go up and take a picture of him in the buff right now and use it as blackmail to stay. It wasn't a bad idea. She could jimmy the lock and be right in before he knew what had hit him.

But there was the matter of his chasing her to get the picture back. It wasn't like the old days, where you could hide a canister of film in a bank deposit box while you were blackmailing someone. All he'd have to do is grab her phone and it would be over. He might be wrapped in a towel while he was chasing her, too.

It sounded kind of fun. And funny.

But he wasn't her type. No actor was her type, especially one like him, who was lauded across the globe. He must have a huge ego. He'd probably *want* her to send the picture out, especially if he had—you know—large man parts.

"Men," she muttered as she scrambled her last three eggs and tried not to think of Beau Wilder naked.

She'd think of getting a job instead. And of Henry.

That's what she'd do.

But she caught herself looking at her reflection in the kitchen window and adjusting her ponytail. Not for Beau Wilder, though. Southern girls loved prettifying. She was simply a well-groomed woman. A starved-for-affection, sexually unfulfilled woman who didn't have a hope in hell of ever having a happily-ever-after, at least not until Henry was grown up and gone.

By then, she'd probably have lost her lusty libido anyway.

Your job's not to burn the toast, she reminded herself, and popped it up just in time. *Your job, Mom, is to watch out for that boy's best interests.*

She set the table for three.
Three.
One mom, two hungry guys.
And pretended she didn't like it that way.

CHAPTER THREE

"My lighthouse," Beau said that morning when he opened his eyes and threw off the quilt, psyched to do battle with ninja guys or terrorists, whoever showed up first. But no one was there. Just a beam of sun warming his feet and the sound of the surf whispering good morning.

Then he remembered. He was in South Carolina, about to star in a sensitive film about love and inner peace, with a little blackmail and betrayal thrown in. And it was Greta he couldn't wait to take on—the gorgeous spitfire with the molasses-cookie voice that made him want to pull up a chair with a cold, tall glass of his full attention and pinch every last ginger-spicy crumb from their conversations.

Even through his hangover, which he coaxed into submission beneath the spindly spray of the shower (taking another one at the set after his run would suit him just fine), Beau couldn't wait to see her. Distractions from the movie were good.

Which was why he couldn't wait to see the lighthouse lamp, too. It was gonna be a big mother, a work of art, layers of glass. Maybe he should wear his sunglasses. It was sunny out—a ray of light could shoot him in the eye and bring that hangover right back.

Lighthouses were cool. To be respected. If there couldn't really be giant Transformers, at least there were these badass behemoth towers lording over the ocean.

So this one wasn't operating anymore. That was a shame. But even so, he couldn't believe his luck staying here. He'd have made an awesome lighthouse keeper. And while he was at it, a rad bridge opener, zowie steam shovel operator, and dope dump truck driver.

All those fun boy fascinations came rushing back—he'd made his living indulging a lot of them, hadn't he?—and he almost grinned while drying off with a coarse white towel. No fabric softener, so he was getting a nice, tingly rub, the way a man *should* dry off in a lighthouse.

Where was the Old Spice?

But he stopped cold when he heard Greta's voice from the first floor.

"Hen-reee!"

What the hey? He didn't look like a Henry. He was a Beau.

Obviously.

And a super-famous Beau at that. Maybe she was thinking of his character Hank McCormick, from that bank heist film. Hank was a nickname for Henry, wasn't it?

He still couldn't believe Greta Gildensturm was nearby, especially when he thought about that scene in *Biker Aliens* with her kneeling in a motorcycle sidecar wearing a purple helmet and a belly-revealing tank top and smacking gum while shooting orange-scaled creatures on the Pacific Coast Highway.

"Hen-reee!"

He made a face in the fogged-up mirror. "It's Beau!" Ouch. Sounding irritated and in charge was going to cost him. "Whatcha need?"

A few seconds later, someone tried to open the door.

"Hey!" Beau wrapped the towel around his middle,

automatically lowering it to sexy position. "Hang on a second!"

She was pushy. Was he surprised? The worst part was he liked it. He wanted to wrangle with her again.

"Hurry up!" called a little voice outside the bathroom door. A little *dude's* voice.

It had never occurred to Beau last night that someone else was around, especially a kid. He slung the towel over the towel bar and began throwing on his shorts and shirt. "I'm coming out, I promise. Give me a second."

"I gotta go *now*! Mom, who's in the bathroom?"

Be nice. It wasn't the child's fault that his mother was screwing up Beau's plans for a perfect getaway where he could indulge all his frustration about *Flowers from the Heart* through wild parties, massive surfing jags on his days off, and secretly viewing the same TV show over and over— all when he wasn't conducting manly forays about the property, which he hoped would involve bonfire lighting, knife throwing, and maybe an occasional fish spearing.

He flung open the bathroom door. A boy with an awesome little Afro and a latte complexion stood there in worn Iron Man pajamas and gazed up at him with big brown eyes, I-don't-give-a-rip-who-you-are eyes, which was kind of impressive, considering the size difference.

"Hey," said Beau.

The universal greeting in the South.

"Hey." Henry grabbed his crotch with both hands.

"Go for it, buddy." Beau grinned and stepped aside. He'd introduce himself later.

Henry raced past him, then turned. "I've got super-powers," he said, and slammed the door in his face.

Well, then.

Beau found himself on the landing behind the metal ladder leading up to the lighthouse dome. If he walked around the ladder to the right, he'd be at the door to his room. To the left was protected territory. Already the opposing door had a sign tacked on it, STAY OUT, with a pretty good drawing of a skull and crossbones, except it had eyes with black dots for pupils and spiky lashes.

Greta's work.

He swung around the ladder—God, that felt good; he'd have made an excellent fireman, too, he'd bet, as long as he could have a yellow Lab on the engine instead of a Dalmatian—and hopped on the second-from-the-bottom rung. He was going up, even though the smell of toasting bread and sizzling bacon downstairs called to him, as did the promise of seeing Miss Venus de Milo again.

"I thought you said you had to leave early in the morning," her throaty morning drawl rang out from below.

At the sound, his bare toes curled hard around the fourth rung. She needed coffee. He could hear it in her voice. Sadly, there hadn't been a coffeepot in sight last night, and he was in serious post-hangover withdrawal himself, as a matter of fact—at least until he got to the studio.

He knew something besides caffeine that would make them both feel better—jolt them to nirvana and back before they started their day—which was why he was holding on to that cold steel ladder for dear life, like a monk. "Early means ten o'clock," he explained. "Super early is eight. Crack a' dawn is six. An ungodly hour's five."

"That's ridiculous. Early is at sunrise."

"So says the late sleeper."

"I didn't sleep late. I was up by seven."

"Seven's roll-out-of-bed early."

There was a split second's silence, and then Henry burst out of the bathroom and froze. "You can't go up there," he said to Beau. "You don't even live here. You should *ask* first."

Beau dropped down to the first rung and stuck his hand out through the ladder, his palm open. "Beau Wilder."

Henry looked into his eyes for a long second. "Who are you, anyway?"

"I'm a good guy," Beau said, and leaned closer to whisper, "Got no designs on your mother, either."

Henry's face puckered.

"That means she's not my girlfriend," Beau said, "and I'm not going to ask her to be my girlfriend."

"So you're not gonna make her cry?" Henry whispered back.

Smart kid already.

Beau felt for him, and for Greta, too, although he could tell she'd spit in his eye before she'd ever accept his pity. "Absolutely not."

The boy grabbed Beau's hand and pumped it up and down. "My name's Henry Clark."

"Good name. Sorry you didn't know I was coming to stay. That must have been a big shock when you woke up this morning."

"I didn't mind," Henry said shyly, "especially if you have superpowers, too."

"I don't have any that I know of—*yet*."

Henry's face brightened at that.

"Have you ever seen the lighthouse lamp?" Beau asked.

"Of course." The boy stuck his finger up his nose but only for a nanosecond.

Beau glanced upward to the empty square space, thought of the price he'd paid—those Lakers seats—to get here, and for now felt no remorse. He looked back at Henry. "Well, I'll be right back. I can't do anything else until I see it. You can come, too, if your mom says it's all right."

"Mom?" Henry screamed at the top of his lungs. "I need to show Beau Wilder the giant lightbulb. It's *important*."

"Okay," his mother called back. "You know that noise we heard last night?"

"Yeah," said Henry.

"It was Mr. Wilder. He knows some of the same people we know in Hollywood. They gave him a key to the lighthouse, too."

Beau shrugged. "They were stupid not to come themselves."

"Yeah," said Henry. "*Dumb.*"

"You go up to the top and come right back down," she said in an urgent but loving faraway mom voice. Beau could just imagine her talking that way from a front porch up to Henry hidden in the branches of a tree. "We've got to go job hunting after breakfast."

Henry's face fell. "What about looking for dead crabs?"

"We'll do that when we get back," she trilled.

"You promise?"

"Yes, now hurry on downstairs. I'm making scrambled eggs."

"With cheese?" Henry wanted to know.

"Of course."

Beau hoped she'd made enough for him, too, but if she didn't, he'd get something at the set. They always had good food on movie sets.

He retrieved his sunglasses from his room, put on his socks and running shoes, hung his leather backpack from his back, then let Henry go ahead of him on the ladder. They got to the next level, a circular dome with a slanted staircase with no railings that rose to the lamp itself.

"Whoa." Beau looked up at the bottom of the light. It was way better than any chandelier he'd ever seen, layers and layers of thick glass gleaming ice blue. "This is cool."

"I know," said Henry. "What's it for?"

"Calling people home. When sailors out on the dark ocean weren't sure where they were, they could see this light shining and knew that if they went that way, they'd find a safe harbor."

"Awesome. What's a harbor?"

"A place where boats stay when they're not going out to sea. Ready to go all the way up?"

"Mom says you can't go without an adult."

"She's right. But since I am one, we're okay."

Henry's face crinkled up, a mass of doubt.

"Honestly. I'm probably older than your mom, even," Beau assured him.

"Okay."

This time Beau went first, and when he got up, he held out his hand to Henry and pulled him the rest of the way.

"You *dangled* me in the air," Henry said.

"I know. At least it wasn't over a pit of crocodiles, right?"

"I wish it had been."

"Me, too."

They stood at the railing surrounding the dome. The beautiful, wide Atlantic spread out before them, the waves rolling in and turning to vanilla milk-shake foam on the glittering sand.

"This is pretty." Beau remembered how much he loved the South Carolina coast. California's was more dramatic, with bigger waves. But there was something special about this shoreline. It was like loving a plain old black pound dog who sat contentedly at your feet instead of a glossy Doberman always ready to fetch.

"I never want to leave," said Henry.

For a second, Beau didn't, either. He lapped up the serenity, tucked it away, would use it later that day when mild nerves took over, as was appropriate on a new set.

Thanks for being a butthead, Callum, he thought sincerely, then felt guilty because Callum—one of those rabidly ambitious actors who wanted to be your friend to see what you could do for him—had obviously cheated on Greta. That couldn't have felt good for her, especially when she was a single mother.

No way he could kick her out now, especially with this little guy in tow.

Beau's chest expanded a little. It was only six weeks. He'd have to curb those wild parties—a good thing for his abs, which got soft when he drank too much—and watch his secret TV show in his room, on his laptop and with earplugs in. No one could know about that.

After another couple of minutes talking about the curve of the earth and giant sea monsters, he and Henry went down all the ladders, Beau descending first. Henry kept talking about a jellyfish he'd poked the day before with a marsh reed.

And then they wound up in the kitchen with Greta. Thankfully, the table was set for three. Beau appreciated that. He really did. She didn't have to do that, yet she had.

And then he remembered that serving him breakfast was the perfect way to lure him into thinking that keeping her around made sense. Smart move. He was already buying in to it.

Henry sat down. But Beau wouldn't. Not just yet. He pushed up his sunglasses, did okay with the light streaming in through the kitchen window, and said, "I'm afraid I never caught your name last night. I'm sorry."

"Lacey Clark."

He liked it. It suited this morning creature, her hair all fluffed and her yellow dress cheery. The alluring eyes and shiny-pink mouth were a little much for the beach. She needed makeup the way a frog needed more green or a sky more blue. But he was back in the South, and women here lived and died by their lipstick colors. He even knew his own mother's: Laguna Peach.

With a skillet of eggs in her hand, Lacey Clark made a mild face at him, slight enough that Henry wouldn't guess her disapproval but sufficient that Beau would. "I grew up here, too," she said. "You don't leave people out at mealtimes, not unless you want to burn in hell—which I don't."

Got it. He was supposed to eat like a robot with its volume turned off and then leave. "I probably won't be around much for meals."

"Awww," said Henry.

"I know." Beau shook his head. "Those movie people are going to force me to eat things like wild mushroom ravioli, beer-battered corn dogs, and filet mignon sandwiches." At least they did on the big movie sets.

"That's no good." Henry grabbed a triangle of toast from the platter in the middle of the table and ripped off half of it with his teeth. "Whatever happened to pizza?"

"They do that, too," he said, "but it's called smoked-salmon-and-caper flatbread. Or goat-cheese-and-olive focaccia."

"Yuck!" Henry said, his full mouth wide open.

"Watch your manners," his mother said primly, then looked back at Beau. "We'll see you at the table when you don't eat on the set." She scooped a small hill of eggs on the guys' plates, put a platter of bacon down, got out some OJ, poured three glasses, and set them on their funny place mats with an elegant hand.

"Mama, where's your eggs?" asked Henry.

"I didn't want any today." There was a peanut-butter-and-jelly sandwich on her plate.

"But you love scrambled eggs." Henry held his fork like a spear on the tabletop.

"Not on Tuesdays," she murmured, then turned pointedly to Beau. "Sit down and dig in."

Henry munched on his third strip of bacon, his brief flare of bad manners not dampening his appetite in the least.

Beau was only trying to be polite by waiting for her to be seated, but Lacey Clark obviously wanted none of that. Still, he refused to sit until she did.

She looked away, took her seat, and fiddled with her napkin before taking a sip of juice—a flustered mom not used to men displaying a knowledge of etiquette, he supposed.

He'd offer her his eggs, but he knew she'd chew his head off if he guessed that she probably didn't have much food in the pantry and fridge—but he did know, of course. And he should have left before she'd felt obligated to feed him.

"Where'd you go to high school?" he asked conversationally. Guilt warred with a need to show he belonged here, that she was a guest in *his* domain.

She put down her toast, her brows furrowed together. "I was homeschooled." End of subject.

"Interestin'," he said anyway.

Henry downed his entire glass of juice while looking at Beau with wide eyes. He was about to choke on the juice, he was swallowing so fast. What was it, a dare? Beau picked his up and drank it down, too. Then Henry went to work on his eggs, his eyes never leaving Beau's.

They were good eggs, too. Beau wanted to bolt his the way Henry was, but he wouldn't take him up on this particular challenge.

"Slow. Down." Lacey looked at Henry, her fork poised in midair.

Henry stared back, and his jaw stopped working so fast. "I gotta run get my magnifying glass."

Beau almost spit out his bacon. "You do?"

Henry nodded. "How'd you get in that man's body? Nathan Ritter told me that real men live inside Pluto and Donald Duck at Disneyland. And now *I* know a dog can live inside a man." He swung his head to look at his mom. "Mom, can we call Nathan and tell him?"

"*Henry.*" Lacey put her hands on the edge of the table. "You're not making any sense."

"Where's *your* magnifying glass?" Henry asked Beau. "Let's go get it."

Beau stopped chewing completely. Karma was such a bitch.

"Are you all right, Mr. Wilder?" Lacey asked him.

"Fine," he croaked like a dweeb. Here he'd called her Greta—really rubbing it in; God, he'd been stupid . . . and *drunk*—and now, *now* . . .

"He's Dudley the Dog Detective," Henry said to his mama. "And I'm so glad out of everyone in the world, he's decided to come live with *us*."

CHAPTER FOUR

"Oh. My. *God*." Lacey stared at their breakfast guest—not that he was a guest; he was an intruder—and put down her fork. "You *are* Dudley. The way you said *Interestin'*, his signature line." She put her hand over her mouth and stared.

Dudley was Henry's favorite cartoon. It had run only one season—sixteen episodes, around seven or eight years ago, before Henry was born—but they owned it on DVD. Henry watched it. A *lot*. She'd even gotten him a used Dudley T-shirt and a Dudley key chain on eBay last Christmas.

"See, Mom?" Henry swung his legs out of pure excitement and kicked her, hard.

Mr. Wilder looked between them. "It was a long time ago." His tone was flat. "You must have seen the reruns."

"That's right," said Lacey, rubbing her shin.

"That was my first acting job," he told her. "A man has to start somewhere. Look at Brad Pitt. He wore a chicken costume for El Pollo Loco on Sunset Boulevard."

"Yeah, I know." She fought a chuckle down behind her napkin. She sensed *he* had to kick something, too. Very soon.

"It's not even in Wikipedia," he said. "I used another name. No one knows but my agent and the creator of the show."

Sure enough, his fist bunched up on the table, and Henry patted it—or maybe petted it. Yes, while Mr. Wilder looked on in fascination, Henry was clearly petting that fist as if the man were a dog.

"Dudley," Henry murmured, "it's okay. Are you hiding from Barbella?"

Barbella was the bad squirrel who committed probably 50 percent of the crimes in the Dudley cartoon.

"No." Mr. Wilder wouldn't glare at him. But he did glare at Lacey, and then he stood. "I'm going now."

Oh, vengeance was sweet. But here she was, taking vengeance against Dudley, the coolest dog detective on the planet. He had a wicked sense of humor, a swagger in his walk, and that trench coat he wore with his tail sticking out was downright sexy—for a dog, of course.

But the best part about Dudley was his voice. It inspired calm, confidence, and total madcap adventure all at the same time.

"Where *is* Barbella?" Henry asked Mr. Wilder.

He pulled on his ear. "Ask your mom. She'll know." He sent her a *hah* look.

Now she had to explain to Henry. She took in his face, happy, aglow. Maybe vengeance wouldn't be so sweet, after all. "Barbella," she said with care, "is still in Boomtown, hiding out."

Henry chuckled. "He's scared of Dudley."

She exchanged a glance with Mr. Wilder. His gaze was shuttered. Maybe he was thinking about getting rid of them again. "Break a leg," she told him.

God, she was talking to Dudley.

"Mom!" Henry chastised her.

"It means good luck," she replied, her eyes still on Mr.

Wilder. She was a little in awe. She *loved* Dudley. He had such an engaging, lovable personality, with just the right amount of devil-may-care attitude to make you laugh out loud. And . . . and here he was. "Henry, that's enough about Dudley now."

Mr. Wilder didn't thank her for wishing him that ridiculous broken leg that all actors craved. Instead, he picked up his backpack, slung it over his shoulders, and at the door looked back. "The surfboard outside is mine. Please don't touch it. I mean, really. Don't touch."

"Surfboard?" Henry ran to the door. "Mom! Look!"

Dudley was eccentric, too, but about important things, like making sure he had argyle socks on every day. They gave him a special pizzazz.

Lacey hated to act at all interested, but part of her wanted to see this amazing surfboard. She peeked outside and saw a bright red board with a yellow stripe up the middle. It was big.

"You're a surfer?" Henry asked him.

Surfers were sexy. And outrageous. Some of them were up to no good—too much partying, some of it maybe illegal. Mr. Wilder had better not be one of those.

"Yes, I'm a surfer," he said. "I flew this board in from Los Angeles."

She wasn't going to ask him why he was treating it like it was made of gold.

"Why can't we touch it?" Henry asked. "I *want* to. Really bad."

Mr. Wilder drew in a big breath. "I just waxed it. And . . . and it's special to me. Nothing can happen to it. I mean, nothing. Soon I'll let you touch it, kiddo."

Soon . . .

That meant he'd given up making them leave.

Lacey's heart soared.

But you're supposed to make him *leave*, she reminded

herself, right as Mr. Wilder tried to trip Henry by hooking his foot over Henry's calf. But Henry caught on and ran away laughing so hard, Lacey's heart couldn't help turning over. He needed guy interaction. Big-time. But a revolving-door policy on men wasn't for her.

"So leaving the board on the side of the lighthouse is a good idea?" She knew she sounded like a nag, but they didn't need to be friend-friends. Just housemates. She wasn't going to make him leave, either. And she knew well that even if she tried, he wouldn't.

He shrugged. "I'm getting it conditioned to this climate and this place. I want it facing the ocean. Just for today. And then I'll keep it in my room."

"How will you get it up the spiral staircase?" she asked.

He laughed. "If I have any problems, I can always haul it up on a rope from outside."

"Haul me up, too!" cried Henry.

Now, *that* was ridiculous.

"Sure," Mr. Wilder said.

"*No.*" Lacey scowled at him just a little, not enough for him to call her on it. But she needed to remind him that he wasn't doing her any favors. She was doing *him* one by letting him stay.

"You're going to sleep on it?" Henry squinted up at his dangerous new friend.

"I won't sleep on it, but I'll have it there to cheer me up when I come home after work." He crouched down to Henry's level, his haunches flexing in an attractive way, his shorts riding up high on his thigh. "You be a good boy today, helping your mom find a job," he said in a serious tone.

"Okay, Dudley," Henry answered, his eyes shining. "I never knew you surfed. But guess what?"

"What?"

"You won't be the first dog who surfs. I saw one on the Internet with Mom."

Great. Henry was still at that age where he could totally confuse reality with make-believe. Five was a magic time, yes. But he was so vulnerable, too. Lacey watched him run as fast as he could to catch a seagull, his feet spraying little arcs of sand.

"Miz Clark," Mr. Wilder said, "I'll leave it up to you how to handle a certain issue while I'm away."

Lacey's chest tightened. Had he changed his mind again? She couldn't stomach the idea of taking Henry away from this glorious place. And she wouldn't. "I told you, Mr. Wilder—"

"Just explain to him."

"*You* try to explain real life to a little boy." She swallowed a lump in her throat. "He's happy the way things are right now. I can't make that matter to you. I wish it did, but as long as it matters to *me*, that's what counts."

He stood, the corners of his mouth creased. "But it's not a good idea, him thinking I'm Dudley."

She blinked. He wasn't talking about their leaving?

"That petting thing." He scratched the back of his neck. "Next time he might want to put a leash on me and take me for a walk."

Relief flooded her, and she chuckled.

"I think he's old enough to get it, don't you?" He put his hands carelessly on his hips and watched Henry play. "If you explain it right. That's the key."

"Yes." She nodded. "Of course. I can do that." She wasn't sure how yet, but she would.

He looked at her sideways, then pulled a wallet out of his backpack and held out two crisp new hundred-dollar bills. "To stock the fridge."

She stared at them a moment. God, they were beautiful.

"Take 'em." He thrust them at her. "I won't be eating here a lot, but I drink milk like crazy, and I like snacks. Usually cheese and crackers. And Peanut Butter Cap'n

Crunch. And please"—he pulled out another hundred—"if you could get us a decent coffeemaker, a grinder, and some dark-roast coffee beans, you'll be saving my life."

She took the money and curled it in her palm. How quickly security could come and go. "I'm not crazy about this. But I'll do it."

"If you need more," he said, "I'll give you more. One thing I don't like is empty cupboards."

"I'll keep that in mind." She tried to sound professional, the way she had when she'd been Monique's assistant and handled her everyday business affairs. But she couldn't wait to get to the grocery store and buy chicken, beans, brown rice, veggies, bananas . . .

They stared at each other a second. They were standing awfully close. She didn't budge an inch. Neither did he.

It's gonna go like that, she told him with her eyes, the fight stronger in her than her relief. Because really, she *was* here first. She didn't have anything to apologize for.

Uh-huh, his eyes said back. He'd gotten the message, all right. But he blew it away, like puff on a dandelion, by saying, "Call me Beau. And I'll call you Lacey. *Miz Clark's* a mouthful."

The smart-ass.

And then he was gone. Henry insisted on watching him run down the beach. Lacey stood in the doorway of the lighthouse, her arms folded, and watched him, too. It wasn't a hardship, and she didn't want to act churlish in front of her son. But neither did she want him to get the impression that she was the same big fan of the guy that he was.

Still, Mr. Wilder—*Beau*—was hot. She had to grant him that. The man looked as fit and fierce as the marine he played a few years ago in *Drop and Give Me Twenty*. He was hot . . . and he'd once played a dog in a cartoon, and now he was starring in a movie called *Flowers from the Heart*.

Lacey didn't get it. What was he doing in a movie with that kind of title?

Monique had acted like it was this artsy love story that she couldn't wait to star in because she'd wanted to add dimension to her résumé. And Callum had only gotten his secondary role thanks to Lacey. She'd worked on Monique for three months to get her to see his charm and talent, and to contact the director to put in a good word for him.

But her strategy had worked a little too well. Monique and Callum had run off to Italy to another movie set. So far, nothing had hit the news about them backing out of the movie here. No one seemed to care. But plenty of photos had been published of them together at LAX, and then at the airport in Rome.

It wasn't right. Why did spoiled people so often get away with being rotten? When the hardworking people got screwed?

And what was Beau Wilder doing in such a sappy movie? Lacey was dying to ask. Monique and Callum had never mentioned him.

"Henry, let's go wow Indigo Beach." She wouldn't waste any more time stewing about Beau, her traitorous ex-boss and ex-lover, or her lack of a future at the moment. It wouldn't do her any good. If she'd learned one thing from Sheena, it was to fake it until you make it.

Meanwhile, teeth had to be brushed and beds made.

Henry didn't know it, but he was kind of a fashionista. At least he would be until he outgrew the size he was wearing now. Monique had had a penchant for dressing her Pomeranian from an upscale pet shop in West Hollywood, and she'd stop in next door to a used children's clothing store and browse for Henry, whom she'd treated like a live Ken doll.

Today he wore his aviator sunglasses with his scuffed black Gucci loafers, custom-tailored blue shorts—made for some little boy who probably lived in a big mansion in Bel Air—and a short-sleeved gray T-shirt.

Twenty minutes after Beau left, Lacey and Henry were headed into Indigo Beach in an orange-and-white 1977 Cadillac Lifeliner ambulance, which she'd borrowed from her friend Patrick. Yes, it was ridiculous, but it was a set of wheels. Patrick had restored vehicles for movie sets for forty years and said he'd pick it up next time he came east on a buying trip, which was a couple of months from now.

She'd need a car by then.

No problem, she thought. And smiled a close-lipped, all-is-well-with-the-world smile while staring straight ahead on Heron Avenue because she was scared. Really scared. And she didn't want Henry to guess.

On their left was a long row of three-story-high beach houses, all different styles standing virtually shoulder-to-shoulder, facing the Atlantic. On their right, another long row of over-the-top beach houses, nearly all of them with widow's walks so the occupants could catch a glimpse of ocean.

Of course, she was used to rich out in Hollywood, super rich, even. But this was rich enough. There was money to be made here, at least in the warmer months. Maybe lots of money.

Their first stop was a clothing boutique called Finer Things with elegant beach saris hung out front, rippling in the ever-present wind gusting off the beach. Lacey held Henry's hand, and they walked inside.

A beautiful blond woman in her mid- to late thirties, the epitome of Southern chic in her chunky gold jewelry and tailored pale-blue linen, looked up from the counter. "Hey." She greeted Lacey with a smile that didn't quite reach her eyes. "I've got a great sale going on."

Lacey gathered her courage and smiled back. "Hi," she said warmly. "I'm Lacey Clark. My son Henry and I just moved here from Los Angeles, but I grew up in the South so this is like coming home. I'm looking for a full-time job and wondered if you could use some help."

The woman's smile dissolved. Maybe she was disappointed Lacey wasn't there to buy clothes. Or maybe that was just her boss face. At any rate, she didn't offer to introduce herself or welcome Lacey to Indigo Beach.

"I know the summer season's going to be gearing up soon," Lacey forged on brightly, "and I can see that your store would be popular with the visitors. Locals, too, I'm sure."

"I'm afraid I don't have anything." There was nothing neighborly about her tone.

"I see." Lacey shot her another nervous smile. "If something comes up, perhaps I could leave you my number—"

"I don't think so."

Wow. That was a punch in the gut.

The shopkeeper gave her a condescending little smile and stood. "I've got to hang some clothes, so if you'll excuse me."

Henry looked up at Lacey. "Can we go now, Mom?"

"Sure."

She was about to walk out when the woman said, "They might be looking for housekeepers at the Beach Bum Inn. A lot of single mothers go there. But if that doesn't pan out, you might want to think about moving inland. You'll find lots more jobs there for someone with your qualifications."

"But I never said I was a single mother. And I was the personal assistant to—"

"Save your story for someone else." The harpy's smile was now severely pinched. "I'm looking to attract a certain clientele."

"Is that right?" said Lacey, and adjusted her purse. She wished she had the gumption to tell this woman she was an unlikable snob and storm out. But something in her felt weak, like watered-down Coca-Cola—ever since the TMZ show. Ever since Callum dumped her.

Her fizz was gone.

The woman moved closer and lowered her voice. "I understand that you're living at the lighthouse." The disapproval in her eyes made them beady. Not a nice look.

"Yes, we are."

"Uh-huh," the woman said knowingly.

Lacey chose to ignore her smug tone. "How did you know?"

"Indigo Beach is a small town." The woman tossed her head, and her heavily hair-sprayed bob didn't even swing. "I make it my business to know what's happening here."

"Henry," Lacey said without looking at him, "go wait on the front porch. But don't go down the steps."

"Okay, Mama." He ran out, anxious to leave a place that bored him to tears anyway.

Lacey looked the woman in the eye. "You don't know me. Yet you seem to have a problem with me. Hardly the sort of attitude a visitor would expect in a laid-back beach community."

The woman gave a short laugh. "You really shouldn't be behaving the way you do when you have a child."

"Excuse me?"

"Beau Wilder was mighty drunk last night, so I hear, when he walked into the liquor store with a floozy on his arm." The woman turned her back and began pushing clothes across a rack.

Lacey was so stunned, she stood still for half a second. She couldn't believe anyone even used the word *floozy* anymore, much less had the temerity to call her one. "I wasn't with him at the liquor store," she said evenly. She was glad her voice wasn't trembling. Her hands sure were. "If this is such a small town, then you'd know he was with a blonde. Not a redhead."

The shop owner looked over her shoulder at her. "My, oh, my. That man sure does have a lot of women in his life. And you're okay with that?"

"If he does, that's his business, not yours. And I'm not one of his women. We're sharing the lighthouse. As friends."

"Friends?" The woman raised her brow. "Let's cut to the chase, shall we? We don't need your kind here in Indigo Beach. This is a *family place*. We've got *wholesome values*. I suggest you do the right thing by your child and move on."

Say something. You're Greta. You shoot aliens. You pour ice-cold beverages on people's heads.

But Lacey stood there with her mouth open and no words coming out. Never in a million years had she dreamed she'd walk up the stairs into this lovely cottage and find a wicked witch inside. She'd forgotten how some Southern belles could be. Suppressed it, actually. She'd seen it happen to Sheena too many times to count, haughty matriarchs or spoiled young marrieds fingering her quilts at craft fairs and talking down to her when they ordered custom ones—or dismissing her work entirely. Fashionable women who barely concealed their distaste for Sheena's mousy hair and faded floral rayon dresses.

The shop owner stopped moving her hangers. "Did you not hear me?"

Lacey whirled around, stumbled outside, and grabbed Henry's hand. "Let's go."

He didn't say a word. He had an instinct for when things weren't right. She was glad he was such a sensitive guy, yet it also required that she work extra hard to protect him from the bad stuff. And sometimes she just couldn't.

At the ambulance, she opened the passenger-side door

and watched her life and joy buckle himself up into his seat.

He looked up and grinned. "Ready."

"Good." She flashed him a smile, relieved that this time he appeared oblivious, and shut the door. No way was that bitch from hell going to diminish him by slighting her.

She refused to look up at the store when she buckled herself into her own seat. "On to the next place," she made herself say cheerily and moved the gearshift on the steering column into reverse.

CHAPTER FIVE

Beau's run down the beach wasn't paying off. Despite the great breeze, his beautiful view of the Atlantic, the cloudless blue sky, and his excellent speed, he was stressed, an odd state of affairs for him. But he had to face facts: He was in a bad movie, and now he was living with a family. He didn't really know what a family was like, at least not a loving one. And his lighthouse—his giant playland and bastion of privacy—was now something he had to share. That meant he had to act like a regular guy.

He hadn't been a regular guy in forever.

He called Oliver, his English publicist, on his Bluetooth. "You ever hear of Greta Gildensturm?"

"Who hasn't?" Oliver grew up in Liverpool. "A bombshell. Bad actress. Says every line like she's Scarlett O'Hara fighting off the Yankees. Who played her again?"

"Never mind. She's here."

"What do you mean, here? On the set?" Oliver sounded slightly frantic, which was unusual. He was the smoothest publicist in LA, totally unflappable in front of cameras and microphones, that British steel in his spine intimidating to all who tried to breach the walls of his clients.

"Not the set," said Beau, his strides long and sure. "She

was in my lighthouse when I got here. Big mix-up in the living situation. Can't do anything about it. She refuses to budge. Neither will I. We've had to come to a truce."

He wouldn't tell him that Lacey had threatened to cause a PR ruckus if Beau attempted to throw her out. Oliver wouldn't take kindly to that. He could be pretty ruthless, and no way would Beau want him to unleash his Hollywood brand of fight on a single mom, however capable of pushing back she was.

"Crumbs," Oliver said. "That's a bit wonky. But she's a looker, isn't she?"

"You could say that. Yes. Yes, she is." So hot that the thought of her right now was causing him some issues that a man didn't want to have in the middle of a run on a public beach.

"Just don't let her on the set," Oliver said.

"I don't plan on it. But why not?"

"You don't know?"

"No. Spit it out, Ollie."

"She's bad luck. Hard cheese, as we say in the UK. Every set she's ever been on, the movie's gone tits-up."

"Inexperienced actors"—which was Beau's way around saying *unskilled* or *untalented actors*—"often appear in disastrous movies. There's a relationship there."

He hadn't had a disastrous movie yet, of course. Emphasis on *yet*. He was running toward one now.

"Yes, I know," Oliver said. "But supposedly the directors went a little bonkers during filming. One wound up in rehab. One quit the business. The IRS came after the third one for tax evasion."

"Why would any of that be her fault?"

"I have no idea. Aside from the dubious acting skills, which we both know is no detriment to some filmmakers, no one in Hollywood would touch her with a ten-foot pole after the third director went to jail. Some kind of theater superstition, perhaps. She was the only actor in all three movies—someone made that connection. And word was that the woman was opinionated. Stirred things up on the set."

That part didn't surprise Beau a bit. She was the girl who'd called Callum out in public, after all. The one who'd fought tooth and nail to get Beau out of the lighthouse.

But his heart rate was steady. He wasn't worried. "Thanks for the heads-up," he said, "although I didn't know I was paying you to be my psychic adviser, too."

"It's a free perk."

They talked about soccer for a few minutes—Oliver had slowly gotten him into it, and now Chelsea was Beau's team, which disgusted Ollie; he was Liverpool's number-one fan—and then he switched over to another call. It was Sarah, his twenty-two-year-old cousin.

"Beau!"

"Hot dog, it's my favorite cousin."

"Your *only* cousin."

He grinned. Being out on the beach alone, he felt relatively able to cut loose. "Good to hear your voice, sweetheart."

"I hear yours all the time. Grady can't stop watching *Jupiter Storm*. And now *Homewrecker*. Did you really drive that truck off the pier?"

"Nope. I got as far as ten feet away. And then they pulled the old switcheroo with the stunt guy. But I'm still a tough guy, right? I've endured the St. Cecilia Ball."

"Dance cards filled with the names of some of Charleston's most formidable fire-breathing dragon matrons and eligible young ladies," Sarah said with a giggle.

"I'm sorry I missed your come-out and your graduation."

"You already told me. You're forgiven. The necklace and the Bahamas trip couldn't replace you, but they went a long way to making me feel special. Thanks, cuz."

"I'm glad." Sarah was like the little sister he'd never had. She was the one family member he actually thought about when he was in LA and wished he lived closer to. "You and Grady doing well?"

"We sure are." Her voice was breathy. "I hear you're in town for this movie. It was on the radio this morning. Someone saw you—pretty inebriated, I might add—at the liquor store on Indigo Beach."

"Did Mom hear?"

"No doubt. But that's not why I'm calling."

"Oh, yeah?" He had a sneaking suspicion. She sounded awfully excited—jubilant, even.

"I'm married," she crowed. "Grady and I eloped to Paris and said our vows in Notre Dame! Mama and Daddy were shocked—but happy."

He laughed out loud. "Lucky Grady. Stealing away the prettiest, sweetest girl in Charleston right from under everyone's noses."

She laughed, too. "You know I'm not sweet."

"Sure you are." He grinned again. "When you want to be. So did you just get back?"

"Two days ago. And guess what—we're having a wedding ball! Soon! I hope you can come." She gave him the date.

"I'll be there." He'd talk to Mike, the director, about rearranging their schedule if it came to that.

"Oh, my God, Beau, I know all Mama's friends and mine will be ringing us off the hook to see if you'll come."

"Remind them that I'm not looking for a girlfriend, okay?"

"Or even one night of forbidden pleasure?" She laughed. "You know there'll be plenty of matrons ready to offer you that. My single friends, too. They're shameless when it comes to you, even the shy ones."

"Nope. I'm a workingman. No time for love *or* flings."

"Okey-doke. Well, can't wait to see you. And Beau?"

"What?"

"Charlotte Wallace will be there."

"Good for her." They'd dated when they were both seventeen—she at her boarding school, he at his, a few weekend dances and parties at home over Christmas and summer breaks. And then there'd been a crazy week when they were both twenty-five and found themselves in Aspen at the same time and they'd had a few nights of fun, torrid sex—and that was that. Neither one had been interested in anything more substantial, or so Charlotte had assured him at the time.

But she'd been dropping hints the last couple of years to his mother that she'd never gotten over him.

"Your mother's ecstatic that she never married," Sarah said. "The most eligible woman in Charleston."

"I know. Mom reminds me every time we talk."

Sarah laughed again. "Oh, boy. This is going to be *so* interesting."

"Hey, it's about you and Grady. I'm going to blend into the wallpaper."

"Sure you are."

He was going to do his best to. He hadn't gone to a Charleston function since he'd gotten his first movie. Last time he had, his dad had been alive. It was going to be surreal, in a way. Something he'd been glad to avoid.

But Sarah mattered. For a girl who'd grown up south of Broad Street, the enclave of Charleston's elite, she was pretty grounded, and he had no idea how. Her mother, his mother's sister, was as obsessed with social correctness as his own mother. Her dad, too, was a legendary attorney who never took a wrong step. Sarah had been in boarding schools since the sixth grade. She was a champion horsewoman. If she had any deep issues about the family, she'd never expressed them to him.

When he hung up, he took the last mile a little faster, ending in a sprint. The studio loomed before him, and when he reached it he was actually out of breath. For a brief second, he forgot everything but the fact that he loved his job.

He took in the familiar layout. It was on a much more modest scale than what he was used to, but recognizable all the same. There were the trailers, two looming warehouses dwarfing a one-story office off to the side, some film equipment near a door, waiting to be moved inside, and then INDIGO BEACH STUDIOS in a dramatic blue space-age font on a sign attached to the largest warehouse.

Sweat poured in rivulets down his back, and he swiped his face on his shirt. He'd worked hard to get where he was, but he was also a lucky man.

No way was he gonna let that luck run out.

CHAPTER SIX

That woman at Finer Things had been a bad apple, Lacey decided. Outside on the porch, she'd had a sign: NO PUBLIC BATHROOM & NO WATER FOUNTAIN. That should have told her something right there.

"I didn't like her, Mom," said Henry, "because she didn't like us. I could tell."

Poor Henry. It made Lacey livid that he'd picked up on the woman's animosity. "Honey, some people aren't nice, I'm sorry to tell you. But we won't give up, okay?"

"Okay."

They parked the ambulance at a meter near the lively intersection of Heron Avenue and Center Street. This junction, which ended in the fishing pier jutting out over the Atlantic, was bustling, the heart of commerce on Indigo Beach and the social hub for visitors and locals alike. Go west on Center, and it led off the island, over the inlet to Charleston.

No one even noticed the ambulance. Apart from Finer Things, a funky artists' vibe prevailed at Indigo Beach. Lacey had already seen dune buggies, lots of motorcycles—several with sidecars—a couple tandem bikes, and some bicycle rickshaws.

There was the post office on one corner of Heron and Center, Tally's Seafood Emporium on another, a surf shop on the third, and Merv's gas station on the fourth. Lacey and Henry had bought dollar hot dogs at Merv's on their way to the lighthouse the other day when they'd arrived, hungry and exhausted, at nine PM after driving fourteen hours.

But thirty minutes later, after checking with all the businesses except the post office, she still had no job leads.

"Mom, what are we going to do?" Henry's sunglasses glinted up at her.

She smiled brightly. "Everyone was very nice." And except for that woman at Finer Things, they had been. Merv had given Henry a free piece of saltwater taffy. And at Tally's, a waitress told Lacey about a woman on Laurel Street who was great at taking care of her own child Henry's age.

"I wouldn't send him anywhere else," the girl had said, and wrote down the child-care giver's number on a napkin.

Lacey took it and thanked her. Things were looking up already. "So you live on Indigo?"

"On the back side." The waitress grinned. "We've got our rich people 'from off,' but us locals refuse to budge or let them turn Center Street into Fifth Avenue. Our mayor's a fifth-generation islander."

That was heartening.

"Check out the whole island," the waitress suggested.

"I've already been to Finer Things."

The woman laughed. "Oh, Lord, you walked straight into the viper's den. That's Biddy, the town bitch. She thinks she did us a favor when she moved here from Charleston a few years ago. She'd like nothing better than to turn the island into a fancy resort. Unless you run in her circles, you'll be fine. She ignores the little people as best she can."

"Thanks for the tip." Lacey felt a lot better hearing that.

"Just don't let Biddy ruin anything for you," the waitress had said. "Indigo Beach is a slice of heaven."

Lacey and Henry walked into the mom-and-pop store where they'd bought their bread, milk, eggs, peanut butter, and jelly. No cashier jobs there, at least not for a month or so. They told her to check back. Right past the grocery store were a couple of restaurants—one Mexican and one ultra-chic, called Bonefish—two bars vying for the same customers across the street from each other, and a small hardware store with a picture of a giant red crab painted on its side.

"Cool!" Henry said, in awe.

Lacey was glad he seemed so relaxed. It had been hard ripping him away from LA, the only place he'd ever known.

The hardware wasn't hiring. She wouldn't check at the bars. No way. Too much potential for trouble. Bonefish said they were accepting new applications but that they primarily hired college students for the summer, and they had regulars returning soon.

But the manager at the Mexican restaurant offered her a job on the spot.

"You can start tonight," he said. "We just lost someone."

"Do you mind if I get my child care lined up first?" She looked at Henry, who sat swinging his legs on a bench on the patio, oblivious to their conversation.

"You mean, you don't have a babysitter yet?"

She shook her head. "But I have a name of someone on Laurel Street. And I hear she's really good."

He threw up his hands. "You come back when you have your personal life organized, okay?"

"I'll call her right now! Please," she begged him.

"Fine. I'll wait." He rolled his eyes, but she wouldn't take offense. He had a business to run, after all, and she should have been better prepared. She'd jumped the gun, anxious to get her new life started.

The babysitter didn't have any openings until the fall. "Sorry." Kids' voices could be heard laughing and shrieking in the background. "I wish I could help."

Lacey smiled at the restaurant manager, but her disappointment was huge. "Do you—do you know of anyone else?" she said into her cell.

"There's a day care on Heron." The woman on the phone paused. "But I wouldn't recommend it."

"Why?" The knot of tension in Lacey's stomach drew tighter.

"Too many kids, not enough supervision. Period. And I'm not just saying that to bring you back to me in September. I'm a mother, too. You'll have to go over the bridge for decent care. A couple of miles down the highway, there's a nice place. But it takes two weeks to get through the paperwork and to get approved."

Lacey's throat was dry when she looked up at the manager.

"So?" He crossed his arms.

"I can't find anyone for two weeks. But could you hold the job? Please?"

He shook his head. "I can't run a business that way. I need to fill this position. Check back in two weeks, and if I haven't filled it, apply again."

She nodded weakly. What was she going to do, tell everyone from now on that it would be at least two weeks before she had day care for Henry? And how did she know she'd like this place over the bridge anyway? She hadn't even seen it.

She and Henry would go in the morning to check it out. No more job hunting today.

They got back in the ambulance. The rest of the street

was residential, but the movie studio, she'd been told in Bonefish, was at the far end.

"Let's go see it," she said to Henry.

"Yeah!"

Why not? She needed time to think—think of what they'd do for two weeks and how long her money would hold out.

The ambulance cruised between two rows of beach houses, big ones, and headed like a heat-seeking missile to the movie studio, which was the last place Lacey needed or wanted to be.

But Beau's there.

She remembered those crisp one-hundred-dollar bills he'd handed her and reminded herself that she wasn't going to rely on anyone again. Yet it didn't hurt that he was staying at the lighthouse, either. She hated to admit that, especially because he was an actor. But she was thinking with her business brain. *That's all*, she told herself sternly.

After five blocks, the road left the front beach and curved around the south tip of the island to the studio, a complex of two large corrugated metal-sided buildings and a small office huddled with some trailers beneath large oaks and pines.

"This is where Mr. Wilder works," she told Henry, her heart pounding hard, although she couldn't see anything— just a few pick-up trucks.

"He had to run real far to get here."

"He sure did." She tried to forget that image of the man, his stride sure, his torso an upside-down triangle silhouetted against the morning sun hovering low over the water. "Mr. Wilder is an actor. You know what that is?"

"Nope." Henry opened the glove compartment and slammed it shut again.

"It means he gets to pretend to be other people. And he

gets paid for it. He stars in movies at the movie theater, and sometimes he's on TV."

"Wow!" Henry's forehead wrinkled. "I must be an actor, too. I pretend to be Luke Skywalker. And Iron Man."

"Yes," she said cheerfully. "It's kind of like that. A long time ago, Mr. Wilder got to pretend to be a dog in a cartoon. Dudley, actually. His job was to be Dudley's voice. But"—she gulped—"Dudley's make-believe. Some people thought him up in their heads and drew him on paper. Then they colored him with Magic Markers and made him into a cartoon on TV."

Henry stared at her hard.

"But Mr. Wilder's real," Lacey plodded on. "No one drew him on paper. He was born a baby, then he grew to be a boy, and now he's a man." *A lotta man, too.* She cleared her throat. "Does this make sense?"

"Yes."

Gosh, his expression was unreadable. She took his hands and squeezed. "So you get it, then? He's not really Dudley. But Dudley would never have happened without Mr. Wilder. He helped make Dudley into that great cartoon we both love. Mr. Wilder spoke into a microphone everything that Dudley would say in the cartoon."

"Okay." Henry sounded unfazed.

Lacey was relieved. She put the ambulance in reverse.

"Does this mean I can't pet him anymore?" Henry still looked hopeful.

Lacey pressed on the brake. "Dudley doesn't live inside him, buddy. So if you pet Mr. Wilder, you're petting . . . Mr. Wilder."

Shoot. She just had to say it.

Henry threw his head back and his arms out and looked up at the ambulance ceiling. Mr. Drama. Part of her tightened up. Had she scarred him for life, ripping his make-believe carpet out from under him?

"That's *dumb*," he eventually pronounced. And then he looked at her and laughed.

She laughed, too. "*I* thought it was pretty funny."

"What did Mr. Wilder think?"

"He thought *you* thought he was a dog."

"I did."

"I know."

They beamed at each other.

God, she loved this boy.

So there. They'd survived that little ordeal, and he didn't seem scarred about anything. She worried too much. She knew she did. But she was trying—*really* trying—to be relaxed. Maybe having a partner made a difference. She had no idea because Henry's father had wanted nothing to do with him, and she'd never let Callum get quite that close. Maybe she'd known deep inside that he wasn't the right guy.

If there *was* a right guy. The jury was still out on that for her. For Henry's sake, she didn't want to be a cynic, but she didn't want to be a cockeyed optimist, either, and leave them open to more hurt.

She pushed down Callum's recent betrayal—still raw, like a paper cut—and thanked God that Henry had always seemed indifferent to him. He must have known somehow that Monique's new love wasn't meant to be part of their family.

She made a three-point turn out of the studio, and they cruised back down Heron and onto a shorter residential street parallel to it—Laurel Avenue, which was one step farther back from the front beach. When it got closer to Center Street, Laurel became a mix of retail, a day care, a twenty-four-hour gym, and smaller food places, including a doughnut shop—"Work there!" Henry yelled; "I just might," Lacey said back—but on both sides of Center, farther out, Laurel Avenue was a solid row of beach bungalows way less ostentatious than the homes on Heron but still darned nice.

"Pretty," Henry said when they passed a funky bed-and-breakfast with plastic pink flamingos all over the yard.

"I think so, too," Lacey said, and meant it.

It was fun, Indigo Beach. No wonder people flocked here.

And then there was Calico, one street removed from Laurel, still parallel to Heron and on the back side of the island facing the marshes and saltwater inlet. On the north side of Center Street, Calico boasted an elementary school, a small medical clinic, a dentist's office, and the animal rescue shelter. But it was predominantly composed of modest brick or clapboard homes filled with "regular" people, locals who had to work for a living.

On the south side of Center, Calico led to the marina and boatyard, passing a few mobile homes here and there, and one unfinished concrete brick building that Lacey couldn't figure out.

The views on the back of the island were just as breathtaking in their own way as the view of the Atlantic. There was the bridge over the narrow inlet, and boats moored at jutting docks everywhere, on both the Indigo Beach side of the water and the other side. A couple of fishing trawlers at a dock on the mainland side lent a charming patina to the scene.

"I'm glad we moved here," Henry said. "I never want to leave."

There was a strange tugging at Lacey's heart. "I don't, either." She put the ambulance in park so they could bask in the view.

"Do we really have to, Mom?"

The sun glinted off the water.

She loved it here, too. Heck, she was back in the South,

and this slice of Atlantic coast was as close to roots as she'd ever get. Her father had been born here. That had to mean something.

"Please find the house we're going to live in," Henry said. "I want to paint my room like a football field. I want a dog. And we're going to run on the beach every day."

She wanted that for him. She wanted it so badly, her fingers trembled on the steering wheel. "I'll tuck you into your very own bed in your own room in that house. It will have a red front door and flowers in blue clay pots on either side. You'll finish growing up there, and when you're a man you'll go out into the world and do great things, and then you'll come back and see me. Maybe you'll get married and bring your wife and kids with you."

Henry smiled. "I hate girls. And I'm never leaving you."

"My chocolate chip cookies are that good, huh?"

"Yep."

"We may have to start off in an apartment. A little one. But that'll make the house even more special once we get to it."

He grabbed her hand, his palm hot and sticky. "As long as it's here. I want to swim with the dolphins I saw today."

"Me, too."

"Promise, Mama?"

She looked down at him, her little boy. And for the first time in her life, she understood what it meant to make a sacred vow. It involved goose bumps. A surge of love. Courage. But most of all, it involved someone else . . . someone who needed you to be steadfast and true to the very end.

"Yes, sweetheart," she said, "I promise." And felt the bridge of that vow shimmer between them, shutting down so many options, leaving open very few. Inside, her warrior self began slowly to gird for battle.

She had a promise to fulfill. And she would. No matter what.

As the ambulance headed back to Center Street, Henry bounced up and down on the orange vinyl passenger seat. "Turn on the sirens, Mom. *Then* they'll know we're coming."

She smiled at the window in front of her. "You know we can't do that. We'd get in big trouble." Her chest was tight, her palms damp.

Where was she going? She looked to the right and left, hoping to see some obvious place to ask for a job. *I need a sign*, she thought, desperate for guidance and lost—lost and afraid and not sure where to turn. She couldn't hide. She mustn't. She had to be brave.

A sign . . . a sign . . .

Her pulse thudded in her wrists. She gripped the wheel and tried to ignore how trusting Henry's profile was, his mouth slightly agape at the wonders around him, his lashes curling long and high against his brow, not a crease of anxiety on his face.

"Look!" he cried, and pointed a stubby finger straight ahead. "I knew you should work there!"

And that's when she saw Beau Wilder in the doughnut shop window.

CHAPTER SEVEN

Beau was in for something new. Hot breakfasts on this movie set? Nah. A personal assistant assigned to attend to his every need? Nope. In fact, he drove his co-stars and director to the doughnut shop. And nobody acted like it was a big deal—Beau Wilder, driving the studio van. There was even an old coffee cup on the seat when he got in. He'd collected a few other pieces of trash, too, from the dashboard before they headed into town.

If you could call it a town. Indigo Beach was a hodge-podge of businesses and residences perched on the end of the world, its fishing pier a giant wooden exclamation point. Anyone with ADD would be immediately over-whelmed by the color and the signage and the endless variety of people he'd already seen in the space of ten minutes from the doughnut shop window. But the island was small enough that after a while, the jumble smoothed out, like the insides of a well-oiled clock on your mantel, the parts in sync, ticking regularly, working as a calm, comforting backdrop to your day.

He could see himself living on Indigo Beach—

If he weren't Beau Wilder.

"There's a hole in your character's psyche," Mike Carter,

the movie director, said from their booth, and held up a chocolate-covered doughnut. His voice was deep and rumbly, like a Harley. "A big round hole that can be filled only by—"

Through the window Beau saw Henry and Lacey Clark on the other side of the street. She looked beautiful. Tailored and vampy, all at once. Henry was the boss in his aviators and slick shorts. Beau couldn't help grinning into the palm he was leaning on.

"Beau?" Mike was a big guy with a bushy brown beard, black leather jacket that read MIKE'S POOLS on the back, and spikes on his black baseball cap.

"Right," Beau said, focusing again on the table talk. "I'm like a doughnut. *We're* like doughnuts."

How come no one was laughing? He looked around at the other two actors at the table, Simone Davis and Adam Monroe, who were nodding like old sages. Simone had taken Monique's role and Adam had taken Callum's.

Beau licked some sugar off his pinkie and gulped his coffee. Avant-garde filmmaking on a regular basis would drive him up the wall. He'd been hoping the other actors would become friends and make up for all the weirdness, but so far he wasn't too encouraged.

Simone was the love interest. Made sense, he supposed. She was pretty, like Monique, but in an entirely different direction. Instead of Monique's sun-kissed blond looks, Simone had long, jet-black hair. Violet eyes rimmed in black eyeliner. A diamond stud in her nose. When he asked her a simple question about where she was from, she stared at him and said, "I know I'm not Monique."

"So?" said Beau. "We don't need Monique. You're fine just the way you are."

"Peoria, Illinois, and I don't want to talk about it," she said back. From then on, she stared suspiciously at him.

He was used to admiring glances, so this was something new—and a little unnerving, as she was sitting right across from him in the booth and had no problem not blinking for minutes on end.

Adam Monroe, whose sharp elbow kept knocking into Beau's ribs, resembled your average European male model in *Vogue*: wounded, suffering, with look-at-me clothes— his collared shirt buttoned all the way up, his jeans too high at the waist and too skinny—and great hair. If Beau put his eyes out of focus a little, the guy resembled James Dean. That was the nicest thing he could think of to say. Adam was a whiner. A pretentious windbag. But Beau would try not to notice. Much.

Mike folded one giant arm over the other. "About that hole in your soul. It can only be filled if your character changes. Change is imperative. It's the substance—"

"Maybe the jelly or custard?" Beau interjected with another grin, then wondered if he was taking his life in his hands by messing with Mike.

"—of your character's journey." Mike lifted his chin at Beau. "Done with the snark?"

"Give the caffeine a chance." Beau maintained a pleasant smile, but he wasn't backing down. "Any minute now we can talk Freud. Or Adler. Maybe even Jung."

Mike placed both palms on the table and leaned forward, the table groaning against his weight.

Uh-oh.

But his blue gaze turned admiring, even friendly. "I like your style, man. You really got the roleplay, didn't you? My over-the-top jab at pseudo-intellectual smugness. You're dishing it right back. Doughnut holes, indeed. What utter crap, right? The irony is that some people fall for it. They think I'm *serious*."

"Stupid heads," murmured Simone.

Adam snorted.

Beau was totally weirded out by the whole conversation,

but he was gonna maintain his Beau cool, come what may with these folks.

"Authenticity." Mike leaned back. "That's all I seek in my actors. Give the role its truth. No bullshit. No fucking doughnut holes." He bit into his chocolate-covered confection and chewed.

Yeah. Okay. The guy was different. But he was actually sharp in his own way, which Beau found mildly irritating. He was hoping to breeze through the whole Indigo Beach experience, but he couldn't risk being on autopilot with this crowd.

If only he had a book called *Artsy-Fartsy Filmmaking 101* to pave the way.

Lacey and Henry were crossing the street now. She held his hand tight as they both watched for traffic. No one could miss her with her *I Love Lucy* hair color and that ponytail swinging back and forth. They were heading straight for the doughnut shop.

Henry saw him and waved like crazy. Beau raised his cup at him in salute. That little kid had a bead on him— the Dudley recognition still shocked him—and rocked aviator sunglasses way better than he did.

"You're going to make Evan come roaring to life," Mike said.

Adam couldn't roar if he wanted to, Beau thought, and kept his eyes on Lacey's boobs, which were awesome. Hopefully, she couldn't tell he was looking directly at them.

"Beau, dammit."

He looked back at Mike. "Yeah?"

"I said I look forward to your take on Evan."

"Not Evan," Beau reminded him. "Xander." The leading man. Still not a great role, but the best of the bunch.

"No." Mike dumped a pack of sugar into his coffee. "*Evan.*"

"Lucky." Simone's mouth curled up a fraction. "You get to die at the end."

"Yeah," said Adam. "No one's gonna cry for *me*."

"You're kidding, right?" Beau looked around the table. Was someone punking him? "Who's playing Xander?"

"I am," said Adam.

Beau crooked a thumb at Adam and looked at Mike. "*He's* Xander?"

"Yes." Mike lazily stirred his coffee with a spoon.

The sloppy clinking noise got on Beau's nerves. "That's a mix-up right there." He shifted in his seat. "Callum was playing Evan. He told me so."

"Callum's not calling the shots around here." Mike softly thumped a curled fist on the table. "Adam is playing Xander."

No way. That little piece of shit Adam was going to get the girl? And Beau was going to be the one who died a slow, lingering death because he was too dumb to figure out he was being poisoned?

This was too much. He'd already memorized all of Xander's lines in the first half of the script. He stood up and knocked over Simone's doughnut, which she'd poised on its edge, like a sculpture. "I gotta get outta here."

"But Beau—" Mike's beard blew the slightest millimeter to the right because the front door opened, letting in a big gust of salt air and Lacey and Henry.

Realization dawned. She was the damned Hollywood jinx, and she and Beau had slept in the same house last night!

This was all her fault.

"Henry, wait!" called Lacey. "Mr. Wilder's speaking with people."

But Henry ran straight to Beau.

It actually wasn't too difficult as an adoring crowd of Beau fans was lined up at the counter, leaving a polite gap between his table and the door. This was the South. After people finished hugging you to death and asking you who your favorite NASCAR driver was and if you went to church and did you like barbecue with mustard sauce or vinegar, they gave you your space—if you were a celebrity.

If not, get ready. Your life was no longer your own. Maybe that was why he'd had to get famous. He didn't want to have to answer any questions deeper than the barbecue sauce one.

Henry was so excited, his sunglasses shook down to the end of his nose. He grabbed Beau's arm and squeezed. "Mr. Wilder! I know you're not a dog now!"

No way would Henry have done such a gorilla grip on a dog.

Beau needed to be nice, although he was pissed at Mike. And sort of at Lacey, even if he kinda-sorta didn't really believe that jinx story. So he sat back down. "I'm glad," he told Henry and managed the shadow of a grin.

Good thing Henry hadn't specifically mentioned Dudley, or Beau might have been forever typecast as a cartoon dog, if that was possible. But maybe being typecast as a dog detective was better than being Evan, the knucklehead loser in *Flowers from the Heart*.

Anything was better than being Evan, actually. This role was gonna cast such shade on his career, he needed to contact Oliver immediately.

"Some other time, folks," he called to the crowd at the counter. "I'm not going anywhere."

They got the message and dispersed.

Henry pulled on his arm again. "Have you had a doughnut?"

"Two," Beau said, texting Oliver at the same time: *Everything gone to hell. Stand by for long-term damage control.* "They were good. Especially the spinach one."

"Yuck." Henry laughed. "You're making that up."

"Maybe I am."

"I want Mom to work here."

Beau glanced up at her. She stood there looking very innocent. Very innocent, indeed. But could she be the reason that *Biker Aliens* tanked? To tell the truth, he always kind of liked that movie. Bad writing, bad acting, bad filming and editing, but her presence in it had lent the cheesy production an endearing, almost defiant, quality, the way the "It's a Small World" ride in Disney World insisted you believe you were really entering a halcyon world of color, motion, and song when you knew damned well you were actually on a cranky old car circling around a bunch of paper puppets.

He hadn't seen her in anything else.

"Henry, we need to go," she said. "Mr. Wilder's busy with his friends and now his phone."

Did he sense a set-down there?

"We need to find the store manager," she added, looking very self-conscious yet also like a bossy Miss Manners type, all rolled into one.

Beau decided then and there he didn't believe in jinxes, or bad luck. Hearing about blackballed Hollywood Lacey was a fascinating factoid for its sheer entertainment value, he supposed. It even added to her allure somehow, ratcheted his guy instincts to protect the soft and vulnerable up another notch. Nothing like a woman tied to the railroad tracks with a train coming on to make a man want to jump in and save her.

But the sooner she went back to job hunting and out of his hair, the better. He needed to tell his movie friends to go to hell, forcing him to die in that crappy role—

"Sorry about the texting," he said to Henry.

"I don't care."

Made sense. He was five. Beau reached into his wallet and pulled out a fifty. "Here. Get yourself a doughnut. Keep the change."

"Wow, thanks." Henry grabbed the money.

But Lacey took the bill from his hand and handed it back to Beau. "A doughnut doesn't cost anywhere near fifty dollars, but thank you. We'll get our own."

Beau eyed her and put it slowly back in his wallet. Surely she didn't expect him to be a man of the people. He was holed up with the Hollywood elite all the time. He hadn't had any practice hanging out with customers in doughnut shops or diners or Laundromats in years, much less learning the ins-and-outs of dealing with a five-year-old boy.

"College fund," he said, thinking to mollify her. "That's what the change was for."

But she would have none of it. "Thanks, but no thanks. I'm taking care of that. And when Henry's older, he'll earn money toward it himself."

Whatevs, lady, he wanted to say. Because he sure as hell wasn't going to admire her for being an on-the-ball mom. That would mean he'd have to notice how much *his* mom suffered in that category, and he didn't want to go there.

"Who are these people, Beau?" Simone asked rudely. She'd been in Hollywood too long herself, apparently. "You grew up near here, right?"

"I did," Beau said.

On the Battery in Charleston. He didn't like to broadcast that fact. And thankfully, most people weren't real up on the details of the Early Years portion of his biography on Wikipedia.

"Are you an old friend?" Adam asked Lacey.

A loaded question if there ever was one.

Beau and Lacey exchanged a look. Maybe they should have thought of a story. But it was too late for that.

"Wait—" Adam clicked his fingers. "I recognize you."

"I'm not her," Lacey said.

"She," Beau corrected her. His expensive prep school education had been good for something. He knew his predicate nominatives up, down, and sideways.

Lacey ignored his little win. "I just look like her," she told Adam, then bent down to Henry. "Here you go." She handed him a dollar and two quarters from her purse and told him to go pick out a doughnut, any doughnut.

Henry scampered away.

"Yes, you are her," Adam insisted.

She, Beau said in his head, a tantrum about playing Evan wanting to burst forth from him like a gargoyle inside a possessed person.

"Your hair, everything about you," Adam added.

"Honestly, I'm not—"

"You're the girl painted on the giant mural on the side of that restaurant in downtown Charleston," Adam insisted. "The Hominy Grill."

The lines between Lacey's brows disappeared.

"You know," Adam went on, "the one with the vintage look. You're wearing a waitress uniform from the '50's. We had breakfast there the other day. Why would you deny it?"

Simone shrugged. "Who wants to be known as the girl from the mural? She's fifteen feet tall. Her nose alone is six inches across."

"It's honest work," Mike said.

"You've got a lovely nose," said Adam. "Perky."

"What's the girl in the mural holding in the bowl?" Simone asked Lacey.

"Grits,' " said Beau. He'd been to the Hominy Grill a million times.

"I've never tried a grit," Adam said.

Beau wanted to puke.

"It's always plural," Lacey told Adam without looking like she wanted to throttle him.

Could she possibly think Adam was cute—*adorbz*—whatever it was women said about men they had the hots for?

Beau sank farther into his funk. He knew without a doubt that he was the only one in the doughnut shop who wished he could toss a chair through the plate-glass window, leap out, and kick some Bad Guy ass. He wished there was a fake robbery at the gas station, or a staged kidnapping on the pier. Something he could shut down with a few well-placed stunt punches and phony bullets while a massive explosion took place behind him on a green screen. A little action to celebrate afterward with Lacey—and a fifteen-million-dollar salary—would clinch the whole deal for him.

Mike smiled at her. "How do you know Beau?"

Henry popped up in front of his mom with a chocolate-covered doughnut—this one with sprinkles. "We live together," he said, "in the lighthouse."

Shoot. Out of the mouths of babes.

Simone giggled. "Really?"

"Not forever." Henry hopped. Just once, a random kid move that Beau found awesome.

"Someday we'll have to leave," Henry added, super-fast. "But we're staying here in Indigo Beach. I'm getting a room painted like a football field, and Mom's buying a house with a red door and plants in blue pots out front." He inhaled a quick breath. "You can come over. She's gonna have chocolate chip cookies all the time."

Lacey's eyes widened. "*Someday*, Henry—" She sounded indulgent and worried, all at the same time.

"Someday *soon*," he told the group. "Mom promised."

At those words, her expression changed subtly. Now she looked scary-sexy, like the bad girls in Beau's movies. But even more like Greta Gildensturm.

He thought it was hot, but something in him also felt for her. "Lacey and I go way back," he jumped in.

"To when?" Simone asked.

There was half a beat of silence, then Lacey said, "We lived next door to each other. Growing up."

Beau wasn't sure where they were going with this tale, but he supposed one story was as good as the next. She'd just better not say he was like a brother to her. He'd had enough humiliation today already.

Mike whistled. "Wow. You grew up on the Battery in Charleston? Where they fired the first shots of the Civil War?"

"Uh-huh," Lacey said, her cheeks getting pink.

She'd better be able to keep this lie going—Beau had his doubts about her acting chops.

"Where all the rich people live?" Adam added. "That's primo real estate."

"Not all of it," Lacey said weakly. "My house was . . . was cozy. Just a little thing. Nothing special."

"Don't be embarrassed," said Mike. "We all know that cozy on the Battery is a small eight-bedroom mansion. Beau's family are gazillionaires, right, Beau?"

"I wouldn't say we have a *gazillion* dollars, Mike." Beau's reproach was mild.

Lacey shot a quick look at him, but it wasn't his fault he'd been born with a silver spoon in his mouth. And he wouldn't participate in an impolite discussion of his family's financial affairs. Rich Southern boys didn't talk money, unless it was to their stockbrokers, CFOs, or fathers, often not until the patriarch was on his deathbed—and even then the subject must be handled with decorum and humility.

"You people down here are so fascinating," Simone muttered, her brows drawn over her nose. "Were you a debutante, Lacey? That would be totally creepy. In a good way."

"Of course, she was," said Adam, "if she grew up on the Battery. No doubt she's here to welcome Beau back to South Carolina, right?"

Lacey put a tendril of hair behind her ear. "Well, when I heard he was coming to town to do a movie, I decided he could use a little company at the lighthouse."

"I need a lot of attention," said Beau. "All Southern guys are that way."

"It was more that he needs to stay anchored," Lacey said. "He's not a movie star around us. He's . . . well, he's the old next-door neighbor."

Beau grimaced at her and hoped it looked like a smile. "That's right."

Henry's head popped out from behind Lacey's dress. "He's not sure if he has superpowers—yet."

And he and his mother took off, leaving Beau alone in this briar patch.

"I get it," Mike said. "She's the girl who got away, the one you talked to across the backyard fence. Is the old flame reigniting as we speak, perhaps?"

"Just friends," Beau said. "No flames." No sex, either. Or kissing. Nothing. Not even a grab of her sweet derriere.

"Living together," Simone clarified, her intensity having moved to her hands, which were folded beneath her chin, her shiny silver nails glinting in the sun like talons.

"Not *together*," Beau said, "but in the same place."

No one believed him. They had their he's-known-as-a-horndog-this-can't-be-true expressions going. He'd have to make this good so they'd stop getting ideas. He looked around the shop, then leaned forward and said in a conspiratorial whisper, "She's just now decided she wants to live a normal life, apart from the high society she's used to. Since I'm back for a little while, I can help her out with a place to stay while she looks for a job."

Adam was into it. "She's obviously a single mother,"

he whispered back. "I wonder if her parents don't approve of her lifestyle and cut her off without a penny."

"Maybe they had a Southern aristocrat all picked out for her," said Simone, "and she fell in love with the wrong guy. And they're pissed."

"Like *The Notebook*," said Mike.

"Too wimpy," said Simone. "Maybe her life's in danger."

These people were getting carried away.

"No, Simone," Beau said. "She really needs a job. That's it." He hated to get deeper into misleading them—not because it was a lie but because he'd need to get his story matched up to Lacey's. That involved talking to her, which usually involved sparks flying.

"Yet she's more than a poor little rich girl," said Mike. "She's also the girl in the mural. There's something iconic about her. Pop-culture-y. Vibe-y."

Beau didn't like how Mike made up words by adding a *y* onto the end of them. But his main concern was covering his butt. He didn't need the tabloids coming down here to investigate his supposedly new live-in girlfriend and then turning around and doing stories on *Flowers from the Heart*.

Beau Wilder plays a man who not only doesn't get the girl, he dies by slow poisoning . . .

He glanced over his shoulder and saw Lacey deep in conversation with the shop owner. Her lips were the color of his mother's favorite tulips. Their hue shouldn't have gone with that red hair, but the whole package worked somehow. It worked really well, the way a red-and-white-checkered tablecloth went with every color of plate you wanted to put on it. Because it wasn't the color, it was the feeling.

She radiated *picnic*. And apple pie and ice cream. Maybe a cold beer and Frisbee, too, followed by a big makeout session under the shade of an old tree by a riverbank.

Henry's face suddenly fell. So did his mother's, although she recovered quickly and grabbed his hand.

Well, hell. It looked like she didn't get the job.

The manager was a fool not to hire her—either that, or he just didn't need another employee. Reality was a bitch sometimes. That had to account for why he reached into the doughnut case, grabbed another chocolate-covered doughnut with sprinkles, and handed it to Henry.

Beau would have done the same thing. Doughnuts made everything better.

Henry gave the man a crooked, sad little smile. When a boy that age knew that the glories of a fried circle of sweet dough dipped in icing didn't outweigh his mother's getting a job, he was too perceptive for his own damned good.

"I gotta say good-bye to 'em," Beau told his movie friends—and he used that term very loosely for Adam and Simone. The jury was still out on whether he and Mike would be friends.

He slid out of the booth. Stretched without really showing anyone, which meant he flexed his abs and thigh muscles. He knew he looked good in his jeans and buttondown oxford—preppy was his style, and no wonder, since he came from a long line of Southern gentlemen—but Lacey didn't seem to notice. She opened the door and was about to walk out.

Wow. Without even saying good-bye.

CHAPTER EIGHT

"Hey," Beau called to Lacey and Henry from his end of the doughnut shop.

Yes, *his* end. Wherever he went seemed to become his territory.

Except for Henry's free doughnut, Lacey's visit there had been a bust. Still no job, and she was starting to worry. Beau's three movie friends all sat and stared at her from their booth. She wondered if she had a large, glistening flake of doughnut sugar on her mouth that the glare from the sun was picking up, but she resisted the urge to swipe at her face.

"Yes?" she called to Beau, who looked mighty delicious in his preppy Southern man clothes, which often involved a needlepoint-embroidered belt. His was black with white pirate skulls.

"Just wanted to say good luck." He didn't crack a smile.

She nodded briefly. "Thanks."

And then something crazy happened. The big man with the spiked cap stood up from the booth and called down to her, "Young lady, *I'll* hire you."

Beau's brows gathered together and just as quickly smoothed out again.

"R-really?" Lacey's fingers tingled with the need to wring themselves, but she held back.

"Yes," Spiked Cap said. "I crave your sort of energy on my set. You're multifaceted, like a diamond."

"*Me?*" That was a poetic thing to say. Or maybe he was just a big fan of Rihanna.

"Pearls, Mike," said the moody black-haired woman. "That's what they wear down here."

"*She's* not wearing any," the skinny guy with the buttoned-up shirt said.

"It's because she *rejects* them," the black-haired woman said with scorn, "and all that they represent."

"And embraces the Every Woman," Adam said. "Hence, that mural."

Lacey secretly cringed. What in the world had Beau told them about her, apart from the rich thing? But she'd heard the word *job*, so she wasn't going anywhere.

"Will you work for me?" the man with the hat said. "I'm Mike Carter, director of *Flowers from the Heart*."

Wow. The director. How had she come all the way back to the East Coast to start over and still find herself talking to movie people?

It was because of Beau—Beau invading her space in the lighthouse.

This was all his fault.

"I don't know." She trained her eyes on the doughnut case, which was colorful and comforting. "Acting. Movie sets. Actors." She hugged herself hard and reluctantly looked back at the movie group. "Except for Beau, whom I haven't seen in—"

"Ten years," he filled in for her.

"—I don't know anything about the industry." It was a bald-faced lie, of course. But the last thing she needed was to go back to a place swarming with actors. The very idea gave her the heebie-jeebies, although around Beau it wasn't the heebie-jeebies she felt—it was some kind of sickness. Made her want to fan-girl lunge at him and kiss him just to see if he was any good at it.

"This whole movie shtick isn't in Lacey's wheelhouse," Beau told Mike.

He was right. But did he have to want to avoid her so badly?

"She's more into—" He was giving her a chance to talk her way out of it.

But then she looked at Henry and realized she couldn't afford to let the subject drop. She thought for a minute. "I haven't discovered what it is I'm good at yet, to be honest."

And it was the truth.

"No wonder," Mike said warmly. "Having gobs of money and prestige is a big distraction."

That hadn't been her problem. She didn't know what her excuse was.

"Here's the good news." Mike's rumble-strip voice competed with the sound of a broken muffler on a car outside and won. "I won't need you on the set, although you'll probably be around it a lot."

"Oh?" Lacey put her hand on Henry's shoulder to steady herself. "Where would you need me?"

This was it. He'd better not imply the casting couch. They never said it out loud—he'd call it something like "coffee girl," or "helper around the office." Insiders would know what he meant, but maybe these insiders wouldn't care. Maybe Beau and the other two had hearts hardened by ruthless ambition, like Monique and Callum. A lot of people were like that in Hollywood.

"I need a babysitter for my twins," Mike said.

"*Mom*," Henry said in the voice he reserved to call her attention to coveted toys he saw on TV or in a shop window.

Lacey tried not to get too excited. Henry did need friends, but maybe these twins were older, and if they were, she'd say no. It wouldn't be the first time a Hollywood type used his perfectly self-sufficient children as a cover for trying to seduce a babysitter.

"How old are they?" she asked casually, but *don't let this be the deal breaker* was what she thought.

"Six," he replied.

Hallelujah!

"A boy and a girl." Mike's face softened, and Lacey knew right then that he was on the up-and-up. "I need someone who's fun and encourages them to read and play outside a lot."

"I like the idea," she said. "But I'm curious . . . why me? Why not some fully vetted person from a nanny agency?"

"My older sister Jo Jo's been watching them since their mother died," he said, "but she left." He paused. "We don't know when she'll be back. She said she needed a break."

Not good, she read clearly in Beau's eyes. She felt the same way. She also wanted to know how long Mike had been widowed, but it wasn't appropriate to ask. Her heart went out to him, at any rate, and to his kids. "I'm really sorry."

He shrugged his massive shoulders. "She put a note on the table in my trailer. It's kind of a mess, actually. I-I haven't had much time to process it, much less find someone, and the movie . . ." He trailed off. "Never mind. I asked because I can see already that you're a good mother, but you have reservations. Naturally. This is out of the blue. I'll call a local agency."

"No," she said, surprised at how strongly she felt about it. Henry ducked out from under the grip on his shoulder and stood a foot away, spinning a stool at the counter with his hand. "Please don't. I'm very interested in the job. I'd love to hear more before I accept, of course. I'll need to know how much it pays, for one."

He named a nice hourly wage that certainly beat any

local waitressing job she'd be able to get, even if her tips were terrific. And no shopkeeper would ever pay her that sort of money. "The hours rack up, believe me," he said. "Some days are eighteen hours long."

Money!

"The wage sounds fair," she said, trying not to show how excited she was becoming. "Anything else I should know?" Before she dropped the bomb of *her* requirements: Henry had to be with her. No way was she leaving him for eighteen hours at a time.

Mike managed a small smile, but then it faded as quickly as it had come. "Actually, there *is* a complication."

Lacey's hope plummeted. "Oh?"

"You'd have to hang out with my late wife's father, too." Mike pulled on his hat brim. "Dickey's old, cantankerous, and never holds back his opinion. He has his good moments, but you have to be patient through the bad." His expression was grim now.

"I think I could handle that," she said tentatively.

"And one more thing."

That wasn't bad enough? "What?"

"He's a pathological liar. It started after his wife died about twenty years ago."

Lacey bit her lip. That was sad. And unhealthy. Would it be okay to have Henry around a guy like that? "I don't know . . ."

"The twins seem to let everything he says go in one ear and out the other," he assured her. "So I'm not worried about them. It's just kind of vexing for the grown-ups in the room."

Up to this point, Beau's face had registered concern, the guy kind, which looked a lot like indifference. But the more Mike revealed, the more deeply etched Beau's facial lines and the harder his expression. At the moment, he looked scary and overwhelmingly competent.

Which also meant super sexy.

Not that Lacey caréd.

Their female companion was busy unwrapping a piece of gum, her leg swinging back and forth under the table, her spiked black heel appearing every half second in the aisle while the guy with the pompadour peered intently at his phone, his thumbs jabbing at it, oblivious to the conversation.

Maybe they already knew about Mike's situation. Either that, or they didn't care.

Like Monique and Callum. They hadn't cared about her or Henry, and they'd lied their asses off. She had experiences with liars, after all, and maybe this time she could put her experience to good use.

She swallowed hard. "I'm still interested."

"Really?" Mike's face lit up.

"Yes. Was your sister able to get along with your father-in-law, even if he's cranky and fibs a lot?"

"I'm ninety-nine percent sure he's why she left. He's only been with us for two weeks. I dragged him off his farm in upstate South Carolina when I saw it was just too much for him to handle. A couple of local guys are going to oversee the place for a while. Dickey really shouldn't be living alone, and he won't go to an assisted living facility. I need to work on him." He shook his head. "The timing couldn't be worse. And the kids really liked Aunt Jo Jo. But I can't neglect him."

"I understand," she said. "About Henry—"

"Bring him, of course," Mike told her. "I'll tell Dickey to watch his manners—and his outlandish tales—around you both. I promise. I'll make sure you're happy, Lacey. Henry, too."

The knot in her chest loosened a *lot*. She wouldn't have to spend a portion of her wages on day care for Henry and fret about how he was doing away from her. They'd be able to take advantage of the weather and the beach and have fun together, all while saving money faster.

She made eye contact with Beau, but he didn't give off happy vibes at all. It shouldn't hurt since he was a stranger, but it did. It reminded her that she was desperate for a friend, someone who'd celebrate her triumphs, big and small, with her.

"You'll have access to my family's trailer," Mike said. "Henry can nap if he needs to—you two can even spend the night if we're doing a late shoot. I'll sleep on the couch in the studio office."

Wow. Lacey was impressed. The guy was bending over backward to get her to say yes. But she wasn't done with her requirements. "Henry and I intend to become full-time islanders here on Indigo Beach," she said. "I need a permanent job."

"We're not ever leaving." Henry spun his stool.

Lacey reached out, took his hand, and stopped the spinning.

She had no idea what kind of job she could get with her background. But she wanted one that she could build on, a job that would mean at least some security for her and Henry. So she didn't want to settle. But she couldn't afford to be choosy at this point, either. This was what happened when a person put all her eggs in one basket and closed her eyes, pretending that it would never fall.

"You can look for something more permanent while you've got the kids and Dickey," Mike said. "I'll get someone else to stay with them—all of them, including Henry—an hour and a half a day. You can take off and job hunt." He shrugged. "This'll tide you over until you find what you're looking for. And you'd be doing me a huge favor, meanwhile."

Yes!

The job was sounding better and better, but she had to

cover all her bases. Her heart tripped and her palms sweated. It wasn't like this was a big business deal she was negotiating, right? It was only babysitting kids and being a companion to an elderly man with some issues.

But it is *a big deal*, her heart reminded her. *It's the first step out of a huge rut.*

"That sounds good," she said. "But what if I find a great job tomorrow? Or the next day? I might. And"—she wasn't sure how to say this—"what if your sister comes back tomorrow or the next day? I mean, that would be great—"

"You're right," Mike interrupted her. "There's no job security here. Which is why I'm just glad you're saying yes. If you get another job, all I need is a couple days' notice. And if and when she comes back, I'll give you an extra week's pay." He had an answer for everything, and no wonder. He was a dad who needed help.

And she was a mother who needed it, too. "Are you sure?" She let go of Henry's hand, and he slid off the stool.

"Positive. Can you start right now?" Mike sounded hopeful.

"Yes." She smiled.

Look how quickly one's luck could change!

She was a nanny now. They never lost their cool. She prayed that being around all the reminders of her disastrous career wouldn't cause her constant agitation, and she hoped she wouldn't see Beau much, if at all. He got her riled up, and she needed to stay serene.

Mike approached her, his hand extended. She shook it and, in that moment, knew that she'd made a great decision. He put his palm down, faceup, and Henry slapped it—hard.

The director took it just the way a dad would. "You got muscles, bro."

Yes, this was going to work. "Where are your kids and father-in-law now?" Lacey asked him.

"Dickey's taking a nap. The kids are back at the studio in the office with a production assistant who can't do her job very well while she's babysitting." He grinned.

More than ever, Lacey liked him. What a guy, to bother to act even remotely pleasant when he had so much on his plate.

He introduced her properly to his table companions, Simone and Adam, both of whom told her—in their understated cool-actor way—that they couldn't wait to see her on the set. Then they followed Mike up front to the register.

Beau lingered while she watched Henry tie his shoe.

"Congratulations on the job," he said. "Weird as it sounds."

"Hey, well, beggars can't be choosers. Thanks."

He loomed over her like a construction crane about to drop a thousand-pound weight. Two women squeezed past them, and one gasped out loud.

"My, oh, my," she said. "It's Beau Wilder!"

"Have a good day, ladies," he said.

But they wouldn't leave until he signed their doughnut napkins.

"Is there anything else?" Lacey asked him when he was through. "You're annoying me with all that fake grinning."

"Yeah, as a matter of fact." His delivery was smooth. Easy. Nothing to capture Henry's notice. "I think it's best you stay off the set as much as possible."

"You're sounding mighty overbearing," she said just as pleasantly. "I have no reason to go onto the set, unless for some reason Mike calls me onto it. Why do you care?"

"I've heard stories. Let's just say you wouldn't win any popularity contests in Hollywood."

"Oh, yeah?" She smiled at him, for Henry's sake. "You're into gossip?"

Beau Wilder shook his handsome head. "Not usually. But where there's smoke, there might be fire—especially around *you*."

Henry pulled hard on the two loops of his shoelace and was done.

"Honey," Lacey told him, "wait for me up front."

"Yes, Mom."

He took off, heading straight for Mike, probably to ask him about his kids, and she turned back to Beau. "If you believe those ridiculous rumors that I'm responsible for three movies flopping and the downfall of their directors, you're not only into gossip, you're superstitious, which I think is the luxury of people with nothing better to do."

"I don't believe in jinxes. But maybe there's something to the causing-trouble part of these rumors."

She put her hand on her hip. "Any trouble I caused, I did for darned good reasons. As an actor, I was invested in the process, okay? Relax. I'm not an actor now. I'm a nanny and a companion to a senior citizen."

"I still want you to steer clear of the set. It's a good idea for a lot of reasons."

"Such as?"

"We're already living in the same lighthouse. There's such a thing as spending too much time together."

He was simple and forthright—like a sheriff in an old Western. But she was no bad guy. And hell if she would leave the saloon. "You're not the boss of me, Wilder. You're only a roommate. And you're welcome to spend all the time you want holed up in your bedroom."

"You'd like that, but I'm not a hermit. Expect to see me living large at the lighthouse."

"Don't even think about it. Not around Henry."

"I do what I want. Lucky for you, I'm not into upsetting kids."

"What are the other reasons I need to stay off the set?"

She saw a shutter go down over his eyes. "Professional ones."

"Oho." She felt a sharp jolt of insecurity at the thought of her failed career. "You're going back to the jinx thing."

"No." His tone was flat. "I'm not."

"Then what is it?"

"You're a distraction." He didn't say it at all in a friendly way. "And I promise you, for your sake, you don't want to be."

The look he sent her, banked and hot like a coal fire, made her toes curl.

"Well—" She didn't know what to say. She *knew* she was a distraction. Her whole life she'd been one. She was waiting for the day that she'd be the star—the one person you didn't want to swat off like a fly so you could move on to better things.

But maybe that day would never come.

"Excuse me," Beau said. "I have a movie to make."

When he brushed by her—an awful lot like the four-star general he'd once played on the front lines of an intergalactic war—the hair on Lacey's scalp stood up just a millimeter higher. Her breasts, for some reason, came to full attention. She was ready to obey his orders, to stay out of his way, even to salute.

The man was insanely charismatic.

And then she remembered he'd been Dudley. Sweet, eccentric Dudley.

"I'll stay out of your way on the set if you teach Henry how to surf," she called to him.

He turned around. "Is he a good swimmer?"

"Yes."

"Are you?"

"Of course."

"Only if you participate, too."

"No."

He didn't change a muscle in his neutral expression, just continued on his merry way.

"Okay, yes!" she cried. Because Henry really did want to learn how to surf. And maybe a tiny part of her wanted to learn, too.

"You'd better wear a bikini," Beau said over his shoulder.

Lacey's knees almost gave out. "I don't have one."

"It's a bikini or nothing."

"Fine!" she said, angry as hell. "I'll get a bikini!"

When he walked out the front door, he was chuckling.

The cocky bastard.

CHAPTER NINE

Beau parked the car down the street from his family's antebellum home on the Battery, a waterfront park overlooking Charleston Harbor and Fort Sumter. Tourists were a part of the landscape, as were horse-and-carriages, moss-draped oaks, and lots of old cannons.

All kinds of feelings came back to him. Riding his bike down this broken sidewalk. Leaning on the railing of the Battery wall and looking down into the green-brown Atlantic—locally defined as the place where the Ashley and Cooper Rivers met.

To Beau, Charleston was a place of war, of battles won and lost, and that was never more true than in his own house. He walked up the stone steps, opened the heavily lacquered false front door with its imposing brass knocker, and strode across the piazza, past two sleeping King Charles spaniels sprawled out like little brown-and-white fur rugs.

"Hey, you two, ever heard of being watchdogs?" he murmured, but didn't hold it against them. It was too pretty a day to bother with burglars.

One of them looked up and blinked. "*Ruff,*" it said with little enthusiasm.

"That's a fail," he told it before he opened the front

door—the real one, this time—and entered his ancestral home, which would one day be his.

Inside, the air was heavy and still. A bouquet of fragrant flowers sat on a recently polished mahogany table. Angela's work. Their longtime maid was probably upstairs now, ironing the bedsheets and watching *The Price Is Right*.

To his right was a formal living room, with windows twelve feet high facing the harbor. It was sunny and bright, his favorite room in the house. Especially because hanging on the wall above the fireplace were three Revolutionary War–era swords that had belonged to a great-great-great grandfather, one of George Washington's generals.

"Mom?"

"In here!" she called from the kitchen in her refined Virginia accent. Mother was from Richmond. She'd kindly agreed to marry a blue-blooded Charlestonian and move here, but her heart would always be in Virginia.

Beau crossed through the dining room—weighty with an antique sideboard, a vast table with seating for twelve, and china and silver housed in a towering cabinet. The walls were lined with old watercolors of rice fields that had been hanging there for as long as he could remember.

He entered the almost vintage-looking space where his mother stood at the sink rinsing a plate, her elegant hands moving slowly, gracefully. She didn't believe in electric dishwashers. She was quite the penny-pincher in some ways, although she took it as a matter of course that one should wear thousand-dollar suits and five-hundred-dollar shoes.

She angled her cheek for Beau to kiss.

"You look good," he told her.

"Thank you." She sounded happy to see him. But they weren't into large displays of affection. She dried her hands on a linen towel, embroidered with yellow daisies, and turned to face him. "You'll never believe it," she said, "Howie Buckner died yesterday."

Whoa. This was how Charleston conversations always went. The local gossip came first.

"I'm really sorry to hear that." Mr. Buckner had lived down the street. Beau remembered the man catching him climbing over his back garden wall once when he was about nine to go fishing in his koi pond. He'd been about a hundred years old back then already, so he *did* believe it.

"You know his baby sister married Peter Larson," Beau's mother went on. "From the sugarcane Larsons?"

"Right." Beau didn't care one iota, but he pretended to.

"I understand you're making a movie on Indigo," Mom said, seguing without any transitions. The gossip part was like taking your first breath at birth, totally necessary but soon gotten out of the way.

"Yes, ma'am."

She projected no judgment—yet.

Just like the old days, he opened the fridge. It was so small, he had to crouch to see inside. It had the curved front of a really old appliance, and it was. He wondered how it could possibly still be running when he grabbed a cold Evian water and took a slug, eyeing his mother as he did.

She waited patiently—she was always polite. When he lowered the glass bottle, she said, "Shall we sit on the second-floor piazza? It's a beautiful day."

"Fine. Is Angela here?"

"She left half an hour ago. She's got to bake a couple of coconut cakes for her church bazaar. She'll be sorry to have missed you."

He was sorry, too. He'd have to come back to see her. He remembered her coconut cake, light, sweet, washed down with milk. She'd chuckle deep in her throat when he ate a fat slice in a matter of a few bites. "I'll never stop making 'em," she'd say, "so slow down."

Endless coconut cakes. Forever. The thought used to make him so happy, he'd laugh out loud while he was chewing.

Angela had been more a mother to him than Mom ever had.

He walked behind her up the back stairs. She always held her neck high, her slim posture erect. She was in a pair of expensive-looking tan slacks, her usual Italian leather low-heeled shoes, and one of her many silk blouses. This one was burgundy. He might have even given it to her. Gracing her ears were some old pearl studs. No necklace. Mom always said she didn't want to look like a Christmas tree. She'd learned that as an exchange student in Paris when she was a girl.

When they walked outside, Charleston Harbor in all its sparkling beauty lay before them.

"Why haven't you done a movie here before?" she asked him.

"I've never been asked."

"You'd think you'd have enough clout by now to make some demands." She kept her eyes on the water.

"Mom, it takes a village to make a movie."

She cut her eyes at him for a split second. The infamous Julia set-down.

"Maybe I should just get home more," he said. "I'm sorry."

She lifted one dainty shoulder. "I understand how busy your life is. Tell me about this movie. It sounds like a tearjerker to me. I read about it online. Or is it an existential treatise of some sort?"

"Both," he said. "The good guys don't win in the end. No one goes home happy. Not really."

"This may kill your career."

"I sure as hell hope I have more traction than that," he said, not daring to show his mother that he was more than a little worried himself. "One mistake shouldn't negate all the good stuff."

"Yes, the good stuff." His mother's mouth crooked up. "Which is pretty much about blowing up things and saving the planet. Or getting the girl."

"And your point is?"

"You shouldn't have taken this one."

She was a mass of contradictions. "I don't get it. First, you diss my other work. And now you're saying this kind of movie is wrong for me, too."

She pursed her lips.

"Besides"—he noted how stiffly she was sitting, but he was her *son*, for God's sake—"I had to take it. I'm contractually obligated. It's a long story."

"Tell me," she said. "I don't have to be at the symphony fundraiser for another three hours."

So he told her.

"You should have taken your father up on his offer to have the contract vetted by an outside party."

Of course, he already knew this. And she knew he knew. But he supposed she had to get her digs in.

"Your father had a good head for business," she said matter-of-factly.

It blew Beau's mind that she could say *your father* with no acrimony. "I know Dad was smart. But I wanted nothing to do with him."

She didn't speak for a second, but she did move . . . oh, yes, she stood up and went to the veranda railing, as if she couldn't bear to hear the ugly truth sitting down, which was that Beau had hated his father, and they hadn't reconciled before he died unexpectedly.

"Well," she said, turning to face him, "maybe it's for the best if your career slows down."

"I thought you said this movie might kill it."

She waved a hand. "Oh, celebrities always stage comebacks. You all seem to have nine lives." Mom never said *y'all*. She thought it was beneath her. So she said *you all* instead. And she'd said it as if he were a stranger. "Or you could always quit. How much longer before you get it out of your system?"

Beau stood, too. "Why don't you get it, Mom? My acting career is not a hobby. I'm not going to quit."

"But you could have a full life right here in Charleston. You've got a family heritage to protect, another generation to produce. You can't very well do that from Hollywood."

He walked over to her and picked up her hand, which was cool and delicate in his. "I know you don't like what I'm doing. But I love doing it. Doesn't that matter to you?" He gave her fingers a gentle squeeze. *Squeeze back, Mom. Go ahead.*

But she didn't.

Was there anyone who really cared if he was happy or not?

She pulled her hand away and looked back out at the water. A carriage went by carrying a load of happy tourists. "What will happen to this place after I'm gone?" Her voice was hollow. "Are you going to sell it to the highest bidder? Someone 'from off'?"

"I didn't say I'm never coming back," Beau told her, "but I'm in the prime of my life. The prime of my career."

"Can't you be in your prime here?" The edge of pique in her tone was as close as Julia Wilder would ever come to pleading. "Charlotte Wallace has turned down three proposals and is still waiting for you to ask her to marry you. And if she's not your type, there are other girls perfectly suited from your growing-up years, not to mention we have all sorts of Yankees moving in—smart young women who run the museums and open fine shops on King

Street. I don't care if you marry one—as long as you *stay*. You owe us that."

"I'm not going to debate with you what I do and don't owe you and Dad's memory. Honestly, I'm not up for it. I have too much on my plate, and I don't think you really want to know."

"At the very least," she said, on her dignity, "you could deign to come to your cousin's wedding ball since you're in town. You missed her debut and her graduation."

Sarah had gone to the College of Charleston, Mom's alma mater.

"I couldn't make it, remember? I was in Africa for her debut. And England during her graduation."

"So says the man who draws eight-figure salaries and can hop on a private jet whenever he so chooses." Mom was frosty now. He'd stepped over her line, and he had to wonder—who did *she* share her emotions with? Anyone?

He felt sorry for her. Because he knew what it was like to have no one there to confide your deepest feelings to. "Well, I'm here now," he said at the veranda doors, "so of course I'll go."

She dropped her shoulders an inch. "Good."

There was a beat of silence. What now? She'd won her little battle.

"I've got to get back for the read-through."

She nodded, but she made no move toward him.

"Did you ever get drunk, Mom?" he asked her. "Or cuss? Or do anything wrong in your life? I kinda wish you had."

"Son, now you're talking plain silly."

But he sensed a slight easing of tension. To celebrate, he did the right thing again and went back to her and kissed her cheek. "I'll talk to you soon, 'kay? And stop worrying about me. I'll be fine."

And he would be. Beau had learned long ago to let things he couldn't change slide right off his back.

Downstairs on the porch, he put his smoky-lensed Costas back on and walked over the slumbering dogs, knowing his mother was still above, listening for his departure, planning further how to capture him in her social net.

"Mom? Go have a drink!" he called up to her.

"Son," she warned him. "Don't talk so loud. We have neighbors."

He chuckled and shut the porch door behind him, glad the duty visit was done.

CHAPTER TEN

Lacey had this—at least, she thought she did. She could manage rambunctious twins. Because that's what Bob and Carol were. She'd discovered that as soon as she saw them both pulling open every drawer they could in the studio office looking for leprechauns.

But handling a rambunctious old man who told bald-faced lies was another story.

Just assume everything he says is a lie, she decided. That was her big plan.

Gotta love big plans.

Dickey Baird leered at her from his perch on the edge of his son-in-law's desk. "Keepin' the young'uns occupied," he said with a cackle. He wore a train engineer's cap, overalls, and a long-sleeved white T-shirt.

He looked like a wicked scarecrow come to life.

The twins were sitting at a table with Henry. All three were passing around her makeup compact and making faces in the mirror. "Yes," she said, "but telling the production assistant George Clooney needed to speak with her on the phone on the set, and then telling the twins there are leprechauns in the office hiding gold—this is where their dad's business is run, Mr. Baird. You know better than that."

"Maybe now he'll stay outta *my* business." Dickey Baird stood up. His head came to her chest. "My, oh, my." His faded eyes twinkled now, clear and sharp. "You can call me Dickey. But only when you wear dresses like that one."

"No matter what you say, I'm not leaving," she told him, stacking papers on a desk. The kids had pulled out a ton. It would take a couple of hours, probably, to file them back correctly. She'd shooed Mike and the assistant out. She needed to get on top of this problem herself.

"When I was six, I was plowing fields," Dickey said.

"So? Kids are different now."

"Anyone woulda told my six-year-old self to look for leprechauns, I'd'a got out my rifle and held me a leprechaun shoot."

"I know you want to shock me," she said. "But you might as well give up."

"I'll pay you three thousand dollars right now to take me home. I got it under the bed. I swear on my mother's grave. You and your boy can jump on a Greyhound bus and take off to Mexico."

"I'm not interested."

"You don't care that an old man has been kidnapped from his own home, where he'd like to die in peace?"

"You haven't been kidnapped. Mike is trying to help you. And you're not anywhere near dead."

"Pshaw. A lot you know about being old. If these bones could talk—"

"You don't need 'em to. Your mouth runs enough for three people. And you're not particularly fond of facts."

"That was called disrespect in my day." He tried to look put upon.

Lacey put her hands on her hips. "Here's the deal. You and I have to get along. I don't know how long you're staying, but if you want me to be able to tell Mike you're doing well, you need to act mature and responsible. Otherwise, he'll be afraid to send you back."

"I'm calling my lawyers."

"Go ahead."

"You're a smart-aleck," he said, "but you won't last. You're too pretty. Jo Jo was horse-faced, poor thing. No man looked at her twice. But you—you'll run off with some gullible guy within a week."

She poked him in his scrawny chest. "Jo Jo *did* run off."

"Not with a man. I drove her off."

"And you're outright fiendish to be proud of it. Don't you dare insult her, or me, either. Only reprobates talk like that, and I'd hate to think you'd reach the ripe old age of ninety-four—"

"Hey, I'm only eighty-one!"

"—and you're still unenlightened."

He went over to the kids, grabbed the compact from Henry's hands, and peered at himself. "These eyes don't look over seventy," he muttered.

"Maybe after that nap you're about to take, they won't," Lacey said, and took her compact back.

He didn't argue with her. "These kids are exhausting."

"No one told you to lure the production assistant out of here and babysit them."

"Someone has to get my son-in-law's attention."

"Come on, kids."

They jumped down from the table and followed her and Dickey, whom she'd linked arms with. "We have to work together, whether you like it or not. Now show me to the trailer."

Dickey narrowed his eyes at her, but he appeared willing to cooperate—finally.

A minute later, he opened the door to a trailer and gestured for her to go in.

She was a little skeptical. "You first."

"Fine." He pulled himself up by holding on to a little stair railing.

She almost felt sorry for his bony old self, but then she remembered he'd run off Jo Jo, looked down her own cleavage with not a bit of shame, and dashed that PA's hopes when she found out George Clooney was not on the line, after all.

She held the door open for the kids next.

Carol came first. She was a tough little thing in jeans and a pink HURRAY FOR HOLLYWOOD! shirt. She had brown eyes, freckles, and two brown braids that stuck out like pokers. "I wanted those leprechauns." She sounded like she smoked two packs of Camels a day.

"Miz Lacey," Lacey encouraged her.

"Miz Lacey," Carol added obligingly.

"You can't have 'em. They live in Ireland, and they prefer to hide from people. Otherwise, they can't make those cookies they make."

"Then I'm going to Ireland," piped up Bob, who was missing both front teeth and finally was lucky enough to get a sentence without any *S*'s.

Who named a little kid Bob? Shouldn't he be Bobby?

But even though she'd have to wear a raincoat around Bob, with all the spit that flew out of his mouth, and Carol tended to be gassy (hopefully, it was temporary), she already loved them both. They were motherless. And now their aunt had left them.

Henry, sweet Henry, sick with joy over making two new friends within seconds of meeting them, came next. He shoved Bob in the butt to get him up the stairs. Bob grabbed Henry's shoulder and wouldn't let go. They were two cogs in a vast machine called Hyperactive Boy Children Who Need Exercise. It could power an entire country and remove its dependence on oil any day, if only someone could figure out how to harness the machine's energy.

"Go," Lacey said weakly. The XY-chromosome machine, besides creating energy, sucked it out of everyone around it.

Finally, she got inside. The interior was dullsville. She'd anticipated more. There was a modest flat-screen TV, an ugly little kitchen, and a tacky lounge area. Halfway back was a double berth on one side, a twin on the other, both as severe as any soldier's cot in a Quonset hut. In the rear, a door exposed the end of a big bed covered in the shiny emerald-green floral quilt from hell.

Mike must have taken the worst trailer and left his actors the luxurious ones.

Henry squealed with excitement and bounced on an overstuffed chair that looked like a giant portobello mushroom. The twins got right to the TV. One of them picked up the remote and started clicking.

"Wait a minute." She took the remote back. "We need to find some games. Or cards. Books, too. You're going to take me on a tour."

"Hey," someone called from the back. "What're y'all doing in my trailer? Didn't you see the sign?"

Shoot. Her heart instantly picked up its pace.

She'd been had.

Beau was here. When he came out of the back room, his nearness made her a little crazy.

But she couldn't afford to be. She had to be like Mary Poppins. Stern. In charge. Unafraid. That was a nanny's usual MO anyway.

Dickey pulled a door hanger that said BEAU WILDER—PRIVATE out of his shirt and started to laugh. Either that, or he was having an asthma attack.

He'd moved fast for an old man. She vowed to be on high alert with him from now on.

Beau strode toward them as if they were on a reality show castle set. He was the master of ceremonies backlit by kerosene-fueled flaming torches, and he was about to throw them all in a plastic moat filled with warm bathwater and electronic hungry crocodiles.

"Sorry," she said, and was annoyed with herself for thinking how handsome and kissable he looked.

She couldn't help remembering that sex dream. It was primal and intimate and more than lust—it had been a crush dream, made of happy and sensual and want, the ultimate sweet escape from obligations and worries—and from what was wrong and what was right.

It was ridiculous and embarrassing to contemplate in real life, but she hadn't let it go. *Yet.* It was too luscious. She still got a rush of warmth to her lower belly thinking of it.

"Uh-huh," he said, as if she'd barged into his domain on purpose.

She refused to rise to the bait. "Dickey, you owe Mr. Wilder an apology."

"Apology, my ass," Dickey said, and threw the door hanger with Beau's name on it on the couch.

"Watch your language in front of the children," Lacey told him. "And you invaded Mr. Wilder's privacy. That's not mature. *Or* responsible."

"So it's come to this." Dickey snorted. "We think namby-pamby signs should keep people out. In my day, everyone kept a shotgun above the door."

"People walked in at their own peril." Beau looked at Lacey as if *peril* could mean all kinds of things.

The dream flooded her brain.

"Exactly." Dickey sighed with satisfaction.

"Let's go." Lacey waved the kids over, and they clomped down the stairs and stood outside the door.

"Wait right there," Lacey told them. "Henry, you know the drill."

"Let's hit up the town sometime," Beau said to Dickey.

And he ignored Lacey, even though she was the one who'd defended his right to privacy.

"Sounds good to me." Dickey saluted Beau then ambled down the steps like an innocent old man.

"I'm sorry." Lacey wished she wouldn't turn red so easily. Thank God he'd been dressed. And alone. God forbid they'd walk in when he had some girl in here . . .

His expression was inscrutable. "No harm, no foul."

She wouldn't think of the possible scenarios, especially with the children present.

"You don't need to worry," he assured her. "I'll keep the door locked on this sorry trailer when I need to."

So he was admitting he'd need to keep the door locked sometimes. Maybe he meant only when he had to take a shower. Or possibly he meant more than that: Maybe he'd have parties in there. And he'd misbehave.

The nanny in Lacey was appalled. But the bad girl inside couldn't help getting a little bit excited at the thought of Beau misbehaving. Kissing her. "You're used to better conditions on the set, huh?"

"What do you think?"

"Yeah, I kinda guessed that."

"Don't tell me it's going to build character," he said, so damned cute when he scowled.

"It built mine. I lived in an RV with pink shag carpet. Moved in when I was three years old. This one's double the size of my family's, so you'll get only half the character building. Just be careful, please, since we have kids around here," she warned him from the first step down to the door.

"You'd better be, too," he said, looking over her head.

"I'm watching Dickey right now. He's taking all three of them to the canteen. At least they're headed in that direction."

"Henry never runs off when I tell him not to."

Dickey was diabolical.

She took off down the stairs. Beau chuckled behind her.

Yeah, he could afford to make fun of her. He was a wealthy man who had a trailer with his name on it. All he had to do was memorize lines and act them out.

Even so, she'd rather have her job than his. She hustled after her crew, whom she saw heading like heat-seeking missiles toward the canteen, where Mike assured her that there were *not* free burgers, hot dogs, and ice cream cones served all day long in between catered meals—Dickey's favorite lie he told newcomers.

"Kids! There's no ice cream!" she yelled after them. "Or hot dogs and hamburgers!"

"We already told Henry," Carol yelled back. "But they do have Nutter Butter four-packs. Dad bought them at Costco as a special treat for everyone."

As Lacey strode to catch up with them—feeling Beau's eyes on her from his trailer—she was grateful that the movie life was behind her.

No more hot lights shining on her face. No more avoiding walking into equipment that could put your eye out. No directors barking terrible orders, or grips eyeing her like she was a piece of meat. No more poorly written scripts, ill-fitting costumes, and hours so long, she'd nod off on the set and wake up with a jolt.

No more auditions in which she felt either overqualified or underqualified to be there, either.

Why had she ever craved that life in the first place?

She couldn't remember. Well, she could, but it was painful. It had something to do with wanting to get away from home, with loving ancient *People* magazines she'd find in the break room at craft shows, with Sheena letting Walt call all the shots and with Lacey becoming the main character of her own life, like so many women were in her favorite books: *Jane Eyre*, *Gone with the Wind*, *A Tree Grows in Brooklyn*, *To Kill a Mockingbird*, *Mistress of Mellyn*, *Pride and Prejudice*.

And then Henry had come along, and she'd happily made him the center of her life. And it was so much better now . . . *so* much . . .

She caught up with them and gave them all a good dressing-down, especially Dickey.

"You don't go anywhere without me," she reminded the children. "Mr. Baird's an adult, but he's not supposed to take you anywhere on his own."

"I want Jo Jo back," Dickey said uncertainly.

"We'll get some Nutter Butters." She saw Beau walking toward the studio, a rolled-up script in his hand. Must be for the read-through.

And then she remembered that she'd see him tonight—and she'd be making him dinner. Not *for* him. If he was there when she made her special pork chops and gravy over sticky rice with sautéed apples and fried okra on the side, it was only because he'd gotten lucky. Some other night, she'd be sure to make canned tuna and mac-and-cheese from a box.

At the canteen, they ate their Nutter Butters, and all the while Lacey asked Carol and Bob about things they liked to do, and what kind of books they enjoyed reading. Henry fell right in asking them questions, too.

"Let's go to the studio library and see what they've got," Dickey said.

"They have a library here? That's so nice!" Lacey helped Carol clean some cookie crumbs off her face.

"A small one," he said. "The local chamber of commerce

pulled it together when the studio decided to open up shop here. They even have kids' books."

"Have you seen the library?" she asked Bob and Carol.

"Yep!" Bob said.

"I love the library," Carol said.

So it was true. Lacey gave herself a proverbial pat on the back. She could handle Dickey. It simply required a little finesse.

A couple of men walked by them as they tried the door to the building, which was locked. "You'll have to go through the set to get in there," one of them said. "Just be careful. We're placing lights."

"Fine," said Lacey. She knew all about that. It would be noisy, complicated work. Unwelcome distractions needed to be kept to a minimum.

She made all the children grab on to each other's waists. Then Henry reached up and took hers. She was the head of a human caterpillar. Dickey walked to her left.

"Stay right next to me, please," she asked him, "and help me keep an eye on the kids."

"I'm not getting paid to babysit."

"I know. But sets are crazy dangerous even if you've walked them before."

"Hmmph," he said, but did as she asked.

Once on the set, the old feeling came back, one of excitement and nerves and possibilities. But she didn't miss being an actress. Not at all.

Everything was going well until she saw a red-bearded grip holding a wrench and twisting a bolt onto a piece of equipment. He looked up and mopped off his face with his free arm. She stopped walking, and Henry smashed right into her.

"Sorry," she said. "I thought maybe there was a bump in the floor. I didn't want us to trip."

But she recognized that grip! He'd been on the set of *Biker Aliens*.

Her temples thrummed with anxiety. She couldn't afford to let him recognize her. Then everyone would laugh at Greta Gildensturm, and Mike wouldn't want a bad actress who'd supposedly jinxed every set she'd been on taking care of his kids and ruining his movie.

Thank God six years had passed and she'd changed her hair color and the style. She averted her face as she walked about fifteen feet away from the grip, and they eventually got to the library.

"All right," she said, and opened the door.

Four faces around a table stared back at her: Beau, Mike, Simone, and Adam. They were sitting with their scripts. Simone was in the middle of some sort of impassioned speech.

The kids ran in, and Lacey's heart sank, especially when she saw blank walls. Then she saw Beau leaning back in his chair in his jeans, looking like denim-blue sin. A hint of irritation—or was that amusement?—glinted in his eyes.

"Where are the books?" asked Bob.

"I love the library!" Carol wailed.

"When I asked you if you'd seen the library, did you think I meant any old library?" she asked the two of them.

"No," said Bob. "I thought you meant the one back home. *That's* the library."

"Yeah," said Carol, kicking at the carpet. "I miss it, Daddy." She looked at her father accusingly. "I want to go home."

Great.

Lacey looked at Dickey, at his innocent old man's face. She was such a sucker. Always had been. Dammit.

CHAPTER ELEVEN

Somehow Beau wasn't surprised when the door was flung open by a red-haired tornado—nor by all the things that happened afterward. He kinda liked it, too. It meant he didn't have to think about the sorry-ass film he was making, plus Lacey looked magnificent restraining the shitstorm she wanted to unleash on Dickey. Her cheeks were flushed and her breasts were about to bust out of her yellow dress with all that heavy breathing she was doing.

"I-I'm so sorry," she told Mike after Carol's little speech about wanting to go home. "I had no idea y'all would be in here."

"You got 'em, Dickey," Mike said affably, although his expression was a trifle grim. "You need to stop that." He pulled Bob and Carol close and hugged them.

"Hey." Dickey shrugged. "The kids have books in the trailer, and they never read those. Maybe they will now."

"We can't go home," Mike told his kids. "We're not done with our adventure here."

Carol looked skeptical, but the hug must have helped because she and Bob both broke away and started wandering the room with Henry, three curious puppies checking things out.

Lacey turned to Dickey. "We interrupted an important meeting. That wasn't nice of you to trick us. You can't make trouble like that again."

Dickey put on his innocent face but didn't deny anything.

"Right," Lacey said to the kids, and put her hands on her hips. They all lined up behind her, a short conga line. "Dickey?"

The old man shuffled over.

"Let's go," she said. "Please get the door."

Dickey opened it. "I invented doors," he told the kids as they walked through.

"Yeah, right," said Bob. "I gotta go to the bathroom."

"We'll stop there," Lacey said.

"I'll bet a guy named Mr. Door invented doors," said Henry. "And then they named them after him."

"I think it was *Miss* Door who invented doors," said Carol.

At least none of the kids are stupid, Beau thought, when the door shut behind them.

Mike stood up. "We probably need to call it a day, too, guys."

Thank God. Beau picked up the script he hated so much and stuffed it in his back pocket.

"Beau," Mike asked him a few minutes later as they were crossing the set, "do you really want to read your lines in the grocery store scene in such an angry way?"

"Yep," Beau said, and looked over his shoulder.

Lacey was behind him—right behind him, a kid's hands grasping her waist. Dickey stood next to her, eyeing her breasts discreetly.

She sent Beau a tight smile. "There's only one way out, you know. It's why I'm following you. No other reason."

"Got it," said Beau.

A ladder moved across their path.

"I think Evan would be sad talking to Clara about Joc," said Mike.

They started walking again. The kids were quacking like ducks.

"Ssshhh!" Lacey said.

Dickey burped.

"Excuse *you*!" Bob said.

"Evan would be frustrated hearing he was being passed over for a promotion he deserved," Beau told Mike, "and angry."

"But he's in love with the boss's wife. And the boss suspects that. Evan can have more nuanced emotions muting his anger, you know, like a shade of regret. Or underlying shame going back to his childhood."

"Yeah, and that'll put my audience to sleep," Beau said. "They don't do nuanced. You told me you wanted authenticity, and I'm playing Evan my way."

A taut silence fell between them as two stagehands lumbered past pushing a giant purple sofa on a trolley.

Lacey smelled damned good. And the kids were getting restless. Beau heard Bob say, "Dumb-dumb," and then Henry said, "Stop pushing."

"That's enough, boys," Lacey said in a drawl like thick caramel drizzled from a spoon.

For a second, Beau wondered if she meant him and Mike or the kids. He could swear he felt her hot breath on his neck, and he liked it.

The path cleared again. "That was an ugly couch," Dickey said.

"That means you actually liked it, then, huh?" Mike shot a wicked grin back at his father-in-law.

"No," Dickey snapped.

"Two can play at your game, Pops," Mike replied lightly. He might be obtuse about Beau's being totally wrong for the part of passive loser Evan. But Mike knew just how to handle Dickey.

They made it to the exit. Adam and Simone were outside waiting for them, both of them on their phones with their backs to each other. The kids burst forth like balls released by a plunger in a pinball machine and scattered across the parking lot.

"Dickey, we're going shopping now," Lacey said. "Do you want to stay here and nap, or come with us?"

"Stay here." Dickey's chin stuck out. "But I'm not napping. It's time for *Doogie Howser, M.D.* I've got a brain tumor. Everyone should be nice to me."

"You don't have a brain tumor," Lacey assured him. "I'll bring you back something from the store. What do you want?"

"Cheddar cheese Bugles," Dickey said right away. "If you bite off the ends and hum into them, they sound just like a kazoo."

"Let's get those!" the kids yelled.

"I'll take care of Pops until you get back," Mike told Lacey, "then I'll just need you for an hour more today. I have some calls to make." He turned to Beau. "Why don't you read those lines again tonight and see if you can get from angry and frustrated to resigned and unhappy by tomorrow?"

"I don't see that happening," said Beau.

If Dickey could dig in his heels, he could, too.

Simone put her phone down for a second. "I'll come over and practice them with you," she said. "I'm Clara, after all. We can work through this together."

Beau shook his head. "I need to settle in tonight. I'm not up for company. Sorry."

Simone walked sulkily toward Adam.

"I'll help him," Lacey called to Mike from thirty feet

away. She was already after the kids. She'd rounded up one, Henry.

"No, thanks." Beau wasn't going to go there.

And now she had Bob. "Carol, if you don't follow us, you'll miss out on going to the grocery store and getting either Peanut M&M's or hard-as-rock candy shaped like tiny bananas out of a bubble-gum machine. Your choice."

Carol ran right over.

"But that's a great idea." Mike was peppy. "I'll get you a copy of the script, Lacey."

"I'm not reading lines with someone who's not even in the movie," Beau said. "She has no idea what the story's about."

"I can still fill in." Lacey had ears like a schoolmarm and sounded sure, even though she looked flustered as hell, her hair falling out of that ponytail and the kids talking a mile a minute about bubble-gum machines that didn't carry bubble gum.

"That really won't be necessary," Beau said.

What was her deal? Didn't she have enough on her plate?

"No, I got it," she insisted. "Mike, please get me a copy so I can read the whole thing before tonight. I'll pick it up when I drop off Bob and Carol."

"Sure thing," said Mike.

"And when will you have time to read the script?" Beau yelled after her. "Why would you need to anyway? You'll just be reading the damned lines back to me."

But she either didn't hear him or was ignoring him as she walked to that weird ambulance, the three kids skipping along beside her. Her hips swung with the assurance of a woman who didn't let life run over her.

Damn her for getting in his way. And for sounding like she was in charge, somehow. She wasn't even in the movie, for God's sake.

"I know I've seen her somewhere," said Adam, squinting after her in his high-waisted pants and buttoned-up shirt, like he was at a Tears for Fears convention.

"She's the Hominy Grill girl," Mike reminded him.

Adam whistled. "She can butter my biscuit any day."

"And I'm going to butter your *face* and leave you out for the coyotes," said Beau, "if you don't shut up. This isn't a soap opera set. So keep it professional."

"They don't have coyotes here," Adam said.

"Sure they do," said Beau. "They always have. But we're talking about my old neighbor. And now she's a nanny and the caretaker of a senior citizen while she tries to land on her feet."

"Yeah, I know." Adam glowered beneath his hair.

"Beau's right," said Mike. "Don't mess with Lacey. Without her, this whole project could fall apart. If my kids aren't happy and Dickey's not happy, my directing will suffer, and so will the movie."

Little did *he* know, thought Beau. Not that he put any stock into superstition or Hollywood gossip.

"Fine." Adam said. "Professional it is. But if she's off limits to me, she's off limits to everyone."

"Of course," said Mike.

Adam stared at Beau.

"Why are you still here?" Beau asked him. It would be a cold day in hell before he answered to that little twerp. He wished he'd come out of the closet. He'd like him better.

Adam stalked off. "Simone! Let's go get a drink."

"I guess." She wore her usual disgusted face.

The two hipsters left together, leaving nothing behind but three boring guys with nothing to do.

"See you later, Beau," said Mike. "We have a lot to do." And took Dickey with him to the trailers.

Okay, scratch that. There was only one boring guy with nothing to do.

Beau.

"I have a helluva lot to do," he muttered to himself as he walked to his car, a rented Saab he'd had to call for himself.

He sat in it for a second. He could go help Lacey.

But he was annoyed with her. And turned on by her. That wasn't right—not when she was in charge of three kids and an old man. He was as wrong to lust after her as it was for Adam to fake-lust after her. Plus, he hadn't been shopping in a supermarket in over five years. Before that, he'd done takeout, and before that Angela had fed him. So he'd be useless anyway, following Lacey around.

Instead, he took off across the bridge to Charleston again and eventually hooked a left onto Highway 17 South. He drove for twenty miles, passing miles of marsh and nondescript ranch houses, a wig shop, then—ten minutes of marsh and pine later—a used-car dealer, a Hardee's, and an abandoned farmhouse until finally he turned right at a stoplight next to a run-down gas station. He went six more miles down a two-lane highway flagged by pines and oaks on either side.

Eventually, he came to the dirt road he was seeking. He took the Saab slowly over the bumps, past a pasture, then through the woods, and finally braked beside a fat oak. Through the tree branches, he caught a glimpse of the cabin. Still the same. But next to it was a house now, two stories. Red shutters on brick. Nothing too fancy. The edge of a blue pool with a short diving board behind it and to the side. His pulse thudded like gravel in his wrists and neck. To the right were the old stables, which had obviously been redone. It had been repainted. The roof was shiny new copper, and there were a couple of new stalls added at the end.

He backed up the car and returned the way he'd come, except he stopped and looked at the horse pasture. More horses, for sure. Sleek, fine horses.

The old anger became fresh again and coursed through his veins like a bad drug. "You sure played us, didn't you, Dad?"

At the sound of his voice, some bullfrogs in a nearby ditch answered him with a flat, unrelenting chorus: *ugh, ugh, ugh.*

"You have it right, boys," he told them, the familiar noise from his childhood taking the edge off. "Ugh. Just ugh."

He took off again down the dirt road, feeling better. Funny how lies didn't get to lie still. The earth spit them out. The wind carried them to someone's ear. It might take years, it might take minutes. But eventually, the truth—however sucky it was—kicked the shit out of the lies, and you had bullfrogs singing and the sun shining and you were stronger than you'd ever been.

Bruised, maybe. But stronger.

And hot damn if you weren't a movie star, too.

CHAPTER TWELVE

George, an orange tabby cat, sat on a kitchen chair, watching Lacey and Henry. They'd just carried him in with the groceries, and now Lacey was putting the food away, including pouches of Whiskas.

"I'm so glad we get to take care of him, Mom," Henry said, scratching George's ears.

When she'd dropped off Bob and Carol and picked up the script, she'd run into Scottie, the animal trainer on the set. "George is old," she told Henry now. "He's let Scottie know that he's tired of being a movie cat and staying with other cats in a pen at night. He wants a foster family to take care of him until Scottie can take him back to his real home."

She wanted to make sure Henry understood that the arrangement was temporary.

"We have to make sure he doesn't go out," Henry said importantly.

"We'll be careful, right? No leaving doors open." She couldn't wait to get him a pet of his own.

"Right."

The space-age litter box, complete with cover and carbon air filters, was in the sitting area, and George was already familiar with it. He seemed content and added a wonderful homey touch to their living space.

"It's been a long day." Lacey blew out a breath and smiled.

"I don't think it was very long." Henry petted George's back. "It went by real fast."

"Good."

"I can't wait for tomorrow."

Lacey chuckled. "You like Bob and Carol a lot, don't you?"

"And I told you, Dickey, too. He's funny."

"I don't know if he means to be, so we need to be careful about laughing, okay?"

"Okay. And I *love* Mr. Wilder. When's he coming home?"

Home. She liked how he said that, although Beau wasn't part of the picture she'd envisioned for them here at the lighthouse. But neither was George. Of course, George was a lot more manageable than Beau Wilder.

"I don't know," she said. "He does his own thing. We do ours."

"Oh," said Henry.

"Remember how it was with Monique? We lived in the same place, but she was busy with other people a lot. Don't forget you've got me. I'm the queen of exploring the beach."

"Yeah, but—"

"But what?" she teased.

"You're a girl. I want a guy here. I like George, but he can't swim with us, and I doubt he has superpowers."

"Well, then," she said, "while you figure out a way to have fun on your own—because I *know* you can—I'm going to make you a nice dinner. Your favorite, pork chops."

"That's good, Mom," he said, "because I'm going to be outside working." He opened a cabinet under the sink and pulled out two dented red Solo cups.

"Building a sand castle?"

"Yep. But you gotta watch."

"I will. I'll keep an eye out the kitchen window." She found a big plastic spoon in a drawer. "Bring all this equipment back when you're done."

"I will." He ran outside with it.

Lacey had a nice half hour chopping, stirring, and frying, in between watching Henry dig and dig, his earnest little face taking his sand castle very seriously.

Finally. As crazy as her day had turned out, she'd moved ahead. She and Henry were on their way to a new life, but until they got there, they had a stable home—with decent food and now a shiny new coffeepot and coffee, thanks to Beau Wilder, although she really didn't want to think about him right then. She had solid work. Soon enough, she'd be able to stock the pantry all on her own. And Henry had friends.

We landed safely, she thought, and went back to her cooking, feeling lucky as she fried the pork chops in butter, garlic, and onion.

George watched her steadily, his tail wrapped around his body.

The lighthouse didn't have a TV set. And she was glad. It was great not having that constant low-level distraction. It had always been on at Monique's. But there was an old radio on the kitchen desk. She had it turned on to WAVF, 101.7, Chuck FM radio. She loved this station. They played everything. Hall and Oates was on, "Kiss on My List," and then "Maggie May" by Rod Stewart.

As she sang along, her heart felt light. And there was something else—peace. She hadn't felt either one in a long time. They went together, she was figuring out.

She filled an old skillet with a thin layer of oil and fried up her sliced okra sprinkled in cornmeal and pepper. Then she slid the little green wagon wheels onto a couple of paper towels and salted them. Meanwhile, the sliced apples were bubbling in brown sugar, butter, and cinnamon, and the pork chops simmered in a thick brown gravy. The boiling Yukon Gold potatoes were almost tender when she poked them with a fork.

Twenty minutes later, supper was on the table. Three places were set.

But there was no Beau.

Henry ate one big pork chop, two scoops of mashed potatoes and gravy, and plenty of sautéed apples and okra. In between, he drank two glasses of milk.

"Gosh," he said, a giant milk mustache on his lip, "this is good. Where's Mr. Wilder? If he doesn't come home soon, my sand castle might wash away. And all the food will be gone."

Lacey wished now she hadn't set a place for him. "I don't know where he is, and if your castle washes away, you can build another one tomorrow. Don't worry, there will be plenty of leftovers for him, too."

"Hey!" Henry sat up taller. "I hear a car!"

Speak of the devil. "Don't stop eating if you're still hungry."

"One more bite." Henry put a forkful of apples in his mouth and chewed.

George leapt down from his kitchen chair and ran up the stairs.

When the front door swung open, Beau walked in with three guys Lacey had never seen before—all of them tan, unshaven, and wearing faded boat shorts and T-shirts. They looked like they'd walked right off the fishing pier.

"Hey." Beau made brief eye contact with her then froze when he realized they were eating supper. "Looks good."

"You were supposed to be here," Henry said.

"No, Henry." Lacey felt brittle and stupid for some reason. Maybe because the three men behind Beau were total strangers and she felt on display. Or maybe it was because she'd been secretly disappointed Beau hadn't joined them. "Mr. Wilder does *not* have to eat with us. He eats whenever he wants."

"I wish *I* could eat whenever I want," Henry said.

"Is that your castle out there?" Beau asked him.

Good change of subject.

"Yep."

"It's cool." Beau was definitely avoiding eye contact with her.

"Supper sure smells good," said one of the guys.

It was a very broad hint. Lacey stood. "I'm Lacey Clark." She looked at Beau. "I don't mind feeding your friends, but I'd appreciate knowing their names."

There was an amused reaction—a snort, a chuckle. And then one said with a snicker, "So, Beau. You're coming home to the little woman these days."

"I'm not the little woman." She sensed the guy's instant whiplash of his neck. He'd had no idea she'd heard. "And if you insist on being rude, you can leave right now." Her ire was up. Oh, yes, it was. God help the next male who sassed her.

There was a beat of silence.

Beau's brow lowered. "These are old friends. And they mean no harm." He looked at them. "Guys, settle down." He lifted his chin. "That's Skipper, Mitch, and Stephen. And they won't be eating the rest of the meal you cooked, but they appreciate the offer. We just had something in Charleston."

"Fine," she said. "Was it at a bar, by chance?"

"Might have been."

"Well, there'll be no drinking here." She eyed his friends. "So I expect y'all will want to hit the road."

"No." Beau clapped his hands together once. "We're gonna play poker. Right here at the kitchen table. And there will be beer."

For the love of—

"Henry," she said, "I need you to go upstairs and get us a book to read."

"Yes, ma'am." He took off up the stairs, but not before high-fiving Beau.

"And you gentlemen"—she indicated Beau's friends—"can step outside for a moment, if you don't mind."

"Yes, ma'am," all three of them said at once, without an ounce of sarcasm in their tone. They shuffled out together like meek little lambs.

"No," she said. "No poker and beer in the lighthouse."

"It's not your lighthouse. And it won't get out of control. We'll wait until Henry goes to bed."

"I know what it means. You'll be drinking all night. Causing a ruckus while Henry and I try to sleep. You've got lines to go over before tomorrow. Or have you forgotten?"

"Ain't gonna happen," Beau said.

"Because you know best, right?"

"Right."

"Doesn't matter that Mike's your director and he wants you to do this."

"My relationship with Mike is my business, not yours."

"He's my boss now." She was glad of that, too.

"His family concerns should matter to you. Not his professional ones."

"Well, you'd think your professional concerns would matter to you. Apparently, they don't."

"Don't put words in my mouth. I can take care of myself."

"Henry's not going to bed for another hour. What're you planning to do until then?"

"Surf," he said.

"Are you kidding me? After you've been drinking, you're gonna jump in the ocean on a big board and try to ride it?"

"Yeah, I'm gonna ride it," he said in a mad-sexy voice.

She felt her neck heat. Was he trying to rile her? Men could wring X-rated innuendos out of any old remark! She hadn't said anything to conjure up bad thoughts, but she was having them now, thanks to him: Beau in a wet pair of Birdwell Beach Britches, the swim trunks all the guys around Indigo Beach wore when she was younger.

Beau doing to her what he'd done to her in that crush dream.

He scratched at his tanned, nearly stubbled jaw. "We're not drunk. Far from it. We've only had a couple of beers."

"You just go ahead then. Break your neck." She knew what she sounded like—a shrew. Good. All that vinegar would stave off any naughty sex dreams her subconscious might be inclined to have tonight.

"I don't know why you're being such a killjoy"—he raked her with the trademark cool expression she'd seen him bestow on all the sexy villainesses in his movies before he bedded them and then either arrested or killed them—"but that's *your* problem."

"Maybe it's because we were having a happy, wholesome night until y'all showed up smelling like stale beer and cigars." She was lying, just a little. The other guys smelled like a walking-talking bar, but Beau happened to smell like hot male. Probably due in part to his fancy Hermès cologne. She'd caught a glimpse of the bottle in his dopp kit in the bathroom.

"We're called men," Beau needlessly reminded her.

"When we get together, that's what we do—have a few beers, smoke a cigar."

There were clattering footsteps on the staircase, then Henry appeared. "Here's the book, Mom." He put it on a chair.

"Thanks, honey." Lacey smiled at him. Reading was wholesome. Henry was like Timmy in the *Lassie* show. He was the most adorable boy in the world. Her heart nearly burst with pride and love, and she knew she was getting carried away, but damn—

Just look at that kid! Don't you see what I see? she told Beau with her eyes. *Miniature perfection—with sand in his pants!*

"You want to watch us surf?" Beau asked him just as another clump of fine silica grit fell out of Henry's shorts. "You can get a feel for it."

Lacey's mouth dropped open. "I'm about to *read* to him."

"I'd rather go with Beau," Henry told her.

"But Henry. You love when we read—"

"Mom" —Henry scratched at his crotch—"surfing's better."

"I'm gonna faint hearing you say that." He was still like Timmy in *Lassie*, Lacey assured herself. But better. At least he had a little rebelliousness in him that was good for the soul.

"Then let's read right before bed," Henry amended and laid a hand on Beau's arm. "I've got two things to show you first."

"What?" Beau's face registered fake adult interest, which was kind of him.

So part of Lacey forgave him. But only a teensy bit.

"One's George, the orange cat," Henry said. "But he's hiding upstairs under Mom's bed."

"George?" Beau turned to her.

"He's one of the cats that belong to your character Evan in the movie. But he's made it clear to Scottie, the trainer, that he's done working on sets. He was meowing in distress in the pen at night. I volunteered to take him home for the duration of the filming."

"But I don't *like* cats."

"Have you ever had one?" she asked.

"No."

"You might just change your mind," she said lightly, ignoring the look of doom in his eyes.

"And the other surprise is out back," Henry said. "A clue. A big clue. But I don't know to *what*."

"Let's check it out," said Beau.

There he went again, being nice to Henry. Lacey followed after them to the little patio facing the dunes behind the lighthouse.

Henry pointed at the cement. There was the imprint of a child's hand. "See? Someone left their handprint here."

Beau peered over his shoulder. "Well, I'll be. They sure did."

Dudley used to say that: *Well, I'll be.*

Lacey sensed Beau was in partial Dudley mode for Henry's sake. He didn't go into full Dudley-speak, but that phrase was a tip of the hat to the cartoon dog.

Sure enough, Henry laughed. "I told you so!" He crouched down next to the handprint and put his hand inside it. It fit almost perfectly. "There's something else: T. BRENNER, 1965." He pulled his hand out and ran his fingers over the words below the handprint.

"Wow," said Beau. "Some boy or girl a long time ago stuck their hand in wet cement, and then it hardened, and now all these years later we get to see it."

"The waves won't wash *this* away," Henry said.

"No, they won't," Lacey agreed.

"Where's this boy now?" Henry asked her.

"He's a grown-up. Older than me and Mr. Wilder." She wondered if he lived on the island still. *Brenner*. She'd have to remember that name.

"Ready to watch me surf, Henry?" Beau had a wild look in his eye already.

Surfers—they were a crazy lot.

"I'll take good care of him," he said over a well-muscled shoulder to Lacey.

"You can have him for thirty minutes," she said, her pulse skipping for a lot of reasons. "Henry, be good. Don't run off, all right? You don't want to be caught on the beach alone after dark."

"Okay, Mom."

She folded her arms and watched them go. Back in the kitchen, she put away the leftover food and washed the dishes. Every few minutes, she'd look out the window, and each time, she couldn't help but smile.

Henry was hypnotized by the surfing.

So was she, in a way.

The guy who called her the little woman had a beer gut and kept falling off his board. The other two were in pretty good shape, and they obviously knew what they were doing on their boards. But there was one guy—Beau—who was in *stellar* shape and played all kinds of tricks with his board on the curling waves, sliding up and down them with an easy confidence.

She was mesmerized by his form and skill.

"Wow," she said on an admiring sigh, and wished she had someone to call and say, *Hey, I'm living with this international superstar right now. He's heartachingly cute and sexy. He's very coordinated on his surfboard, and I can just imagine how that would translate into the bedroom . . . .*

But she didn't.

Her pulse rate picked up again when Beau came in from the surf and put Henry on top of the board while it was on the sand. Beau helped him with positioning. Lacey laughed out loud when Henry crouched and tilted on a pretend wave. And then big male and little male started walking to the house, the red surfboard under Beau's arm.

She looked at the clock on the radio. Thirty minutes on the nose. The other guys started to straggle in behind.

"It was awesome!" Henry said, and ran straight up the stairs to the tub, shedding more sand along the way.

Thank God she had a broom always at the ready.

Beau stood there dripping on her floor in wet shorts. "He had fun watching."

"Yeah, I could tell." She forgot about the broom and the pool of water she'd have to mop up and got all shivery. Beau's body was too much for this small living space. She turned away and heard him climb the stairs to change clothes.

The other guys took turns going inside a van to change. It was awkward, but she was grateful. The lighthouse had one bathroom and no spare bedrooms. Not a great place to bring a lot of men who needed to change out of wet clothes.

The now dry visitors eventually streamed in—with her watching the door, so George wouldn't get out if he decided to show up—and then she picked up Henry's book. She waited for Beau to come back down, and when she did, she turned to them all and said, "Please keep the volume to reasonable levels. Absolutely no smoking in here. And I'd appreciate if you'd go easy on the drinking."

"No problem," one guy said.

"Yeah, we got it," said another.

"Good." They weren't such bad guys. So she managed a halfhearted smile.

"You sleep well now," said the potbellied one.

They all beamed and nodded—except for Beau—who

was reaching into a small cooler on the floor by the table. He looked mighty askance at her, although she didn't know why he should.

Had she said anything about the cooler?

No.

She shot him a mildly disdainful look in return—no way was he gonna get to her—and then went upstairs, rinsed out the crescent of sand in the tub, and tucked Henry in. A short chapter in his book came next. His eyelids started drooping almost immediately.

"Good night, sweetie." She kissed his forehead. George was curled up behind his knees. "We need to get up and get out of here a little earlier tomorrow. Are you excited to go back to the movie studio?"

"I can't wait," he mumbled. "I'm gonna dream about it."

"Are you?"

"Yep. And about surfing, too. Good night, Mom."

" 'Night."

From downstairs came the laughter and talking of men playing poker. Men she didn't know playing poker, led by Beau, who only last night had partied hard enough to wake up this morning and need sunglasses in the kitchen.

She picked up Henry's book, brought it to her room, laid it on the bureau. And then she got out her knitting. She didn't get to it often, but it was time to catch up. She was making a little afghan for Henry in his favorite colors: royal blue, purple, and yellow. God, it was going to be an eyesore, but he'd love it.

Why not go downstairs and work on it? Beau's guests thought she was pretty nice. They'd smiled at her. And yes, maybe her presence would keep them in line.

So she put on her secondhand Chanel reading glasses tossed away by Monique and plunked herself down in the armchair across the way from the kitchen, in the kitschy sitting room with its '60s-era sofa and coffee table. About twenty feet of empty space yawned between her and the guys at the kitchen table. When she turned on a tall lamp with a Tiffany shade and got to work, George swaggered down the stairs and decided to lie on the sofa and watch.

Home, she thought, but she couldn't relax. There was the sound of twisting beer caps and clinking poker chips nearby. And the aura of Sex God that Beau gave off without even trying. No girl could be at ease around that.

CHAPTER THIRTEEN

Beau looked over the top of the worst hand of cards he'd been dealt since he learned how to play poker at age twelve and silently cursed his luck. Lacey wasn't going to sit there and knit—and jinx his game while she was at it, was she?

Apparently, she was.

And had.

He'd just picked up a jack, and he needed anything below a five. The fat orange diva cat watched him through half-slitted eyes and whipped his tail.

Beau released a silent sigh. He knew what Lacey was trying to say. No one was going to push her around in her own living space. But now that she was knitting away, the whole vibe in the kitchen went from easy to tense.

"I know what you're doing," he called to her in a neutral voice.

"Oh?" She looked up from her needles, her little glasses perched precariously on her nose.

"And it's not gonna work," he said flatly.

"You think what you want." She shook her head and got back to work.

Ten minutes later, he caught her stealing a glance at the table, which now had eight beer bottles on it instead of four.

Her eyes narrowed.

Lord save him from her prudish ways.

None of the other guys looked happy, either.

"I think I'm calling it a night," said Mitch.

"Me, too." Stephen looked over at Lacey, his eyes a little fearful.

She ignored the hell out of all of them.

Skipper pushed back his chair. "I'm losing too much anyway."

"Shit," muttered Beau. There went poker night.

Lacey's knitting needles flew as his guests excused themselves from the table.

"Good night, Stephen, Mitch, and Skipper," she said when they huddled at the door, looking beaten. "I never figured out who was whom. Maybe next time."

They mumbled their good nights.

Beau shut the door behind them and felt Lacey's silent triumph. It came off her in waves, even though her face didn't register a bit of smugness. She was all concentration and contentment, looking at that hideous blanket she was making.

He turned to her. "You know there will never be a next time."

"Is that right?" She peered closer at an invisible stitch gone wrong.

He came up close, stood there looking down at her. "You're being ridiculous. But since you're being my lighthouse wife, I'll be happy to take on the role of lighthouse husband. You just say the word, Miz Clark."

They were like an old married couple already, weren't they? Fighting and having power struggles. Might as well have sex, too.

She glanced up at him, her spectacles sparkling. "What's that supposed to mean?"

"I think you know."

"You've been a movie star too long." She stood, left her glasses and knitting in the chair, and walked around him—outside of grabbing and kissing distance—to the sofa, where George lay. She sat down next to the beast, picked him up under his orange tabby arms, and stretched him like a big sock until he made it over to her lap and settled in. "I can't believe what you're suggesting."

Her tone activated an ancient, little used thing called his conscience, which Beau quickly tamped down. "Don't get all sanctimonious with me. You lived in Hollywood. You ran with Callum and his crowd. They weren't saints by any means."

"I might have been stupid at the time, but it gives you no right to proposition me like I'm some starry-eyed ingé-nue grateful for your attention." As she petted the cat fu-riously, it looked up at her with a mixture of devotion and annoyance.

"Call it a sexual cease-fire," Beau said.

"Because I don't go for late-night poker games among men I don't know in my own living quarters—I'm a prob-lem?" She stood, George sagging between her arms, one feline leg dangling low. "And you want to solve it by sleep-ing together?"

"I'm pretty sure it won't solve anything. And I'm sorry I missed your dinner, if that's why you're punishing me."

"I'm not punishing you."

"You set that third plate." He felt guilty, but dammit, he was a bachelor back in his hometown with old friends nearby.

"Henry wanted me to."

Aw, hell. They were dumbass friends, admittedly, none of them cooler than Henry. "I told you I don't know when I'll be around."

"Whatever," she said airily. "You do your thing."

"I will. And keep reminding yourself that not everything's going to be on your terms."

She dumped George on the stairs. "My terms are sensible."

"And my terms are fun."

"For *you*." She went to the kitchen table, ignored the mess of poker chips and beer bottles, and rearranged the salt and pepper shakers.

He switched them back. "No one ever said you had to choose between the two."

"I'm a mom." She strode to the sink, turned on the cold water, and they both watched it run together into a dirty coffee cup.

"You can be a fun mom," he said, and turned the water off.

"I am." She slipped away from him again, grabbing the broom by the fridge.

She was already a hot mom.

"But there's more to being a parent than being fun." *Sweep, sweep, sweep.*

"I get that."

She paused and leaned on the broom, looking like Cinderella. "You can't, really. Not until you love a child."

"Okay, so I'm not as smart as you about kids." He picked up the dustpan, squatted down, and held it to the broom bristles. She swept in some invisible dirt. He stood, grabbed the broom from her—which she relinquished easily—put it away with the dustpan, then turned back to face her. "But I know a helluva lot about women, including women who put everyone else first and let life pass them by."

"*My* life is most definitely not passing *me* by." She pushed all the kitchen chairs under the table, then glared at him. "I'm getting the strong impression that if you don't get what you want when you want it, you start causing problems."

"I don't cause problems—" He pulled out a chair and flipped it around.

"Now you're just trying to make me mad!"

"I merely take action." He sat in the chair, his arms resting on the back. "Having hot sex with you is action. It's preferable to fighting, isn't it?"

"You're the king of scene-stealing, you know that?" she said from the other side of the table.

"Well, what was it called when you bullied my friends outta here?"

"Sitting in a chair knitting is bullying?"

"You know it was. You can do a lot of things from a chair." Let her guess what he meant.

She didn't say anything, but from the way her mouth parted ever so slightly, she'd read his mind. Like a champ. Wasn't hard, he supposed. He was coming on stronger than a cup of Starbucks triple espresso dumped into a glass of straight bourbon.

"Which is why I'm saying if we're going to fight, we might as well kiss and make up." He stood, pushed the chair back in, and started walking around the table. "A *lot*. Just to even things out. When Henry isn't looking, of course. Or that damned cat."

She stood perfectly still, watching him. He had one more step to go before he could take her in his arms and kiss away her pique. But she made a last-minute beeline to her backup armor—George, who was pissed at being interrupted in his ablutions—and picked him up anyway. "I know what you're trying to do. You think seducing me is going to make me turn all 'little woman' on you. I'll cook, I'll iron, I'll just stand by and do nothing when your suspect friends come over, and I'll sleep with you in the bargain. Well, Mr. Wilder, as fine as you are, it's not going to work. I won't be your lighthouse wife."

And she flounced—*flounced*—up the stairs, with

George's tail whipping like a kite tail in a gale beneath her arm.

But Beau was a man in lust. Everything tended to go in one ear and out the other except the good stuff.

She called him *fine*?

Nice compliment.

And *really* nice ass.

CHAPTER FOURTEEN

The next week passed in a gigantic blur for Lacey. Mike hadn't been kidding about the schedule. And she had movie experience, so she shouldn't be surprised. But even so, she was caught off guard by the unrelenting pace of filming.

On the upside, things were going well with the kids and Dickey. She'd figured out that the more she paid attention to Dickey, the fewer stories he fabricated. And the kids were good kids. All they needed was someone to take charge. Henry was exhausted but having the time of his life.

She, on the other hand, was strangely wired. All the time. She avoided the set as much as possible. Besides being a bad place to take kids, she didn't want to run into Beau *or* that grip who'd worked on *Biker Aliens*.

She couldn't sleep, and if she thought of anything beyond her job requirements and her new routine at the lighthouse, she felt scattered. Nervous.

All her insecurities came back. She'd been the poor kid. The one who lived in an RV. And then she'd been an awful actress. Monique, too, obviously hadn't appreciated her organizational skills or her friendship, and Biddy at Finer Things thought she wasn't of the right caliber to work with her upscale clientele.

Something about Lacey shouted *unworthy*.

Except when it came to Henry. She knew they were meant to be together and that he was happy. As a matter of fact, so were Bob, Carol—even Dickey, in his own way. And George was her number-one fan.

Today, as usual, she woke up wondering if Henry had slept well. George had taken to curling up with him at night, and she loved seeing boy and cat in the mornings. She swung out of bed and peeked in—they were both asleep.

Her heart also lifted at the smell of coffee downstairs. Someone else had made it.

Beau.

She felt spoiled, even though she knew he'd really made the coffee for himself. The coffeepot, the beans, the grinder—they were his domain. He'd made that clear. For a fraction of a second, she allowed herself to imagine what it would be like to have someone make coffee for her every day—

What it would be like to have *Beau* make coffee for her every day, to let him be her lighthouse husband . . .

"No," she whispered to herself in the bathroom mirror.

In the shower, she had her usual fleeting thoughts of lathering up with him. But she put her head under the spray to douse the fantasy.

"You're pathetic," she mouthed to her reflection as she dried off.

Why couldn't she just forget about him? Was it those manly toiletries hanging around the sink? Maybe it was the fact that he was a famous guy with over-the-top good looks and charisma (try saying that in one breath).

So she was normal. It really wasn't fair to expect her not to react to him on a primal level. Every night, she begged her inner Aphrodite to bring back that dream she'd had the first night he was there. But instead her dreams were restless and fragmented—stressful. She was used to that. Having a respite in the form of another Beau dream would be so *welcome*.

She raced to her room in her short terry robe and got dressed. Afterward, she laid out Henry's clothes—a Harley-Davidson T-shirt and khaki shorts—waking him as she opened and closed his bureau drawers by singing his favorite song.

"Mom," he croaked. "I'm hungry."

"I thought your name was Henry."

He grinned, as if they hadn't had the same conversation every morning for forever. Then he hugged George, who opened one eye and closed it right back. Lacey sat on the edge of the bed and held Henry's hand. They talked about Bob and Carol and laughed about Dickey's latest story, that he knew the president of the United States. They'd met in a tire store, according to Dickey.

"Mom, the president lives in the White House. That's far away, isn't it?"

"Yes." She sighed. "I guess Dickey really wishes he could meet the president."

"He lied. You don't let me lie."

"Well, you know better. But I think with Dickey, he sometimes believes his own stories or wants to. He could be too sad, thinking about his wife who died all those years ago. And his daughter, too. He lost her only three years ago. She was Mr. Carter's wife."

Dickey was the only grown-up Henry called by his first name, maybe because Dickey acted more like a peer than an adult.

"That's sad," said Henry. "I like Mr. Carter."

"Mike is a good guy. So for his sake, too, we'll be nice to Dickey. If his stories get too crazy, I'll tell him, okay?"

"Okay."

While Henry was getting ready for the day, she went downstairs and made a hot breakfast: scrambled eggs with cheese, sausage, and buttered English muffins. George got half a pouch of cat food in the morning next to his water, and she left him extra on the kitchen sill in case they stayed late on the set.

Beau brushed by her on his way to the coffeepot.

She wanted him so bad. She was shamefully, sinfully hot for him.

"'Mornin'," he said in a pleasant enough voice, but there was a tension about him.

She wondered how filming was going. Mike hadn't said a word about it. "Good morning." She gave him a polite little smile.

They'd barely seen each other since the night his poker buddies had come over and he'd proposed being her lighthouse husband. Breakfast was the only time their paths really crossed.

He returned every night later than she and Henry did, and honestly, she had no idea if he was working hard with Mike and the other actors at the studio—or socializing with them or local friends somewhere on Indigo Beach or in Charleston.

Whatever he was doing, he still managed to look awesome. She wanted to kill him because she knew that she looked semi-witchy from lack of sleep. But she'd tried to make up for it by wearing her aqua-blue shirt with the darts beneath the bust and cutoff Levi's that she made an inch or two longer than Daisy Dukes. Butt cleavage was a no-no in her mommy world.

He sat down, already in his running clothes. "Where's the kid?"

"Here!" Henry came running over from looking at a big book of sailing ships in the sitting area.

They ate together, not talking much. Time was running short. They all had to get to the studio by seven thirty. Lacey couldn't imagine how Beau could run after the big meal he partook of, but he did, every day, right after he rinsed off his plate and put it in the dishwasher. Lacey and Henry spent another ten minutes at home, brushing teeth, cleaning up, petting George a little more, and pulling together a plan for the day before they jumped in the ambulance and got to the studio about the same time Beau did.

"I'm tired," said Henry.

"Me, too." Beau downed his glass of OJ.

Lacey couldn't help wondering what he'd done the night before. He didn't look a bit tired. "We've been getting up really early," she reminded Henry.

"And we didn't get home until after dark." He crammed half an English muffin in his mouth then, at the look on her face, spit half back out on his plate. "Sorry."

He was trying so hard to impress Beau.

"It's a fast pace we're keeping," Beau told him. "But are you having fun?"

"Yes." Henry's eyes were full of get-up-and-go. "But I don't see you very much. At lunch *or* dinner. And you haven't been to the beach with us, either."

"I know. I'm sorry, man. I've been working. I hear Dickey, Bob, and Carol have come over here to swim and eat lunch every day."

"Yep. But we still need to go surfing. You and me. Mom, too."

"You're right, we do, but first"—Beau looked over at her, and his mouth crooked up—"your mom needs to get a new bathing suit."

Lacey blushed. She had yet to look for a bikini. And she wasn't sure about surfing anymore, at least for her. She didn't need to be almost naked and wet next to Beau.

"She's got her blue one," said Henry.

"Yeah, but surfer chicks need bikinis." Beau was adamant on that point.

"What's a bikini?" Henry laughed.

"It's a bathing suit cut in half. Your belly button shows."

Lacey looked askance at Beau. "Don't listen to Mr. Wilder. Surfer chicks can surf in one-piece bathing suits, too."

"Ohhh," said Henry. "I'll bet bikinis are better."

"You're corrupting my child," she murmured to Beau.

"Bikinis can save the world," he whispered back, sending wicked chills down her spine. "Guess what, Henry?"

"What?" Henry sat stiff as a Popsicle stick.

"I found some clues."

"You did?" His eyes were huge.

Lacey put her chin in her hand, highly amused but not showing it. Clues to what?

She supposed it didn't matter. As long as they were called clues, Henry was into it.

"That treasure chest in my room," Beau said. "I opened it, and it's filled with a bunch of boy stuff. Like an old Hot Wheels car. And a baseball glove. You wouldn't believe what it says on it."

"What?" Henry was practically floating out of his chair, he was so excited.

"Well, you know that handprint outside, the one that belongs to T. Brenner?"

Henry nodded fast.

Beau leaned forward. "This glove belonged to a boy named Timothy Brenner. So that *T* outside probably stands for . . . Timothy."

Lacey could see it in his face, how much he'd loved being Dudley! And she couldn't help it—there was nothing sexier than a man who was good to your child.

Nothing.

That damned shower fantasy came roaring back.

"Wow." Henry's gaze was locked on Beau's. "Now we know his name!"

"That's totally cool." Lacey really thought so, too.

"When can I see that glove?" Henry asked like his life depended on it.

"Tonight." Beau stood and stretched. "I'm taking the evening off."

"Oh?" Lacey tried not to look at his exposed belly, but she did anyway, and he caught her. "You—you've got toast crumbs."

"Right," he said drily, and gave one cursory wipe to his abs. "Mike says no filming tonight. It's his wife's birthday. He's taking the kids and Dickey out in Charleston."

"Oh." Lacey felt so sad for Mike and his family.

There was a tiny lull. She stole another look at Beau's body—the back side, just a sweeping glance—and was glad he didn't catch her.

He was busy walking to Henry's chair. He gripped the top rail, and Henry stretched his neck backward to look up at him, total hero worship in his eyes—which scared Lacey.

"I figured we could make up for not hanging out much." Beau grinned down at her boy. "We could have dinner together tonight ourselves. That is, we'll go out if your mom doesn't have any other plans. How's that?" He held out his hand over Henry's head, palm down.

"Yes!" Henry awkwardly slapped it. "Mom, can we do it?"

She looked between them. "Sure," she said, feeling discombobulated. "That sounds . . . nice."

"Are we gonna surf?" Henry asked Beau.

"We'll do that another day. You need to keep on your mom about getting that bikini."

"All right." Henry grinned and ran upstairs to get his special Tonka truck to take to the studio.

"I'm going," Beau said easily.

But Lacey's heart was racing. "You have a lot of

obligations. And I know you've got friends to see while you're here. Honestly, you don't have to worry about Henry and me."

"I'm not worried."

"You're good at saving people in the movies"—she hardened herself against him by remembering him that first night, coming in drunk and saying good-bye to his personal assistant—"but we don't need your pity."

She saw an answering flicker of hardness in his eyes. "I don't pity you. I just like the hell outta Henry. And you're okay, too, Miz Clark, when you're not defending yourself against the world. I've seen you with Henry. And Dickey. You're not the iron maiden you want me to think you are beneath your totally riveting wardrobe."

She blushed so hard, she was incapable of speech. So she busied herself by picking up Henry's plate and silverware. "How are your scenes coming along?"

"Poorly."

They stared at each other a second.

She could see very clearly what he wanted from her. She wanted it, too, but it was a dumb idea. She'd already offered him her own brand of help, reading those lines with him. "You'd better get going."

"Lacey—"

"No, Beau."

"I was only going to tell Henry to eat the last Pop-Tart if he wanted it. What'd you think I was gonna say?"

"Nothing." She picked up her coffee cup and poured herself another half cup. Beau's brew. It was perfect. She'd miss it. She wrapped her hand around the warmth and tried not to worry.

At the door he turned around. "See you tonight."

A flush heated her cheeks. He sounded like he was looking forward to it.

"See you," she replied, and buried her face in her mug.

He lingered a second too long. "You're definitely not an iron maiden," he said with a grin. "And I wish you'd wear those shorts *every* day."

"Go!" she yelled at him.

At the studio, Dickey was waiting with the paper. "I found you a real job, Lacey girl." He held up the classifieds. "The sooner you get outta here, the better. Mike won't know what to do with me, so he'll be forced to send me home."

"Mike wants you here," she reminded him. "You'll be lonely at home."

"I'm not lonely. I got all them cows. You ever sat in the middle of a cow pasture? Those girls come strolling over and make a big circle around you. A man feels loved with a bunch of bovine noses pointing right at him."

"I'm sure that's a wonderful feeling. But you've got people who love you, too."

He didn't look impressed.

"What's this job you think is good for me?" She steeled herself for an outlandish lie.

"Lexus car dealership right over the bridge. They say they're looking for a new salesperson."

"Show me."

It was true. The job was a mile away from Indigo Beach on the Charleston side of the waterway. After an initial trial period, it was full-time with all the benefits.

She wasn't interested. She knew nothing about cars. And probably a high-end dealership like that would take one look at her and send her packing, the way Biddy did at Finer Things.

"That was really nice of you to share with me." She kissed Dickey's hollow cheek. "But I'd be terrible in sales. Especially cars. And I'm assuming they're looking for someone with experience."

"You have experience." He got an extra ornery look in his eyes. "Every day you sell these kids on the day's events.

You make it sound fun and jolly that we're going to the lighthouse, and then you pull an old switcheroo and make it educational. They don't even know, the poor saps. But I do. And I'm sick of identifying seashells and dead crabs and talking about sand erosion, ocean tides, and the moon."

"We won't do that today. I thought maybe we'd go shopping instead on Center Street. You could use some reading glasses. Bob needs a pair of flip-flops. Carol and Henry want comic books. We'll eat at the Mexican restaurant."

"Great idea. I like those señoritas serving margaritas." Dickey chortled. "Beau's been hanging out at El Burrito almost every night. All the actors head over there after they're done filming for the day. The crew, too."

Lacey remembered that sort of scenario well, everyone from the set going to their favorite cantina to have a drink after a long day of shooting.

Dickey leered at her. "There's a raven-haired beauty Beau's seeing, a woman named Maria. She's the owner. That woman has *curves*."

"Oh." Lacey felt weak inside. "Who Beau Wilder socializes with is his business, not ours."

"Maybe she'll be there today. I'd like to catch a glimpse of her."

"Maybe so." She tried to smile, but she wished now she'd chosen another place to go, not that she was jealous of this restaurant owner. But the possibility of Beau bringing another woman to the lighthouse didn't sit well with her. The place was too small for him to carry on with someone while she and Henry were there.

And then she remembered: The whole story might be a big, fat lie. That made her feel better. Because hell *yes*, she was jealous! She wanted Beau in *her* bed. At least in her fantasies. If he took up with another woman, those would have to cease. She wasn't so desperate that she'd imagine making love to another woman's man.

Mike called. "Can you run over for a minute before you go shopping? There are a couple of props you could pick up for us at the hardware store, if you don't mind. I've got a list."

"No problem."

"And there's a wet suit jacket, too, for Adam's character, from the surf shop. We won't need any of these things until tomorrow's shoot, but since you're out and about . . ."

"I'll be happy to."

"The set's extra precarious today. Just leave the kids with Dickey in front of the TV. You'll be back in three minutes."

So she told her charges not to move upon pain of death, then scooted as fast as she could to the set. No telling what Dickey could get up to in three minutes. Mike handed her the list, and she was almost gone when she literally bumped into the grip with the red hair.

"Steady," he said. "It's dangerous around here."

"Right," she squeaked against his chest.

He pulled back and tipped his head. "What's your name?"

"Lacey." She felt sick from nerves. "Lacey Clark." *And please don't recognize me.*

"Oh. Okay. Hi, Lacey."

She'd never shared her real name on the *Biker Aliens* set. Everyone had called her Greta. It just seemed to fit.

"Nice to meet you," she said fast, and ran off.

"I never introduced myself!" he called after her. "It's Archie! Archie West! Can I call you sometime? And haven't we met somewhere?"

She pretended she didn't hear him. Half a second later, she pulled the set door shut behind her just as her phone rang. Her hands were trembling when she answered. Maybe Mike had something else to add to the list. No way was she going back inside to talk about it, though.

"Yes?" She started striding back to the trailer in her too-loud flip-flops. God forbid she'd ever see Archie West again. But she would—how could she not?

"It's Sheena," her mother said in her hummingbird voice. "We're on Indigo Beach."

In an instant, Lacey's heart soared, and she forgot all about Archie West. Sheena was *here*. She'd meet Henry. Finally. And Beau, too, probably.

No. She couldn't meet him.

"We can only stay the afternoon," Sheena said. "Where are you?"

Lacey's bubble of excitement popped. But she clung hard to the knowledge that her mama would meet her grandson. "In fifteen minutes, we'll be at the lighthouse. Can you Google it?"

She could keep Beau out of the way for just one afternoon. Piece of cake.

CHAPTER FIFTEEN

"Everyone, take a fifteen-minute break." Mike sounded worn out.

It had been a long morning, and Beau was ready for a break, too.

The actors scattered in little clumps. Adam and Simone, Beau noticed, hung out together a lot. The other minor players also had their pals. Beau was the only one who didn't. He was bending over backward to make sure his superstardom didn't intimidate anyone. But as nice as he was trying to be, he had nothing in common with the rest of the cast. They were either posers like Adam or fighting their inner demons like Simone.

Apart from Mike, there was no one "normal," someone doing his or her job without giving off a lot of annoying or angsty vibes. At least he could relax with Mike. His artistic temperament was offset by a very practical nature.

"I build pools," Mike said to the cast on their first day. "And I build movies."

Beau was off to his trailer to catch up on his phone messages.

"Hey, wait up," Mike said.

"Sure."

They headed down a corridor with no one in sight.

"I called that break for more than the usual reasons." Mike's arms were huge as they swung next to Beau's.

"Oh, yeah?" He might need to add a few extra pounds to his barbell. "What's going on?"

"I need you off my set, Beau." Mike's tone was casual.

"What?" Beau had his hand on the exit door.

"I'm thinking about firing you. I have very limited time to film. And you're ruining the movie, my friend."

Beau gripped the doorknob harder. "*I'm* ruining the movie?" He couldn't believe what he was hearing. "But the script—Mike, it's got issues."

There was no way he was ruining this movie.

"It's my fault, man. I thought I caught glimpses . . ." Mike trailed off, his tone regretful.

"Glimpses of what?" Beau wasn't one to beat around the bush.

"Glimpses of authenticity." Mike wasn't backing down, either.

Beau wasn't used to this kind of talk. Hell, he wasn't used to taking second billing. Getting a crappy trailer. Working with cats. Enduring scene after scene of sensitive story that had nothing to do with the real world . . . only "the inner life," as Mike called it.

Inner life, Beau's ass. What someone was on the inside didn't matter—it was how that person acted on the outside, what he did, whom he loved, whom he rejected. It was his choices that mattered, not all the bullshit inside, the muddy, confused soul questions that racked him. "Could you elaborate?"

"Sure." Mike heaved a gusty sigh. "You make entertaining movies, but you have to know that you may have created your brand a little too well. You're no longer a channel for a character to shine through. You're Beau Wilder. That's all I'm getting from you on the set. And I needed

Evan. You told me at the beginning that you had concerns. I really believed that once you got into the scenes, you'd overcome them. But you haven't. So you need to leave for the rest of the day and think about whether you want to come back tomorrow."

Shit, was all Beau could think. He had no idea artsy-fartsy film people could be genuine badasses. "If I don't come back? You have someone waiting in the wings ready to take over?"

"Yep," said Mike. "I might be a pool guy nine months of the year. But for three months, I'm a goddamned director of what I hope will be a magnificent film. And I don't mess around."

He apparently didn't.

Beau didn't know what to say. It crushed him to hear that Mike was unhappy with his performance, but hell, the truth was, Beau was unhappy with it, too. He was outright miserable. "I don't like the script. I can't stand my character." He didn't say it with any animosity. In fact, he felt guilty. And embarrassed. "Maybe I ought to just quit right now."

"You could."

Damn. The guy wasn't even gonna make a case for his staying. "Are you saying I might not be as good as you thought I was?"

"Yes."

That sucked. A big one.

"But you need to think about whether you're as good as *you* think you are." Mike poked him in the chest. "That's the crux of the matter, man."

Beau tipped his head, considering his boss's words. Wow. No, really. *Wow.*

Not as good as he thought he was . . .

And Beau thought he was pretty damned good. He'd never had any doubts. Not once.

Until now.

"I hate you, Mike," he said slowly.

Mike chuckled. "Welcome to the Insecurity Club. It's not all bad. There are goals to shoot for. They make things exciting. Really exciting."

Beau hadn't been excited in a long time on a movie set. Not really. The last time he'd been challenged was a good five years ago, and since then . . .

Things hadn't changed. They'd stayed the same. *He'd* stayed the same. But he hadn't seen a problem with that. He liked the lane he was in. Why change when he didn't have to change to get what he wanted?

And he didn't want this movie. No, not by a long shot. He'd just been in a scene with seven cats. What did they add? Nothing! And they were all over him, rubbing on him, meowing, purring their little hearts out. It was sheer torture.

So . . . why was he still conflicted?

It was an ego thing. Had to be. The idea that Mike would be walking around forever thinking, Beau wasn't as good as I thought he was. As *he* thought he was.

He couldn't get fired from a movie, even a strange one like this that no one would ever see. His professional reputation was on the line. He owed Mike his best work. He already knew that—

And I thought I was giving it.

He had a lot to contemplate.

"I hope you'll come back," Mike said. "I don't want to shove my version of Evan down your throat—I'm open to seeing a valid interpretation on your part. But right now, you're not moving beyond your brand, man. I know you're under pressure by the Hollywood honchos to stay Beau Wilder. But I need more. Way more. If it's too much for you to give for whatever reason"—he locked his hand onto Beau's shoulder and squeezed—"it's okay. We part friends. And professional colleagues."

Beau shook his head. "I'm not leaving." He couldn't blow something up and then just walk away—which was a revelation of sorts, because he did that in his movies all the time. "Unless you fire me, I'm coming back."

Mike nodded soberly. "Okay. We'll see what happens tomorrow. Take the rest of the day to figure out what you have to do to make it work in the morning. I'll tell the others you got called away by your PR guy for a couple of important telephone interviews."

Beau didn't even remember opening the door and leaving. He'd been cut off at the knees for the first time since he could remember. If he didn't respect Mike, he wouldn't have cared and he'd still have his knees.

But he did respect the director of *Flowers from the Heart*. For some reason, he did, even though he and Mike were on two different planets in a lot of ways.

And then he remembered: three years ago today, Mike's wife had died.

He felt like such a jerk for making the guy's hard day even harder.

"You're *here*?"

The throaty voice to his right in the parking lot managed to pull him at least partly out of his funk. It was Lacey. She was walking in a tight circle, her flip-flops slapping the tarmac, a phone to her ear.

"In fifteen minutes, we'll be at the lighthouse," she was saying. "Can you Google it?" She stopped walking. "Great. I'll see you there. I'm going to have more than Henry with me, too. I've got a job. I'm a nanny. And a caretaker." She put a tendril of hair behind her ear. "I'll explain when I see you. 'Kay. Bye, Sheena."

Sheena.

Who was that?

She looked up and saw him. "Hey."

"Hey." He put his hands in his pockets.

"My mom's in town with my stepfather. I'm meeting them at the lighthouse."

"That's cool."

She looked at Mike's trailer. "The kids and Dickey think we're going shopping on Center Street and eating at the Mexican restaurant."

"Maybe you can take your mom to do that, too."

"We'll see. She's not a big adventurer."

"Really? Does she still live in an RV?"

"Yes." She seemed to look almost through him. This visit was obviously a big deal.

"That sounds adventurous to me."

"I guess so. Either that, or she's got a commitment problem." Lacey paused, her eyes wary. "Do you mind that I've been feeding the kids and Dickey every day from our pantry?"

"No. Not at all."

"I can ask Mike to give me some money for bread and milk."

"It's no big deal."

"Okay. But I'll be doing it again today with my mom and stepfather. That makes seven people eating lunch at the lighthouse. And George. Cat food isn't cheap. But I'm paying for that." She tipped her chin up. "You're not going to pull that lighthouse husband thing, right? As in, I owe you a favor for your largesse?"

"Hey, that's a great idea."

She sent him a droll look.

"Do you need any more cash to make a store run?"

She shook her head. "Mike pays me every three days. Next trip to the grocery is on me."

"You don't have to do that."

"Yes, I do. I don't want to owe you, Beau."

"You've uncovered my dastardly plan. How else am I going to get someone to sleep with me?"

"Sarcasm doesn't suit you."

"That outfit sure suits you. I never had a nanny fantasy until now."

She crossed her arms over her breasts. "So how's the filming going?"

"I told you already."

She winced. "Still not good?"

He nodded. "In fact, I'm going to take you up on your offer to read with me. If it's still open."

She shrugged. "Sure it is."

"Maybe tonight after we get back from dinner. Unless your mother and stepfather are staying." He'd been looking forward to the night out with Lacey and Henry, but now that Mike had spoken, he didn't much care about being Mr. Sociable that evening. He had a lot of thinking to do. He needed to make a scotch-and-cigar run.

Her eyes looked sad when she shook her head. "They're leaving in a couple of hours."

"That's too bad."

"Yeah, well."

He got it. *That's life.*

She cocked her head at Mike's trailer. "I have to go. Are you already done for the day?"

"Yep." Maybe she was going to ask him to go with her. But he'd have to turn her down. He had work to do.

"Can I ask you a favor?" And she told him about Mike's list of things to shop for. She couldn't take the time to do it now. Could Beau pick everything up in the next couple of hours? She didn't want to wait until that evening. The shopkeepers were expecting her.

"Sure," he said.

"Thanks. Mike won't need the stuff until tomorrow. And please, take your time. It's going to be a little crazy at the lighthouse. You might want to come back to your trailer afterward and look over your script before we rehearse tonight."

"Not a bad idea."

She looked guilty when she hurried off, and he wondered why.

Maybe it was because she'd asked him, the big movie star, to pick up props. It was crazy. This whole experience was, he thought as he retreated to his trailer, determined to keep his priorities straight. His lines came first.

He wasn't averse to being alone, usually. But today it bugged him. He pulled the script out of his pocket, sat down on the plump brown chair, and looked at the title: *Flowers from the Heart.*

Good Lord. He could hardly bear to read those words, they were so sappy.

But he dug in, sinking deeper into the chair, and decided to read the entire script over, see if he'd missed anything he could grab on to. Twenty minutes passed—twenty long, agonizing minutes—and he still hated it.

He sighed and turned another page. He had enough talent in his little pinkie to carry a blockbuster movie. So what was so hard about this little story from hell?

He had no idea. Getting off the studio site seemed to be the temporary answer. He'd run Mike and Lacey's errands, and then he'd drive to the lighthouse. Take a peek at her parents. Go surfing. Do something out in the sun. Maybe play with the kids. Talk to Dickey. Share a joke with Lacey. Learn more about her from her mom and stepdad.

You weren't invited.

She'd known he was free, too, and instead had sent him off to shop for her.

A stab of self-pity hit him hard in the gut.

Pussy, he told himself. He was going. He didn't care who wanted him there or who didn't. It was his lighthouse, too.

The keys to the Saab were still in his front pocket. He stood, shoved the script in his pocket, and left the trailer. He ran Lacey's errands at the stores, although he added one item at the surf shop—a cute little bikini. He guessed her size: *V* for voluptuous.

But no amount of busywork or sexy thoughts about Lacey suppressed the annoyance he felt about the script and his determination to fix the problem.

At the lighthouse, he pulled up next to a modest RV. No one was outside.

He'd be interrupting their lunch. But he'd charm everyone to pieces and while he was at it, get a boost of adrenaline looking at Lacey.

When he opened the front door, George was sitting on the stairs like an Egyptian statue. His eyes blinked once when Beau walked in. Lacey and her gang sat around the big table, eating. She put her sandwich down and pushed back her chair, her perfect oval face registering some confusion. The kids were laughing and crunching on chips. A small, skinny woman with her nearly colorless hair in a tight bun and wearing no makeup stared up at him, half a sandwich in her hand.

She was Lacey's mother?

Beau couldn't believe it. She was muted, like a black-and-white photograph, nothing like her daughter.

Next to her, a man with slick, obviously dyed black hair and heavy jowls took a huge bite out of his sandwich, his eyes bugging out when he saw Beau.

"Hey, everyone." Beau grinned, but he was still pissed at the world in general.

"It's Mr. Wilder!" the children announced.

Huzzah for him.

Dickey chuckled. "If it isn't the sailor, home from the sea." He looked at Lacey's mom. "Think you know him? Think again. How many people are aware that he's a Naval Academy graduate and flew missions over Afghanistan?"

"I never went to college, Dickey," said Beau. "Or fought in any wars. But I did play an intergalactic pilot."

"You sure did," said the Elvis guy. "You saved the world in *Zodiac Force*. What was your name? Commander—"

"—Britton was the name," Lacey jumped in, her eyes conveying some kind of secret message to Beau. "I wasn't expecting you."

Yep. But she remembered his name in the movie. It was a huge blockbuster, but still. He liked that she knew about it.

It was embarrassing that he wanted to impress her. But he somehow kinda did. What had happened since he'd come to Indigo Beach? First, he wanted to impress Mike. And now Lacey. He was usually the one waiting to be impressed.

"Would you like a sandwich . . . Mr. Wilder?" Lacey asked politely.

Mr. Wilder? He shrugged. "I'd love one, thanks. But I'll get it. Sit and eat."

"I'm done." She wiped her hands on her napkin. "Would you like ham or turkey?"

She was being deferential. He didn't like it. Not at all. "Turkey, please."

The little woman with the bun was watching Lacey curiously now.

"Sheena"—Lacey stopped right before she got to the counter—"this is Mr. Beau Wilder. Walt's right. He's a movie star. He's one of the actors in *Flowers from the*

Heart. Beau, this is my mother Sheena and her husband Walt Runey."

Sheena nodded, just barely. "Hello, Mr. Wilder."

That was a helluva name for this slip of a woman.

"Welcome to Indigo Beach," Beau said with his usual gracious manners. He'd been taught right. "Please call me Beau, Mr. and Mrs. Runey."

This was the South, and they were older than he, so he followed the rules upon first meeting someone—you went by the last name until given permission to do otherwise—and noted that neither of them offered to have him call them Sheena and Walt.

So be it.

He sent a look Lacey's way. What was going on with them? And why wasn't *she* calling him Beau?

Mr. Runey—Walt—shook his head. "I can't believe it, a real celebrity right-chere." He chuckled, but his eyes were shrewd. "Lacey, get me a beer if you got one. Either that, or I'll send Henry out to the RV to fetch me one." He winked at Beau. "Gotta remind 'em who's in charge."

Beau went to the fridge and grabbed a beer. "Catch," he said, and tossed it to Walt.

He caught it but just barely.

"Lacey's busy, and Henry doesn't fetch," Beau said easily, but his tone was cooler than the other side of the pillow. He'd met roosters like ol' Walt—weak men, every one of 'em—and it pissed off every Southern cell in his body.

Sheena stared at a place mat. Lacey's mouth hung open just a little. There was a beat of silence.

Then Walt pointed at Beau. "You're good! I was just testing you!"

Beau didn't laugh.

But Dickey snorted. "I like you, Walt. I like you something *fierce*."

Dickey, Beau could tell, was lying through his teeth.

"Can we be excused, please?" Henry asked his mother on behalf of Bob and Carol, too. He was sitting to Sheena's left.

"Sure." Lacey sounded distracted as she poured Dickey another glass of milk. "Y'all go play outside. But stay in front of the window where I can see you."

The kids stopped to pet George before they made their exit. Beau noted that Sheena didn't get all warm and fuzzy when Henry left the table. No quick squeeze around the shoulders or a kiss on top of his head. No remarks, like, *You be good out there, honey!*

Of course, his own mother was like that, too.

Poor Henry.

"Here you go." Lacey handed Beau a plate with a sandwich.

Her lips were thin. Something was going on.

He sat down across from Sheena and Walt and kept a cold eye on Walt while he took his first bite. Let the man squirm. He epitomized the worst of Hollywood stereotypes of people from below the Mason-Dixon line. The amiable, polite Southerner with an abundance of common sense and wit—which characterized 99 percent of the Southerners Beau knew—didn't get nearly the screen time dopey outliers like Walt did.

"Whatcha doing here, Wilder?" Walt asked with a grin. He seemed oblivious to Beau's disdain. "Shouldn't you be making a movie?"

Beau swallowed. "I have the rest of the day off. And I live here."

Lacey dropped a plate. George scrambled up the stairs.

Sheena's eyes widened.

"But Lacey and Henry stay here," Walt said.

"Mr. Wilder does, too," Lacey replied softly.

"We're roommates," Beau explained.

The Runeys looked at each other.

Lacey looked at *him*.

Dang. The atmosphere just got really weird.

CHAPTER SIXTEEN

Lacey smiled at her mother, but her temples were buzzing with stress. "I'm not only helping out the movie director," she said firmly, "I'm also Mr. Wilder's paid housekeeper and cook. He was being too kind calling me his roommate. But I'm not the least bit embarrassed to earn a living through hard work, so you don't have to spare my feelings, Mr. Wilder." She sent him a steely look.

"Well," he said, and she could see he was thinking fast, "my housekeeper in LA couldn't come out. Lacey's doing me a favor. I didn't want her to feel like the hired help."

"Although that's exactly what I am," she said with a sure nod.

"Fancy that," chirped Sheena.

No way was Lacey going to let her mother get the wrong idea. "I wasn't going to tell you two since you're here only for the afternoon, and Mr. Wilder values his privacy. He pays me to be discreet." She smiled around the table, conveniently not meeting Beau's eyes. "Would anyone like a brownie?"

"A' course," said Dickey.

Sheena nibbled on the edge of hers. "I'd love to see the rest of the place."

"Me, too," said Walt. "I want to take a gander at that light."

"Well, let's go," said Lacey, trying to sound upbeat. "I'll be happy to show you around."

Sheena looked up timidly. "Unless, of course, Mr. Wilder—"

"Beau," he interrupted Sheena.

"Unless you object," she said.

"Not a bit," he answered. "Make yourselves at home. Dickey and I will head outside for some fresh air."

Lacey took Sheena and Walt up the ladder to the light first.

Sheena's eyes widened. "Mercy."

"That's a fine light," Walt said.

They walked out onto the balcony.

"Would you look at that." Walt took in the Atlantic Ocean.

"You sure are lucky." Sheena gripped the rail with her bony little knuckles.

"I know." Lacey loved how the wind blew her hair straight back.

The kids suddenly appeared in view. They ran to the water, with Beau chasing after them.

Neither Walt or Sheena had called Henry by name yet. And when he'd called them Grandma and Grandpa, they hadn't hugged him, said how happy they were to be his grandparents. Luckily, Henry hadn't seemed to notice their lack of interest or enthusiasm about him—yet.

She wasn't going to force the issue. There wasn't time. They were about to leave. She was already miserable and trying hard not to be, and if she brought it up now, she'd get so worked up about it, she'd feel even worse.

They went down the ladder again.

Sheena drew in her chin when she saw her bedroom. "You have the master?"

"Because Henry's room is attached." Lacey brought them through to his cubby of a room.

After a brief, silent perusal—couldn't they see how cute Henry's room was? How perfect it was for a little boy?—they returned to hers.

"Doesn't seem right that the employer gets a small bedroom," Walt said. "I'm thinking you and your boy could move into that room"—he indicated Beau's current one—"and give Beau this one. A man needs his space, especially a movie star, I reckon."

Your boy.

"I agree," said Sheena. "It don't seem right at all."

Traitor, Lacey thought for the umpteenth time since she was a little girl. Sheena always chose Walt over her.

"It made more sense for us to move in on this side," she explained. "Mr. Wilder didn't mind."

"No, I didn't," Beau said bluntly from the doorway. "Henry needs his own room, and he'd much prefer to know his mother was sleeping on the other side of that door than me, don't you think? I like sleeping on the south side of the house, anyway."

Sheena sent him a nervous smile. "That's awfully kind of you to treat your help so good."

"This is the twenty-first century, is it not?" Beau said grandly, and put his arm up on the doorjamb. "I'm not lord of the manor, Mrs. Runey. I don't consign my employees to attics or basements." He grinned, but Lacey saw it didn't reach his eyes.

It was embarrassing that Beau could plainly see how unappealing her parents were. But it was more—this awkward situation made her recall those days growing up when she pretended she wasn't related to Sheena and Walt. All that angst and loneliness came rolling back. The guilt, too. She wasn't supposed to feel that way about her family.

It was past, it was *over*. But something illogical still

clung: that something was wrong with her to have these feelings. Something was wrong with *her*, not Sheena and Walt.

Walt gave a blustery sigh. "I think it's time to head to Alabama."

So much for their whirlwind visit.

"Too bad you're leaving." Beau put his thumbs in his jean pockets. "I'd like to take you to supper. I'm already taking Henry and Lacey."

"You *are*?" Walt's brows shot up in disbelief.

Of course he'd think it nonsense that a celebrity would want to take little old Lacey out.

"We're eating in Charleston," Beau went on. "It would be a shame not to have you go with us. You could always stay in your RV overnight and leave bright and early in the morning. You can plug it in to the outlet in the back. Or if that doesn't suit you, a mile down the road is an RV park."

"We saw it on the way over here," Sheena said.

"Surely you'll want to stay and spend more time with Lacey," Beau said, "and your grandson."

Lacey was grateful, but he was pushing it a little hard. In fact, he was being lord of the manor, probably without even trying.

Still, she couldn't believe when Sheena and Walt said yes, they'd stay.

"We'll move to the RV park," Walt said. "It's that much closer to the bridge, and I'd like to get settled in and take a nap, too, before we meet up again."

"Sounds like a plan." Beau was upbeat, and Lacey marveled at his ability to stay so polite and charming to her family. "We'll pick you up at six thirty."

When they went downstairs, all three kids were sound asleep on the couch, piled up on one another, while Dickey snoozed in the armchair. On the coffee table, a laptop still ran a cartoon.

Outside, Lacey felt hopeful again. "See you soon." She smiled and kissed her mother's cheek. Beau and Walt were discussing the gas mileage the RV got.

"All right," Sheena said, passive as ever, but then added, "I'm excited for you. I think he likes you."

"*No.*" Lacey's heart pounded. "The boss is off limits. Totally. I would *never*—"

"But he wants you to go to dinner. And you're living in the same lighthouse."

"Don't tell me you want me to throw myself at him."

"Well . . ."

"*Sheena.* If I marry, it'll be for love. Not security. Honestly, please get it out of your head. I'm not even interested in him."

"Why not?"

"He's my boss, for one." How many times did she have to repeat that lie? "I have professional standards."

"What else?"

"He's"—she looked at him—"he's all wrong for me. He likes the West Coast. I like the East Coast. We don't match. There's no spark. And he's so good-looking"—she was desperate—"he's almost . . . ugly. I'm not attracted to him at all."

There. That should do it. But just in case—

"And he's taking us out to a simple dinner only because he has to eat," she added. 'So don't get too excited about that, either."

Sheena didn't look convinced. "Should we dress up tonight?"

"A dress will do, and you always wear those. Don't read into this, okay? I'm just excited to spend more time with you."

"All right." Sheena squeezed Lacey's hand.

Lacey was touched by the gesture—she was starving,

actually, for her mother's approval, so she got a lump in her throat. And though it may have been too much to ask, she wished Sheena would do even more, like throw her arms around her. But the hand squeezing was the extent of her mother's physical affection.

Beau shook Walt's hand. And he continued to charm Sheena, suggesting that the dress she wore now was perfect for the evening.

When they pulled away, Walt waved out his driver's-side window.

"And they're off," Beau said, "but we'll see 'em again."

"Thank you," Lacey said softly. She was too embarrassed to tell him that Sheena hoped he had designs on her. "You were really nice. And maybe a little hard on Walt, but I have to admit, I loved it."

"How long did you have to live with him?"

"Too long."

They watched the RV until its taillights disappeared.

"It's pretty obvious your mom is a scared rabbit," Beau said. "What kind of hold does Walt have on her? Or was she always this way?"

"I don't know. Whatever the reason, he takes full advantage. I never saw him hit her or be openly verbally abusive. But he never let her think for herself, either, and she went along with it. Still does."

"I got all those props you asked for."

"That was nice of you. Thanks."

"You're welcome." He pulled his keys from his pocket and went to the Saab. "I got you a bikini, too."

"You're kidding me."

He leaned in and pulled out a bag. "Just look at it."

She peeked inside. "*Where* is it?"

"It's in the bottom. That itty-bitty brown thing in the corner."

She sent him a chiding look. "I can already tell I can't afford this. I get my bathing suits at Target. Thanks, but you'll have to return it."

"Oh, come on." He pushed the bag into her hand. "Just this once take a present someone offers you."

"What do you mean, *just this once*? Have you been around when other people offer me gifts?"

"No, but I can tell you try to give them back. You say things like, 'Oh, this was too expensive!' and 'No, I really shouldn't.' "

"You're wrong. I've never done that."

He didn't have to know it was because no one had ever bestowed an expensive, personal gift on her. Sheena and Walt hadn't. Callum had always been broke. So had her other actor boyfriend, the one who'd fathered Henry.

Of course, she treasured Henry's little crayon gifts more than any fancy present.

"Then keep your record going," Beau said. "There's no need to take it back to the store."

"I can't even see it"—she shook the bag—"or hear it. It will fall off in heavy surf."

"Nah." He had a twinkle in his eye. "Just tie the top on tight. And your booty will hold up the bottom."

"My booty?"

"I say that with all due respect for a very smart woman—who just happens to have a gorgeous body."

Her insides went hot as she pulled out a bikini top and dangled it in the air. A little gold clasp in the center winked in the sun. It was one of those expensive designer suits.

"Oh, hell, no." It was her favorite expression when she was really ticked off. "If you respect me, you don't gift me with an almost invisible, expensive bikini when I'm not even your girlfriend. That's something a guy buys a woman he's in an actual relationship with."

"Fine." He leaned against the car. "I won't deny that I think you're hot and would love to get you in my bed. But that doesn't mean I don't respect you, too. I knew that if you didn't like the gesture *or* the bikini, you'd tell me. You shoot from the hip, and I was willing to take the bullets on the off chance you'd be pleased. Okay?"

"It goes back to the store." She held it out.

He took it, reluctantly. "You're being difficult."

"And your point is? When I want to get a bikini, I'll find one myself. Same for a lover. But thanks for giving it the old college try, Mr. Movie Star."

"If you're playing hard to get so I'll lust after you even more, it's working."

"Keep thinking I'm just playing," she said, his grin making her insides heat. "Meanwhile, don't you have a movie to focus on? A career to save?"

"Unfortunately, yes. Mike's about to fire me."

"That's bad."

"I'll admit it sucks." He squinted into the sun like a young Clint Eastwood. "It's why I'm asking for your help. I'd appreciate your working with me right now. I need a breakthrough."

"I thought you were the guy with all the answers. And I was the Hollywood jinx."

"Maybe your jinx will smash into my bad karma and they'll explode, leaving nothing but good stuff behind."

He made it sound so . . . sexual.

"Um, okay," she said. "Where?"

"We don't want to wake anyone up. How about out here?"

"Best set ever," she said.

"No place to hide," he said, taking in the wide-open vista.

"If it's no good, we'll know it. And nip it in the bud." But she wondered as they walked in tandem to the place where the waves met the sand exactly what she was getting herself into.

CHAPTER SEVENTEEN

They passed a horseshoe crab carcass in the sand. It was lying upside down, its belly exposed. "That thing is *ugly*." Beau stretched out the first half of *ugly* until it snapped like a rubber band on the second half.

No Southerner said that word flat-out plain.

Lacey chuckled. "But it's fascinating, nonetheless. Beautiful, if you just think a little differently."

He peered closer. "Look at those legs. And the scary weird tail. It looks like something that belongs in the pre-historic age."

"That's what makes it cool. Henry loves them."

"Kids always see the best in things." He always had. Part of him still wanted to. When he was with Lacey and Henry in the lighthouse, he dreamed he could.

"Children appreciate anything genuine." Her glossy lips curved in a wistful smile. "That's why we love na-ture. It can't lie, and that's compelling."

Neither could her smoky eyes. Behind those thick lashes, she kinda wanted him. Or *a lot* wanted him. But she was holding back, and she was a smart cookie to do so. "Okay, Miss Crocodile Hunter. Or should I say Dr. Phil?"

She laughed, and his heart lifted at the sound. He

liked this chick, no doubt about it. And the like was a lot more than his usual. It bordered on out-of-control, way-over-the-speed-limit, resisting-arrest, and heading-into-jail-time like.

At the water's edge, they stood about five feet apart with their scripts.

"I've read the whole thing," she said.

She'd make a hot teacher. "What do you think?"

"It's a good story."

Damn. He didn't want to hear that.

"But what do I know, right?" She shrugged those smooth, tanned shoulders. "I'm that jinx. I was in bad movies."

"Hey, Greta is revered on the cult movie circuit. You have lots of fans." He was a huge one, way bigger than he wanted to be.

"I suppose that's nice."

"And I'm Dudley, don't forget."

"But Dudley was awesome."

She had no idea how much it meant to him that she and Henry loved Dudley. It got him in his Dudley place, which he'd hidden since he was in first grade and invented that dog as an imaginary friend. "Dudley had about three viewers. Best thing that ever happened to my career was that show getting canceled. I might have kept at it."

"The way I did. My next two movies after *Biker Aliens* were worse. I should have walked away. But looking back, I think I wanted to put the final nail in the coffin of my acting career."

"Why?"

She kicked at the sand with her manicured toes. "Acting's not for me. Something about it calls to me and always has. But I know in my bones it's not the thing I'm supposed to do—and my reviews prove it." She chuckled. "I'm sidestepping something else. Besides being Henry's mom, that is."

"Have you figured it out?"

"No." She looked so lonely saying that.

He wanted to pull her close, bite that shoulder . . . "Well, don't give up."

"I won't." The wind snatched at her hair. "But it's hard when you don't know what you're looking for."

They were quiet for a second while a wave washed over their feet.

"Let's read your most difficult scene with Clara," she suggested.

"You know, this would be a lot more fun naked."

"You'll do anything to change the subject."

"Is that a scar on the back of your calf?" He bent down.

"Yes." She twisted to see it better. "My first ride on a motorcycle, I got burned by the muffler."

"You look branded."

Her pupils got bigger, even in the sun.

"It's sexy." He knew his voice was huskier than usual, a dead giveaway that he was turned on.

"You think everything's sexy."

Everything about *her*, including that tilt to her mouth, the one she employed when she was trying hard to be a good girl. But he wouldn't say so.

"Show me one of yours," she said, "if you have any. As long as you won't be arrested for indecent exposure, that is."

He pulled his shirt off and lifted his arm.

She came closer. "Ah. On your triceps. A couple of them. How'd you do that?"

"Fell in an oyster bed. They're like knives. I've got a few more on my butt, too, and lower back. And a couple on the edge of my right foot."

"Oh, my gosh. How scary." She touched the muscle with the edge of her fingernail and the pad of her index finger.

He flinched, and a rush of heat swelled his groin.

She jumped back a step. "Sorry."

When he put his arm down, he wished she could touch him like that again, but lower, trailing her finger along the length of his thigh, moving upward—

And he'd really better stop thinking along those lines, or he'd embarrass himself.

"Luckily, it missed the artery," is what he said instead.

"You *are* lucky, in so many ways. So let's kill this scene. At least your part."

"Fine." He felt a fist of anxiety in his gut. Mike's words came back: Maybe he wasn't as good as he thought he was.

"Take your time." Her voice was soothing, but it also activated every nerve fiber in his body. "Unless you want to talk it over first. Maybe we should."

"Nah. I'm gonna go for it."

So he did. They read five pages nonstop.

"Okay," she said carefully. "That's enough for now."

"What do you mean?"

She looked up at the house—no movement there yet—then back at him. "You definitely don't have a feel for this guy. It's okay not to like him, but you have to be able to relate to him somehow—dig in."

"Mike said the same thing. But I don't know how. We have nothing in common. Nothing. I've tried finding a connection."

"Do you know his story?"

"Well, yeah." And he went on to explain Evan's background and his problem.

"No, I mean the story before the script. Like, from his childhood."

"No." This was getting a little crazy for him. "Why should I? I know acting theory, but making something up that the screenwriter never included . . . that seems bogus to me."

"You have to find a way to *get* Evan, so bear with me."

She sat on the sand and patted it. He sat down next to her, his hip touching hers. "Let me tell you a story about his childhood. A brief one. Something I think might have happened to him that made him love cats so much. Something that everyone on the planet can relate to, even non-cat-lovers."

Beau groaned. "I'm going to hate it. And I don't see the point." All he had to do was extend his arm, drape it over her shoulder, and they'd be looking out at the ocean as a couple.

"Just wait."

So she told the story, and Beau pondered the waves—and her sexy toes—as she did so. After five minutes of solid talk, she was done.

"So that's why he likes cats," she said, "and in a way, it's a metaphor for why he can't get a grip at work. Why he'll always be middle management. Why he lusts after the boss's wife and knows from the beginning that not only will he never have her, but he'll ruin himself just by loving her."

Beau looked at his knees. He was spooked.

"Are you with me?"

Slowly, he nodded. "You just made all that up?"

"Yes."

"I'm feeling him." He looked into those eyes of hers, so big and deep and understanding. He wished he got people as well as she did. "It's like Evan was Frankenstein's body parts, and he just got zapped to life. Where the hell did you learn to do that?"

She grinned. "I don't know. I guess driving around in an RV with people who aren't that fond of you, and doing it for years and years, forces you to inhabit your imagination."

"I still don't like him." Beau had to be honest. "I'd like to kick his ass. Rough him up. Make him drop and do two hundred, not twenty."

She laughed at the allusion to his old movie. "That's

okay, as long as you can poke around in those lines and feel a real guy in there."

He jumped to his feet and pulled her up by the hand. "Let's read again."

"Sure."

He backed off about ten feet, and they started over. The sun blinded him, bounced off her calf scar, made the pages of the script searing white.

"You're not worth it," Lacey said as Clara—hard, hard Clara with the sharp edges. "You bow out, give in. You never *fight*."

"You don't understand," he said as Evan, "what it means to be David when Goliath has already rigged the match."

"The game's not rigged. That's an excuse," Lacey said in character.

And he felt it then, the dark walk of a seriously wounded man who couldn't see anymore, who'd given up. This time . . . this time something happened. Something in him tripped, fell, and he allowed himself to be cut wide open.

"Be with me," he told her, shaking a little inside at the bleeding, the newness, the change. "I think about you— all the time." Because it hurt him—*Evan*—too much to think about himself.

He walked up to her, took her elbows.

Waited.

Their gazes locked.

She pulled her script up between their bodies and glanced swiftly down at it. "Um, I-I can't be with you. Don't even say that."

Her voice trembled. She was in character—or was she? Did she feel as turned on as he did?

"I don't give a shit what anyone says," he murmured while marveling at the perfection of her porcelain skin. He leaned down to her. "Did you hear me, Clara?"

"Y-yes." She blinked those bedroom eyes. "And you're going to get fired."

"I don't care what happens to me." He pulled her closer. Evan was desperate, but *Beau* was even more so. "Just . . . just kiss me."

"No," she whispered. "No, Evan."

Her mouth was *that close*.

Beau fought the compulsion to kiss her. It wasn't in the script, but it should be, dammit. If it were, Evan would *win* the girl.

She tilted her chin up. Her breath, sweet and warm, bathed his jaw. An inch. One inch, and he'd be in heaven.

She took a step back, lowered her script. "That was it."

He drew in a breath, pulling air back into Beau's lungs, breathing out Evan's despair.

"That was Evan," she said quietly. "And it was *so* strong."

"I think I get it now."

"I can tell." She grabbed his hand and tugged.

Sex and turn-on and warm skin . . . his fingers curled around hers. He was in the horny-as-hell zone—too fast. Way too fast.

"This calls for some serious acknowledgment." She yanked his hand again and took a step toward the waves, the taut angle of her body deepening her cleavage. "A christening of sorts of the new, improved actor."

"Let's go," he said.

They took off running together, their strides not matching at all, their arms alternately pulling too hard apart and hanging loose. But there was syncopation between them anyway, a miniature pulse of attraction right where the V of tender skin at the base of their fingers joined. They jumped, lunged, tried to skip over the waves, shouting primal nonsense all the while, and kept going until they fell flat on their faces together.

He was laughing so hard, he didn't even notice when he came up and got hit in the side of the face with a big wave. And she didn't notice that her sexy aqua-blue shirt had slipped, exposing more than enough lace-covered breast that he needed to keep his lower half underwater, or someone would have to call the porn police.

The kids flung open the lighthouse front door and came racing out.

"You didn't tell us where you were!" cried Henry. "Swimming without us?"

As they rushed toward them, screaming and shouting in the waves, Beau was a blur of emotion. Still half Evan. But part of him had woken from some kind of slumber. He wanted to pick Lacey up and kiss her. She was a genius. And the kids, the sun, how he'd looked like a fool running through those waves . . .

The lightheartedness of it all cleared something out. He didn't know what it was, but everything was good. He couldn't wait to see Mike. Get back on the set. Experiment with this new feeling of letting go, leaving the Band-Aids off.

An hour later, after a private phone call to an influential old friend of his in Charleston—who happened to be the mayor—they dropped Bob, Carol, and Dickey back with Mike, along with those props Mike wanted. Beau got a chance to tell Mike that he was ready for the next day, that he was looking forward to it. Lacey hugged the director and told him that she knew he was strong and that his wife was watching and so proud of him, her father, and the kids.

Dickey was oddly quiet for Dickey. No wonder, considering the anniversary they were acknowledging. But Mike wrapped his arm around the older man's neck and said, "Let's go celebrate Jasmine."

His late wife. Dickey's daughter. Bob and Carol's mom.

"I don't know," said Dickey. "Last I heard, the bridge

to Charleston was out. Drawbridge went up and didn't come down. Some woman had triplets on the side of the road, delivered by a nun and a music teacher en route to a carnival. We'd better stay put and watch *Seinfeld*."

"A carnival?" asked Henry hopefully.

Beau exchanged a bemused look with Lacey.

"No, honey," she said low.

But it was too late.

"I want to go to a carnival!" Bob cried.

"Is there cotton candy?" Carol asked.

Poor Mike.

"There's a putt-putt course not far over the bridge," Beau told him. "I used to go to it as a kid. They had race cars, too. And a few pinball machines."

He hadn't thought about that place in years. He'd go with his dad and Ricky. He double-checked on his phone that the little slice of child heaven still existed—it even had cotton candy—then gave Mike the address.

Mike's crowd seemed happy, and everyone wanted Henry to come.

"But I want to see my grandparents," Henry said.

Lacey squeezed his shoulder. Beau could tell she was very happy Henry said that.

"I'll take you to the fun park another day," Beau told him.

He felt pretty good when they left, until Henry reached up and took his hand, which shook Beau up a lot. Henry didn't have a dad. Henry probably wanted one. That wasn't Beau's territory. But he could act like a big brother.

Yes, that's what he'd do.

He stopped and spit as far away as he could.

"Why'd you do that?" Henry asked.

"Because I can," Beau said back, and dared Henry to outspit him.

Henry tried but couldn't do it.

"I have an unfair advantage," said Beau. "Spitting's my superpower."

"It *is*? I knew you had one!" Henry did one of his fist-pumping jumps. Pure childhood adrenaline.

"Good Lord," said Lacey with a bemused grin. "I'm supposed to get in a car with you two?"

Beau was gladder than ever that he'd said he'd take Lacey and Henry to his favorite casual eclectic restaurant in Charleston. He'd done it to make things easier between him and Lacey at the lighthouse. Sure, if the outing won him points toward breaking down her sexual defenses, all well and good. But the truth was, he honestly just wanted a little downtime with an interesting and beautiful dinner companion, someone he'd like to linger at a table with and talk to—and Henry made everything fun.

But his plans had changed after he'd met Sheena and Walt and seen the writing on the wall in that family. Now, for reasons he didn't bother to try to understand, he was all about making Sheena and Walt—bless their flinty, ignorant hearts—regret how poorly they treated their hardworking daughter—and by default their grandson, who was also Beau's partner in mystery solving and, let's face it, his big-time buddy.

No one was gonna mess with Henry.

And—to borrow a great movie line—no one was gonna put Lacey in a corner.

CHAPTER EIGHTEEN

"Ready to go?" Beau asked everyone when he parked the Saab along the Battery wall.

Lacey couldn't help noticing how incredibly handsome he was with his five o'clock shadow, and his excitement made him even cuter. He wasn't a movie star right now. He was Beau. Friend. Roommate.

Possible lover?

No.

She mentally girded herself not to be charmed.

Behind them, huge antebellum mansions faced the harbor, which was blue and only mildly choppy today. What a beautiful place this was, full of so much history! Not to mention wealth. And to think that Beau grew up here . . .

A horse-and-carriage waited nearby for passengers. Everyone got out of the car.

"Look at that horse!" Henry said. "And the water!" He immediately walked up some steps to the sidewalk and railing fronting the harbor.

"Take a look, and then we're going to get in that carriage," Beau called up to him.

"Really? With the horses?" Henry's face lit up, and he did a little hop holding on to the railing.

Walt and Sheena followed him up, while Lacey and Beau pulled up the rear.

"What's happening?" she murmured for his ears only.

"You'll see."

"Beau, I don't like surprises."

He put his hand on her lower back to guard her step, and she couldn't help enjoying the gentlemanly gesture.

"At the last minute," he said, "I got an idea for a way to pay you back for helping me with the script, okay? Just go with it."

"Bad idea."

"Let me be nice. Or are you gonna try to send this back, too?"

"It's not that. It's Sheena."

"What about her?"

But Walt came up right then and asked a question about Fort Sumter, and they didn't get to finish the conversation.

They took a carriage ride to the pier—which included scrumptious appetizers and drinks—cold shrimp, pimiento cheese on crackers, local beer, and Veuve Clicquot—as well as a bottle of chocolate milk and Cheetos for Henry.

When they clambered aboard a luxury sailing yacht—Lacey almost fainted when she saw it—she tried again. "Sheena thinks you have designs on me," she whispered to Beau. They were hanging out near the bow of the boat, but the forward hatch was open and the others were down below, exploring the interior, so she had to monitor her volume. "This is going to make it so much worse. We should have just gone to Shoney's or something."

"Tell her this is how movie stars roll," Beau said low, from mere inches away. She couldn't help being thrilled at his nearness. "Because it's true. Especially those of us who are high on ourselves and like to flaunt our wealth."

She laughed. "You're not high on yourself."

"Tell her I am anyway. It will make her hate me, but don't do it until after all the fun's over. Until then, we want her to love it."

"You're so strategic."

"For a good cause."

She felt embarrassed. Awkward. Their fists were wrapped around a metal line. She was extremely aware of his hand, warm and big, abutting hers.

"Admit it," he said. "Won't it feel good to get their approval for one night?"

"I guess. But I don't need it."

"I know. But why not enjoy it while it lasts? And enjoy all this showing off?"

"Okay. I-I'm sort of overwhelmed. I'm not trying to be ungrateful." She looked into his eyes.

"I get it." His concern was sincere.

She really didn't need that right now. She wanted to fall into those eyes, and she had this wish . . . that his fingers would cover hers on the line and they'd kiss.

Stupid. She needed to get a grip. So she was glad when Henry, Sheena, and Walt chose that moment to come back on deck. She and Beau walked to the stern and sat in the cockpit with them while the captain pointed out notable sights. They had a wonderful time basking in the beauty of Charleston's skyline and got a special surprise— especially Henry—when three porpoises streamed alongside the boat.

It was magic. And with every passing moment, Lacey was drawn to the man who'd arranged this outing, as much as she realized that to Beau, it was probably nothing. He'd seen the entire world. But when she saw true fascination in his demeanor when he stood next to Henry at the railing and watched the porpoises . . . her crush grew even more.

Don't go there, she told herself, over and over.

Don't fall in love.

After the sail ended, they had an exciting private tour of Fort Sumter, something that Lacey would never forget. Beau was proud, she could tell, of all the living history in his hometown. Henry, too, was completely enthralled.

"Where's everyone else?" Lacey asked their host when Sheena and Walt walked ahead with Henry. She had a feeling Sheena was trying to give them some alone time. She didn't want her mother to scheme on her behalf. But she was glad that it meant Henry got to spend more time with his grandparents as a result.

"It's after hours at a national park," Beau said, the pressure of his hand on her back—*again*—sending delicious tingles up her spine. "I had to pull some major strings, but it was my pleasure."

"I can't wait to tell my mother," she murmured. "I'll say it was an abuse of your power and prestige. She's from a holler in West Virginia. She won't appreciate that."

"You go, girl. But hold off. Bask in her approval till we get home." He was standing way too close to her, and her rebellious body loved it. "I like to see you being appreciated."

She had to get out of this sexually charged dynamic, so she stopped for a second to adjust her purse. "I don't know what you mean."

"You're a hardworking single mother who's done a damned good job with her boy. What's wrong with someone spoiling you now and then?"

"Because—" She felt the heat in her face and couldn't continue.

"You're just not used to it."

"I know. I feel kind of sick. Off." She pushed her hair off her face. "Maybe it was the sailboat ride."

He laughed. "Someone needs to spoil you more often, that's all."

What he was saying was so different from anything she'd ever heard before. He was like a good-looking alien impersonating a human and invading her planet. She wasn't sure what to do with him—stun him with a phaser and send him back to *his* planet, or stun him with a phaser and lock him in her room as a permanent play toy.

Half an hour later, they dined alfresco near the monument upon filet mignon and local shrimp at a beautiful table set with flowers, a white tablecloth, and gorgeous china and silver. The vast Atlantic Ocean was their backdrop.

"Mr. Wilder, I can't believe you arranged this." Sheena looked almost fearfully at the string quartet playing a soft baroque concerto in the background.

She took the words right out of Lacey's mouth. Beau had done all this, only because she'd helped him read today? It was a little over-the-top—wait, way over-the-top. But magnificent, nonetheless.

If this was how movie stars rolled, she liked it.

"This is the best day I've ever had," said Henry after he'd finished his piece of chocolate cake. "Can I walk over there, Mom?" He pointed to a low ledge on the side of the monument.

"Sure, honey."

"Watch me, Grandpa!" he said to Walt, and bolted.

It broke Lacey's heart when Walt didn't say anything back. But at least he and Sheena followed him with their eyes.

"What do you think of him?" She didn't mean to speak

out loud. But she had, and she wanted to know. She was *desperate* to know.

Walt took bite of cake. "Should we really discuss this now?" he said with his mouth full. "We're having a good time. And Mr. Wilder's not interested in hearing our family business."

"Doesn't bother me," said Beau. "But I can go hang out with Henry if you'd like me to."

"No." Lacey was firm. "There's no need. I'm only asking a simple question."

But she knew it was more than that. She was on fire, and she was about to lose it emotionally. She could tell. Her bucket of resentments, worries, and hopes, which she'd kept to herself for so long, was about to overflow.

Stay calm, she told herself. *Be Henry's mom.* And then she thought of Beaver Cleaver's mom. *Act like her. Not Lucy Ricardo.*

"He's a nice boy." Walt sounded peeved to be forced to reply.

"Very polite," added Sheena.

Lacey was seriously disappointed, but she couldn't give up. "Are you ready to claim him as your grandson?"

Sheena sighed. "He can call us Grandma and Grandpa," she said slowly, "and we won't object."

Walt didn't look too happy about that. "You've adopted him under California state law?"

"Five whole years ago." A tremor of anger went through her. "It's permanent. How long will it take for you to use his name? How long will it take for you to be happy you're his grandparents?"

Beau's gaze was grave.

Walt shook his head. "I've got nothing against the kid. But you've backed yourself into a corner taking him on, and your mother and I can't help you with money. We know you've moved back east, but you've made your bed, and you have to lie on it."

"I never expected your financial help." The deep hurt made her numb. "Only your love."

"I'm not comfortable talking about this anymore." Sheena shook out her heavy cloth napkin and put it next to her plate. A server came by and removed it for her.

"Devra doesn't give us a bit of trouble," Walt told Beau as if they were best friends and Lacey wasn't listening.

Beau wasn't biting. The angles of his face in the shadows were hard and unyielding. "You should know something. Lacey planned this whole evening for you two. Completely last-minute. She's got mad networking skills, your daughter."

He'd already done more than he should, and now he was really pushing it. Lacey appreciated it, but he had to stop. This was *her* battle.

She sent him a look, but she couldn't read the one he sent back. He was in full splendiferous movie-star mode.

"You planned this, Lacey?" her mother asked, almost suspiciously, but she did lay her hand on her heart.

Lacey shrugged. "I suppose you could say I arranged it, yes."

But it would be a lie.

"Who footed the bill?" Walt's long, scraggly sideburns—and his nosiness—bothered Lacey more than ever.

"I did," Beau said right away. "Lacey caught a discrepancy on one of my bills. Saved me overpaying by five figures. It was the least I could do."

She thought Beau was incredibly exasperating—and attractive—at that moment. The contradiction wreaked havoc on the equilibrium she was trying to maintain before her mom and Walt.

Sheena shook her head. "She was always good at math."

Had to be. No one else was there to teach Devra, so if Lacey didn't learn it, Devra was screwed.

"Good for you, Lacey," Walt said.

Was that a smidgeon of respect she heard in his tone?

She smiled weakly, fairly overcome by the whole evening's events. There were the porpoises, the chocolate cake, Beau's hand on her back, Henry's laughter. And now lukewarm approval from Sheena. Walt, too, observed her blandly with no trace of his usual defensive scorn.

"I wish—" Sheena's dreary aura lightened just a tad.

Lacey's hope meter shot through the roof. Could Sheena possibly want to live near her and Henry, or something equally wonderful?

"What is it?" Lacey could almost see her mother wearing something like a vibrant navy-blue tunic, white cigarette pants, a big gold bangle bracelet, and cute flats—and hugging Henry close.

Sheena gave a little shake of her head. "Never mind."

A seagull dive-bombed toward a whitecap in the distance. Lacey fixed her gaze on it and swallowed the lump in her throat.

"Is there something you need, Mrs. Runey?" Beau asked. "A cup of coffee, perhaps? Some more cake or wine?"

"No, thank you." Sheena looked away.

What more could her mother possibly want after the lavish experience she'd just been given?

"Sheena wishes Lacey had a man in her life," Walt explained without being asked, "especially with all the responsibilities she has now." He angled his head at Henry, who was flapping his arms slowly while he watched the same seagull soar low over the water in search of more dinner.

"*Walt.*" Lacey glared at him. "Please."

But Walt obviously didn't mind continuing. "Once Mr. Wilder and this movie depart Indigo Beach, what are you going to do, Lacey? Where will you go?"

"I'll have another job." She was tired of defending herself.

"Of course you will," said Sheena.

Good. At least some of the glow of the amazing dinner and tour was still lingering.

Walt crossed his arms over his chest. "You're like a boat without a harbor."

A very easy metaphor to come by considering that a boat was putt-putting out of the harbor at that very moment.

"I have a harbor," Lacey insisted. "It's Indigo Beach. Henry and I like it there. And what about you? We never lived in one place, ever, when I was growing up."

"The RV was our home," said Walt, "and the circuit of craft fairs. Year after year we went to the same ones."

"We never had a hometown," Lacey reminded him.

"But we had steady work," said Sheena, "a trade we could carry with us. Walt's birdhouses and my quilts. Hometowns are all well and good. But you need a place inside you to rely on, too."

How come Sheena had never told her any of this when she was growing up? She could have used that kind of advice.

"What's your trade?" Walt demanded to know.

"I don't know yet." A puff of wind drove a strand of hair into Lacey's mouth. She felt small and stupid.

Sheena and Walt hadn't changed. They would never apologize for how they'd brought her up. They wouldn't see how much they'd held back from her as parents.

But the thought that really obliterated her was that *she*

hadn't changed, either. She'd always sought their approval. And she'd always been adrift, and now she was adrift with a son. Walt and Sheena had valid concerns.

Oh, my God, she thought, *Walt and Sheena are* right.

CHAPTER NINETEEN

The very idea that Walt and Sheena were right—and that Lacey hadn't changed and might never be able to—scared her so much, she was mute.

Only the sound of Henry's battle noises in the background broke the long, dull silence. "Kaboom!" he cried, pretending to shoot off an invisible cannon.

"I think I'd better tell you another reason we're here tonight," Beau said, casting her a quick glance.

Something in it made her wary. She couldn't tell which of his former leading men he was being right now. His tone was one she'd never heard before.

"What is it?" asked Walt.

"Your daughter's a catch," Beau said slowly to Sheena— not Walt, "and I'm bending over backward to impress her. I'd marry her in a skinny minute if I could get her attention."

What?

"But I'm a California guy now, with a high profile, and she wants to stay local and grounded. She's made it clear she's not interested, and I get it."

"You really shouldn't have said that," Lacey said immediately. How could he? He knew she didn't want her mother to think he had a crush on her!

No apology was forthcoming. He just looked hot and in charge.

She'd get back at him later, somehow. Maybe she'd dance on his surfboard. But at the moment, inside she was a limp piece of shrimp left out in the sun too long, like the one on the ground near Walt's chair.

What to do? How to get out of this current mess?

And how was she going to fix her life?

"What do you mean, *not interested*, Lacey?" Walt looked both scornful and ignorant, which meant things were back to normal. "Beau's a rich movie star! Damn, girl, what kind of man are you waiting for?"

"I'm not a gold digger, Walt." Lacey glared at him. "And I'm done with this whole tacky conversation."

How was that for a movie speech? Short and to the point.

"Don't forget"—Walt refused to be shut down—"even apart from all the money you'd get your hands on"—he looked at his new BFF—"'cause you're a nice guy, Beau, and I know you'd let her have the checkbook"—he turned back to Lacey—"you were Greta Gildensturm. Greta damned Gildensturm!"

"Oh, God." Lacey put her head in her hands. "Please don't mention that name."

But Walt kept going. "Beau's a *real* actor. You'd be moving up in the world. You should be grateful. Maybe you'll get another chance in the movies. You'll have connections. Like Will Smith's son. That kid's movie blew, by the way."

"Please shut up," Lacey told him.

Nope. It didn't work.

"It's time," Walt continued his grand speech, "for you to make a good decision." He slapped the tabletop. "Just one. Sometimes I think you're flakier than three bowls of Total."

Sheena shrank lower in her chair, while Lacey almost levitated out of hers.

"Whatever you say about the decisions I've made since I left home," she said to her stepfather, "you'd better not be suggesting that adopting Henry wasn't a good one. Because I will not tolerate that bullshit attitude from you, Walt."

"I'm talking about you floating *around*," he said, evading the accusation.

"Please don't swear." Sheena frowned.

"Sorry," Lacey replied, "but I was taught to float around by the masters—you two. I'm not holding it against you, but you need to lay off criticizing my choices. I'm doing the best I can. Except for the cussing. I could do better there."

"We're doing our best, too," Sheena said.

"We never cuss," said Walt.

"It's not the worst thing in the world to do." Lacey gazed steadily at him. "I never left a twelve-year-old girl for three days with her sick little sister while I went off to a drunkfest wedding three states away with my adoring wife."

"That was my sister's wedding," Walt said, "and we couldn't afford to pay for four train tickets." He shrugged. "By the time I was twelve, I was in the coal mine."

"And I was sewing shirts full-time," said Sheena.

"You're lucky all you had to do was babysit." Walt chuckled.

"That's what I'm good at," Lacey said. "Watching out for other people. Whether it's Devra or Monique or Dickey or Bob and Carol, or even Mr. Wilder. At least these days I'm getting paid. Although I remember the other parents at the craft fairs had me babysit their kids, too, and they'd give me a dollar here, a dollar there. Y'all took every dime."

"That went straight to buying food for the family," said Walt.

"And your beer," Lacey reminded him. "I wouldn't

have minded giving it all to you, either, if you'd said thank you. Even once."

"Well, I never," said Sheena.

She always said that when she was shocked—*shocked*—at Lacey's behavior but couldn't think of a damned thing to say back.

All the points she'd gotten for supposedly arranging this spectacular evening had been used up.

Beau raised a hand. "Mr. and Mrs. Runey, I only told you I had a thing for Lacey to let you know that I think she's got a lot going for her, not to make you angry at her for turning me down. She has every right to. I'm sure she'll rack up many proposals before she accepts one."

He should stick to scripts. That was the most unromantic speech she'd ever heard.

"A bird in the hand," Walt reminded them all.

"Lacey, darlin', I have a hard time believing you'll ever do better than this man right here, who obviously loves you very much," said Sheena.

Was Sheena referring to the man who'd damned her with faint praise by checking off the she-has-a-lot-going-for-her box? Who believed she would *rack up* more proposals?

Lacey had had it.

She looked at Beau, who apparently thought he was off the hook. "All right. I've changed my mind. I *am* interested, Mr. Wilder." She paused. "Maybe I shouldn't call you that anymore. Especially since we've made out. Twice."

Which was a big, fat lie. Only in her dreams.

Beau's eyes didn't narrow and his amenable expression never changed, but she sensed his entire body shifting to high alert. "But you said you'd never want to move to California, or marry a guy with brown hair, or a guy who plays poker, or a movie star—"

She liked how he equated "movie star" with "guy with brown hair" in his impromptu list.

Two could play at this game.

"Maybe you could try to convince me," she said, "since you're crazy about me and all. Isn't that what a guy really in love would do? Especially after you told me that I was the center of your universe?"

Beneath his polite facade, Beau was definitely agitated. And maybe angry. But so was she.

Sheena clasped her palms together. "That's a fine plan."

Lacey would call her in a week or two and tell her that it hadn't worked out, but meanwhile she liked seeing her mom shine from within with approval of her. Walt had never grinned at her the way he did now.

It was like chocolate, in fact. Totally addicting.

She still wished Walt to perdition and Sheena to a room filled with current women's magazines. They weren't easy people to be around. But she loved being on their good sides. It was sick and wrong. But that was what families did, drove one another crazy, to desperate measures sometimes. At least *her* family.

"See?" Walt was close enough to punch Beau's arm. "She came around."

Lacey laid a hand over Beau's, and even though she was mad at him she nearly lost her breath from how good it felt to touch his warm male skin. He had a few little hairs on it. Tickly. Super manly. She could envision him breaking into her cabin in the woods, throwing her over his shoulder, tying her up, and ravishing her in a cave, with her express permission, of course. Somehow this scenario involved a sheepskin rug on that cave floor. And maybe a little fire nearby. And champagne . . .

"It's not a done deal by far," she said, veering off from her delectable daydream. "So stop getting your hopes up, everyone. But at least I'm thinking about it. Does that sit well with you . . . Beau?"

His eyes were full of a deep, dark message she was afraid to read. It brought her straight back to that imaginary cave, but this time it was pitch black. Lots of cold stone ledges. And he was in charge.

"You bet it does," he said softly.

Her insides cramped up. And her breasts tingled. She was a mess around him. He'd better not try to kiss her.

She hoped he did.

Nope. He wasn't going to.

Maybe she'd kiss *him*. For extra points with Sheena. And to irritate him. Because he sure as hell had irritated *her*. Besides, he was totally kissable, and she'd said they'd made out already.

So even though she hated PDA—it was tacky, tacky, tacky—she did kiss him, the way people kissed in the movies in the olden days, before they started showing tongue action.

Sheena actually gasped aloud her delight.

You and me. The thought jumped into Lacey's head while her lips were smashed against his. *Together. On the bed, on the floor, on the beach, in the Saab. Fun sex and long sighs and hot, hot pleasure.*

Thank God no one knew what she was thinking. This PDA was really working for her, even as she sensed that she was messing with a mighty force, and she'd better watch out.

Beau pulled back after three hot seconds.

"Time out," he murmured.

She was disappointed. She'd hoped he would have said, *You vixen*, as if he were still the masked bandit from that great medieval action-adventure movie he did with Johnny Depp.

He stood and yanked her to her feet. And then he moved

her in one fell swoop so that his back was to her mom and Walt and they were at least twenty feet away. In their own little world, sort of, if you forgot about all the catering people and musicians watching, in addition to Walt and Sheena.

But somehow, it still felt like their own little world. Maybe it was the giant fort behind them. It lent Lacey a sense of security.

"You went too far," he said.

"You started it. How could you?" She saw Henry behind him, oblivious. He was balancing on a ledge, facing away from her toward the sea.

"Too late now. And your fake kissing sucks. What were you thinking about?"

"None of your business. You'd better kiss me again. And make it an extremely tacky fake kiss. Otherwise, they won't believe us."

"These days the kisses in movies are real."

"Even if you're not attracted to that person?"

"Of course."

"So you've had to kiss someone you weren't attracted to? Not Emma Stone, right? You must have loved kissing her."

"Shut up," he said and grabbed her hips. "You know this might wind up in the *National Enquirer.*"

"So be it. No one will ever guess it's Greta this time. I've got my new hair." She whipped out her huge sunglasses. "And these."

They started kissing again, for real. Her sunglasses forced her to tip her chin and neck up, giving him even greater access to her mouth.

Her lips molded to his warm ones, and their bodies pressed close. As his exotic aftershave tickled her nostrils and his scratchy face reminded her what a brute he could be—a luscious thought—she realized she wanted him. Not only that, she *had* to have him.

Us, she was thinking as their tongues collided. He was good at this, *very* good, so good she couldn't think at all. He was all heat and sex, and she was ready for him. They really needed to find a private place . . .

He pulled back, but she fought against it.

"Henry," he reminded her, and she finally released her mouth from his. "That was plenty long," he added with a gleam in his eye. "We were extremely tacky."

She loved tacky now. She was totally into PDA and wanted to do it again. "Did he see?"

"I don't think so. He would have come running over."

"Good. I'm sure we satisfied Walt and Sheena." She straightened. This was all his fault. She had nothing to feel guilty about.

The rest of the evening was the most wonderful hour and a half Lacey had ever spent with her mother and step-dad. They smiled at her, hugged her even, and spoke to her and Henry much more than they had earlier. You couldn't change Walt completely—he was still an ass, pointing out the fact that the motorboat they took back to the pier was not his favorite color, burnt orange.

"I paint most of my birdhouses that color," he said. "My second favorite is pine green. You'd think more boats would be that color, too."

But other than that one blip, Lacey basked in their approval.

She tried not to think that it was all based on the false premise that Beau was in love with her, and she was ready to give him a chance to court her.

"You sit up front," Walt told her when they got back to the car.

Wow.

At the RV campground, everyone got out.

"We'd better say good-bye now." Lacey hoped they didn't notice that Beau wasn't holding her hand. They needed to be careful around Henry. "I know you'll be leaving early tomorrow. Rush-hour traffic gets bad about seven."

Sheena looked at Walt, then back at Lacey. "I don't think so. We're staying for at least another few days."

Walt nodded. "Yep. Not going anywhere."

"B-but why?" Lacey was both horrified—she'd have to keep up the playacting with Beau, which wasn't part of the plan—and ecstatic because Henry would see them more, too. *That* was a wonderful thing.

So was kissing Beau, but she wasn't supposed to *think* it was wonderful. And poor Henry—she couldn't have him thinking his mom had a boyfriend.

"We want to get to know Mr. Wilder better," Sheena said, her face still glowing.

"And Henry," Lacey added forcefully. Then remembered to smile.

"Of course," Sheena said, semi-brightly.

Hallelujah!

"Devra can hang on a few more days," Walt said. "Hell, the store opening isn't for another week."

Was the world ending? Lacey had to wonder.

"We'll be here," Sheena said, "waiting for your call."

Like devoted grandparents.

"Maybe we don't have to wait," Walt said. "We could hang out with you on the movie set."

"I don't think that's possible." Lacey loved and hated the idea. "I mean, I have a lot of people to look after already." They could be with Henry, doting on him. *All day*. She'd have to fend off questions from Sheena about Beau. *All day*.

"It's not as if you have to look after *us*," Sheena said.

Lacey imagined her mother watching her get fooled by one of Dickey's lies. The very notion that Sheena might see her look foolish made her tense. "I'll have to ask the director. But don't count on anything."

"How could he object?" Walt said. "Two more adults, watching out for the kids and an old man."

"Exactly." Sheena beamed at Beau.

They were coming. Whether she liked it or not.

Lacey had created a monster.

CHAPTER TWENTY

"Excuse me," Beau said.

They were back at the lighthouse. Back to some sanity.

Lacey was brushing her teeth, and the door to the bathroom was wide open. Henry was in bed, sound asleep. She mumbled something and moved out of the way. Beau grabbed his own toothbrush—the electric kind, of course, to keep his celebrity smile whiter than ever—and got to work himself.

Two adults, one tiny sink. Usually, he waited for her to finish, but tonight he was barging in. Hell, she'd left the door open, almost like a dare.

"I get what you're doing," she said around her toothbrush.

"Oh, yeah?" he said around his.

She nodded vigorously.

He shrugged.

She finished first. He had a good view of her from behind. Then it was his turn. By then she'd already left. She was downstairs, turning off all the lights.

He followed.

"You're mad," she said, straightening the coffee table in the sitting area, where Henry, Bob, and Carol had been coloring. "But so am I. You were trying to be nice. But then you had to go all high-concept family drama on us. Me. You. Together. If only."

"Out of the kindness of my heart."

"Or an insane desire to be in control of everything around you because you're used to calling the shots. Or was it because you're simply accustomed to playing the hero who rescues everyone else?"

"Hey—"

"But it wasn't quite far enough to get their approval. They needed me on board the love train, too. So what was I supposed to do?"

"Serves you right you have to hang out with Walt until they decide to leave."

"Every cloud has a silver lining. I plan to bask in their approval for a week, and we'll get back to normal when I call them and say we've broken up. Hopefully by then, they'll have bonded with Henry and we'll have taken one teensy step forward to becoming a normal family. It never would have happened without your crazy generous offer to help, so guess what—I'm not mad anymore. And you shouldn't be, either."

"Why not?"

She stared at him. "Because I'm ready to be your lighthouse *date*. Not your wife. You can woo me. But I make no promises."

"For real?"

She nodded slowly. "You're a movie star. You can have anyone you want. And I just didn't care to be one of those women, succumbing to your obvious charms."

"So . . . why now?"

"I've decided you're succumbing to *my* charms. I can live with that. You're a lucky man, Beau Wilder. And don't get comfy. The last thing I need is to become a cliché. I refuse to let it happen."

"Oh, yeah?" He came close and put his arms around her.

"I might decide to revert to our previous roommate relationship at any moment. But kissing you at Fort Sumter reminded me that it had been a long time since I'd made out with someone who knows what grits are. Someone who loves Southern sunshine and who notices whether the carriage horses are well fed and watered and who rubs their noses and talks to them. A guy who buys Cheetos and chocolate milk for Henry, too. I've never kissed anyone like that, actually."

He couldn't help but laugh a little. "No way could you ever become a cliché."

And then they kissed.

She was warm and soft and willing.

But she was more, too. She had a spark he couldn't get to, and like a moth to a flame, he sought it. But it eluded him, and the lack made him crazy with a need to get this woman in his bed. He pulled her into his room and shut the door.

To hell with the slanted ceiling. These four walls were going to see some action. Finally.

"Watch out for your head," he told the woman he'd been lusting over since the first minute he'd met her.

Lacey looked up. "I see what you mean." She knew she sounded calm, but inside, she still couldn't believe it. She was here. In Beau's lair. She'd studiously avoided it, tried not even to look in its general direction, since he'd arrived.

"Let's get naked," he murmured against her neck. He was already caressing her waist and rear end with bold hands.

She had to remember to breathe. "People don't get naked on first dates. At least, I don't."

He was kissing her ear, her jawline, and then he went for her mouth again, a full-on assault, his lips slanting over hers, his tongue coaxing one second, demanding the next.

She gave it back, and they kept it going, the push-and-pull of foreplay sensitizing every nerve ending in her body.

When his hand moved higher to cup her right breast, she moaned.

Kissing him was what she needed. Getting skin-to-skin with him. She'd thought it was sun, vitamins, and a job. But it was this. His mouth over hers, his palm flat now and rubbing hard circles over her breast.

"Consider how many hours we've already spent together." He played at putting a hickey on her neck, his man fingers pulling her closer, up against a hard-as-granite erection.

"Oh, my," she whispered, and tilted her own pelvis in for better traction.

That stopped all the talk for at least thirty seconds. They kissed, he unbuttoned her blouse. They kissed again, and she unbuttoned his shirt. But she didn't get a good look at his chest, which was one of her favorite parts of him. He was already nuzzling at her breasts with his mouth.

"I'd call that at least two dates a day." He pushed down one bra cup with his chin and twirled his tongue around her nipple. "This means we're on something like our forty-second one."

"That's true." He could have said the Eiffel Tower was in Kansas City and she'd have agreed with him. Because now he had her bra unfastened, and he was suckling deep on her breast, his free hand pinning her tight to his body.

"Woo," she managed to gasp out. "It's an actual word. Not just an exclamation. That's what I said you could do."

"This is my version of wooing," he said back, and bit gently on her nipple.

"Oh!" she cried softly, and buried both her hands in his hair. "You're so good at it. Please don't stop."

She finally got to run her hands all over what she'd admired from too far away when they'd been on the beach:

that broad, muscled chest and the washboard abs that disappeared into his jeans. She loved the fine golden hair curling over his pecs, his clearly defined biceps and triceps. This man was a prime physical specimen, and she was so turned on, she had to say something about it. "You're hot."

"Thanks." His grin was adorable, as if he'd never heard anyone say that before. "But not half as hot as you."

"You're certainly polite for a movie star," she said.

"I'm not being polite." He picked her up to put her on the bed. "I'm going after what I want. And that's *you*."

"So you think I have a lot going for me, huh?" She couldn't help getting prickly at the memory of what he'd told her mother and Walt.

He paused a beat. "Sometimes I value my dignity a little too much. And I didn't want you to think I was going overboard. I should have said that if you were a princess in a castle guarded by alien beings shooting radioactive light arrows, like the ones in *Biker Aliens*, I'd storm it anyway. I'd glow green—just for you."

"Wow. That's way better."

He kissed her again. Her arms were wrapped around his neck and shoulders, and her legs dangling over his arm. Dammit if she didn't get a little choked up at being treated as if she was something special. "You can't carry me to the bed, you know."

She'd hit her head on the ceiling. So would he.

"Fine." He alternated between breasts, adoring them with his mouth. Biting, kissing, laving the tips with his tongue. "I guess we'll stay right here."

Her body clamored for him. "We can't stand here all day."

"*I* can."

His voice was sexy-rough, his mouth sweet and hot on her breasts, and a dart of acute desire flashed between her legs. All it would take was arching her back just a teensy bit to press her flesh even harder against that hot, magic mouth of his, and her exquisite torture would end in a flash of fireworks.

With her skirt and panties still on.

This was way better than her dream.

But she didn't get the chance. Beau put her down right then and there on the wide-plank floor and pulled the rest of her clothes off, then held her waist and pulled back for a better view, devouring her with his eyes. "You are a glorious sight."

She blushed. "Thank you."

"No, thank *you*." He kissed her gently, promising more, and while he did, he caressed her inner thigh, sending her a silent message to move her legs apart.

She did, and he cupped her sex, his mouth never leaving her own.

Dear heaven. She couldn't take anymore, not with him still half dressed. She didn't want to climax all on her lonesome, so she forced herself to squeeze her legs together.

He pulled his mouth off hers. "What are you doing?"

"This." Shyly, she unbuttoned his jeans and started to slide them off his narrow hips. And then she smiled.

"What?"

"Is that a *gold* waistband on your underwear?"

"Isn't it shiny?" He sounded proud. "They're kind of like Underoos for grown-ups."

"Oh, my gosh." She loved them. And she loved how much *he* loved them.

"Don't be shy. Go ahead, take a better look." He stepped out of his khakis.

"Those are somethin' else." But it wasn't really the briefs that caught her eye. It was the whole man, especially the package the briefs covered.

"I like bling on my clothes. But being a Charlestonian, it has to be hidden bling."

"It's time to lose the bling," she whispered.

"You want to help?"

"I'd rather watch," she squeaked and sat on the edge of the bed—thank God—because she needed the support. Beau Wilder naked was awesome to behold.

His erection jutted upward, and she, um, didn't know what to say. It was a doozie. But you didn't tell a guy that, right? Not unless you wanted him to make love to you all day and night . . .

"Yeah, enough of me already." He tackled her on the bed.

She laughed. He kissed her. He wanted more—so much more—as did she. They were so primed to do the deed that she spread her legs within seconds. His hips fit between her thighs perfectly. His pride-and-joy—for surely it had to be—pressed hard against her swollen juncture. All he had to do was move it an inch to the left, and they'd be home.

It would just happen. It would be *right*. She enjoyed a second of almost total perfection, then slid out from under him. "I wish," she said with a sigh.

"We can't?" he said back, and pulled her to him, sucking on her bottom lip, teasing the seam of her mouth with his tongue, his hand caressing her hip, dipping to her waist, then up to her breast and back.

"No." She knew she sounded miserable to his ears. She didn't want to be a downer, but this was going to be difficult. "Everything else, okay? But not that."

"Okay."

He gave in so easily. She wasn't expecting that.

"I'm a gentleman," he explained, brushing her hair back from her face. "I coax—I don't coerce."

She kissed him hard. "It's not that I don't *want* to. But if we have sex, we're moving to the next level. And we both know that can't happen. So . . . I just want to have fun with you, Beau. There's so much we *can* do."

"I'm all for fun," he said, his kisses slow and erotic, his mouth occasionally leaving hers to tease her breast.

While he worked above, he spread her legs with his own—how warm and manly his limbs felt against her thigh and calf!—and toyed with her feminine sheath, his hand taunting her until she moaned, and then finally entering her with two fingers while he mimicked making love to her with his mouth on hers.

She came so fast and long against his fingers and hand that when her spine fell back against the mattress, she gave a little sob. She didn't remember ever having that kind of powerful, crazy release before.

"Mmmm," he said, utterly relaxed. "I loved watching that. Hearing it, too."

She stretched out and grinned, feeling good. Filled. Happy. "You made it happen."

He started kissing her again, and then she remembered. She had to get out of there. Quickly. Otherwise, she was getting in too deep. But there was something yet to do, and she couldn't wait to see Beau Wilder lose it. To be at her mercy.

That was her big fantasy.

And she was going to make it come true.

"I can already tell you're scheming," Beau said.

"And?"

"I'm all for it."

She laughed.

He loved when she laughed. Something in him always lifted. "But let's make it easy." He picked up her hand and put it on his erect member. "No tricks, babe. Not tonight when we're just getting started."

"Are you sure?"

"Yeah."

So she started stroking him. Her hand felt incredible. She had no idea that he intended to go right back to pleasuring her, so when he did, her little gasp of surprise pleased him.

His woman, flashed through his head.

They kissed all the while and played. He talked a little dirty to her and she laughed again, then she talked a little dirty back to him. They kept their hands busy in those hot, aching-for-touch places because otherwise, they'd wind up where they'd started, with him between her legs again, pumping into her with all he was worth, her legs wrapped around his back.

That daydream alone was enough to send him over the edge, but he held on until she was ready, and when she reached the precipice, they went over it together. It was hot and erotic as hell.

"There's something to be said for limiting one's options," he said, and pulled her up into his arms. He loved that she was limp as a rag doll.

"There is."

A second later, she stood on long legs and grabbed her things off the floor, giving him quite the view. And before he could stand to kiss her good night, she was at the door.

"Good night." She smiled. "See you tomorrow."

"That's it?"

"Uh-huh."

"I guess I'll take it." He winked.

She was back to being fussy Lacey, so her eyes widened at the wink, but she still wore a smile when she pulled the door shut. He had nothing left to do before going to sleep but watch his secret TV show. He'd discovered it about ten years earlier on one of those cable channels that showed old series. He watched two whole episodes, too, scrolling backward the last three minutes of each one to catch the ending again.

And then he fell asleep, dreaming of hoot owls, Lacey naked, Lacey smiling at the stove—clothed—and him and Henry surfing with that mystery kid, Timothy Brenner.

CHAPTER TWENTY-ONE

Lacey had been Beau's lighthouse date the last five nights. She was sleeping *so* much better. All that bristling energy she'd had each day . . . gone. In its place was a languor that served her well with her three little charges and Dickey.

Stressed about Dickey's fibs?

No longer. She giggled at a few, and even brushed off the one that sent her running to Sheena to tell her that she was wanted on the set as an extra. Dickey claimed Mike needed Sheena to play an attorney, and Lacey had been so excited at the idea of seeing her mother dressed like a modern woman—a professional, at that—she never even questioned Dickey.

Freaked out when Bob accidentally stuck a penny up his nose?

Nope. She made him blow it out.

And when Henry and Carol couldn't settle down to do their math problems, she set up an adding and subtracting station with grapes and cookies, and they finished their worksheets in a flash.

"Good morning," Beau said again that morning.

But he meant way more than that:

You're hot.

I want you.
Let's do it again.
Soon.

"Mm-hmm," she said back, turning bright red, "good morning." She was barely able to speak. Move, too. When she thought of the things he'd done to her last night— particularly that one thing he'd done with the . . . the thingamajig—her legs almost went out. She crossed them under the table to remind herself to be good.

Henry came downstairs. "Can I bring Timothy's base-ball glove with us today, Mom?"

They'd gone through the trunk and looked at some of Timothy's drawings. And then there were pictures, sweet pictures of him with his parents in front of the lighthouse. The oldest he'd been in any of them was right around Henry's age. This was definitely a trunk holding early-childhood memories.

"I don't know," she said. "It's pretty old. And it was in that trunk. Maybe the lighthouse owner doesn't want us messing with Timothy's toys and books and everything else in there."

Henry said, "Awww, shoot," but he was hungry, so he got to work on his breakfast. When he finished, he ran upstairs to brush his teeth.

"So your scenes are going well?" she asked Beau.

Maybe he couldn't remember any of last night. She was a nice girl. She didn't *do* kinky.

But she had last night. They were running out of op-tions, running out of willpower. And she couldn't wait to do kinky again, God save her soul!

Sheena and Walt were still here, torturing her with their nosiness about her supposed romance with Beau. She needed some kind of release from all the pressure, didn't she?

"Filming's going much better." Beau slapped peanut butter on a piece of toast. "Although I think I need another little story from you before Wednesday. I just can't wrap my head around that scene. Evan lets another guy punch him in the face. And he *cries*. Part of the reason he cries is because he's slowly weakening physically, too, from the poison." He shook his head. "This role may actually be the end of my career. I can sense the yawning abyss."

"No, it won't be," she said, "for two reasons. Who's going to see it? Just little pockets of artsy types at a film festival or two. And you're going to do such a good job, no legitimate critic will be able to fault you, even if you do think the script is terrible."

He was in his running clothes, and seeing his worn Coke T-shirt literally hang off his broad shoulders and brush over his flat abs made her breathless. She'd run her hands over those shoulders. Grabbed his back. Kissed his neck. Gone farther south, holding nothing back.

That last memory made her flush—and made her want to do it again.

They'd played, romped, laughed, and made out—and somehow managed to do everything but have actual intercourse. And it was because she had a strategy that he backed her up on. If he hadn't, she never would have paid him repeat visits. She got in and out of there. *Fast.* Before she could change her mind.

With a guy like Beau Wilder, who was always at the sexual ready, like a prize bull, it didn't take much foreplay to get her to the point of no return, either. And when she reiterated her parameters last night (which she did every night)—when she'd said she was willing to do everything *but*, and if didn't like it, he could take his favors elsewhere—the man had flipped her over on her back and shown her exactly how creative he could be with his fingers and his mouth and something else that was simply too outrageous for words. Let's just say that evening, the salad would be short one ingredient.

She cleared her throat now. It was all coming back too clearly, the whole hot, crazy fifteen minutes.

She knew what they were doing was inappropriate. She was a single mother. She had responsibilities. No way could she count on Beau to be anything beyond the man who brought her to the peak of sexual pleasure every night and then some. He'd taken her way over the peak to that anti-gravity zone where reason didn't matter, where *common sense* was a dirty word, where a girl floated in a bubble of bliss and forgot all her troubles—and all the lessons she could swear she'd already learned—for a few heady moments.

Don't think about last night, she told herself. *Don't let* him *think about last night, either.*

Maybe he regretted how . . . interesting it got.

A rusty meow came from the living room. George watched them with half-closed eyes and pretended he hadn't just begged for some human attention.

"He's been sleeping with me, you know," Beau said. "He comes in the middle of the night and leaves before morning." He paused. "Like someone else I know."

His slow, sexy grin made her almost choke on her coffee. He'd never mentioned their liaisons outside his bedroom before, and today of all days? Right next to the refrigerator he'd raided with erotic intentions after midnight last night?

Oh, God, she'd been an utter hoyden.

And he was the devil.

"Yeah, but I drop by to visit well before the cat," she whispered. "And the only reason I do is because you can't come to *my* room."

"I hope I'm paying you back well for the inconvenience."

How could he speak so politely about it all?

"Um . . ." She nodded quickly, unable to finish that sentence. She'd be polite, too, if it killed her.

He took a sip of coffee, but she saw his amusement. And a flame of lust in his eye that he kept banked in the kitchen, at the studio, on the beach. But it was always there. She recognized it now and crossed her legs tighter.

"I have to give the cat credit," he said. "He's playing all of us."

"He is." She managed a short chuckle. "He starts with Henry, goes to you, and winds up back with Henry in the morning. And he sits on my lap every night after dinner."

A dinner Beau rarely was there for, although Sheena and Walt were, of course. She wondered if Beau was really hanging out with the gorgeous owner of the Mexican restaurant. Or was he simply trying to avoid her mom and stepdad?

But she couldn't ask. He owed her nothing. She owed him nothing.

She'd do well to remember that.

"You making a grocery run today?" he asked her with a straight face.

She stopped chewing. "Do I—do I need to?"

He shrugged. "I kinda think so." If he were an angel, he'd be a warrior one with his noble brow, beautiful man's body, and that clear, guilt-free gaze.

"I see," she said, then nodded. "Sure. Sure, I can go. What exactly did you need?"

"Nothing." He lifted his mug one more time and grinned.

Grinned!

And that was when she knew for sure he hadn't forgotten last night at all.

"You son of a—" No, she wouldn't insult his mother.

He was chuckling now, softly.

She leaned forward. "I'm not the one who—"

And then he grabbed her wrist across the table and kissed her. In broad daylight.

She was so astonished, she didn't have time to react.

"You're funny," he said when he pulled back. "Are you ever going to let us slow down? Or are we always going to go full throttle?"

She blinked, flustered by her body's intense visceral reaction to him. "Um, I don't think we should talk about this."

"Have it your way." He stood—he was so close!—making her sexual agitation all the worse. "Tell Henry filming ends at three today."

Normal. That's what she'd try her best to sound like. "Mike told me."

"Great. I'm taking you both to the Sportsman's Shop. We'll get gloves and play catch."

But he'd kissed her in the kitchen. How could she act normal? "Sheena and Walt will want to go, too."

"Fine. And we're going to surf. You'd better be ready with that bikini."

Then he ran out the door in his sexy running shorts, his backpack over his shoulders, and was gone.

"Let that be a lesson to you," she told herself as she watched him go down the sand. "Actors always run away. You know that, silly woman."

"Hey, Mom?"

She turned around. Henry stood there with George draped over the back of his neck, like a cougar he'd shot in the woods. Henry held his front and rear paws while George blinked sleepily up at her.

"Oh! Are you sure he likes that?"

"He loves it!" Henry grinned.

George wasn't objecting, so she let it go.

"Who were you talking to, Mom?"

"Myself, sweetie. Mr. Wilder said 'bye." And she told

him what Beau had said about the Sportsman Shop and surfing.

"I can't wait!" Henry squatted down and let George slide off his neck.

Lacey watched him explain everything to the cat, who closed his eyes and ignored him. A minute later, she couldn't get the lazy grin off her face as she climbed the stairs to brush her teeth. Beau had kissed her at the breakfast table.

And she was crazy to be so excited.

She needed to forget it ever happened. To him, it was no big deal, she was sure.

When she passed his bedroom door, which was open, exposing a nicely kept room, she got a rush of feeling in her pelvis. It was all so cheap and tawdry—fast and furious—and she was loving every minute of it. And now that he'd kissed her, she was even more convinced that there was no way they could slow down on those sheets. Things got dicier then.

She consoled herself that the rest of her day she spent as a wholesome mother to Henry, nanny to Carol and Bob, and friend to Dickey.

And she hadn't forgotten what she needed to do: find a job. She figured that if the car dealership advertisement disappeared from the newspaper, that was a sign she should stay on course at the studio at least for a while longer. But it had been almost a week, and the ad was still running. They wanted to expand their sales staff now that they'd moved to a bigger location and were willing to train people from the ground up.

Seeking enthusiastic, career-driven employees, the ad said, *who appreciate quality*. It was a little snobby—but the car brand was, with good reason. It was top-of-the-line.

You don't belong in a car like that, she told herself. But she'd go. If only to practice. She needed to try, and she should take advantage of the fact that Sheena and Walt could watch the kids and Dickey. She'd rather not force Mike to round up a production assistant if she could save him the trouble. Her interview was at eleven.

"Don't believe Dickey," she told her mother in a low voice right before she left Mike's trailer, "if he tells you y'all need to run somewhere on the studio grounds. Just stay here in the trailer and let them watch a movie. If you get in serious trouble, call Mike. He can be here in two minutes or less."

"I've got Dickey's number by now," Sheena said. "He says he played the fiddle at Doc Watson's funeral and that he and Dolly Parton are friends. When are we gonna see Beau next?"

"Tonight. He's taking us to the Sportsman's Shop for baseball gloves. You and Walt can ride along. He's been super busy with filming."

"How's it going with you two?" Sheena's tone was a little intense.

"I don't know."

"How could you not be sure? Is anything happening?"

"Some things." Heat rose up Lacey's neck. "I mean, we're . . . talking."

"I see how it is." Sheena nodded. "Don't be the cow who gives up her milk for free. Not if you want to keep him, honey."

"Please don't go there."

"I know how you modern kids do things—"

"I'm not a kid anymore. I'm a grown woman. And I won't lose my head. I promise you."

"But you almost *have* him." Sheena's eyes were hopeful. "He's going to get bored. He's a *movie star*. Do you want him to get away?"

"I want what's best for me and Henry."

"It's not too late. If he wants to take Henry to get a ball

glove tonight, he must still be infatuated with you. *Stop everything.* You know exactly what I mean."

Lacey inhaled a deep breath. "I don't want a guy I'm forced to manipulate to love me. I want a man who does it all on his own. And until he comes along, I'm *fine*."

"Humph," said Sheena.

From the other end of the trailer, Walt said, "Who's ready for some NASCAR?"

All the kids squealed.

"I wanna drive a race car," yelled Carol.

"I want to be the man who puts all the stickers on 'em!" said Bob.

"I knew Dale Earnhardt, Senior, before he died," said Dickey. "We was good friends."

"Who's that?" asked Henry.

"The best race car driver who ever lived," said Dickey.

"What was his favorite food?" Henry could go on forever asking Dickey questions. He'd caught on that he'd always get a good answer, never an *I don't know*.

"Bacon and hamburger pizza," Dickey said right away.

The three kids looked at one another.

"Cool!" they all said at once.

"Hey, you," Dickey called to Lacey.

"I only answer to Lacey," she said, "Or Your Majesty."

"Come here, Lacey girl." He was wearing his evil scarecrow grin. "I got something to tell only you."

She didn't trust him for a second. "We don't tell secrets around here, Dickey."

"It's not a secret," he said, "just a juicy tidbit of news you won't want me to tell the whole world."

Juicy tidbit, her butt. He was gonna tell another lie.

She put both her hands on her hips and sidled over.

"Lean down," he said.

She did, like the Tin Man when he was still rusty. "Tell me."

"Beau Wilder's in love with you," he whispered in her ear, like they were in fourth grade.

Her heart leapt into her throat, but she refused to react on the outside. "Now why would you go say that?" she whispered back. "You're just causing trouble."

But her pulse was wild, her hands damp. Beau Wilder . . . in love with her?

Dickey chuckled. "Yes, he is."

"What's your proof?"

"His eyes," Dickey said. "Dead giveaway."

She tried to be mad at him. She tried very hard. Instead, she shook her head and patted his shoulder. "You haven't heard him say it. *That's* proof."

"There's all kinds of proof."

"Well, it doesn't matter anyway," she said and walked briskly away—as briskly as one can in an RV—threw her purse over her shoulder, and left, telling herself she was relieved to get out of the madness for a while.

But the truth was, she needed time to recover from Dickey's outrageous comment. Forty-five minutes she sat at the dealership waiting to be interviewed—and thinking about Beau Wilder's eyes and Dickey's latest lie.

For surely, that's what it was.

He must have guessed that she was crushing on Beau. Who wouldn't? And Dickey was taking advantage of her vulnerability. That was right up his alley.

The interviewer, a man in his late thirties who was the dealership's general manager, looked her up and down. "Way too sexy."

"*Pardon me?*" She'd run home to change. She was wearing a simple striped skirt—rose and darker rose—and a white short-sleeved sweater. Neutral pumps.

"Women won't trust you, and that's who we'd be hiring you for. You need black or navy blue skirts and dresses.

No reds, oranges, yellows, or pinks. Toned-down makeup. Conservative approach. Expect ten-hour days. You'll start at three days a week. No benefits. If you improve, you'll become full-time."

He told her what kind of commissions she could expect. "But that's the best-case scenario. You might have to work up to that."

"Oh," she said faintly. "Why am I limited to selling to women?"

He shook his head. "Men don't want to tell their friends they bought a car from a woman."

"I could prove you wrong."

"Can't risk alienating the clientele. But with a little work, you might do all right. You've got a good sales personality: warm, approachable . . ."

Lacey's heart hammered in her chest. "Does this mean I have the job?" She wasn't even sure she wanted it.

The guy threw her application on the desk. "What have you been doing the past five years, before this job at the Indigo Beach studio?"

"I worked in Los Angeles, mainly as an assistant to a minor celebrity. But I can't get you a reference. I wasn't fired, but we had a personal conflict that forced me to burn my bridges."

"Who was that?"

"I'd rather not say. I promised to keep everything confidential." Which wasn't true. But she didn't want him to remember her from the infamous TMZ story.

"Your résumé is pretty sketchy. But if it's true about Los Angeles—"

"Of course it's true."

"We get all kinds here looking for a job, Miss Clark."

"I understand that."

"But if that LA job happened, then you've had some experience working with wealthy people."

"Yes. I have. I'm patient. I'm organized. And I know how to please."

He shrugged. "Maybe if you get Mr. Wilder in here to vouch for you—"

"Is my getting the job contingent on that?"

"It might show us how enthusiastic you are."

"That's asking a lot. Mr. Wilder's busy making a movie."

"You have to be bold to sell cars."

She stood and kept her hands folded in front of her. "Thank you for your time. But I feel I need to remind you, sir, that we don't live in the Stone Age. I look perfectly professional right now. I could sell cars to men, too. Better than most of your men, if I was challenged to do so. I'm afraid, however, that my answer is no."

"Wait—are you turning *me* down?"

"Yes."

"I haven't even offered you the job."

"Well, now you don't need to."

He shook his head. "Not a lot of work out there right now on Indigo Beach other than restaurants and housekeeping. But you know that."

"Yes, I do. And both occupations provide good, honest work. Good-bye." She walked out with her head high, but inside, her heart was heavy.

On the way out, she saw a well-dressed middle-aged couple looking at a sleek sedan.

"Can you answer a question for us, young lady?" the man asked.

She stopped. "I'll try."

He must have assumed she worked there.

"Why should we buy this car instead of this one?" He pointed to a car the competition was selling in the paper and thrust some papers in her hand. "Here's my research. Before that young fella comes back to make the hard sell, I want a second opinion."

She looked at the ad and all the information they'd compiled—crash ratings, gas mileage, other specs, frequency of repair, customer satisfaction, et cetera—then opened the door of the car they were standing next to and peered inside. Afterward, she read the sticker on the door and leafed through the research he had on it.

"The price is the same, just about." She handed the papers back. "And everything else is about equal, too."

"Yes," said the man's petite partner expectantly.

A guy in a suit was walking toward them—apparently, this couple's salesman—and with him was the manager who'd interviewed Lacey.

"You been married long?" she asked the couple.

The man nodded. "Twenty-three years."

"Will you be keeping this car a while?"

"Ten years at least." The woman's expression was none other than stalwart. "We buy nice, but we hang on to things we love."

They held hands.

Lacey smiled. "Have you inspected the backseats?"

"That's about all we haven't checked," the man said. "We've test-driven both."

"Get in." She opened the rear door.

The general manager and the salesman were approaching faster.

The couple slid inside the backseat.

"Miss Clark? Can we help you?" The general manager's tone was friendly, but she heard his underlying tension.

She ignored him and said calmly to the husband and wife, "I'd buy the car that most reminds you of your necking days. Think how quickly the past twenty-three years have gone. Time's precious. Make your backseat still matter."

The woman's mouth fell open.

The man chuckled.

"Miss Clark? What's going on here?" the manager persisted.

Lacey kept her head in the car.

The woman patted the seat. "I like this one," she said, almost shyly to her husband. "It's comfortable."

He grinned at her. "I like it, too."

Lacey chuckled. "Do you need to go check the other one?"

"I don't think so." The husband eyed his paperwork. "The backseat dimensions are smaller on the other one." He looked at his wife. "You're tiny, but—"

"The more room, the better," she said.

They both laughed.

"Have fun with it." Lacey grinned at them, then pulled her head out.

The two men frowned at her.

"Sold," she said simply.

And walked away.

There was a Target a mile down the road. She stopped and bought herself a bikini—a blue-and-white diamond pattern. And all the way back to Indigo Beach, she sang "Royals," by Lorde, at the top of her lungs.

Something had shifted for her.

It wasn't that she didn't have enough skills. She had too *many*.

Narrowing them down was the key.

CHAPTER TWENTY-TWO

"So we've got the gloves," Beau said later that afternoon at the cash register at the Sportsman's Shop. He was glad to see Henry so excited.

"I love mine." Henry beamed with pride. "Now I'm like Timothy Brenner."

Exploring that trunk full of toys, drawings, and photos with the little guy had really turned into a fun activity for both of them.

"See, Grandma and Grandpa?" Henry held up the small leather mitt for Sheena and Walt to see. "I'll write my name on the side, too."

"Very nice," said Sheena, not like a grandmother would but like a Sunday schoolteacher: prim. Showing attention to the boy because it was the right thing to do.

Beau already recognized when Lacey was upset. And right now her mouth thinned. Her eyes clouded, and she pretended that nothing was wrong. But he sensed her frustration with her mother. Her sadness, too.

"Gotta condition the leather when you get home," Walt told Henry. "Oil it, put a baseball in the pocket, then tie a big rubber band around it, and leave it out all night to soak."

"Okay." Henry punched the glove. "Will you help me?"

Walt paused a fraction of a second. "Sure. We need to get the oil."

So they all waited for Walt to find it, and then he actually bought it because Beau had already completed his purchase, which included several soft T-balls for throwing and a T-ball stand.

As much as Lacey thanked Beau for the gifts, it was Walt's buying that oil for Henry's glove that put the sparkle back in her eye. And for that, Beau was glad.

"Hey," he said at the car, "Mike and his crew had a great time at the old fun park I used to go to." It was a harmless enough memory. He had to have some remnants of his childhood to cling to. "Why don't we visit since it's only a few stoplights away? Buy some cotton candy and ride some go-carts and play a round of miniature golf?"

"Yeah!" Henry said.

Lacey high-fived him.

Walt and Sheena were definitely less enthusiastic, but they didn't outright object.

"Mike said there's pizza and frozen yogurt there, too, if anyone's hungry." Beau took a quick glance in the mirror at Lacey in the backseat. Just because he could. "I think they can even wrangle us a fresh cup of coffee."

"That suits me," said Sheena.

"They have a NASCAR wall, too," Beau added. "Signed photos of all the best drivers. Some memorabilia."

Walt perked up at that.

Beau didn't really know why he was trying so hard to help this family have fun. It had to have been Henry. A child deserved a happy family. Of course, he really liked seeing Lacey happy, too. She was one of those people who wore her heart on her sleeve, and damn the consequences. He had to admire that. Plus, her spunk came with a whole lot of sex appeal.

Too much. All he could think of was the coming evening when she'd slip into his room and they'd get it on. Best way to end the night ever.

Lacey and Henry sang "Old McDonald Had a Farm" in the car while Beau called out the various animals.

By the time they wound up at the concession area, they were a festive little party, if you didn't pay much attention to Walt and Sheena, who pulled up the rear like the guards who walked behind the queen's carriage—solemn and unflappable. Henry got to swing between Beau's and Lacey's hands, and even though it looked too cozy for words, Beau was aware of a distance in Lacey, much more pronounced since they started fooling around at night.

Maybe he should stop. What if she was protecting her feelings? She'd already been dumped by Callum.

"Five tickets to miniature golf and the go-carts," he told the teenager at the window.

"Children his height have to ride with someone," the teenager said.

"He'll go with me." Beau looked down at Henry. "Is that all right?"

"*Yes!*"

Henry's gap-toothed grin never failed to please him. The kid was nothing if not enthusiastic about everything they did together.

Lacey smiled shyly at Beau—that distance again—but her eyes glowed with soft happiness. Henry's doing, no doubt. Beau found her irresistibly sexy at that moment.

Maybe he was being selfish. All he had to do was call an old girlfriend in Charleston, or crook a finger at one of the several attractive women he'd met at Indigo Beach—the manager at the Mexican restaurant, for example—and he'd slake his sexual appetite.

But he didn't want sex with any woman. He wanted sex with Lacey.

Why, he wasn't sure. It wasn't the thrill of making a fascinating or difficult conquest—although she was both. But he'd never been that type of guy, etching notches in a proverbial bedpost, and neither were any of his close friends. They were secure and successful enough to get their egos pumped in other ways.

Maybe it had to do with the fact that when he was in bed with Lacey, hot and furious as their sessions were, he felt exposed in a way he never had before. Exposed, but comfortable somehow, as if he didn't have to try to be the Beau Wilder everyone expected him to be.

It was a relief. And a turn-on. A *major* turn-on.

"How about the cars first?" he suggested once they were inside the pavilion. He remembered the intense excitement he used to feel as a kid seeing the race cars and the batting cages and the golf course. "And then we'll stop for snacks, followed by nine holes of miniature golf."

"Sounds good," said Lacey.

The place wasn't at all crowded, which was nice. No lines. They started walking toward the cars. He could still feel the drive to impress his father, the utter joy when his dad noticed anything he did, the security he'd felt being Garrison Wilder's son . . .

"I want that one!" Henry cried now, picking out a royal-blue car.

A man leaning on the railing separating the track from the customers turned at the sound of Henry's voice.

Beau stopped walking. His heart jerked into his throat then started beating double time.

After a few steps, Lacey turned around. "Beau?"

Was it really who he thought it was? He took a few steps forward. Stopped again.

The man took off his baseball cap. His hair was receding. "*Beau?*" He was wearing a shirt that signified he worked there.

No damned way. "Ricky?"

"Rick, now," the man confirmed with a nervous smile. He *should* be shaking in his boots. "You caught us between the afternoon and nighttime rush."

Beau said nothing.

"What are you doing here?" Rick asked, then added cautiously, "It's nice to see you."

Nice. What a lame, lying word.

The wall of hatred came up. "Hey, everyone." Beau was unable to keep the coldness out of his tone. "It's time to go."

Lacey raised her brows at him.

Hell, yes, he was ignoring the man's question.

"What's wrong?" Her voice was thin, worried.

"Mr. Wilder! Mr. Wilder!" Henry pulled hard on his hand, so hard the child was leaning at a forty-five-degree angle. "Let's get in the blue car!"

Remember the kid, Beau said over and over in his head, his big hand encased in Henry's two little ones. *Just damned well remember the kid.*

He didn't know if he was talking about Ricky or Henry.

Or maybe himself.

"Do you need some coffee?" Walt asked him. "When I get headaches, that always helps."

"Sumpin' ain't right," Sheena murmured, then looked at Ricky with a pointedly cool stare.

So Sheena was going to be a hard-ass and go to bat for him by glaring at Rick. Any other time, Beau would have been amused and flattered. Right now, he felt like shit—the worse kind of shit he'd felt in over a decade.

A dark hole of despair loomed somewhere beneath his feet. Couldn't anyone else feel it there, waiting to pull him down, and not just him but all that was right with the world, all that was good and wholesome and honest?

It was why they had to leave.

Lacey could take Henry back another day. He'd survive

the disappointment. Not riding in a go-cart was probably good for the kid. Teach him that people broke promises. Might as well learn while he was young . . .

"Don't go," Ricky said awkwardly. "Stay as long as you want. For free. I'll refund your money. I own this place now." He opened the gate to the track. "Come on over and pick your cars."

Henry raced right over.

"We'll leave if you need to," Lacey said gently, standing next to Beau, "right now. I can tell Henry you're sick."

"Look at this, Mr. Wilder!" Henry pointed at the blue car. "It's number four! I like that number!"

"Cool!" he called back and tried to focus on Lacey's sweet scent. "He needs a go-cart ride." It was all he could get out. But he meant it.

"Fine." She must have sensed there was to be no debate. "I'll go with him."

"No." He could handle this. If he could play sensitive Evan, he could play Beau, the star who didn't let down hopeful children. "I'll take him."

"Okay," she said, "but as soon as you cross the finish line, we're out of here."

He gave a short nod. Moving his legs in Ricky's direction was like lifting cement blocks. He finally got close. But everything in him wanted to run away. Or punch the guy's lights out.

He knew how Ricky could afford to buy this place.

Ricky stuck out his hand when he got within range. "Hey, man. Good to see you."

Beau clenched his jaw. That was the one thing he couldn't do. He couldn't shake his hand, even with all these people staring. A handshake meant something—something he wasn't willing to give. He walked past the guy's outstretched palm and got in the car with Henry.

"*Beau*," Lacey said in a softly chiding voice.

He wouldn't look at her. "Let's go," he commanded. Henry squirmed next to him. "You in your seat belt?"

"Yes, sir."

"Thank you," Lacey said to Rick when he helped her into her car.

"My pleasure," he said low.

Beau's hatred ratcheted up another notch.

Walt got in his car next.

"Ma'am?" Rick said politely to Sheena.

"No, no," Sheena told him. "I'm going to watch."

Let's get it done, Beau thought, and looked awkwardly down at Henry. He was making revving engine noises with his mouth, lost in his own race car daydreams, which was good. Beau directed his gaze straight ahead.

"On your marks, get set, go!" called Rick.

It was the longest three laps in any car of any size Beau had ever taken. For Henry's sake, he beat Walt to the finish line and let Lacey win.

"Wow, that was great." Rick adjusted his ball cap. "Really great. Y'all should go again."

"Please, Mr. Wilder," Henry begged him.

Beau sucked it up and did it again. This time, a lump formed in his throat. He rounded the curves, his face shielded from the viewing section of the track, and took in big gulps of air while Henry screamed his delight. When the pain became nearly unbearable and Beau's vision blurred at the edges, a guttural sound came from deep in his chest, the noise drowned by the go-cart engines.

This time when they got to the finish line—in first place—Beau turned to Henry. "Wait here for your mom to help you out. I gotta go to the bathroom. Meet you up front."

He leapt out, strode past Ricky without a word, and stood outside the entrance to the park.

Three minutes later, the rest of the group joined him, and he took off toward the car.

Lacey caught up with him. "I told Henry we'd do min-iature golf another time," she said brightly. "I said we need to get back to the beach and use our new gloves."

Beau said nothing. But he nodded that he'd heard.

Henry raced to his side next. "That was awesome." His inner gasoline gauge was always on FULL. "I want to go back there. Can we another day?"

Beau took another couple of strides. "I might not have time." He knew what he was doing to the boy by saying that, and he still did it.

Pain all around.

Pain everywhere.

"Oh," Henry said.

Get used to it, kid.

But Beau's heart, try as he might to harden it, responded to Henry's disappointment anyway. "We can still play catch. And surf." He wouldn't look at Henry or Lacey. He felt like the Terminator. *We will surf*, he imagined himself saying like Arnold. *We will throw a sphere and catch it.*

At the car, Walt and Sheena eyed him with interest. He stared stonily back. *Don't ask*, was his silent message.

Walt opened his mouth to speak but then shut it.

Smart man.

Beau was in no mood to talk.

All the way back, Lacey was the only adult who said anything, but Henry was happy to talk with her. They dis-cussed the two go-cart races in great detail, especially the second one.

"And then we passed you, Mom," said Henry. "At the finish line, the man that Mr. Wilder didn't like high-fived me."

"Cool," said Lacey faintly. "And, uh, it wasn't that Mr. Wilder didn't like the man."

Beau didn't know what to say.

"You had to go to the bathroom," Henry explained to

Beau helpfully. "When I have to go to the bathroom, I can't think of anything else."

"Right." Lacey trailed off.

Beau heard it in the boy's voice. He obviously wanted to know what was going on. Beau had been the same way at age thirteen—hurt and confused by the grown-ups in his life.

Imagine that uncertainty at age five—*five*—and a guy you look up to, a man who's your friend, tells you he doesn't have time to go back with you to the fun park he made you leave after promising you could stay.

Beau looked in the mirror. "The truth is, Henry, I don't like that man. I knew him when we were kids."

"Ohhhh," Henry said, and Beau could swear he saw some tension dissolve in the boy's eyes. "Was he a bully?"

"Nope." Beau couldn't believe he was revisiting this sorry part of his past. "Let's just say we were friends, and then I found out that he wasn't a real friend. He was hiding something. A secret. And it's not nice to hide secrets from your friends."

"What was it?"

"I wish I could tell you, but it's not really my secret, or his. The person who started it is gone now. So it really shouldn't matter anymore, but it does."

"So the secret is why you and that man can't be friends?" Henry's little-boy voice was sad.

"Yes," said Beau. "I'm only friends with people who are honest with me."

"Okay." Henry leaned forward. "I'll be honest with you, Mr. Wilder."

Beau shot him a small grin in the rearview mirror. How could he not? "And I'll be honest with you, too, Henry."

It was the right thing to do with people you cared about, even if it broke your heart.

Or theirs.

The rest of the car's occupants were silent during this exchange, but now Sheena sighed loudly and looked out the window. "I'd like to be dropped off at the RV park. We'll see you tomorrow."

Walt cast a glance at Beau, and in his eyes, Beau read some pity. For him. From Walt.

Wow.

"I'll leave the oil with you," Walt said, "for the glove."

Not *Henry's glove*. Just *the glove*.

"Fine," Beau answered with a slight nod, his eyes on the road. "I'll take care of it."

The car went around a sharp corner, and Lacey's gaze never wavered from the scenery outside her passenger window. At the stoplights, same thing. Her shoulders drooped, but her expression revealed nothing. She kept her arm around Henry the whole time.

A few minutes later, with Walt and Sheena safely deposited at the RV park, Beau felt a lessening of the tension in his neck. He knew the adults in the car wanted to know what was wrong with him—how could he hold a childhood secret against a man he hadn't seen in years? Why had he freaked out—in his own restrained way?

At least two of those adults were out of the way now.

"Let's play catch," he said as soon as he put the car in park at the lighthouse.

So they did, for a good fifteen minutes. Beau made sure Henry wasn't facing the sun. Lacey never dropped a ball. Henry did, many times over. But he laughed most of the time. Only once did he show frustration and say, "I stink."

"Don't worry about it," Beau told him, and tousled his hair. "We'll get that glove in better shape by tomorrow. How about we take a break now and do a little surfing?"

"Yay!" Henry threw his glove up in the air and caught it.

"You don't have to," Lacey said quietly as Henry ran inside to get on his bathing suit and say hello to George.

She told him to give the cat a new bowl of water, too. "Obviously, something really bothered you at the fun park."

Beau kept his eyes on the surf. The sun shone brightly. The sea was almost an emerald green. The tide had just turned, was coming in. The waves needed to be thigh-high to be just the right height for a beginning surfer.

"My dad had a secret second family," he said. "I didn't find out about it until I was thirteen. I walked in on him with his mistress, Tula. Rick was her son. *Dad's* son. My half brother."

CHAPTER TWENTY-THREE

Lacey couldn't believe what she was hearing from Beau. How shocking—and how bizarre—that his father had had a secret family.

When Beau turned to face her, his eyes were hard. Yet there was something hollow there, too.

"Tell me about it," she urged him gently.

He threw one arm over the other and squinted at the sun.

She waited, knowing that listening was the best gift. She couldn't remember the last time any adult had really listened to her. Henry did—Henry listened, always, especially when he read him stories. It was a balm to her soul, his attention.

"All right," Beau said eventually, his tone a little hesitant. "Dad and I used to go out hunting or hiking almost every weekend, hanging out in the country, like so many Southern dads and sons. Most of the time, we'd swing by Tula's house and pick up Ricky first. At least once a year, we'd go to the fun park. Usually around one of our birthdays."

She wanted to stay perfectly calm to ease his agitation, so she merely nodded.

"But usually we were in the woods," he went on. "After guy bonding time, we'd go back to Tula's, and I would spend an hour or two with Ricky, climbing trees, exploring. Dad always said he felt sorry for them, Tula being a widow and all." He shook his head. "I used to talk about our exploits—mine and Ricky's—all the time at the supper table with Mom."

"Did she know that your father was more than friends with Tula?"

He sighed. "All through high school, I never thought she did. I went away to boarding school—my choice. They wanted me to stay in Charleston and go to Porter-Gaud. But I couldn't stand to be near my father after I found out." He shifted his weight and looked down at the sand and scrubby turf. "My senior year—at graduation—I learned my mother had known about the arrangement all along. Dad told me. Gave me one of those man-to-man talks. He'd thought I'd understand by then. He said, good wives knew their men needed an outlet. They put up with it. And everybody was happy." He gave a short, bitter laugh. "But he was wrong."

"Did anyone else know?"

Beau shrugged. "I'm sure most of Charleston society had it figured out. But you don't talk about those things."

She glanced at the house, glad Henry was taking his time coming out. "What happened to you and Ricky?"

"When I found out what was going on, I never went to see him and Tula again. Once we met up when I was home for Christmas my junior year in high school. He tracked me down, waited outside the house, and followed me down Broad Street. He caught up with me in a parking lot, and we had a fistfight. I broke his nose. He chipped one of my teeth."

"Was that his intention—to fight you?"

"I don't know. I never gave him a chance to talk. And I never will."

They stared at the sea for a few seconds together.

"I'm sorry if I'm intruding where I shouldn't go," she said, "but now that you're older, you must know it wasn't his fault."

Beau spit on the sand. "He knew the whole time we'd climbed those trees. We were best friends. But Dad told him to keep his mouth shut. Tula, too, I suppose."

"He was just obeying his parents."

Beau grimaced at the word *parents*.

Lacey regretted causing him pain. "I-I'm sure he hated keeping the secret. He was only a kid."

Beau shook his head. "Maybe it wasn't his fault. I don't care. But I want nothing to do with him or his mother. She used to make me something she called ranger cookies— just for me, she said. I felt special. Dammit, I felt like *I* had a second family. And I liked it. I liked *them*—"

He took off toward the house.

"Beau!" She followed after him.

"I told you what I did because you're easy to talk to," he said over his shoulder. "But I have a limit."

"I get how you'd feel extremely hurt by the entire situation."

He didn't answer at first. He grabbed his surfboard off the side of the house and put it under his arm. "It was more than hurt. I was a pawn on my dad's chessboard. All those Saturday mornings with me, he was just looking forward to getting laid."

She couldn't imagine how devastated he must have been. Disillusioned. "Surely he enjoyed spending time with you." She found her own voice trembling with emotion. "Doing all those father–son things."

"Yeah, with Ricky there, too. Both his sons."

She didn't know what to say.

"It's over and done with, for the most part," he said. "After Dad died, he left Tula a bunch of money. She and

Rick were dirt-poor. That fun park belongs to him thanks to Garrison Wilder's largesse. And now Tula has a fine stable of horses and a big new house."

Even when he was hurt, he looked rough and tough around the edges. "Did you ever make up with your dad?" she asked. "Or talk to your mom?"

"No, about my dad. And yes, I confronted my mom. But she won't discuss it."

"I'm sorry you can't talk with her about it. Maybe it would help."

"I'm done trying. There's only so many times you can delude yourself before you say, *Enough*."

"I know that feeling."

There was a beat of silence.

"You'd better go in and change," he said. "Tell Henry to look behind the door of my bedroom. I've got another surprise for him. And then y'all meet me on the beach."

"You got him something else?"

"He's five. He can't learn to surf on this board." The shiny red one.

Her mouth dropped open. "You got him one?"

"Sure, a soft one. In fact, I got two. One your size, and one his."

"You're kidding. When?"

"The other day when you were on the pier fishing with Dickey and Mike's kids. I ran to the surf shop during my lunch break, and I've been waiting for a good time to get them out."

"You didn't have to—you're spoiling us—"

"I like to. And there are no strings attached. Don't you even dare think that."

"No. Not when Henry's involved, I wouldn't." She stared at him a moment, then leaned in and kissed his cheek. "Thank you."

"You're welcome."

"You're not changing into swim trunks?"

"No." He took off toward the water in his cutoff khakis, his back straight and proud, his shoulders thrown back, his hair whipping in the wind.

What was it like, she wondered, to know that your childhood had been a lie?

Let the sun warm Beau's heart. She thought of her own mother and Walt, of how disjointed their relationship had always been. *And warm mine, too.*

Half an hour later, she was laughing. Henry had taken to surfing like he was born to it. She couldn't figure out how his tiny body could stay upright on the new blue board Beau had given him, but he did, three times out of four, for at least five seconds before falling off.

And he was loving every minute of it.

It thrilled her to see Beau's face, too, how light his expression was, how easily he laughed despite the story he'd told her mere minutes before. His board was on the sand at the moment. He'd given them a friendly lecture and then a demonstration on how to get up, and now it was their turn to practice.

"That's right," he said to Henry as he coasted forward. "Put your arms out. They help balance you."

The waves that broke near the shoreline were small enough that Henry could manage quite well.

Lacey clapped. She told Henry, "Way to go!" And she tried hard not to notice Beau's abs.

"Time to teach your mom," Beau said when Henry had a good fall off the board not long after. "You sit on the sand and watch."

"You can do it, Mom," Henry encouraged her. "And if you wipe out"—she loved to hear him use surfer talk—"you just get up and do it again."

"Thanks," she told him with a grin. She was excited.

But she was also nervous. She didn't want to look stupid in front of Beau. With Henry, it was all right. She wanted him to see her be okay with failure.

But Beau was another story.

"You watched me explain to Henry, so you know what to do." Beau hung low in the water, watching her, his hair slicked back and sexy. "Do you have any questions?"

She bit her lip, and a wave knocked her sideways. But she held her ground. "Yes. What's so special about that red board of yours?"

He didn't say anything for a few seconds, and she could read the reluctance to tell her on his face.

"Never mind," she said. "You don't have to tell."

"No, it's okay." He dunked his head backward to keep his hair wet. "It's a little involved."

"I don't mind."

"All right. It starts with Dudley. The reason no one knows I was Dudley is because I'm the show's creator, so I made sure that fact stayed a secret. Until Henry figured it out."

"*You're* Harmon Jennings?"

"Yep."

"That's so cool. Your name came first under the cartoon magnifying glass during the rolling credits."

"Yeah." He grinned.

"Wow. I won't tell. Promise." She felt so honored that he'd shared such a confidence with her.

"Thanks. So anyway, I produced the show myself with some money I got when my grandmother died. I put every cent I had into it. The sound guy I worked with—whom I'd vowed to secrecy—died not long after that first season. And the animators never knew I was the voice of Dudley. I was working with them under an alias, and we never met face-to-face. They were cheap, all I could afford, out of Japan."

"I thought they did a wonderful job."

"Me, too. As for the TV connections I had to make to get the show on the air, I worked through my old agent. He knew I wanted to keep my ID under wraps."

"Why?"

"A bunch of reasons. I didn't want to deal with my parents and their petty judgments about how I was supposed to live my life. Plus, it didn't make me much of a chick magnet, saying I was Dudley."

"Some chicks think it's cute."

"Oh, yeah?" His tone got sexy.

A big wave knocked her sideways again. "Not saying *I* do."

"Hmmm. You sure?"

She followed his gaze downward and realized that her suit was plastered to her skin. Her nipples were like little party hats, and her bikini bottom had inched down on the right side, below her hip.

"Shoot," she said, blushing a little, and pulled the garment up again.

"I'm not complaining." Beau's voice was silky smooth.

Her entire body responded to that tone, especially her breasts and lower belly. She wanted him. Always. It was getting to be a bit of an issue, really. "Henry's watching."

"I'm not doing anything."

"Liar."

He laughed.

He was undressing her with his eyes. "Back to your story," she said.

"All right. Another reason I kept the show secret was that I was hoping Dudley would be my bread and butter while I explored all my options in LA. I was starting to audition for movie roles, too. I wasn't sure where I wanted to land at that point."

"Sounds like a good plan. A creative one."

"You're being awfully nice to me." His eyes gleamed with humor, but his voice promised sex. "Sure you don't have an ulterior motive?"

"No." She clung to her board, and tried not to think about them in bed together.

He laughed again, then dunked under a wave and came back up. "Back to the surfboard. I got it in LA with the little I had left over after I'd paid everyone who worked on Dudley. I was broke. I didn't want to tell anyone what I was doing—it was embarrassing that Dudley failed so fast—but I was also proud of myself for creating what I thought was a great show."

"It *was* a great show."

"My parents were totally against my moving out to LA. They wanted me to stay in school, become an attorney or doctor. They never supported me financially or otherwise. So when I got the board, I made a vow. I'd always follow my heart, even if it meant I had to do it alone and I crashed and burned, the way I did with Dudley. I'd get up. Get back on the board. Sounds corny. But it never fails me. Whenever I start to doubt myself, I go surfing, and things become clear again."

This guy was more substantial than Lacey had ever given him credit for. And she liked it. She liked it *too* much. "Are you following your heart now? As a movie actor?"

"Yes. But I'm still learning."

The sun beat down on her shoulders and back, but it felt good. She wished she could float with Beau in the surf, kiss, even make love. "That's a good story. But it's sad, too, in a way. Surely you have some human support these days."

He shrugged. "Of course. But people let you down. And I'm not excluding myself from that observation. I can be a jerk. Like I was today, with Henry."

"You had a shock. Henry's fine. Look how happy he is now."

They both looked at him on the beach. He was on all fours, gazing down at a clam hole spouting water.

"He's a great little guy," Beau said.

"And you've been a good friend to him."

But she wasn't going to get emotionally attached to a man who wasn't sticking around. Plain and simple. She couldn't waver on that fact. All she had to do was take one look at Henry, and she knew she wouldn't.

CHAPTER TWENTY-FOUR

Lacey was back in mommy mode. "Okay," she said brightly to Beau, "I'm ready to try this surfing thing. I just have to get up and stay there, right?"

"You got it." He sounded genuinely excited for her, and that—even more than the way the sun glinted off his wet shoulders and chest—flooded her body with crush feelings.

So much for mommy mode. She turned her back on him—*smart girl*—poised herself above her board, and waited.

And waited.

A huge wave knocked her off her feet and she lost the board.

The next two were too small.

And then one went by that she regretted not taking after it was too late.

"That was a good one," he said, keeping his distance. "It's okay to go for it and miss it. You'll get a feel for the board."

She kept her back to him. "Okay."

And then it came. The wave. It was just the right size, and it seemed as if it would break at the right moment.

"Go, Mommy!" Henry called from the beach.

She did go. She put her board down, glided forward, scrambled onto it, wobbled left and right, and for one whole second she was on her feet, her hands out.

And then she fell off the back of the board and landed butt-first on the sandy bottom. A wave flowed right over her, holding her down a moment, and then she pushed up to the surface, spluttering.

"I did it!" she yelled.

Beau was right there, grinning and holding on to her board. "On your first try, too. You Clarks are naturals."

She grinned back and turned to face the shore. "Henry? Did you see that?"

"Yes!" he cried. "Do it again!"

So she did. For a whole fifteen minutes without stopping, she caught waves, fell off her board, and experienced a few heady moments as she found herself standing at least five more times, a beautiful ocean wave carrying her on its back toward Henry.

It was heaven.

And she was worn-out. Fast. Surfing burned calories, apparently.

"You ready to go in?" Beau said.

"*Yes*." She was panting. She wondered if her waterproof mascara and twelve-hour lipstick had held up, and then she decided she didn't care. "I'm coming out here every day I possibly can from now on."

"Great," he said. They began walking through the waves to the sand, where Henry was building a castle.

"It's playtime," Beau said. "It's why I love it." He cast a glance at her. "I suspect you don't get much playtime."

"I do," she said, "with Henry."

"But not on your own."

"No."

"Then I'm glad I got to help you with that. Every adult needs to play."

She flushed. Was he thinking only of surfing? Or of what they did together at night in his bed, the way she was?

"I do feel different," she babbled to cover up that she was highly attracted to him, not only his body but to his heart—more than ever, in fact. "I feel like I don't have to worry so much. As if things will fall into place."

Henry came running up then and grabbed her around the waist, burying his sandy face on her wet belly. "Mom, I told you we picked the right place to live forever."

"I'm so glad you did, Henry."

Beau met her eyes then. She felt the hum of attraction between them. It was powerful.

And dangerous.

Especially when she found out he could dance as well—if not better—than she could. In the kitchen, she turned on the radio. The old one-hit wonder about a guy named Mickey was playing, and Beau grabbed her hand. "It's not a shagging song, but we can make it one."

What most touched her about him at that moment was that he meant the Carolina shag and nothing else. No Austin Powers double entendres. He got her. She got him. They'd grown up knowing how to shag, and it was pure joy and something they were both proud of.

She felt the best she'd felt in years.

Happy. That's what the feeling was. Oh, she could feel happy with Henry all the time, but this was a happiness that ventured beyond their borders—it encompassed this man, this place, the whole world . . . .

Life was good.

"Hey, Mickey!" Henry shouted while he avidly watched them dance.

Lacey was out of breath. Yes, things were going well. Too well, maybe. But she'd take it. She'd claim it.

When Beau finished twirling her the tenth time, she admitted to herself she was crazy about him. But a few seconds later, when he clasped her close for a millisecond, her back side butted up to his front, their hands locked in an embrace around her middle, she realized she was in love with him.

Love.

It was the dumbest thing she'd ever done, to let him stay there at the lighthouse. She was just like all the other girls, after all.

When the song ended, she went straight to the radio and turned it off. "That was fun," she said, and blew out a breath. Her heart was still going a mile a minute. She was afraid and exhilarated, all at the same time.

"*Mom!*" Henry chided her. "Don't stop. I like to see you dance."

"But it's time to order pizza." She twisted her hair up and stuck a pencil through it. "I'm starving."

"Me, too!" Henry was always starving for pizza, and his enthusiasm was a great distraction when she was feeling so frazzled.

So in love.

Beau seemed oblivious to her feelings, thank goodness. He grabbed a beer from the fridge. "That was *fun*," he said, and high-fived Henry. "Your mama can dance."

"I know," Henry said, puffed up with pride.

That night they had sausage and pepperoni deep dish delivered, and watched *Toy Story 3*, even Beau. She'd hoped he'd go out, but he insisted he was tired. She sat nowhere near him and let him and Henry carry on their own dialogue about the movie. They cracked her up every once in a while, despite her resolve to stay cool and above it all.

They're my guys.

The thought spun into her head, like a good twirl during the shag. It was wrong. She couldn't let herself indulge in dreams like that.

So when Henry was in bed sound asleep, she went straight to the bathroom and filled the tub. Routines. They'd get her through. She read a book, had a glass of wine, and when she got in her pajamas, she felt better.

No wonder everyone loved the beach and wrote sappy slogans about it, which they then embroidered on pillows or painted on driftwood and placed in their homes. Where the sea met the sand was a magical place, one that never stayed the same yet always did, no matter the storms in people's lives . . .

The mystery was intoxicating and comforting all at once. Lacey wanted to snuggle in bed, read, and listen to the shush of the nighttime waves pounding her window, and she also wanted to dance, to twirl again—

To make love.

She shut the book. Henry had been asleep only an hour. Downstairs, Beau was talking on his cell phone. He laughed at one point. Who was he chatting with? An old flame? A best friend? His agent? Maybe it was Mike or a new friend from Indigo Beach.

Suddenly she wanted to know everything about him. The sex romps they'd had up until now made her shy, look away the next day when he met her gaze for too long. But now she wanted to study his face, peruse his body, take her time.

Taking her time, though, would be the kiss of death. It would mean that she was allowing herself to get emotionally involved. She couldn't afford to do more than play with Beau Wilder.

Fifteen minutes later, there was a soft knock on her door. "Lacey!"

Even his whisper—hoarse and demanding—made her insides melt.

She knew she shouldn't be excited he was out there, but she was. With trembling arms, she pushed aside her bedcovers and stood, vowing to rein in her crush, which was like a runaway horse sprinting over higher and higher hurdles.

She went to open the door. "Yes?"

"Hey." Beau's handsome face loomed a few kissable inches away. "I was talking to my cousin earlier. She's having a post-wedding ball in Charleston this Saturday night, and I was wondering . . . would you mind going with me?"

Every cell in her body flushed with extreme pleasure at how nervous he sounded.

Did he like her, too? She was acting like a teenager, and it was embarrassing, but he was asking her out—

To a ball.

She'd never been to anything like that. Monique used to go to charity balls in Hollywood, which required formal gowns, beaded clutches, satin slippers, and a passing knowledge of dancing. But they were public events. Monique always had a date, but they seemed more obligatory social functions than romantic evenings out.

Somehow a private ball seemed different.

More like a *real* date.

"You'd be doing me a favor," he said. "If I go alone . . ."

"You'd be besieged." That was a no-brainer. Her dazzled feelings began to settle down.

"Yeah. I hate to use the word *buffer*, but that's what you'd be. I promise you'll enjoy yourself, though. I'll make sure you have a nice dress. And your hair done, if you'd like. I'd be super grateful if you came."

"Um—" Could she stand being with him as a date who wasn't really a date? Was she that desperate? "—okay."

Apparently, she was.

"Are you sure?" He studied her face.

She tried to school it to be perfectly polite and easy. "Oh, yes." She nodded for emphasis.

He winced a little. "I'm sorry if I asked you wrong."

"Yes." She shook her head. "I mean, no, I totally get it."

He gave a short laugh. "You don't have much time to shop. Do you think Sheena and Walt would watch the kids and Dickey tomorrow so you could find a dress?"

"Probably."

"Great. I've already called Gwynn's. That's the store my mom always goes to. They know you're coming, and they'll get you set up."

"You called already?"

He shrugged. "I'm a little OCD about making sure I'm ready for events I attend. The fewer surprises, the better. And women like balls. I figured you'd say yes to *that*. Not to me."

She lifted a brow. "You're a confident man, Beau Wilder. Maybe you had someone else lined up if I hadn't worked out."

"And if I had? Would you have cared?"

She hesitated only a fraction of a second. "Of course not. I would have thought you were smart. Did you?"

Beau would never look sheepish, but he had the grace to shoot her a self-deprecating grin. "I thought of asking Simone if you said no. But it would have been torture."

Lacey laughed. "At least you're honest."

"That's because you're my friend. My *real* friend." He put his hand on the doorjamb. "Thanks, Lacey."

"You're welcome." She knew she wasn't being honest with him about her feelings. But she couldn't afford to be. It would only make things awkward.

"There are some things I'm not sure of, though," he added.

"Oh?" She opened the door a little farther.

"Yeah."

Something electric arced between them.

"You're right not to be sure," she said softly, recognizing the sexual invitation in his eyes. "At least not with me."

His mouth tilted up at the corner. "Good night."

"Good night."

But neither one of them moved.

Go back to bed, you idiot, she ordered herself. But the pull of his gaze was too strong, so strong she felt compelled to open the door wider. He tugged her out into the hall, leaned against the ladder leading to the top of the light-house, and kissed her.

It was exactly what she'd craved—being tucked into him, connected to him, skin on skin, tongues exploring.

His hand ran up and down the back of her nightgown. "I want *all* of you."

"I want you that way, too. But it's not gonna happen."

"Why not?"

She shook her head slowly. "You're Beau Wilder. You're *leaving*. That's what movie stars do."

He sighed and tilted her chin up. "I know. But I'm not asking you lightly. I care about you, Lacey. Don't you care about me?"

"Of course I do." *I love you, you idiot. Can't you tell?* "We've gotten to be very good friends."

"I'm not a jerk. I'm not out to sleep with you and then never call. I'll call. And I'll come see you and Henry."

"As in, we'll have a real relationship?"

"I call that a real relationship. I don't ditch my friends."

It was her turn to sigh now. "I don't want to keep being friends with benefits, Beau. Maybe these few weeks we can delude ourselves it's okay—we're at the beach, living together in a lighthouse. It's a special time and place. But there's something wrong with making an arrangement like this last."

"*Why?* Isn't that a helluva lot more honest than a lot of so-called romantic relationships?"

"I never said I wanted a romantic relationship. But if I do, it's going to be with someone I can actually see every day." She shoved off his chest.

They had a staring match. After a few intense seconds, he looked down at the floor.

So she won. That told her something right there.

He returned his gaze to hers. "You know I can't be that guy."

"I *do* know. And I don't hold it against you. So stop looking so guilty."

He raked a hand through his hair. "It's not just because of my job, either. It's also because of what I've seen with my parents. I don't want to be like my dad and fool around on a woman I've promised to love and cherish forever. I hate him for what he did to Mom."

"You're not your father. But I'm not telling you that to persuade you to be my boyfriend. The last thing I need to do is convince a man to be with me. He needs to be running after me in the middle of a hurricane, as far as I'm concerned."

He chuckled and drew her close. "You're funny. You've got spunk."

"No," she said softly, "I've just had several bad experiences with men. And I think I've finally learned it ain't worth it, playing games. Even for mind-blowing sex, which I have with you. And don't tell me it's not sex because we haven't had intercourse. You've gotten way into me. Deep into my soul. I've let you there."

He kissed her temple. "I know. Thank you. Let me there again. Right now." He ran his hand up her nightgown.

She leaned her head on his chest and let him stroke her thigh and butt. "Go for it. You know the rules."

He held her hand. "Come on. Let's see how many times you can ring the big bell in fifteen minutes tonight."

She was already wet when they were next to the bed. He pulled off her nightgown and started kissing her breasts, suckling hard on one while kneading the other.

"Beau," she whispered, and cried out when he spread her legs and fingered her. She fell back on the mattress, her legs wide open. He knelt in front of her sex and started the torture: nuzzling her folds, licking lightly over and around the nub that was her greatest pleasure point, driving her insane with longing.

He took her to the brink, pulled back, then did it again.

When she finally crashed and burned, her skin was flushed, damp, hot. Her nerve endings were seared. She rolled to the side of the bed, pulled up her knees, and buried her face in his chest.

"You always take everything from me," she murmured, and ran her hand over his pectoral muscles.

"Not everything," he said, still kneeling. "You always have that reserve."

She giggled. "That's right. I'll be using some of it for you." She spent the next five minutes showing him exactly how.

"Don't leave so fast this time," he said afterward, his muscled legs splayed on the quilt.

"I should."

"But don't."

She thought about it a minute. "Okay, this once." She stretched out beside him and wrapped her leg around his. "Why do you want me to stay?"

His eyes were warm. "This room gets lonely."

She smiled. "You have all of Timothy's stuff in here."

"Why do you think I went through it? I got bored."

"No, it's 'cause you're Dudley. Dudley never leaves mysterious trunks unopened."

"There's that, too."

They both grinned.

She decided to get brave. "Can I ask you something?"

He stroked her hair. "Sure."

"Dickey says you hang out a lot with the manager at the Mexican restaurant. The pretty lady with the big smile. He says y'all are having an affair."

"That's Maria." He smiled lazily. "And you believe Dickey, of all people?"

She shrugged. "I wasn't going to ask, but I just now decided that we're good enough friends that I can indulge my nosiness—without you calling foul."

"Trust me. We're not having an affair. She's a very nice woman, and she manages a great restaurant. She's thinking about getting into other things, and we've talked about it a few times. End of story."

She sighed, feeling happy about that, which was a problem, she knew.

"Believe me," he murmured, "you're enough woman to satisfy any man."

"Besides which, it would be creepy for you to go back and forth. I'd have to quit on you."

"Can't have that," he said, and wrapped her in his arms again.

A few heady minutes later, his phone rang.

He groaned, got up, grabbed the phone out of his shorts on the floor. "Hi, Susan."

My agent, he mouthed, and waved at Lacey to stay put on the bed.

"I should go," she whispered.

He shook his head vehemently.

So she caved in, sat up on her elbow, and listened. It was impossible to tell what the woman was saying, but she sounded very excited.

"For real?" Beau was terse, but his whole posture changed. He had been leaning on the bureau, but now he pushed off and stood straight. "Okay." He nodded. "Okay."

Lacey could hardly bear it.

He hung up and looked at her, something new in his expression.

"What is it?"

"Neal Danvers liked my audition tape. He wants to see me about his next movie."

Lacey forced herself to smile at him. "Look at you grinnin' like a bird-fed cat. He's one of the best directors in the world. Congratulations! *What* movie?"

"No title yet, but they need me in Canada a week before filming here stops."

"What will you do?"

"Ask Mike to hurry it up. Film all my scenes now." He sat on the edge of the bed, his hands fisting the quilt.

The man wanted to leap up and get himself to Canada. And Lacey couldn't blame him.

They looked at each other a long moment. Inside, her heart was in a million pieces. But that was her fault. Not his.

"See?" She sat up and swung her legs over the bed. "This is your life. And it's good. Let's not mess with what's working. You gotta paint or get off the ladder, Beau."

He said nothing, but she wasn't surprised. What was there to say?

CHAPTER TWENTY-FIVE

"It'll do." Simone's usual frown lifted at the corners. She was at the lighthouse helping with Lacey's hair and makeup.

Lacey sat in front of her vanity in her new strapless ice-blue satin gown from Gwynn's. She absolutely loved it. Simone stood behind her, and they both peered into her aged mirror with one little crack running across the lower left corner.

They'd struck up a friendship of sorts. The droll actress had taken to knocking on Mike's trailer door when he sent her on break. She was too cool for kids, but if one of them invited Lacey over to see a drawing or to help with a math problem on a worksheet, Simone sidled over, too. And if Dickey had a hankering to play cards and tell a long story, she'd join him in a hand of rummy, say nothing, and nod.

Sometimes she'd sit with Lacey over a pot of tea and talk in a low voice about how things were going on the set when the other trailer occupants were taking their naps in the back.

Lacey was thrilled that Beau was doing well.

"He should act poisoned all the time," Simone said flatly. "He's so sexy trying not to die. And the cats *adore* him."

Now she crossed her arms and scowled into the mirror. "What's it like giving up your old way of life and then showing up at a society ball as a nanny? Will you keep it a secret? Or tell? If you do, will your Battery friends freak out?"

Lacey hated lying, but she couldn't tell Simone the truth about who she was—or rather, who she *wasn't*. She was stuck. Mike wouldn't trust her anymore, and she would hate that. He might even fire her. "I don't care what they think. They know I'm still here in the Charleston area and that I'm trying to start over."

Simone gave a knowing little laugh. "That's right. Posing as a working-class waitress on a giant mural is a decided signal." She put a bobby pin in one of Lacey's ringlets. "They shouldn't have been surprised you're trying to make your own path, riches and status be damned."

Lacey smiled, but it felt painful. "Something like that."

Her friend picked up the eye pencil. "Your usual cat eyes will be a little too much for this crowd. How did you do your makeup before you went rogue?"

"I think I was into the natural elegance look, very Martha's Vineyard–Kennebunkport."

"You think?" Simone sneered. "You don't even know?"

Lacey shrugged. "I had a maid slash stylist."

"Like Anna in *Downton Abbey*?"

"Totally."

"Oh, my *God*." Simone rolled her eyes, then drew back and gazed at Lacey's face. "This is what you need tonight to get back to your Carolyn Bessette-Kennedy look. A sickle of coral across the lips. The merest hint of blush on your cheekbones. A sweep of neutral shadow with a little iridescence and *no* false eyelashes."

"I don't wear those anyway."

"You're kidding." Simone stood back and stared. "Those are your real lashes?"

Lacey nodded.

"You poor girl. You're freaking *lush*. You'll never achieve the Kennebunkport face."

"We can try."

Simone sighed. "Not gonna happen. Your boobs are too big for the wholesome Junior League look anyway. The closest you can get is Cinderella—midway between innocent and naughty. She did run away to the ball, after all."

"I guess," Lacey said miserably. "I really—I really don't want to stick out."

Simone raised one heavily penciled, pierced eyebrow. "Honestly? You scream *salt of the earth*. Own it. You were never meant to be a snooty Southern socialite. Turn around and face me."

Lacey twisted in her chair, away from the mirror.

Simone sighed with satisfaction when she finished. "I'm a genius."

"How?"

"I thought halfway between your usual vampy look and wholesome would be bland. But it's not. It's this."

Lacey turned toward the mirror, and shining back at her was a pretty girl who looked comfortable in her own skin.

"There's a vulnerability about you now," Simone said. "But you're also nobody's fool."

Lacey gazed at her reflection a long time. Who was that girl looking back at her? Had she been there all along? Or was she someone new, fresh? Someone ready to start over—not get sidetracked by a man?

"You did an amazing job," she said slowly. "Thank you."

"You're welcome." Simone plopped down on her bed. "So what will they think of you and Beau showing up together? Will they assume you're together now?"

A flash of hurt went through Lacey, but she waved a hand. "They know Beau will never settle down, especially with me."

"Who said anything about settling down?"

Lacey wouldn't tell her that she had a daydream that she could do just that—cook for three, reserve hotel rooms for three, have three bikes in the garage. Then two, after Henry grew up and left. That was one thing she didn't want to be, a mother who clung to her children forever because she didn't have her own life.

She suspected Sheena had never forgiven her for moving away.

She knew she had to put up a barrier between her and Beau that night, so she focused on her job. "I'm a buffer, Simone. That's it. A female bodyguard of sorts."

"I don't believe it." Simone made a skeptical face to match her words. "He could have any woman on the set. He could have asked me. Or one of his old Charleston friends."

Lacey picked up her new silver clutch purse. "We'll see."

"Do you like him?"

For once, Lacey wasn't going to lie to her. "Yes," she whispered.

A beat of silence went by.

"Then go after him." Simone's voice cracked—so unlike her. "Just do it, Lacey. Be brave and inspire the rest of us."

Twenty minutes later, Beau and Lacey were in the limo he'd rented to drive to Hibernian Hall in Charleston. He was a little nervous. He hadn't seen these people in years—his mom and dad's people. They knew his family history, and they'd pretend not to. He'd pretend not to.

No wonder he became an actor.

But Lacey looked incredibly sexy and sleek in her dress from Gwynn's, her heels high and vampy. The slit up the side revealed a long, toned leg, and her breasts curved high and inviting above her neckline.

If she only knew what he wanted to do to her right now with her dress off and her heels still on, those luscious legs wrapped around his hips.

"I feel rich." She held a glass of champagne in her beautifully manicured hands.

He took a large swallow from his own glass of bubbly. "You look like a million bucks."

"So do you." She smiled, her lips a pretty coral pink. "You wore something like that in *Poppies*, when you and Angelina Jolie crashed the party at the Russian ambassador's house. That bow tie is amazing."

"Thanks." He was wearing a white dinner jacket and a new bow tie made from real peacock feathers. "A local artisan company called Brackish makes them. I get them sent out to LA for the Golden Globes and People's Choice."

Not the Oscars. He'd never been nominated.

They rode along in silence while the limo crossed the bridge. The lights of Charleston and the Ravenel Bridge span lent a pink glow to the sky.

"Darn," she said. "I forgot my purse."

"We can turn around."

"No, don't," she said. "I don't need it."

"It's no big deal. I'm in no rush to get there. Don't you need your girl stuff—like lipstick and a brush?"

"It would be nice." She sat up a little higher.

Beau tapped on the window and told the driver to turn around.

On their way back to the island, Lacey said, "What a difference."

A necklace of lights stretched across Indigo Beach. A small gaggle of them signified the town center, where the doughnut shop was and the restaurants and Merv's, but the light show was modest in comparison with Charleston's. The sky above the island was pitch black.

"We're lucky," Beau said, "to be at the edge of the world, and it's still so natural."

"I know."

But it wouldn't last forever, would it? He'd be moving on. This colorful yet still pristine place would be no more than a memory.

Back home, Walt was in the kitchen, making a pot of decaf coffee.

"I wondered if you'd turn around," he told Lacey. "You left it on the table. Sheena's upstairs reading a book to Henry in bed."

"Thanks. I won't bother them." Lacey picked up the purse, a little beaded thing, and smiled at Walt.

It definitely reached her eyes, too.

Walt followed them to the door. At the last second, Lacey gave him a little hug. "Thanks for staying."

Back at the car, Beau noticed that she seemed more relaxed. Her eyes were softer, her shoulders lower.

"Walt and Sheena are doing well," he said.

"I think so." She smiled. "I have hope."

"Good. The fact is, they're still here. That says a lot."

"I agree."

They were back to the bridge a minute later, a minute that they filled talking about where she and Henry would most likely live on Indigo when she got the job she needed. She told him about the interview at the car dealership.

"He was an idiot to let you walk away," Beau said.

"It wasn't the job for me anyway. I'd rather clean houses or wait tables until I find something that suits me better. I'll keep looking over the next few weeks, before shooting ends."

"Yep." It hit him hard then that his time with Lacey and Henry was going to end sooner than he was ready for it to. He wanted to sling her onto his lap right now and kiss the dress right off her.

"Don't look at me like that," she said.

"I can't help it. You're beautiful."

She looked away. "And available."

He felt a new tension between them. "I don't expect you to give *me* credit, but give some to yourself. You're way more than available. You're amazing."

"Thanks." She shrugged a pretty shoulder. "Sometimes I forget."

He hated to see her at all despondent. "It's easy to get buried under worries." He knew about that.

"Do you ever have any?"

"Of course. It's not easy maintaining a career at my level. It's constant work. Even when I have time off between movies, I'm always doing something: PR junkets, reading new scripts, networking. And then in the back of my mind, I have Mom to worry about."

"That's nice that you *do* worry about your mother."

"Let me tell you about some people you'll meet tonight, Mom included." That would distract them both. "You're going to love my cousin Sarah."

"What's she like?"

He told her how crazy and fun she was, and then he described a lot of other people they'd likely meet. One thing he realized as he spoke was that he liked most of them. Yes, Charleston had its share of people you wanted to steer clear of, as any town would, but on the whole the folks here, whatever the tax bracket, were full of common sense, independent as hell, and always ready for a good party.

He saved his mother for last. "She's tough. She'll be polite. Even warm. My mother would never dare be ill mannered. But when I tell her I met you on the set of *Flowers from the Heart*, I guarantee that she won't go out of her way to get to know you. Don't take it personally."

"Wow," said Lacey.

"She's a lady," he said, "but unless you're from a select

Southern family that meets her approval, you won't get farther with her than a short, polite conversation. On the other hand, I wouldn't be surprised if she shows her feathers tonight and ignores you just to get to me. She's annoyed that I haven't given up my hobby of acting in films and moved back home."

"That's terrible," Lacey said. "Does she really treat your career as if it's a hobby, after all these years you've been at it?"

"Yep. She'd still rather I be a local judge. A well-respected doctor at the medical university here in town. Or the financial adviser to all her friends."

"Maybe it's less about the job and more about the fact that she wants you around."

"Could be."

"What does she do?"

"She loves her garden, and she's on a lot of boards," he said just as the limo pulled up in front of Hibernian Hall.

"Thanks for the heads-up about everyone." Lacey's eyes widened at the sight of the well-lit, colonnaded structure, the site of many of Charleston's more elegant parties. "Oh, boy. Never thought I'd wind up at a place like this."

"You'll do great." He held out his arm. "Shall we go?"

She took it and held on tight.

You're getting in deep, he thought as he walked her up the steps into the cavernous building. He wanted her now, more than ever. She was so sexy in that dress, yet such a lady, too.

As he predicted, they were besieged immediately.

Beau's back, went 'round the ballroom. He could see the news literally traveling from person to person. *And who's the woman with him?* was the next question.

Sarah rushed up with her new husband, Grady, and threw her arms around Beau's neck. "I'm so glad you're here." She grinned at Lacey. "Hi, I'm Sarah. I'm thrilled Beau brought you with him. You're Lacey?"

"Yes," said Lacey, all signs of nerves gone. "And I'm really happy to be here. Congratulations."

Beau introduced her to Grady.

"Oh, my God, she's Southern," Sarah said with a squeal. "Please marry Beau and make him move back home."

"Enough sass, cuz." Beau winked at her.

"Hollywood has been good to him," Sarah told Lacey. "But South Carolina can be even better. I mean, look at the studio, right here on Indigo! He never needs to go anywhere else to make a movie."

Sarah didn't know what she was talking about. But Beau let her imagine that a film star at his level would never have to leave his small town again and still be able to maintain a career.

While the two girls talked, Grady leaned closer to him. "For my own sake, I'd love to have you back. Sarah's such a dynamo. I could use some backup or a place to go when she gets those bees in her bonnet that she tends to get."

Beau laughed.

"I've got another reason, too," Grady added. "It's top secret. A baby's coming. And it's gonna need every uncle he or she can get."

"That's excellent news." Beau clasped his hand—hard. He was missing out, living so far away, wasn't he? "Congratulations, man."

"Crazy times, huh?" Grady shook his head, but his pride was obvious in his grin.

Sarah did seem to have an extra glow, Beau thought, as she and Grady got called away by their other guests.

"I like her so much." Lacey's eyes were sparkling.

"I knew you would."

They shared a happy smile, and he couldn't deny it.

Lacey was definitely one of his favorite people. That was all he'd say. No point looking further. But she was, and he was exceedingly glad she'd consented to be his date.

More people came up to talk to them, and then his eyes lit on his mother. He'd offered to stop and pick her up, but she said she was going early to help Sarah and her mother make sure everything was in place. She was with a man he thought he recognized but couldn't place. He was distinguished looking, lean and tall—about as tall as Beau—with silver hair and bright-blue eyes. When he met Beau's gaze, he nodded and didn't bother to smile. He was older, but he was a guy's guy, no doubt about it.

And he was passing on a message, obviously, when he put his arm around Beau's mother's shoulders and squeezed while she was talking to a circle of friends.

Mine, that gesture said.

Beau could hardly contain his surprise. But he did. You didn't show your ass in Charleston, not at a party, at any rate.

"Let me introduce you to Mom." He dragged Lacey away from Lionel Simons—pronounced the Charleston way, *Simmons*—who was being his usual charming self.

Lionel was an attorney and running for the U.S. Senate. He was noble. Good-looking. And he'd never disappointed *his* family.

"He was so nice," Lacey said.

"Was he?" Beau wasn't really listening. His mother looked up into that silver-haired guy's eyes with something more than mere friendliness.

Mom wasn't a flirt. Something was going on.

"Yes," said Lacey. "He wanted to know all about the movie. What I was doing there. And he never batted an eye when I told him I was the director's nanny. He was a real gentleman."

Good for Lionel.

"I think he wanted to ask me out, too," she said. "He was about to get my number."

"What?" Beau stopped walking. "You're *my* date. And he's married."

"He *was* married. He's a widower now."

"Marilyn died?" Beau's chest constricted at the idea. She was such a lovely woman.

"Yes. Of cancer. Two years ago. It's so sad."

"That *is* sad." He wished he'd known. He and Marilyn had been in the same class in elementary school. "I'll need to go back and talk to Lionel later. Usually, Mom tells me this stuff."

"He stayed by her side throughout the whole ordeal," Lacey said. "Quit work and everything."

"You had this talk while I was standing right there?"

"Yes, but you were talking to the Prestons about Mrs. Preston's arthritis and Mr. Preston's new shotgun."

"Okay." It had been the type of conversation he never had at social affairs in Hollywood.

"Anyway, Lionel picked up on the fact that we were just friends."

"How?"

She cringed a little. "He asked, so I told him that I was the buffer tonight."

"*Lacey.* I was hoping to leave them guessing. No one here really needs to know my private business. We practiced, remember? You say you met me at the studio. When people ask if we're dating, you say, 'We have a lot of fun together,' over and over if you must, but let them come to their own conclusions."

"But I asked him not to tell anyone. He agreed to keep it to himself, and I know he meant it. He's a *really* nice guy."

"Fine, but please try to stick to the plan."

She tossed her head, her curls bouncing around her ears. "Hey. I'm being your buffer. But you also said I'd have fun, too. So . . . I was having fun. I won't tell anyone else. Promise."

"Beau," said his mother when they reached her hallowed presence. Several people broke apart and drifted away to let him and Lacey through.

He kissed his mother's cheek. "You look beautiful."

She did, too. She worked out four days a week, went to the finest hair salon, wore the most expensive makeup and clothes, and looked ten years younger than she was.

"Mom," he said, feeling strangely unsettled—usually he enjoyed teasing her with his devil-may-care Hollywood persona—"this is Lacey Clark. She works for the movie's director."

"Nice to meet you, Lacey," his mom murmured graciously, her small but polite smile set in place.

It was weird, considering how he'd lost respect for her long ago, that Beau felt a surge of pride in his mother. She could eat supper with the U.S. president or the queen of England and never lose her cool. But she was equally good with people who were considered nobodies. Being gracious was her thing.

"Lacey"—he turned, expecting her to be visibly nervous—"this is my mother, Julia Wilder."

He couldn't wait to find out who the possessive man was next to her.

"Your son has told me a lot about you, Mrs. Wilder," Lacey said with a warm smile.

His mother laughed. "Did he now?" She looked up at Beau as if he were a mischievous little boy.

Beau grinned. He liked seeing his mother so lighthearted. "I obviously didn't scare Lacey off with my description, either."

Still smiling, his mother laid her hand on the arm of the man next to her. "Do you remember Walker Calhoun, an old friend of your father's and mine? We'd see him in Flat Rock in the summers on occasion."

"Ah," said Beau, "that's where I recognized you. It's been a long time."

"It has," said Walker, and shook his hand. Good, firm grip. "I'm glad you're here, Beau."

Walker and his mother exchanged a glance full of meaning.

What was going on here?

When his mother made the introductions between Walker and Lacey, Beau was impressed. Lacey came across as quietly confident and . . . enchanting. He'd use that word with her. Because she was.

Even so, Walker drew his attention.

"Your mother and I have something to tell you. In confidence." Walker's tone was friendly but resolute.

"I'll go," said Lacey.

"You don't need to," said his mother. "We just ask that you keep it quiet for now."

"What?" Beau didn't feel cordial at the moment. He felt ornery.

"Wish me luck." His mother's eyes twinkled—he couldn't remember seeing that happen before, *ever*. "Mr. Calhoun's asked me to marry him. And I said yes. You—and Lacey—are the first to know."

CHAPTER TWENTY-SIX

Beau congratulated his mother and her fiancé. But Lacey was surprised that his acting chops didn't serve him well enough to cover his obvious discomfort with the news. Or maybe he simply didn't want to hide his feelings.

As soon as she delivered her own congratulations, he steered her back into the crowd.

"I can't believe this." He looked genuinely grim.

"Why are you upset?" She winked at an old man leering at her through a monocle, his silver-and-gray-striped vest gleaming under the crystal chandelier overhead.

"I don't know," Beau said. "I need a drink."

They did their best to circumnavigate the crowd, and after two brief stops, one of which was to say hello to the mayor and the other to meet Beau's *real* next-door neighbor, they got to the bar. Lacey stood by a potted palm. Women didn't get their own drinks in Charleston, not unless they wanted to be besieged by ten men begging her to let them get the drink for her. So Beau waited in line while she people-watched, and then he came over with a dry martini for her and a scotch on the rocks for him.

They sat on an out-of-the-way bench with a great view

of the ballroom floor but enough privacy they could get away with having a conversation.

In a low voice, he told her about Sarah and the baby—top secret, of course.

Lacey grinned. "That's so great."

"I know." But he still sounded glum. "A lot's going on."

"Is that it? You feel left out?"

He shrugged and took a gulp of his drink. "Kind of."

"You could fix that easily. You don't need to move back. Just visit more. Call them on the phone. Skype."

"Yes, but caring from afar isn't the same as being here."

"Well, what's stopping you from moving back then?"

"Being a Hollywood actor. As you know."

"Some of them make it from other places."

"That's true. But more than ever, after this movie, I'll need to stay visible. I can't be seen retreating. Nor do I want to."

"But you'd like to control the whole world from your mountaintop, and you can't. That bothers you."

"Yes." He swirled the ice in his drink. "Apparently, I can't have it all, and I thought I could."

"Are you sure you really want it all because you genuinely *want* it?" she asked gently. "Or is it because you're scared to choose? Ask Robert Frost about those two roads diverging. It ain't easy."

He winced. "Tell me about it."

She wished she could hold his hand and assure him that everything would be okay. But she couldn't know that it would be. This was his problem, not hers. He had to resolve it on his own. "Look on the bright side," she said. "Most people don't have your options. They're looking at Door A, B, or C, and one of them has a hungry lion behind it. You're looking at Doors A through Z, and each one has a Porsche or a trip to Cancun or a diamond ring."

"Hey, my problems are different, but I still have them. There's a hungry paparazzo behind at least five of my doors."

"True." She grinned at him and saw that she'd cheered him up a little.

"Which door are you behind?" His voice was low and sexy. "I want to open that one."

"I'm not anyone's behind-the-door person." She stirred her drink with her pinky because looking at him was making her hot and bothered. "As I told you the other night." She licked her pinky and smiled.

"Hey. Stop the flirting." He grinned. She grinned back. "You told me that when you were naked. I had a hard time focusing."

"*Beauregard?*" A stunning blonde approached, her pert little breasts highlighted by pointy darts on her ivory gown. She also had thin, toned arms and a sprinkle of freckles across her nose.

Lacey had a feeling her buffer duties were about to begin in earnest. She stood with Beau, who took the woman's hand and kissed her cheek.

"Charlotte," he said, "good to see you," and introduced her to Lacey.

She had a sophisticated smile, enigmatic and alluring. "I've heard that you're babysitting the director's children," she told Lacey. "How charming. Do you have a degree in early-childhood education?"

"No." Lacey shrugged and smiled. "I never went to college. I learned from the school of hard knocks."

"*Fascinating.*" But Charlotte made clear that she was riveted only by Beau when she immediately returned her limpid gaze to him. "I've been waiting so long for you to come home," she chided him softly.

"Here I am," he said, "but not for long."

He made it sound as if it were not only not a big deal

that he was leaving—but that he was looking forward to it, which hurt—although Lacey should probably give him a break. Charlotte was making a full-court press.

He told her about the movie in Canada.

"How amazing, Beau." Charlotte sounded sincerely impressed.

"So what have you been up to?" Beau asked her before she could say more.

"Do you really want to know?" she asked archly.

"Sure." He made quick eye contact with Lacey.

Be the buffer. Please.

"I'd love to know, too," said Lacey, doing her job.

Charlotte put a lovely finger beneath her glossy lower lip. "Let's see . . . I'm about to make partner at Bettany Associates, *and* I'm president of the Junior League."

She turned just enough shoulder in that Lacey felt a trifle de trop.

"Great," Beau said, and moved over a couple of inches to include Lacey back in their circle. "But I'm not surprised."

"Remember Aspen?" Charlotte said out of the blue, artfully tilting her head.

Beau took a swig from his glass and nodded slowly. "Great time."

That was forced. So Lacey guessed that what happened in Aspen he obviously wanted to stay in Aspen . . .

Charlotte laughed and shook her head. "*C'était fabuleux. Vous étiez fabuleux.*"

It was fabulous. You were fabulous.

Beau drained his whiskey glass. "Forget about Aspen, how 'bout them RiverDogs? Bill Murray still part owner?"

"Yes," said Charlotte. "Such an elusive man. Though not as elusive as *you*."

Lacey resisted rolling her eyes. "I think I'll find Sarah again. It was nice to meet you, Charlotte."

"You, too, Lizzy."

"*Lacey*," Beau said.

"Oops." Charlotte tossed her beautifully coiffed head. "Sorry."

"It's all right," Lacey said. "*Si Beau était à moitié aussi bon un amant à Aspen comme l'homme est maintenant, vous étiez une femme chanceuse . . . mais pas aussi chanceuse que moi.*"

If Beau was half as good a lover in Aspen as the man is now, you were a lucky woman . . . but not as lucky as me.

Charlotte's eyes widened, and her flawless brow furrowed.

Lacey was a natural at learning French. It had been a requirement of her job with Monique, who'd bought her Rosetta Stone, brought in a tutor three times a week, and spoke the language to her constantly. Even Henry knew a few words and phrases.

She walked off before Beau could say anything. If he could sleep with Charlotte, he could also make small talk with her. Lacey had already earned the pricey gown, purse, and shoes by being his full-time cook and house straightener. She didn't owe him a thing, especially sexual favors.

Sarah made her dance with three eligible men in a row.

"Go to war, Miss Mitchell!" Sarah cried. "Get Beau jealous."

"He won't be," Lacey assured her.

"He should be. You're the prettiest girl here."

"No, I'm not."

Sarah took her shoulders. "You *are*. You're real. You came in here as Beau's equal and then some, and you've charmed the socks off everyone here. There's nothin' prettier than a confident woman who's not spoiled. And Beau can't keep his eyes off you. I've been watching him all night."

Lacey's entire middle was full of butterflies. Everything going on around her was big. Bright. Full of possibilities. And she was changing. Slowly but surely she was, and she wasn't sure what it all meant . . .

So she did dance with several hotties in tuxedos. She was completely captivated by their attentive manners and their mischievous Southern wit—how she'd missed that! She found herself laughing out loud, not only with them but with the people they introduced her to, including several girlfriends of Sarah's, who worked with her at the bank, and Grady's buddies from pharmacy school.

After that, she was whisked away by Lionel Simons. At the start of the second dance, a slow one, she saw Biddy What's-Her-Name, the shopkeeper from Indigo Beach, go by in the arms of her dance partner, an older man with a paunch and a red face.

Biddy caught a glimpse of her, too, and looked sharply away.

Lacey couldn't help chuckling.

"What is it?" Lionel asked her.

"Oh, just someone I met on Indigo Beach. She didn't care for me."

"I know why," he said immediately. "She's jealous. You're beautiful, Lacey. A breath of fresh air in this old ballroom."

"Moonlight Serenade" was a sexy song, sultry and slow with those clarinets and jazzy vibe.

"Lionel," she said, "you're going to give me a big head."

"It's not mere flattery." He clasped her hand harder for a brief moment. "I didn't want to come tonight. It's bittersweet going to someone else's wedding ball. It reminds me of all I lost. But now I'm glad I did. Thanks for helping me have fun."

"You're very sweet." And someday soon, some woman

would snap him up. It wouldn't be her, of course. Her heart had already been given away—

To the gentleman who was tapping on Lionel's shoulder. "Thanks for taking care of my date for me."

Lionel stepped back and looked at Lacey with a wistful smile. "It was my great pleasure."

"Thanks, Lionel." She smiled back at him.

"He's got a lot of nerve, trying to put the moves on you in front of me," Beau murmured in her ear after Lionel left.

"He wasn't. He just needed someone to listen to him."

Beau pulled her closer. "What if I need that, too?"

"Then I'm here." His mouth was dangerously close to her ear. "For now."

For a split second, Beau brought them to a halt. "Aw, Lacey."

"It is what it is."

They started moving again.

"You deserve more," he said.

"We all do." She closed her eyes.

They breathed together. She luxuriated in the feel of her breasts against his hard male chest. But even more intimate was the way the fingers of his right hand were laced with her own and dropped to their right side—you could get closer that way—while everyone else merely clasped palms and held them up for the world to see.

They were alone together, in their own little world.

And it was utter bliss.

She loved him.

How many times must that knowledge light up the darkest corners of her heart? It was like being awoken at three AM by a flashlight shining six inches from your face, inciting feelings of misery, panic—

Inevitability.

Her heart sped up, her breath shortened. The music—she didn't feel it anymore.

"Let's get out of here," Beau said.

He must have felt it, too.

It had something to do with doom, with the world ending, with the need to run through the streets holding hands to escape the dark thing that was soon to rout them.

But what was there to fear?

Nothing.

They were smart, capable people, both of them. They weren't naive. They were survivors. They most certainly didn't need to conjure up Disney dramatics in lives already roiled with drama, but it was there anyway . . . this need to escape together.

Now.

There was no going back.

"We're going to my house," Beau said. "Can you walk in those heels?"

"Sure." Expensive leather made all the difference.

They skipped out a side door and bypassed the line of waiting limos. Beau held tight to her hand. They walked south on Meeting at a fast pace, the nighttime air cool and refreshing on Lacey's skin. Beau's profile was stern, unyielding.

They didn't speak. There was too much to say, and at this point words—even music—couldn't capture what was going on between them.

It was big, bigger than they were.

Lacey was scared. But she was going to go with it. She was with Beau. She could handle anything with him.

Charleston at night was beautiful, mysterious . . . exciting. They took a left on Tradd, then a right on Church—"This is my new favorite street," Lacey said—then turned left at Stoll's Alley and right on East Bay.

"We're almost there." Beau stopped for a second, braced her face between his palms, and kissed her. Hard.

They looked into other's eyes. She saw so much in his, and her heart couldn't bear it—the separation that was soon to come.

"No," she whispered.

"Don't think of it," he said.

They resumed walking.

His home was a mansion. Not just a house. It was opulent in a tastefully elegant way. Lacey tried not to look right or left, or she'd gawk at everything in sight, especially the antiques. They went straight up three flights of stairs, which were old and steep, a few steps slightly crooked—which Beau warned her about—and entered a boy's bedroom.

His room.

"Yes, this house has ghosts," he said before she'd asked, as if a clock were ticking somewhere. He pried off his shoes, kicked them away, and started working on unknotting his bow tie. "It was built in 1785. I think I saw one once, right here. A guy in a puffy shirt." He grinned, threw the tie on the bureau, then turned her around, unzipped her, and helped her shimmy out of her gown.

"Really?" She turned around to face him in her lacy underthings—Beau's treat, too, from Bits of Lace.

He stripped off the little scraps of silk. "If he's here right now, he's really wishing he were alive again."

She chuckled. The flame between them grew even stronger and hotter. She pressed her stark-naked body against his and kissed him, openmouthed, long.

Possessive.

He was hers.

Time kept ticking.

"I love you." Little tears sprang to her eyes while she unbuttoned his tuxedo shirt. "And I know you love me."

While he caressed her hips, her back, her breasts—whatever he could reach—she yanked off one of his shirt-sleeves, and then the other. "To hell with hiding and being worried about getting hurt. It aches too much to hold it in, and if this winds up being another huge mistake, sleeping with you—which is what we're about to do—well, I'm gonna own it. Hoist it up on a flag for the whole world to see: Oh, say can you see, the love in me."

"It can't be that way." He let her unbutton his pants and slide them over his thighs, past his knees, and to his feet.

He shoved them across the floor with his right foot.

She pulled off his trouser socks, kissing each calf as they were exposed.

"I'm not going to be another Callum," he said. "Or my father. You're not going to love me, Lacey. We're saying good-bye. We're creating a memory. That's it."

With a kiss on his flat belly, she rid him of those ador-able gold-banded briefs, and then he was naked along with her. She leaned the side of her head against his erec-tion and wrapped her arms around his butt. "Stop the bullshit and say it back. Say that you love me, Beau, or I won't respect you in the morning." She looked up. A little bit of Greta came out and tinged her smile with threat.

A beat of silence went by.

But his hard expression remained that way. He pulled her to her feet. "You can take that chance. You have Henry. I'm on my own. I've got to be careful. There's no backup."

"*You* chose this life, Beau. It didn't choose you. You have the power to be connected, and you know it. The question is, what's holding you back? The fame and for-tune? You're afraid to lose those? I say, what good are they if you don't have anyone to share them with?"

He gripped her shoulders. "You're more like Lucy Ri-cardo than you think. I hate to tell you this, but when I leave here, I'm going to be fine. This temporary craziness is a distraction from what I love to do, which is being in the movies. That's all I want. It's all I need."

She threw herself on his bed and leaned back on her elbows, one leg propped at the knee. "Leave me if you must, Beau. But don't you dare go without admitting the truth. I'm more than your temporary craziness. You love me." She held out her hand. "Throw me your cell phone."

He stared at her a second, walked slowly to his crumpled pants, pulled his phone out, and tossed it to her. She played with it a second, found an album he'd downloaded that she loved, and then the room was flooded with the transistor-radio-quality sound of an iPhone blasting Etta James singing "At Last."

His eyes narrowed a little, but there was the slightest tipping up of his mouth. "The more things change, the more they stay the same. What year are we in?"

"Doesn't matter, son. Love's timeless. Come here." She beckoned him with a finger.

He slid onto the coverlet with her. The double bed squeaked in all the old places, the sound as familiar to him as the sound of his beating heart. Time had moved through the years, and he'd moved with it, carrying the good, the bad, all so close to his chest . . .

She laid her hand on his jaw. "*You will not act with me.* You hear? Especially in this room. This is where unhurt Beau used to sleep. When you still believed in good and believed you could trust the people you loved."

He said nothing, her big, terrible lion. He had that wild mane, the cheekbones and eyes of a jungle warrior masking a heart that would take on everyone else's woes if he could.

"This is where you'll reclaim yourself," she said, combing his hair with her fingers, "where you'll reclaim that little boy, the hurt teenager you've been ignoring, and yes, that bitter young man you've been empowering all these years—so you can claim me. I'm your woman. And you're my man. But until you stop lying to yourself about how you're just fine and you don't need anyone—which you do only so you can delight in proving to your poor mother and your long-dead father that they truly fucked you up—you won't be making love to me."

His pupils sharpened to little points. But still he said nothing. She didn't care. Her heart should be beating hard, but instead it felt like the calmest moment of her life.

"And if we don't make love, Beau Wilder, you can bet you're gonna stay out of my life. You're either my lover or my ex-lover. You're not gonna be Uncle Beau. Or my latest job reference. We're not going to see each other someday and make nice at a cocktail party. You either break my heart, or you give me yours. Either way, you lose your soul. And the same goes for me. There's no in-between."

Etta kept singing. Thank God for her. Because at the moment, Lacey wasn't sure what was going to happen next.

"You done?" he said, his voice rusty, like an old nail that needed pulling out of a two-by-four.

She nodded.

He lifted her hand and kissed the knuckles. Slowly. And then he turned that palm over and kissed the middle of it.

She was turning to jelly right there. This was something new. Slow. In defiance of that ticking clock they'd always kept running at the lighthouse, oblivious to the fact that it was counting down to zero for them for real.

He still hadn't said he loved her.

Etta was singing "All I Could Do Was Cry" when he tugged her on top of him, moved his hands up her waist, cupped her breasts, ran soft thumbs over their tips. She closed her eyes. His hand slid up her neck, and he played with her hair, his fingers raking through the strands. When she opened her eyes, he lifted his head and suckled one of her nipples, his other hand—rough in the soul-churning way that a man's hand is on a woman's skin—cradling her back.

"Oh, Beau," she whispered.

She leaned down and kissed him, the smacking sound of their lips, sighs, and murmurs of pleasure the only sounds beyond the music.

And then he rolled her beneath him.

She kept her gaze on his. *You know what this means.* She wasn't backing down.

His mouth was more pliant now; his eyes, less shadowed. He took his sweet time, covering her entire body with soft, deliberate kisses—his tongue licking where he was inspired to, his hair soft as corn silk against her stomach, her elbows, her calves, and her feet.

When he reached her femininity, he lingered long, kissing her legs wide open until they dropped like lead weights to her side, and then returned to her heat, the center of her primal need for him.

He licked around the portal to her womb with all the reverence of a new explorer, thrust his tongue inside with the boldness of the one who knows he's destined to write his name on its walls one way or another.

She arched, she cried.

As he flirted with the nubbin of flesh above—flicking, sucking, circling, marking—she clenched around his probing fingers, marking him back.

They were one, whether he admitted it or not.

He was hers.

And she told him so, but not with words—with notes on a scale that came from deep within her, a wailing song of pure pleasure.

After it was over, he crept up to her face, his stiff mem-

ber dragging up her belly, and kissed her. "You're beautiful," he whispered.

She wrapped her legs around him, threw her arms over
her head, let him worship her breasts until they hurt, a good
hurt that she'd never forget, the sweet pain that came with
loving Beau Wilder.

He sensed her exquisite agony and tried to kiss it away,
but she wouldn't let him. She pulled him in, into their
own world of love and suffering that no one else knew or
could know.

She went low, beneath him, forcing his arms to lock
above her, and taunted him with her mouth, taking him
deep, sucking, exploring, savoring the length of him. She
claimed the base of his shaft with her curled hand, promising him a warm, moist place to sheath it.

But just as abruptly she left it, wet and spiking upward.
She moved back up his belly to his face, where she let the
haze of desire curl around them like smoke, her breasts
pressed to his chest, her eyes looking deep inside him,
seeking out the darkness to dispel it with her light.

"I do love you, Lacey Clark," he said, and with a sav-
age cry captured her hands and drove long and hard into
her, alternately filling and emptying her, a constant re-
minder of what they could and couldn't have.

She kept him there. She let him go.

He sought her. He ran away.

And finally, neither of them had any choice. They
stayed in the beam of light, and it took them up together.

"I love Henry, too," he said when it was over. "I love you
both."

She snuggled into his arms, and tears pooled in her
eyes. "See? Telling me didn't kill you. And your loving me
isn't going to kill me, either."

He kept stroking her hair.

"Feel better now?" she asked.

He sat up on an elbow and perused her face as if he'd never tire of it. "I feel like me." His eyes were more clear—and trusting—than she'd ever seen them.

Bless his heart. Bless his large, loving heart! She knew she was going to lose him, but for a few minutes—on a night she'd never forget—that big ol' heart of his was hers.

For a slice of precious time, Lacey's dream had come true.

CHAPTER TWENTY-SEVEN

Yeah, Beau was rattled. Who wouldn't be after bearing his soul to the woman he loved? He was owning some pretty scary feelings. Yet he also felt more free than he had in a very long time. He had a revelation: Freedom and messiness went together. You had to make choices every day, tough choices. But if you chose right, it could lead you to heady places.

He used to know that! How could he have forgotten so easily? Embracing snug security had come with serious limitations, risk minimizers that had led him to boredom.

That was his problem. He was bored. Until he'd knocked on the door of the lighthouse.

"Beau?"

It was his mother out in the hall. He'd intentionally left his jacket and Lacey's purse on the stairs so he wouldn't surprise her in case she came back early.

Sucked that she had.

Lacey reached up and kissed his neck.

"Yeah, it's me, Mom," he called. "And Lacey. We'll be out in a second."

He heard her footsteps creaking across the floor as she went downstairs.

"This is awkward," Lacey said with a smile in her tone.

"It sure is." He kissed her. "But we're not kids." This was his family home. Someday it would be his.

As they dressed, Beau kept that feeling close, that the good stuff only came when he let go. The reward was huge: Lacey. And Henry.

"We've got to work this out," he said. "I'm not willing to go back to before."

"Before what?" she asked softly.

"Before telling you I love you."

She came up close in her bra and panties and left a lingering kiss on his mouth. "You've given me a great gift. Thank you."

And then she turned away and shimmied into her gown. Something about seeing her back alarmed him. "Lacey?"

"Could you zip me, please?"

Gently, he pulled up the long, silent zipper, loving how the fabric clung to every curve of her body as he did so.

She turned to face him, put her hands on his arms. "As much we love each other, I've got a boy watching. And learning. I have things to prove. To him and to me."

"I want to be part of that. If this is just a logistics problem, we can fix it. Hell, we wouldn't be the first couple to do a long-distance thing."

"*Beau*. You're about to be in a Neal Danvers film. You're entering Oscar territory. How many of his leading men have won? *A lot*."

That was true. It was a heady thought. But sobering, too. *Oscar territory*.

"You're not going to have time to devote to us," she said, her whole face brimming with love, understanding, and sadness. "There literally won't be enough hours in the day. You have to push. Henry needs stability. And I—I need to pull myself together and make something of my own life. For years I've been at the beck and call of other people. First with Sheena and Walt. Then with Monique. It's *time*."

"What will you do?"

"I don't know yet." She lifted on tiptoe and kissed his cheek. "You've treated me as if I matter. Henry, too. Your love has given me courage. Thank you."

"What's going on here?"

She sighed. "Nothing that I want to happen. But it *must*."

"I don't think so." Heat built inside him. "I think you're giving up and trying to write *The End* to another bad script in a lifetime full of them, except for the one where you got Henry. This story between you and me ain't over."

She looked away.

"Don't do that." He took her arms and made her look at him. "Stop lumping me in with all the bratty men in your life who've done you wrong. I told you that the first day I met you." He was tired of feeling detached from his life. On Indigo Beach he'd had a respite from it. *She'd* given him that. And now—"You tried to lock yourself away in the lighthouse with Henry. It didn't happen, did it? But you're attempting it again now. You're still afraid, Lacey, and I get it. You've been smacked down by life more than once. But I didn't take you for a manipulator. You squeezed a confession out of me, and now you're throwing it in my face."

She yanked away. "That's low. And I'm not throwing it in your face. I just told you what a gift your love is." Her eyes grew shiny. "I'm going to miss you, and what we have is special. But it doesn't mean the rest of our lives stop. They can't."

"But you're the queen multitasker. What's the rush to shut us down? I'm here. I'm ready. Don't pretend you're not knocking me around with this man phobia of yours. You're swinging it like a hammer."

"That's easy for you to say." Her face was pale beneath that riot of red hair, and her eyes too big. "When have you ever really had to take risks? You've been content being *the* Beau Wilder. As long as you don't go too deep, you're happy."

He shrugged, but his heart was slamming in his chest. "It's worked for me."

"Not on *Flowers from the Heart*, it didn't. And it won't with Neal Danvers."

"I know that. And despite my learning curve on this film, I've done all right, in large part thanks to you. So what's holding *you* back from some success of your own?"

They stared at each other.

"I see," she said. "You think I'm jealous."

"Not jealous. Afraid. But of what? You admitted I gave you some courage. What do you need it for? I want to know."

She released a sigh. "I'm always afraid of messing up Henry."

"Stop. He's a lucky kid. He's thriving."

Her shoulders sank. "When you're responsible for another person, life changes. You see shadows where there weren't any before."

"Can I take a stab at this?"

"Go ahead."

"You talk a good game about wanting to focus on *you*, but that's what it is. Talk. If you really wanted what was best for you and Henry, you'd let me in. But it's pretty obvious you're willing to sabotage your own happiness—and his—because of Sheena and Walt."

"How dare you say I'd sabotage my own son's happiness!"

It pained him that she looked at him like he was the devil. "Am I really off the mark here?" he asked gently. "You think that if you become everything you want to be,

Sheena and Walt won't love you or Henry. You've got to stop needing their approval. They'll love you both if they're decent people. And if they don't, good riddance. You've got me to love you two, no matter what."

Her lip trembled. "It's not that easy. I love my mother."

"I love my mother, too. But I've put my foot down with her."

"Have you?" Lacey wiped at her eyes with shaky fingers. "In a way, you two are alike. Appearances are so important to you that you haven't taken any risks in your career until now and they were forced upon you."

He scowled. "Showing reasonable caution is a good thing. It keeps us alive."

"Not when you're an actor. Caution is the death of art, and you know it."

"I don't have to hear this." He whipped away from her, looked out the window at the lights ringing the harbor. But she was right. She was right, dammit, and it pissed him off. "I'm nothing like either one of my parents," he said low. "I'm not an elitist."

"No, you're not. But you fight so hard to keep up the image on film of the Every Man who does extraordinary things, you've conveniently forgotten that you're all that and more in real life. You won't acknowledge the real Beau. You stick with the shiny movie guy. You have since your father died."

There was a beat of silence.

"Until you," he admitted quietly. "But things are changing in me. Because of you. *With* you. And you're still going to walk away?"

She sighed. "It's not me walking away, Beau. It's *us*. Our paths have intersected here on Indigo Beach. I'll always carry that with me. I'll carry a piece of *you* with me. But we're both going in different directions that we *need* to go in, and you know it."

He shook his head. "How come it's so easy for you to articulate this? And to follow through?"

She had no answer.

"You were all about passion mere minutes ago," he reminded her. "You can't keep it up? You got a finite amount to go around? If that's love, it's pretty damned feeble. And it's not a lot of comfort—you carrying a piece of me with you. I don't like that. I want it back."

"Oh, Beau." She bit her lip and looked awfully sad.

"What?" He was in no mood to feel sorry for her.

"No one's ever broken up with you, obviously."

"And your point is?"

"I don't mean to hurt you. This hurts *me*." She gave a little hiccup that might have been a sob. "And believe it or not, I'm looking out for you at the same time that I'm protecting myself. There's nothing wrong with that."

"I get it," he said calmly. "Compartmentalize when things get too big. Try to control what you can. So what box does love go in? Or is it something you check off on a list?"

She ran her palms down her face, and when she dropped them, her eyes were shiny and wet. "Maybe we should clarify where we both stand, and you'll stop playing the blame game."

"Fine." He wanted to take her in his arms, kiss her tears away. But how could he?

She inhaled a breath. "Are you willing to stay here on Indigo Beach? Turn your life upside down?"

"No. I can't do that."

"And I'm not willing to take Henry to Canada and then God knows where after that."

"I get that you want to stay—"

"But let's go further," she interrupted him. "How would you feel about having Walt and Sheena in your life permanently, showing up to your future movie sets, meeting your directors and cast mates?"

He glowered, thinking of Walt and how unimpressed Mike was by him. Poor Lacey, being saddled with that guy.

"Your expression is answer enough."

"Sheena's not bad." He knew full well he was damning her with faint praise. But what the hey—she was a tough nut to crack, and it upset him how she wasn't all over Lacey the way a doting mother should be.

"Let's consider how your mother might treat me," she asked, "a girl from the wrong side of the tracks entering her high-society world. I suspect the tolerance she displayed tonight would wear thin, fast."

"Probably. And I'd have to give her ultimatums, which she'd ignore. And then she wouldn't talk to me for six months after each one."

"Do either of us really want to go through that?"

Her eyes were bleak, but he couldn't look away.

"Looks to me like the case is closed, solicitor," she said quietly.

Wasn't she cute, using one of his lines from his last movie. Either that, or she was mean.

All right, she was mean. She was a goddamned witch. He'd never call her the B word. Not his Lacey. But he could at least envision her as a witch at a cauldron, making love spells that threw a man off his game enough that she could then drum up a curse on him that would last forever and ruin all hope for future love or fabulous movie roles.

Who'd want a man who'd had the rug whipped out from under him to star in their next action-adventure movie? And what woman would want a man who was lovesick about another woman he couldn't have? His sex life was over, and as of right now, he didn't care. Make him a eunuch if he couldn't have Lacey. Send him to Siberia and freeze his penis off.

Wait. He took that back. The last thing.

Actually, the last two things.

See? He was messed up. Weird thoughts were entering his brain. He should have listened to his agent.

Lacey is a genuine Hollywood jinx.

"I guess we should have known this was doomed from the start." His heart was a chunk of broken granite thumping painfully in his chest when he dialed the limo driver on his cell phone. While it rang, he added, "We're the walking wounded, after all, from messed-up families and lots of baggage. We never stood a chance."

She looked down at the floor. "I hate to see you so bitter."

"Bitter, my ass. I'm mad—mad that I ever knocked on that lighthouse door." The driver answered, and while Lacey watched, Beau gave him instructions to pick her up outside, then hung up. "I'm sleeping here tonight, and in the morning, while you and Henry are at the studio, I'm moving my stuff out and staying on Kiawah Island at the Sanctuary." It was a five-star hotel he'd always wanted to try. "Might as well. Only have a few days left."

"You could stay in your trailer at the studio lot and save money. Or the Beach Bum Inn."

Really? was the look he sent her.

"Oh, yeah. You don't need to save money." She straightened her shoulders. "I'd better go now. Will your mom be downstairs?"

"Probably."

She shrugged. "I'll handle her without you."

"You don't have to. I can walk you out."

"I'd rather you didn't. If she's going to fly at me, let her do it now and get it out of her system. Maybe she'll feel guilty when I tell her it was all for naught."

"I'm sorry about Henry." Thinking of him made a lump come to Beau's throat, which he swallowed down. "I'll see him at the studio and tell him that I have a lot of work I have to do. He knows I'm leaving soon, so hopefully he'll be okay."

"He's not your problem."

Dammit, he wanted him to be; he wanted to be connected, to matter to someone, to have other people matter to him.

"So don't feel burdened," Lacey said. "But I appreciate your caring."

He nodded.

She left.

He listened to her walk downstairs. Leaving him. For good. And with a heavy heart, he acknowledged that she was right.

The case was most certainly closed.

CHAPTER TWENTY-EIGHT

"Hello, Mrs. Wilder," Lacey said in the foyer of Beau's family home.

Mrs. Wilder sat in her well-appointed living room. "Hello, Lacey." She was holding a magazine open on her lap. Two dogs rested at her feet.

There was a brief silence. A yip from one of the dogs.

"I'm sorry we intruded," Lacey said. "Beau wanted to show me his childhood home, and . . . and . . ."

"It's all right." Mrs. Wilder sent her the enigmatic smile of a wealthy woman who was long used to holding sway over a room of partygoers, charitable board members, or servants.

Lacey nodded. "Well, good-bye then."

"Good-bye." Mrs. Wilder turned a page.

Lacey turned the doorknob and was about to step outside.

"Lacey?" Beau's mother called quietly.

She took a step back, her heart pounding. "Yes?"

"Is there something wrong?"

Lacey's eyes smarted. She nodded. "Beau and I won't be seeing each other anymore."

Mrs. Wilder looked steadily at her. "I'm sorry to hear that."

Lacey blinked back tears so they wouldn't fall. "Are you?" Her voice went up. "I don't ask that with any malice or disrespect. But I got the impression from Beau that I wouldn't be the sort of partner you'd want for him."

"Beau doesn't know everything," Mrs. Wilder said mildly. "If he talked to me more, he might discover I'm not the dragon he credits me with being. I want him to be happy. That's all. I don't care if it means he marries our maid, Angela, who's seventy-two years old this week." She gave a little chuckle.

Lacey managed a smile. "I'm glad to know that before I leave."

Mrs. Wilder stood, put her magazine on the table, and walked to her, her arms folded over her chest. "I like you, Lacey. I haven't known you long. But I like your spirit. I think you could hold your own with Beau."

"I think so, too," she said, her hand on the doorknob again, "But I don't think his heart is in settling down anytime soon. And I have work to do myself. A lot of work."

Mrs. Wilder tilted her head in charming fashion. "If I can be of any assistance, please let me know."

"Thanks. And I want you to know—your son loves you. He's told me so. In fact, I think he's gotten a good shock, seeing you with your fiancé tonight. I think it made him realize that you have a heart, after all."

Mrs. Wilder's forehead furrowed. "I feel so bad for him. He was wounded deeply by what happened. I assume you know?"

Lacey nodded.

"At the time, it felt like the right thing to do—to hold our family together. Now"—she shrugged—"I would have done differently. I'm older and wiser. Not so afraid. But back then, it was a different story."

"I suggest you tell Beau just that."

"I've tried. He claims he wants to talk about it. But we end up arguing and worse off than before."

Lacey was sad for her. "Have you tried writing him a letter?"

"No, I haven't." Mrs. Wilder uncrossed her arms, rested her hands lightly on Lacey's shoulders, and pressed her cheek to hers—the Julia Wilder version of a hug. "Thank you for the suggestion. And I wish all the best to you."

"To you, too."

"And Lacey"—she got that attractive twinkle in her eye, the same one she had at the wedding ball—"if you love him half as much as I love my Walker, don't give up hope."

"You're very sweet," Lacey whispered.

She felt Mrs. Wilder's eyes on her back as she exited the piazza, her eyes stinging and finally brimming over. The lights of the Battery suddenly became great starbursts when she found herself on the sidewalk in front of the limo. The driver leapt out and opened the door for her, and she slid inside the vehicle.

It was a lonely drive home. She dreaded telling Sheena and Walt what had happened. Henry, thank goodness, she could talk to in the morning.

Twenty minutes later, the limo crossed the bridge again to Indigo. How long ago Sarah and Grady's ball now seemed! And as Lacey predicted, Walt and Sheena didn't take her news well. Their disappointment was heavy.

"Will you still work for him?" Sheena asked.

"No."

"We might as well leave tomorrow morning then," Walt said.

Sheena simply shook her head.

Lacey wished—futilely, she knew—that Sheena would say, *No. Lacey needs us. We're staying at least another day to help her through.*

"Henry and I will stop by the RV on the way to the studio, to say good-bye." She walked with them to the door, hoping for a hug. "Good night, Sheena."

"Good night." Her mother was as prim and proper as ever in yet another colorless dress.

The name *Sheena* made no sense. Lacey wished her mother *would* be like a wild woman in the jungle, hug her fiercely, and protect her from glowing yellow eyes in the dark. But nothing in Lacey's family ever made sense. Except for Henry.

After Walt and Sheena left, she went upstairs and stood over his bed for a good five minutes, watching him breathe.

It was another beautiful morning. The table was set for two.

"Where's Beau?" Henry asked.

Lacey waited until he'd sat down.

And when she told him that Beau had special work to do and had to live elsewhere until he left Indigo Beach in three days, Henry simply cried. He didn't move. Two rivers of tears poured down his cheeks. His nostrils flared in and out. Hiccups and moans came from his throat.

She pulled out the chair next to him, wiped his face with a paper napkin, and had to work very hard not to cry, too. What had she done to her son? She never should have opened the door that first night.

"You'll see him at the studio," she promised him brightly. Then gave up. It was horrible to lose a friend. Why was she trying to pretend it wasn't?

"Aren't you sad, too?" Henry asked her.

"Yes," she said. "I feel awful inside. Like there's a rock in my stomach." She hugged his shoulders tight.

He leaned into her. "You danced with him, Mom. We surfed together. He was our *best* friend. He was gone a lot because of the movie, but he was still the best friend we ever had. I could tell that if he didn't have a movie, he'd have been with us all the time."

"He does like us," she said. "But the thing is, he always has a movie. That's his job. When this one is over, he'll go on to the next one. It's in Canada, far away."

"Can we visit him?' "

Lacey shook her head. "But you can write him." Surely, Beau wouldn't mind the occasional card or drawing from Henry. She laid her hand over his and squeezed. "When he's gone, we need to make new friends. Here in Indigo Beach. And I promise we will. We've only been here a month." It seemed so much longer. "Imagine how many friends we'll have after a whole year! You'll meet a lot of them at school."

Henry's mouth quivered. "Bob and Carol are leaving, too, aren't they? And Dickey?"

Lacey nodded. "Everyone at the studio will leave when the movie's done shooting. We've got two more weeks. Except Beau. They're finishing his part now so he can get to his new movie."

Henry bowed his head. "I'm going to miss *everyone*."

"Me, too," she whispered. "We'll save money to fly out to California to visit Mike, Bob, and Carol. Dickey will either live with them or somewhere here in South Carolina. If he's here, we'll go visit him, too, okay? And not just once."

Henry nodded.

At the RV, Lacey told Henry to sit on the front step while she ran inside to pick something up. "Then Grandma and Grandpa are coming with us to the studio."

Inside the vehicle, she put her foot down. "You can't leave yet. Henry needs you. At least stay until the afternoon. He's had a big shock this morning. I can't have y'all go, Sheena. *Please*."

"We need to go," Walt insisted.

Lacey took her mother's hand. "*I* need you, too. We both do."

Sheena looked at their linked fingers a few seconds, then up at Walt. "Truth is, I'm not feeling my best this morning for traveling anyway," she said in a thin voice. "I think I've got a sinus headache. I wouldn't mind staying put another day. And if we do, I might as well rest up at the studio."

"I don't want to spend another day in a movie trailer with that Dickey character," Walt said.

Sheena sighed. "I'm asking you to. But if you can't, get a rental car. Go to Devra's."

"What?" Walt's ridiculous hair moved back on his scalp.

"I can drive this RV," Sheena said stoutly. "You think I've spent this many years in it and don't know how?"

"I'll take the RV—*you* get the rental car." His face was blotchy red.

"Fine," Sheena returned lightly. "Let me get my things." She walked to the back, opened a closet, and pulled out her purse.

Lacey didn't say a word.

Walt sent her a black look.

Sheena bent down and pulled open a drawer.

"Okay!" Walt said. "We'll stay. But I'm not at all happy about it. Just so you know."

Sheena stood up and turned to him. She didn't smile. But she looked . . . perkier somehow.

Lacey loved it. She loved it so much that her knees wobbled and her heart pounded against her ribs. She went back and gave her mother a hug. "Thank you so much."

"It's good we're staying," Sheena said with all the

awkwardness of someone who wasn't used to fighting for and getting her way.

"Yes." Lacey smiled broadly. "Yes, it is. Henry will be so happy. I am, too."

When she walked by Walt, she managed a brief "Thank you" for her mother's sake. But that was all he was getting.

At the studio, no one noticed how quiet she and Henry were when they arrived with Walt and Sheena. One of the minor actresses—a glorified extra named Gina with a regular role, that of a diner waitress—had collapsed and been rushed to the hospital.

"Her appendix almost burst!" shouted Bob.

"It didn't," said Carol, "but she screamed a lot."

Henry's eyes were wide.

Simone shivered. "Mike said they wanted to cut her open on the way to the hospital, and they would have if the bridge had been up." For a girl who prided herself on being cool and a little bit dangerous, she was surprisingly shaken.

"I took out my own appendix," said Dickey over the game of rummy he recruited Walt and Sheena to play at the RV's galley table.

"Oh, yeah?" Henry wanted to hear more and slid in next to him.

"Don't listen to him," Sheena warned Henry.

Wait—was that some grandmotherly nurturing Lacey heard in her mother's voice?

"I did it with my favorite hunting knife." Dickey laid down three tens and took a card from the stockpile. "I didn't have any needle and thread to sew it up, so I pinched the wound shut with a clothespin and got myself to the doctor."

"Coooool," said Bob.

"I'm outta here," said Simone with a shudder. She descended the stairs and shut the door behind her. A whiff of salt and firewood smoke—Indigo Beach smells—wafted up.

Lacey wished she could bottle that scent. "Dickey, you really shouldn't tell the kids you took out your own appendix. This is serious business, what happened to Gina."

He looked up at her with innocent eyes.

What was going through his head? Whatever it was, attention seemed to help reduce the fibbing. She laid a hand on his bony shoulder. "How about grilled cheese and tomato soup for lunch?"

His eyes lit up. He loved grilled cheese and tomato soup.

"I'd like chocolate cake," said Walt in a sulky voice.

As if anyone would want to bring him some. He was here under duress. He still didn't care about Henry.

"We don't have any chocolate cake," Lacey found herself saying sharply. "And quite frankly"—she folded one arm tightly over the other—"we never will."

"Never?" Bob's face scrunched up. "Never, ever?"

"I want some chocolate cake . . ." Carol trailed off on a huge whine.

"My mom doesn't mean never for *us*," Henry explained to his buds. "She just means when Grandpa's here, we won't have it."

"No, Henry," Lacey said lamely.

But of course, he was right.

Oh, God. She really shouldn't start something with Walt. It had just come out of her.

There was an awkward silence.

"I only meant"—she locked gazes with Sheena—"that I'm tired, is all. I'm tired of making chocolate cake, over and over, and sharing it, and then no one seems to notice. Or appreciate it. And sometimes, sometimes I want to quit making it ever again."

"Are you hiding some chocolate cake?" Dickey asked.

"Yeah," Bob said. "Is this a game?"

"What are you talking about, Miss Lacey?" asked Carol. "You've *never* made us chocolate cake."

"Dang," Walt said, oblivious, "I can go get us all some at the bakery on Center Street if you'd like."

But Sheena sat perfectly still, looking at Lacey. In her eyes there was some kind of connection. Understanding. Lacey blinked repeatedly to make sure she wasn't imagining it. But it was still there.

Mom love.

Sheena shifted in her seat, then looked thoughtfully at her husband. "You do that," she said firmly. "You bring us back a whole chocolate cake, and while you're at it, stop at the grocery store and get us two cartons of whole milk to go with it. And some vanilla ice cream. A jar of sprinkles, too."

The kids all clapped and yelled about what color sprinkles they hoped Walt would get. In the midst of the hubbub, a cell phone rang.

Lacey looked around. "Whose is that?" It didn't sound like Walt's. Sheena didn't have one.

It rang again, and Dickey finally put down his cards and pulled a mobile device out of his jacket pocket.

Lacey had no idea he even had one. It had never rung before. It was shiny silver, with a large number 88 emblazoned on the back.

"Junior?" he said.

There was an animated twang of a voice from the phone.

Dickey chuckled. "I saw that race. You tell him he'd better clean up his driving."

The twangy voice went on.

"I don't know, Junior. I don't travel much anymore." Dickey was complacent. "I appreciate it. I do. Your daddy meant the world to me. But you're doing him proud." There

was a pause while he listened to further unintelligible ex-
hortation, which leveled off into mild chat, a laugh, and
then silence.

Lacey was fascinated. Bob said something to Henry,
and she put a finger over her mouth.

"Thanks for checking in," Dickey said into the phone
and cracked a smile. "Talk to you later." He clicked off
the phone and stuck it back in his jacket pocket.

Everyone was staring at him.

"Who *was* that?" Lacey asked.

"Dale, Junior." Dickey picked up his cards again and
looked at Sheena. "Your turn."

Sheena stared at him. "You know Dale Earnhardt, Junior? The NASCAR driver?"

"NASCAR!" Bob exclaimed to Henry.

"Yes," said Dickey.

"NASCAR!" Bob then said to Carol.

"He gave me a phone so he could reach me," said Dickey.
"I talk to him before each racc."

Bob looked up at Lacey and opened his mouth, but
Laccy cut him off.

"Yes, NASCAR," she said softly, still stunned at Dickey's revelation. He really did know Dale Earnhardt, Junior!

"Can I see your phone again?" Henry asked the old
man.

"Sure." Dickey took out the phone and held it up.

"No way," said Walt, as if he'd just seen a miracle.
"Number Eighty-Eight. Can I hold that?"

Dickey passed it over.

"Can I hold it, too?" Henry squealed.

"Me, too!" yelled Bob.

"And me," wailed Carol.

"Everyone can," Dickey said. "Sheena, are you going
to go or not?"

Sheena looked back down at her cards. "I-I'm thinking."

"Dickey, where did you meet the president of the United States again?" Lacey asked him.

"I was visiting Dale, Senior, and he had a tire store opening in Dale, North Carolina, to cut the ribbon at. The president was in North Carolina on a campaign stop, and he wanted to meet Number Three. So he came to the tire store. I got a picture in my wallet."

He pulled out an ancient billfold, tugged out an old photo, and passed it around.

There he was with Dale, Senior—Number 3—and a former president of the United States of America, in front of a bunch of tires. A little guy hung on to Number 3's leg.

"That's Junior," Dickey explained. "Not much higher than a grasshopper."

"Lord, save me," Lacey said, and leaned against the galley counter, shaken to the core.

Not all Dickey's stories were lies, after all. Which meant that the one he'd told her about Beau being in love with her might have some truth to it.

No, her heart said. *Beau wants to be in love. But he's not ready.*

Maybe he is, her head replied, *but* you're *not. So it doesn't matter.*

Yet somehow it did.

CHAPTER TWENTY-NINE

Until Gina collapsed, Beau's morning at the studio had gone pretty well, considering that he was still reeling from his breakup with Lacey.

Not that they'd ever been officially together.

Oh, no.

He really didn't have anything to feel rotten about.

But he still did.

He told Mike that the sooner he got done with filming at Indigo Beach, the better.

"We've been going great guns," Mike said. "If we make a push—put in a few extra hours, have dinner brought in—we can wrap your scenes tonight."

"I can't tell you how much I appreciate it, man." Beau's head hurt. He'd sat up until four AM in his dad's old library, thinking and drinking. "It'll be nice to have an extra couple of days in Canada to settle in before I meet with Danvers."

"Wow." Mike chuckled. "From me to Danvers. I feel pretty special." He sent him an affectionate grin. "It's been a pleasure to work with you."

"You, too." Beau couldn't believe he was saying that, considering he still wasn't a fan of the script. But he meant it. "You've challenged me. It's been good for me. You brought out skills I didn't know I had."

"They were there all along."

"If so, your directing's responsible for my discovering them."

"I can't take much credit. Most goes to you. And there's one more person to thank—Lacey. The tide turned for you after you read with her."

"You're right."

At that point, all hell broke loose when across the set, Gina collapsed. They lost a solid two hours.

But afterward, Mike pulled everyone together and demanded focus. "Let's show Gina the show will go on. We know she's going to be fine, so we don't need to worry about her, all right?"

Even so, Beau wasn't going to push anymore to finish his lines that day. It was too much to ask everyone.

But Mike surprised him. "Beau's wrapping tonight. So we need to pull it together even tighter to honor all the hard work he's given us."

Everyone clapped.

Beau was touched. "Hey, only if it's not a hardship. Today's been rough already. Gina's on our minds."

"We can do it," Mike said.

"Who's going to play Gina in the two coffeehouse scenes?" Adam asked.

"You all know her as my kids' babysitter, Lacey Clark." Mike grinned. "She didn't want to do it, but I convinced her she'd be helping us send Beau on his way."

All the blood in Beau's head rushed to his feet. No way. Lacey was going to be on the set? In a scene with him? Of course, she wanted to send him on his way! He knew damned well the acting opportunity itself didn't interest her.

"Oh, good!" said Simone, and clapped her hands again.

Beau had about an hour to prepare himself for Lacey's arrival. He had two scenes to film.

"You all right?" Mike asked him five minutes into shooting. "You're not quite on target."

"Sorry." Beau didn't explain. And he wasn't going to use Gina as an excuse when it was Lacey he was thinking about.

He pushed aside his feelings of doom, regret, anger, and wistfulness, and recommitted to the scenes. He became Evan again. The scenes went so well that in the middle of the second one, when a cat arbitrarily wandered onto his lap in the big armchair he was sitting in, he kept going with his lines of dialogue, petting the darned thing the whole time.

"That was perfect," Mike said. "We couldn't have scripted that in."

Finally, Lacey arrived.

"Hi," she said stiffly to Beau before he could say hello himself.

"Nice to see you," he said. And it was. She was so damned beautiful. "Thanks for helping to expedite my departure."

"My pleasure," she murmured, tying on her diner apron.

The irony in her words was rich.

"So you have a line." He didn't want to stop talking to her. He wished everyone else would go away.

"Yeah." She blushed. "Never thought that would happen again."

And then they had to separate.

Mike gave directions, camera guys angled their lenses. Beau slid into a booth with Simone and Adam across from him.

Get into character and stay there, he told himself. *No matter what.*

"Lights, camera . . . action!" Mike called.

And Beau was Evan. The scene proceeded well for a couple of minutes. Then Lacey walked up with her pot of coffee, which was actually cold.

He pushed his empty cup over to her, ready for her to say, *Having a good morning, folks?*

"You don't have to take it black," she told Beau, "just because *she* does." And she dumped a bunch of creamers and packets of sugar on the table.

What the hell?

"Cut!" Mike yelled. "Lacey, that wasn't the line."

She bit her lip and looked down at Beau. "I know it wasn't."

Beau sat frozen. He was going to stay Evan if it killed him.

"But it's perfect," Lacey said. "Evan's such a poser around her." She angled her head at Simone. "I just *know* he doesn't take his coffee black. He's been denying himself cream and sugar—real pleasure—because of her ascetic sensibilities." She blinked unhappily at Simone. "And you're such a bitch. You know he wants to doctor his coffee. And you love that he doesn't."

Simone laughed. "What the hell are you doing, Lacey?"

Adam, painfully polished in his European-style suit and tie, snorted and lowered himself farther in the booth. "This is crazy."

"Lacey." Mike's voice was still mild. "I appreciate your take on the scene, but you're not the director. Say your line—the one in the script."

"I wish you'd try it my way." Lacey's cheeks were red. "See what happens. Otherwise, this scene is flat. The script's brilliant for the most part, but it breaks down for about three pages. Right here."

"If you felt this way," Mike forged on with the patience of a saint, "why didn't you tell me before now?"

"Because I was the babysitter. But now, I'm in the scene. It has to be good, Mike. One of the best ones in the movie. Believe me."

Beau wanted to chuckle. He knew just what she meant. Greta needed to break her curse.

"That's the climax scene," Mike said. "We're filming it tonight."

"Well, if you don't change this one, the climax won't work," Lacey said. "I'm sorry, but that's the truth."

"Can we take a break?" Adam called over to Mike.

"No," Mike said. He was staring intently at Lacey.

Beau recognized his thinking face.

Meanwhile, he now knew how Lacey had gotten her reputation as a Hollywood jinx. He took in every quivering part of the woman he loved—her lips, her hands, her voice. He wished he could bottle the passion she was showing right now.

She was completely outrageous.

But she had a point.

This scene bordered on filler.

Maybe Mike was the type of director who would listen to her instead of throwing her off the set or starting rumors about her.

"A little ad lib never hurt anyone," Beau said with a shrug. "We could try it. Loosen everyone up."

"This scene *is* kind of tedious," Simone said.

Mike sighed. "Okay, we'll do it. But it's going to take up your precious time, Wilder."

"I'm okay with it," he said.

"Everyone, back in character," Mike said. "Lights, camera, action—"

After Lacey delivered her new line, Beau looked up at her as Evan. "Are you trying to save me from the hell I'm in?" he asked her softly, and ripped open one of the creamers she'd thrown on the table. "'Cause it's working."

He poured the cream in his coffee and stirred, but he kept his gaze on hers.

Lacey's eyes widened, but her hand on the coffeepot remained steady. "I meet a lot of you bankers here." She swallowed. "After a while, you figure out pretty darned quick who needs a healthy dose of cream and sugar—and who takes his or her life black."

Adam, in character, said, "Black all the way."

"Me, too, baby," said Simone, and kissed Adam in triumph. "The merger is on. If Evan doesn't lose his cool."

"Got that, Evan?" Adam said.

Beau would have told him to take a hike.

Evan was too weak to do that.

"I don't think you're giving me much choice," he told Adam's character, then looked at Lacey-the-waitress. "Want to ride off into the sunset with me?"

She paused a fraction of a second. "And miss the rest of my shift? Sorry, you'll have to merge with someone else." She winked at him and walked away.

"See?" Adam said in character to Evan. "She's not a cream-and-sugar kind of gal. She's a realist, like most of us. I suggest you follow suit."

Simone laid a hand on her husband's arm. "Leave him alone."

Which was way off script. She was supposed to despise Evan as much as Adam's character did at this point.

Mike kept filming, and when they wrapped, he was happy with it. "I liked the way it evolved with Simone's character, especially. You showed us something new: You're on the fence about Evan at this point in the story. So when the climax happens, the audience won't know whether you're going to distract Adam and maybe lead Beau to the poison antidote or not. Lacey was right. It's better."

Every single word Beau had said to her in character as Evan? He'd cheated. That had been Beau talking. It felt good to get the feelings out. He never would in real life. But now they were on film forever.

Lacey's part was over. She'd ditched the coffeepot and chatted with Mike, Adam, and Simone. Beau went over to say something. He didn't want to look churlish. And he was dying to be near her, anyway.

"Lotta balls," he said to her when the others drifted away.

"I can't help it," she replied.

"It worked."

"So it did. I do think it's better now."

"You've got a gift." She had a lot of them.

"I don't know what for," she said. "Certainly not acting or directing. No one would ever listen to me. I'm too impulsive."

"You should do story consultation," he said. "People who are good at that make a lot of money."

"Do they have to live in Hollywood?"

"Pretty much."

"And being male might help."

"Probably."

"So I guess that's out for me," she said, but she didn't look unhappy.

He wanted to kiss her so badly. "Good luck."

"To you, too. Henry will be sending you postcards from Indigo Beach. And maybe some drawings."

"I'd love that." Beau was seriously not enjoying the feelings welling up in him at that moment. It sucked, sometimes, to be a major movie star. No one needed to hear him say so—it was whining, for sure. But damn. Sometimes he wished he could vent with someone who cared about him—someone other than his agent. Susan cared, but her livelihood was intertwined with his, and any bad vibes made her naturally nervous about her own family's welfare. He didn't like indulging his misgivings with her.

"Excuse me." A redheaded grip came up to them. "Sorry to interrupt, Mr. Wilder, but I just figured something out." He was staring avidly at Lacey.

Beau thought he was pretty obnoxious. "We're busy. Maybe later."

But Mike, Adam, Simone, and a couple of extras came over, so the moment to talk alone to Lacey was lost.

"You're not going to believe this, Mr. Carter," the grip said to Mike.

"I have to get back to the kids," Lacey said, and started untying her apron.

"She's Greta Gildensturm." The grip crooked his thumb at Lacey. "You know, the motorcycle chick from *Biker Aliens*? I worked on that set. See? Look at her picture."

And he held up a smartphone with a photo of Lacey as Greta on it.

"Oh, my God," said Adam.

"What did I tell ya?" The grip chuckled.

Lacey looked up, her face white as a sheet. "Here." She thrust the apron at Simone. "Could you return this to Costumes? I'll get the rest back this afternoon."

Simone took the apron and stared at her. "I never saw *Biker Aliens*. But I've seen pictures online of Greta."

"Lacey," said Mike. "Is it true? I saw that movie once when I was really, really drunk. But now that I think of it . . . ."

"I saw it, too." Adam raked a hand through his hair. "How could I not have seen the resemblance? I must have recognized you at some level because I thought you were the Hominy Grill girl." He paused. "Are you?"

"No," Lacey said. "But I'd rather be identified as the waitress in the mural than as Greta."

"You said you were a Charleston society girl who'd broken loose," Simone's voice went up half an octave. "I'm so confused. You're Greta, too?" She turned immediately to Beau. "Why are you being so silent? Isn't Lacey your old neighbor?"

Beau locked gazes with her. There was no way she could lie herself out of this one.

She knew it, too. He saw it in her eyes. But he also could tell she wasn't up for confessing. "She's not my old neighbor, nor is she from Charleston," he said. "That was all my doing to protect her privacy, so don't come down on her for it. Lacey Clark did play Greta Gildensturm, as you can see in the movie credits—but she doesn't go around telling everyone. It's old history."

"Wow," said Mike.

"God," said Simone. "I was so rooting for you—the rich girl joining the masses. Making it on her own."

"Let me tell you," Lacey said, "it's just as hard, if not much harder, making it on your own without any nice social connections. I'm sorry I lied to you, Simone. I'm sorry to all of you."

"Didn't you just dump a pitcher of margaritas on Callum McDonough's head?" the grip asked. "It was on TMZ. But your hair was black at the time."

"Yes," Lacey admitted.

"No shit—that was you?" Simone wore a look of utter disbelief.

"Surely you understand now why I kept this to myself." Lacey beseeched the whole crowd but paid particular attention to Mike. "It's because of people like you"—she glared at the grip—"who treat me like an exhibit at the zoo."

"Hey, don't get mad at me," the grip said. "*You're* the Hollywood jinx. You should have stayed away. Now this movie's doomed."

"You're a jinx, Lacey?" Simone's eyebrow went up. "How come? I don't know this story."

"I don't, either," said Adam.

So the grip told them. "But she's very cute, as you can see. Who'd ever guess such mayhem would follow her?"

A horrible hush fell over everyone. Simone leaned on Adam.

"Thanks a lot," Adam told Lacey. "Did you even think about us when you came here?"

"Shut up, Adam." Mike's face was pale. "I've heard that story, and it's ridiculous to blame Lacey for what went down on those three films. I don't believe in jinxes. But if any of you breathes a word of Greta Gildensturm's presence here to the press, I'll be pissed. We don't need any disruptions on the set. It's not like we have forever to finish shooting this movie. I have a day job to get back to."

"I'm so sorry, Mike," Lacey said.

Beau wished he could hug her. But it was a bad idea for a lot of reasons.

Mike looked at her, a furrow on his brow. "You should get back to the kids. Everyone else, ten-minute break. Grab a snack while you can. We're not stopping until Beau's scenes are done, which means pizza on the set for dinner."

Lacey pushed right past everyone without looking at them—her sweet flower scent still affected Beau as much as it ever had—and raced out.

He went after her.

"Beau! How could you?" Adam called to his back. "Misleading us like that about Lacey."

No time to turn around. Beau flipped the bird at the

film's leading man instead. This was his last chance to talk to Lacey—Henry, too. The boy would be sleeping tonight when they finished filming.

He had to say good-bye.

CHAPTER THIRTY

Lacey's heart felt as if it were breaking. Again. Wasn't there a limit on how much hurt a heart could withstand?

Beau crouched on the asphalt tarmac next to the trailer, his hands on Henry's shoulders. "I'm gonna miss you, Henry." His face was so serious. "We're great trackers together."

"I know," said Henry in a small voice. "Soon everyone's leaving. Even George." His voice cracked. "Most of the time he just wants me to pet him. And that gets boring. But I'll miss his meow."

Beau gave a weird laugh, and Lacey could swear it was to keep from crying.

"You know what? I'm going to miss George, too," Beau said. "I never thought I'd say that about a cat. But guess what—I won't miss him nearly as much as I'll miss you."

He and Henry shared a long hug.

Lacey had to wipe her eyes on her arm.

Beau patted Henry's back. "You'll make new friends. I promise."

Henry nodded. "Okay."

The trust Henry put into the adults in his life! Lacey remembered doing the same as a little kid. Now she knew the other side. No matter how hard she tried to protect her boy, he wound up getting hurt sometimes. And the worst part was, it wasn't always outside forces at work. A lot of the time it was because of the choices *she'd* made as his parent.

It was both vexing and terribly sad. But most of all, it just was. And she could either constantly berate herself, or learn from everything that happened. Maybe by the time she was eighty-two, she'd be wise.

Henry went back inside.

Beau looked at her gravely. "I have a feeling things are going to be different around here tomorrow."

"Me, too," she said. "Good thing you're getting out now."

"Probably so. But I'm worried about you."

"You don't need to be. I brought this on everyone, and I'll ride it out, whatever happens."

The air was still between them.

"Thanks for everything," he said. "The breakfasts, sharing Henry with me, and all the listening you did."

"Thanks for the surfing, and for being Henry's friend." She winced and crossed her arms over her chest. "And thanks for, you know . . ."

He chuckled. "The great sex. You shouldn't have mentioned that."

Because then he took her in his arms and kissed the hell out of her.

I love you, she said with her heart.

But it's over, her brain reminded her lips, which were responding with total fervor to the good-bye kiss to end all good-bye kisses, a regular tour de force.

"Wow," she whispered when it was done. "I feel like I'm in the movies. And that was the last scene."

"It kinda was."

"Except I'll see you in the theaters." She sounded like a stalker. But she didn't mean it that way. She just meant she loved him with all her heart, and if it weren't for Henry, her life would be in a million pieces after he left.

"And maybe I'll pop in sometime, when I'm in town."

She couldn't tell if he was fishing—her heart sped up at the thought that he might care enough to stay in touch—or if he was trying to let her down with a polite platitude.

"Give it some time," she said, her voice softer than she wanted it to be. She prayed there wasn't a trace of wistfulness in it. "We don't want to confuse Henry."

"Good point." He nodded, looked away, over her head. At his bright, shining future, no doubt.

"One more thing," he said.

"What?"

"You're not going to believe this, but I'm actually sad Evan's going to die tonight."

"I am, too," she said earnestly. "He was a sensitive guy."

"Not that. The bastard brought me to Indigo Beach. To you and Henry. For that alone, I wish he could live, although he doesn't deserve to."

She wanted to laugh. It was funny, in a way. But instead her head seemed to fill with hot sand, and her nose tickled, and her eyes—some dandelion fluff must have flown into them.

"Good-bye, Beau," she whispered over the gravel in her throat.

"'Bye, Lacey."

And that was it.

In the trailer, Sheena had just finished making her a cup of tea. "Come in the back."

The kids were fine. They were playing the Game of Life with Dickey. Walt was taking a nap sitting up in an armchair.

Lacey followed her mother. Her heart was shattered, her life nearly was, and she knew for a fact that she'd never, ever be kissed like that again.

"Drink this." Sheena put the cup in her hands.

Lacey took a sip, her eyes brimming.

"I know you don't feel like it, but you'll be okay," Sheena murmured.

Lacey kept sipping, her eyes down in her cup, locked on its shadows and the finely etched lines of the porcelain.

"And I already heard that that damned redheaded grip told everyone about Greta Gildensturm." Sheena's tone was soft.

She wasn't blaming her daughter for anything.

Yet, Lacey reminded herself. Let Walt get involved, and surely he'd find a way to accuse her of something. But right now, at this moment, Sheena was on her side.

The knowledge gave Lacey the wee bit of energy she needed to look beyond the cup's rim. "You heard the news before I even got back to the trailer?"

Beau had caught up with her, and they'd walked back together in virtual silence, until the end when he'd asked to see Henry.

"I was over at the canteen buying some chocolate bars," Sheena said. "And the girl behind the counter was on the phone with her friend, telling her the whole story."

Lacey sighed. "Good thing you and Walt are leaving."

"Why? Are you expecting something else to happen? It's already pretty damned crappy in your world. Except for Henry, that is."

She'd said his name.

Lacey held on to that. It was one tiny knot she could tie on the end of her rope. She was dangling over a yawning abyss of potentially bad press for the movie and herself— even Beau—but her mother had made her tea. Had cursed on her behalf. Had even called her grandson by name.

It was something.

A tortured hour went by. Lacey pretended that she was a happy mother, babysitter, and caretaker while Sheena did all the real work of tending to the kids and Dickey. But eventually Sheena grabbed Walt and they took the ambulance to the lighthouse to feed George before escaping to their RV for the night.

Lacey and Henry stayed at the trailer on the studio lot because filming didn't break until midnight. A very weary Mike wound up sleeping in Beau's trailer, but before he grabbed his toothbrush and went, he told Lacey that Beau was headed to the airport to a private plane waiting for him on the tarmac, ready to take off at two AM.

"I have a feeling about this Greta story." He yawned.

"Me, too." She bit her lip. "I'm so, so sorry."

"I know." They stood in silence for a few beats. "On the good side," he said, "there will be lots of buzz."

"And the bad side?"

"It's going to wreak havoc on the set. It's already going to be different without Beau around. The other actors wanted to impress him."

"Even though he wasn't an artsy kind of actor?"

"Yep," said Mike. "He's a good man. A leader. He might not have been into this script, and he struggled with his own approach to it, but he also brought out the best in the rest. That's what guys who play heroes do. They stick to the mission."

She smiled sadly. "Handsome, rich, talented, *and* inspiring."

"And obviously in love with you."

"What?"

"Didn't you see how he delivered those lines to you? That was Beau talking. Not Evan."

"No. Beau's too professional. He wouldn't have broken character."

"Of course he didn't. But he found a way to be himself and Evan at the same time by ad-libbing. Ad-libbing always comes from the deepest parts of us. It's not like reading lines someone else gave you. It's *you*."

"Then that would make Simone and Adam self-centered opportunists."

Mike raised a brow. "And?"

"Okay, so I know they're kind of self-absorbed, but really, you're reaching too far."

"Oh, yeah?" said Mike. "You're someone who's always giving other people cream and sugar. And you won't let yourself have fun."

"Mike—"

"Hey, give me a minute here. You took care of my kids and father-in-law. I let you stomp all over my scene this morning."

She hung her head. "In that case . . ."

"All I'm saying is that you deserve happiness," Mike said. "And having lost my wife, I can tell you that you need to grab it when you recognize it. Nothing else matters, really. I know that now. Every morning I wake up, and my wife's gone. I'd put up with the entire world's crap, Lacey—not just my own—if I could just have one more minute with her."

Lacey sighed. "I have to hug you now." So she did, long and hard. "Oh, Mike," she whispered. "You're such a good guy."

"I know." His rumbly Harley voice soothed her.

When she drew back, she was smiling. "Hopefully, we're just panicking about the Greta story."

"I hope so, too."

They walked to the back of the trailer to look at the kids in their bunks. Dickey was in the master bedroom, snoring away behind a shut door.

"It's been fun here on Indigo Beach," said Mike. "I hate to leave. For a lot of reasons."

"We have two more weeks." Lacey didn't want him to go, either.

He shook his head. "I don't know."

They shared a look, and she felt so awful for screwing everything up that she headed to the hideous plush couch near the front of the trailer and sat down. "If for some reason we don't get time to talk, I just want you to know how much I love Bob and Carol and Dickey. And—"

"No, Lacey." Mike sat down next to her. "We're not saying good-bye now. We're going to hope for the best."

She leaned her small shoulder onto his huge one. "For a guy who makes downer art flicks, you're very much like Little Orphan Annie."

He laughed. "She's one of my heroes."

Early the next morning, the first sign that things were different was the Mercedes with Georgia plates that was parked near the trailers. A woman Lacey had never seen before appeared to be sleeping in the front seat.

But maybe not. She stirred, then scrambled to get out of the car when Lacey shut the trailer door and began to walk slowly in the direction of the canteen. The kids were sound asleep. Dickey was in the galley, playing Concentration. Mike was rolling out of bed at that very moment to come over from Beau's trailer and watch everyone while Lacey got them both coffee.

The woman caught up with her. "Excuse me?"

"Yes?"

"Aren't you the woman who played Greta Gildensturm?"

"Yes." Of course the woman didn't know her actual name. No one in LA ever did.

"I'm a retired reporter with *Variety*, the entertainment periodical based out of Hollywood."

"I know what *Variety* is."

"They're sending someone out here this afternoon, but

they asked that I come to let you know that if you give us an exclusive article about your time on the set, we'll pay you twenty grand right now. I can write you the check. Twenty-five if you can give us any information about Beau Wilder and his role in the movie."

"No, thank you."

"Are you sure?"

She nodded.

"Could you tell me where Mr. Wilder is?"

"He's gone," she said, walking faster. "I have some-place to be. Sorry."

The woman stopped in her tracks and let her go. "If you change your mind, just call the *Variety* office!" she called after her.

"It's not gonna happen," Lacey said over her shoulder.

She kept walking, her flip-flops slapping on the tar-mac, the soft morning breeze off the ocean gently pulling at her hair. That early in the morning, the studio lot felt like a ghost town.

A sudden flash of longing for Beau swept her. She wished he were with her, walking to the canteen. They'd be the first ones there. They'd talk to the guy who ran it— he arrived at six—and then Beau would lean on the coun-ter and together they'd smell the first coffee of the day brewing. And life would be good.

Indigo Beach wasn't going to be the same without him.

Part of her regretted promising Henry they'd stay. Part of her wanted to move on, as she always had.

But she'd promised.

And her heart would be broken anywhere, she told herself. Heck, if she were in the Virgin Islands right now, or France, or Italy, or anyplace she wanted to visit, she'd still be heartbroken.

The coffee at the canteen was excellent, but her day got worse. Her heartache hurt worse. So did her head, her whole body. She'd had little sleep lately, and an avalanche of reporters had descended upon the studio by noon. They all wanted information on Beau Wilder and why such an action-adventure movie hero was appearing in an artsy movie sure to be jinxed by Greta Gildensturm, who'd only recently poured a pitcher of margaritas over Callum McDonough's head and was known to bring bad luck to every film set she walked upon. Not only that, they'd heard Greta and Beau had been living together at the lighthouse while the movie was being filmed. Was there romance in the air?

There were so many juicy angles to this story that the *Today* show even flew down a reporter to get the scoop.

Mike had a plan. He asked Walt and Sheena to come over and get the kids in the RV. He gave Sheena a hundred bucks. "Could you take the children back to the fun park, please? And Lacey, can you get Walt to drop you off at your car and then hole up at the lighthouse with Dickey? If reporters follow you, fine. Just don't answer any questions if you can help it. Maybe we'll get some filming done in the meantime."

"I'm going to the fun park," Dickey said. "Lacey's in a funk."

"No, I'm not."

"It's about that woman, isn't it?" Dickey asked. "The one who runs the Mexican restaurant?"

"No." She was so frustrated, she could hardly get the words out. "She's a moot point, Dickey. Beau's *gone*."

The old man's shoulders slumped.

"Not only that," Lacey said, "Beau told me himself he's not seeing her."

"Yes, he was," Dickey insisted. "It was a secret. He promised me a trip to Gibraltar, Spain, if I didn't tell."

"He's not like that. He doesn't bribe people. He's a man of good character. But if for some other reason, he did promise you a trip to Spain, I'm sure he'll follow through."

"Not anymore." Dickey glowered. "*I told*. But facts is facts. He was seeing that woman."

"Hey," she said softly, "go to the fun park if you want. But I'd love company if you'd rather have a nice, quiet day on the beach. George could use some TLC, too."

So Dickey wound up going with her, after all.

She was really grateful to Sheena and Walt for their help. But there wasn't time to tell them. Reporters swarmed everywhere.

It was stupid. Honestly. The world had so many real problems that needed addressing. What happened on Indigo Beach, a small island on the edge of the world, shouldn't matter that much.

Lacey went surfing. The reporters who followed her onto the beach got tons of close-ups of her wiping out, but she did it anyway. She loved the repetitive nature of it—get up, glide, fall down. Over and over. Sometimes it seemed as if she'd never master the skill. You had to be a natural, like Beau, she thought. And then she remembered what he'd told her and Henry about hard work and persistence, and how they paid off when it came to surfing.

And obviously, to his life. Look how far he'd come, despite the pain of his growing-up years.

Don't give up on yourself so soon, he'd told her in the water.

He might be rich and famous, and she was a poor unknown, but their brains were on a lock. Their hearts had been, too.

"Are you sure Beau Wilder's not your boyfriend?" one newly arrived reporter asked her, either not knowing or not caring that fifteen other journalists had already asked the same question. "A source says you two have been seen in Charleston kissing at Fort Sumter and slow-dancing at some ball."

"Beau's a great guy," she said. "We have a lot of fun together."

She was only saying what Beau had told her to say: neither confirm nor deny, although really, she should simply deny.

But part of her refused.

"Why are you driving that old ambulance? It's *weird*," the same reporter asked.

"'Cause it rocks," she said. "It kind of helped save my life, too. So did the friend who lent it to me—and all the wonderful people I've met since I got here on Indigo."

"Tell me more!" the guy begged.

But she'd said enough already.

Back at the lighthouse, Dickey was snoozing on the couch with George on his chest when Lacey got a call from Mike.

"How's filming?" she asked, her heart in her throat. "They followed me out here. Hope you got a break."

"They double-teamed us." Mike sounded pretty bad for Mike. "I'm trying hard to ignore them, but the crew, the actors, everyone's agitated. I have to shut filming down. We can reconstruct the sets we still need to use back in LA—which will take a whole month away from my day job, unfortunately—but it has to be done. We'll finish up there. *Flowers from the Heart* will be completed, so don't worry."

"Oh, Mike." She got tears in her eyes. "Of course I'm worried. I'm so sorry."

"Don't be," he said. "It's all part of the business. Usually, this side of it—the cheesy tabloids, the Hollywood rumors, and all that jazz—it doesn't affect me. Wilbur's Ears doesn't get a lot of attention. But I should have been prepared for anything with Beau Wilder on the set. He's a big name. Unfortunately, I wasn't as ready as I should have been."

"It might have gone just fine without me there," she said.

"It's not your fault this jinx is following you around."

"It is, though. I brought it on myself by speaking up on the sets I was on. It got me unwelcome attention. I just need to never go on a set again in my life."

"Wrong. If you were a man, they would never have attached this label to you. Don't stop speaking out."

"Mike, thank you."

"You actually helped yesterday—once I got past the rather dramatic way you added your two cents." He chuckled.

"I'm not done apologizing," she said. "I lied to you about who I really am. Not just the Greta story. The Hominy Grill girl one."

"That was Adam's fault. He recognized you."

"But I ran with it. And then Beau and I didn't want people to know we were strangers living together in the lighthouse. For me, an old-fashioned Southern girl with a mother who wants me married off, it seemed a bit unseemly, especially because he's this sexy movie star. I didn't want anyone thinking anything remotely shady was going on between us, not with Henry in the mix."

"I get it," he said, "and what's more, I admire you for being creative. So shush about the past. We're already packing to go home. I can't lose momentum, and I've got us on the last flight to LA for the evening. I have an admin guy staying behind to oversee the set packing. I'm pulling Dickey's clothes together right now. He doesn't know it yet, but he's coming with us. Let's meet at the doughnut shop one more time to say good-bye. I'll need Bob and Carol, too. Can all of you be there in an hour?"

"Yes."

"I've already talked to the kids on the phone. They're heading back from the fun park. But can you break the news to Dickey for me, meanwhile? He's not a phone kind of guy."

"Yes, I'll tell him." She couldn't help it. Her lips started to tremble. "Henry and I are going to be devastated to lose all of you."

"It breaks my heart, too." Mike was quiet. "And I wish I were there to help with Dickey. If you'd rather wait for me to do it, I'll find a way to get over there."

"No," she said. "Leave it to me." She'd figure out how.

"One more thing, sweetie." Mike's voice was extra gentle. "I've heard Henry talk about George a lot, but the trainer needs you to pack him up."

"Oh." Could it get any worse? She pressed her hand against her eyes.

"You have his carrier?"

"Y-yes."

All at once.

All at once, everyone was leaving.

CHAPTER THIRTY-ONE

Dickey was in a sour mood when she picked up her purse and George's carrier, and told him it was time to go.

Right as they were leaving, someone drove up in a sleek gold Lexus.

Lacey rolled down the ambulance window with the little hand crank. "Can I help you?"

The person didn't look like a reporter. She was an older lady with beautifully done hair and bright red lipstick. "I'm the property manager from the office in Charleston," she said in a kindly voice. "I've had a few inquiries from the press today about the occupants at the lighthouse. Are you currently residing here?"

Lacey's heart began to thump painfully. "Yes, ma'am. I am."

The woman winced. "I'm afraid you're going to have to move out. We had a temporary lease co-signed under the names Monique Bonnay and Callum McDonough. His agent signed off on the rental agreement via fax, and the keys were mailed out to him at his agent's request, which is something we don't normally do. Now you see why. Apparently, Mr. McDonough lent out the keys, which is highly inappropriate. No one else is listed as legal occupants, so you'll have to go."

"He has it for two more weeks," Lacey said. "Please. My son Henry and I have taken wonderful care of the place. We're not hurting anyone."

The woman shook her head. "I'm sorry. You've already had four weeks of staying here illegally, quite frankly. I'll give you until tomorrow by noon to move out. We'll take care of the cleaning. It will come out of Mr. McDonough's and Miss Bonnay's deposits, which we intend to keep because there was a serious breach of trust."

What could Lacey do?

Nothing but roll up the window and drive away. Her hands were slippery on the steering wheel. She and Henry had no place to live. She had eleven hundred dollars saved up from her employment with Mike—Beau's taking care of the food had helped a lot.

But eleven hundred dollars wouldn't last long.

When she got to Walt and Sheena's, she prepared herself to say good-bye to them, too.

Sheena's face was one giant frown. "I hate that this is happening." They were outside the RV. The kids were playing nearby at a picnic table where Lacey had set George's carrier. Dickey and Walt were chatting by the barbecue grill. "This means you're unemployed."

"I know," said Lacey. "I'll find a job." She told her about losing the lighthouse, too.

"Oh, my goodness." Sheena shook her head. "What will you do? Where will you and Henry go?"

"I don't know." Lacey knew her voice was about to crack, but she wouldn't let it. She took in a deep breath. "I just found out. I need to think."

Dickey went to hang out with the kids and George. Walt sauntered up to the women's tête-à-tête. "Not good news at the studio," he said.

"I know." Lacey looked away from him, and waited.

"Maybe you shouldn't have worked there," he said.

Bingo.

"Shut up, Walt," said Sheena. "If you believe in jinxes, then you're mighty foolish."

Lacey looked at her. *Thanks*, she said with her eyes.

But Sheena didn't appear to notice. She was watching the kids and Dickey, her bony little arms crossed over her floral dress.

Lacey wished she could enjoy her mom's taking up for her more, but she had some pretty emotional good-byes to deal with at the doughnut shop, too. "I have ten minutes before I have to leave. I can take Bob and Carol with us in the ambulance. Should Henry and I say good-bye to you before or after we say good-bye to the others?"

"Before," said Walt.

"*After*," said Sheena, at the same time. "We're going to the doughnut shop, too."

Walt glowered. "We need to get on the road. People drive crazy around here at rush hour."

Why was it that Walt always treated getting on the road like a battle he needed to strategize for? Just get on the damned road and drive. Take the bumps as they came. That was Lacey's philosophy, and it was how she'd wound up here at Indigo Beach.

She swallowed. "Henry, it's time to say good-bye for now to Grandma and Grandpa. We're also heading to the doughnut shop to say good-bye to everyone else. That includes George. Remember we were only babysitting him for the trainer?"

"Yes." Henry looked up at her, his mouth sulky. She recognized the look. He was on the verge of big-time tears.

"I'm so sorry, honey. I promise we'll get a cat someday."

"I want George." Henry kicked a tuft of grass. "How will I explain to him that we're not friends anymore?"

"You'll always be friends," Lacey told him. "But he misses his owner, too."

"What about us?" said Bob. "We're leaving for California."

All three kids stared at one another.

"I'll miss you," Carol told Henry.

"Me, too," Henry said.

"You're ugly," Bob said to Henry.

"You smell," Henry said back.

It was supposed to be funny, but neither one of them laughed.

"I want to go back home." Dickey shook his head. "California's about to fall into the sea."

"What?" Carol's stricken little face looked up at him.

"Don't worry." He patted her head. "I've got a rubber raft for us to float in when the big one hits."

"Stop it, Dickey," Lacey said.

She had to face facts: Everything was really, really bad right now. Way worse than it had been when she'd left LA. At least then, she'd had hope—she was moving across country. Opportunities awaited. Now she was at her final destination, and everything was falling apart. She and Henry were losing so much more in a month than what they'd left behind after her six years on the West Coast.

He still had no idea they had to leave the lighthouse, too.

It was too much.

Henry stoically walked to his grandmother and looked at her stomach. "Good-bye, Grandma." His voice came out in a pathetic whisper. And then he wrapped his arms around her middle.

Slowly, Sheena wrapped her arms around his head. Lacey sucked in a breath. *Don't give up too soon.* She saw Beau in her mind's eye, crouched low in the surf, his arms spread like wings, making figure eights in the water while he talked to her about surfing, about life . . .

"Walt, we're not leaving right now," Sheena said, still holding on to Henry.

"What?" Walt was disbelieving—again.

"You call Devra." Sheena looked at Lacey. "We found out this morning she's pregnant. She's feeling just fine, and she's in her fourth month."

"She is?" Lacey put her hand on her heart with the wonder of it . . . little Devra, all grown up and becoming a mother herself. "I'm so happy for her."

"That's a cousin for you," Sheena told Henry.

Lacey almost fainted when her mother said *that*.

Henry looked up at his grandmother, his hands flat on her stomach. "Cool," he said, much less impressed than Lacey by Sheena's pronouncement, and slipped away to go back to George.

Walt pulled out his phone. "What do you want me to tell Devra?"

"To drive on up here with Kevin," Sheena said.

Walt put the phone down. "She's not driving anywhere. Not while she's pregnant."

"What do you mean? We drove all over the place in the RV when I was pregnant with her. She'll be fine. And if she really wants to stay home, we'll let *her* make that decision."

Go, Sheena!

"What's going on?" Lacey asked, feeling a bit fragile, like an egg about to roll off a counter.

"We're going home with Devra in their car. You and Henry are staying here in the RV. We'll take care of the monthly fees until you get on your feet."

"What on God's green earth are you talking about, woman?" Walt said.

"Our daughter needs us."

"That's right, she does."

"You know I mean Lacey."

"She brought this on herself."

"And we're going to help her get out from under it," Sheena said. "You know darned well we would have appreciated some support when we were younger. We're taking six months off and staying in Devra's in-law suite above her garage. She's been wanting us to move in, anyway."

"*No.*"

"Yes."

Walt's nostrils flared.

"You're going to take a break from the road," Sheena said. "You can build up new inventory in Kevin's garage. I can sew. We'll both take walks. You're in terrible shape, and you know it. Sitting your ass in that driver's seat every day isn't helping. You like taking all those pills?"

Walt finally looked a little abashed. "Well—"

"We have two grandchildren to think of now," Sheena said, "and their welfare is important to me."

Walt swiveled his gaze to Henry, who was busy again with his buddies. He didn't have to say good-bye quite yet to his grandfather. "I guess it's not a bad plan."

Lacey folded her hands in front of her to keep them from shaking. "Are you sure?" She looked between Walt and Sheena both.

"Yes," said Sheena. "You don't need to doubt us. We're not changing our minds."

"I can't thank you enough." It came out as a whisper.

"There's no need." Sheena's voice was soft. "This is what family does."

Even so, Lacey's eyes filled with tears. She hugged her mother first, and then Walt. He was a bit stiff, but he didn't outright reject her, which was nothing new. He'd never pushed her away—but he'd never run toward her, either. Maybe someday.

"I'd better go now." She smiled, feeling shy of a sudden. "I'll see you in a few minutes." Then she remembered. "Oh, wait! You're coming, too."

It would take a while to get used to the idea that it appeared her family was behaving in the loving way she'd always thought a family should. She'd never dreamed it would happen for real. She hoped Devra would be receptive to starting up a sister friendship. Maybe talking about babies would help.

"We like these people, too," said Sheena.

"Even Dickey." Walt looked at the old man and snickered.

Everyone liked Dickey way better than they did Walt. He had nothing to snicker about.

"You can come with us in the RV," Sheena said to Dickey. "We can't all fit in that ambulance."

Lacey got the kids strapped in. George meowed in his cage in the back. And she followed the RV to the doughnut shop, the place where her dream to stay in Indigo Beach had first started coming together.

CHAPTER THIRTY-TWO

"Can't make it, Mom," Beau said from his bedroom in Los Angeles almost three months after he'd left Indigo Beach. The Neal Danvers film had gone off without a hitch. His scenes had wrapped the week before. "I have to go to China. There's no way I can miss this trip. I'm going with the director and two co-stars. I'm on a roll."

He really was.

"All right," she said in her cool, contained way. "We'll miss you."

She and Walker were getting married, eloping to the British Virgin Islands, and were hoping Beau could go with them. If he hadn't had the trip to China, he would have invented something else.

Surprisingly, the flap surrounding his involvement with *Flowers from the Heart*, the movie doomed to fail because of Greta-the-jinx's presence, had only increased his cachet. Doing a small, independent film had jolted Hollywood out of its assessment of him as the go-to good-guy hero. A lot of critics predicted his downfall, said he was a fool to take risks.

But he'd learned something doing that film, so when he worked with Neal Danvers, he was a better actor than he'd ever been. Neal, a dynamo of a director, spread the word.

As a result, even before anyone had seen *Flowers from the Heart*, new scripts were coming in—scripts that challenged Beau in ways that both scared him and excited him. They were Oscar-level. And he was being looked at for the lead in all of them but one—the one to be filmed in China, and it was an ensemble cast of A-list actors, many of whom had won or been nominated for Oscars.

Meanwhile, the buzz for Mike's movie was building.

Beau thought he was at the top of his game before, but now he was really breaking out, coming out from behind his comfortable hero persona, slowly but surely.

He wasn't acting anymore to hide from the truth.

He was acting to reveal it.

Huge difference in his whole approach, he'd found out.

Too bad he was unhappier than he'd ever been in his personal life. He punched a number into his phone. "Beau here. Any news?"

"She's still in the RV," the private detective he'd hired said. "And she's still cleaning houses."

"Really?"

"I've seen her look for jobs, but none apparently have panned out. It's a tough economy."

"She sent back the wet suits I got her and Henry."

"I'm not surprised," the detective said. "She pawned their surfboards."

Shit. That really bothered him. But Beau refused to ask the detective anything more personal. He was dying to know if Lacey was dating anyone, but that would be stooping too low. He only wanted to make sure she was financially secure. She'd made no move to stay in touch beyond one drawing Henry had sent a week after Beau had left the beach. He'd written back a postcard. And then all communication stopped.

"I don't know how much bigger we can make the ad," he said.

"If she's ignoring a full-page ad, she doesn't want to move in." The detective's tone was dry. "Some people are too proud. Or they have their own plans."

"It's right on the front beach, too." Beau had bought a twenty-five-room beach house on Indigo with a kitchen on each of the three floors, installed a house mother—his friend Maria, the manager from the Mexican restaurant, who'd been ready to retire—and hoped Lacey would find her way there with Henry. "I told them to keep an apartment open for her, but I can't do that much longer."

"I don't know what to tell ya. The lady's independent."

"Get your secretary to take out another ad, please. This time say a local surfing instructor will give free boards, wet suits, and surfing lessons to the kids who live there every week, every season of the year. They'll need to pass a swim test first in the pool in the backyard. I'll hire a swim instructor, too."

"Fine."

"I should have thought of this stuff already." Beau felt slightly abashed. He was glad to have some connection still to the little paradise that was Indigo Beach. "I want to keep this place going, whether Lacey shows up or not."

He hoped she would. Every day, it was the first thing he thought of when he woke up. Every day at eight AM he called Maria and asked, "Did she come?"

The answer was always no.

"See you next week," Lacey told the beach house owner at 212 Heron, who happened to be Biddy Cromwell.

Biddy was a bitch, no doubt about it. But after interviewing to work for other cleaning services, Lacey was determined to get her own company going, so she'd dropped off exactly one flyer at Finer Things. She'd counted on

Biddy hiring her. She knew she'd be too intrigued not to, and with an anchor client like Biddy, maybe Lacey would have an opportunity to stand out.

The strategy worked beautifully. Biddy's friends hired her, too. They couldn't resist.

It wasn't as if Lacey couldn't take any of Biddy's rudeness. When you'd already lost the man you loved, little minds and hearts like Biddy's had a tendency to matter not a whit.

"Did you dust the tops of the kitchen cabinets?" Biddy asked her.

There was always something Biddy tacked on at the end, something crazy that she'd spent a long time thinking about. But she'd just asked Lacey to clean Finer Things twice a week, so that was extra money in her pocket right there.

"No, I didn't. I'll get that right now." Lacey knew her cool unflappability drove Biddy bananas. She always tacked on an extra hour to the visits she paid the woman's house, so she wasn't worried about being late to her next job.

"I'm not paying you extra to stay past your three hours, either," Biddy said. "You could have gone faster."

Lacey didn't say a word, just pulled a chair over to the counter and pulled out a dust rag. Since she'd already been charging Biddy and Friends double what other housecleaning services were charging, and they'd all jumped at the chance to hire her, she was at peace with staying a little longer.

"You're already way too expensive," Biddy remarked, as she always did at least once per visit.

"But worth every penny," Lacey said back, looking her right in the eye. "I'm thinking about raising my rates, as a matter of fact."

"You can't do that! You just started."

"I might." Lacey took a swipe across the cabinet top.

"How many people can say their house is cleaned by a genuine cult film icon who was not only on TMZ for bad behavior but danced with Beau Wilder at a Charleston society ball?"

Biddy glowered and left the room.

Lacey chuckled.

That afternoon, after she'd run a few errands and picked up Henry at his after-school program, she opened a package that had come to their P.O. box. Callum's agent had tracked Lacey down, said that she'd received a number of things left at the lighthouse, which the cleaners had handed over to the property manager, who'd forwarded the items to the agency office in LA. It had taken forever for the box to reach Lacey, and she had no idea what could be in it. She'd been her usual thorough self packing out, but you never knew what little boys could leave behind.

Inside was a DVD of *The Waltons*, that old TV show. Attached was a Post-it note with the property manager's logo on top: *found in blue bedroom*, which was Beau's. That was odd. Maybe a previous tenant had left it and it had fallen behind the bureau or under the bed.

And then there was a pack of Batman playing cards—definitely Henry's—and an old painted wooden box with a seal balancing a rubber ball on its nose. Both had Post-its that read, *kids' room*.

Well, the wooden box had originally been in the trunk in Beau's bedroom. But Henry had fallen in love with it and kept it in his room, filling it with shells. Sure enough, when Lacey unlatched the lid and opened it, the shells were still inside. She looked at the bottom: TIMOTHY BRENNER was carved with a penknife into the surface.

She smiled to herself.

Two little boys had loved this box.

The cleaners hadn't recognized it since it had been in

the trunk for so many years. They'd assumed it was the tenant's.

Lacey decided then and there to give it back. It belonged in the trunk in the blue bedroom.

"The lighthouse is locked up right now," the property manager told her when she called. "And I'm in downtown Charleston. I'd really rather not have the box back. You could stay right there on the island and give it to the Brenners' niece. She'll return it to the trunk at her leisure. She has a key."

Lacey and Henry were both excited to finally be doing something to find out more about Timothy Brenner.

"I wish Mr. Wilder were going with us," Henry said as they drove the ambulance down Heron Street. "He's Dudley. He'd want to know more about Timothy."

A shaft of pain struck Lacey's heart. "You can always write to him and tell him what we find out."

"That's a good idea."

She was glad that Henry stayed so busy at his new school and with new friends that he seemed to have recovered from losing the many good friends he'd made when they'd first arrived at Indigo Beach. There were still nights when something reminded him—a surfer on TV, an orange cat in a commercial, or a reference to Iron Man, his and Bob's favorite superhero—and he'd lie in bed and cry, missing Mike's family and George, but most of all Beau.

They got through those episodes together, and Lacey was relieved to note that they were becoming fewer and farther between.

"That's so kind of you to return it," the older woman named Nancy Brenner said twenty minutes later. They were sitting on her sofa. She lived in a beautiful old clapboard house.

She fingered the surface of the box. "I remember seeing this in the trunk."

"I'm sorry we removed it," Lacey said. "We never intended it to leave the house. The cleaners got confused when they saw it in Henry's room and assumed we owned it."

"A natural mistake." The woman smiled kindly down at Henry. "Would you like to keep this box?"

"Yes, *ma'am*," Henry said in a rush.

She handed it to him. "I'm sure Timothy would want you to have it."

"Thank you very much." Henry ran his fingertip over the top. "I love this seal. That ball will never leave his nose."

Nancy laughed. "You're right."

Lacey was so pleased for her boy. "You're very kind," she told Nancy. "Did you know Timothy?"

Nancy shook her head. "I wasn't even born when he was there. But I knew of him."

"We've been so curious to learn more," Lacey said.

"We found his handprint in the cement outside," said Henry, his voice taut with excitement. "My hand fit right in it."

"And we've seen pictures and drawings." Lacey smiled down at Henry, who was looking up at her with that clear, trusting gaze that always reminded her how lucky she was to be his mother. "Timothy seemed like such a nice little boy. Like Henry, as a matter of fact."

He grinned. "We both like playing catch."

Which reminded Lacey of Beau again. She needed to get Henry on a T-ball team.

Nancy laughed and stood up. "Here." She walked to a bookshelf and removed an album. "Let me share some more pictures with you."

She sat between them and slowly turned pages. The family history at the lighthouse sprang to life. "Here"—

she pointed at a young couple—"are my aunt and uncle, who were Timothy's foster parents."

"*Foster* parents?" Lacey was intrigued. "But he had the name Brenner."

"They'd had him since he was an infant, and it was an informal agreement between Aunt Ida and Uncle Tom and Timothy's parents that they'd raise him with their own last name until his parents could afford to come back and get him. That was almost six years. I know it broke Aunt Ida's heart when his parents returned. She used to confide in my mother that she hoped they never would. But they were good friends of Uncle Tom's. So what could she do?"

Lacey sighed. "I can't even imagine how hard that must have been for them to give him up." She couldn't imagine ever having to do that with Henry. "It must be why everything's been kept in the trunk all these years."

"Yes," said Nancy, "memories. She wanted to keep them. But they were hard to see on a day-to-day basis."

"That won't happen to me, will it, Mom?" Henry said, peeking around Nancy's lap to Lacey.

"No, honey! Absolutely not." She bent far enough forward to extend her hand to him without crossing the album on Nancy's lap. Henry grabbed her fingers. "You're stuck with me forever."

He grinned. "Good."

Nancy's eyes went a little bright at that. So did Lacey's, she was sure. They exchanged a silent look of understanding.

"I hope you two come back and visit me again," Nancy said down to Henry. "I like being able to talk about my family with people who are interested."

Henry bounced in his seat. "I want to come back *soon*."

"We'd love to," Lacey said with a grateful smile.

"Good." Nancy beamed. "When we're done looking at this, I've got some homemade cookies to share with you."

"Yum!" said Henry.

Lacey felt as if they'd made a new friend.

The album was filled with pictures of Timothy and his foster parents playing on the sand, sharing picnics, and laughing.

"All those years after he left, he never came back," Nancy said. "He'd sign his name on his parents' Christmas card, but Aunt Ida got the impression the family wanted to keep contact at a minimum. And after a while, those childhood memories faded for the boy, as they naturally would. But see?" She turned to the last page. "Here's Timothy grown up."

There was a picture of an adult man holding the raised arms of a little girl standing in front of him.

Lacey's entire body went numb with shock.

"He came back with his own little girl." Nancy's face softened. "He told Aunt Ida and Uncle Tom he'd never forgotten them. And he wanted his daughter to see where he'd been so happy. He intended to take her back to the lighthouse every year. Sadly, he died only a month after this picture was taken. An ordnance explosion at his military base. He was buried with full honors, and his grave is at Arlington: Staff Sergeant Timothy John Clark."

Lacey burst into tears.

"My goodness!" Nancy said, and laid a hand on Lacey's arm. "Are you all right?"

Lacey couldn't speak.

"I know it's sad," Nancy went on, "but it's happy, too. Aunt Ida and Uncle Tom knew Timothy loved them, after all. They died within a few years, themselves."

"Mom!" Henry raced to her side. "*Mom!*"

But Lacey was inconsolable. "I'm okay," she said. And went right back to crying.

Nancy stood again. "Tea," she said firmly. "Tea will do the trick."

Lacey remembered that day on the sand. Very vaguely. She'd only been three. But she remembered the waves. The waves and her father's arms. Sheena had made that tiny frock with the giant appliquéd butterfly on the front. Lacey used to dress Devra in it. Every time she did, she'd tell herself that her mother had to love her if she'd made a dress as beautiful as that.

"Mom?" Henry's eyes were huge.

She hugged him close. "I'm fine," she said. "*We're* fine."

Nancy returned but with sherry, not tea. "You must explain," she said. "But drink this first."

Lacey dutifully drained the tiny crystal glass. Henry held tight to her hand. She sniffed, smiled at him, and sat up. "I'm the little girl in that picture," she said in a shaky voice. "And Timothy"—the man she knew only as Jack Clark because that was how Sheena referred to him when she'd shown Lacey his army induction photo—"Timothy was my father."

CHAPTER THIRTY-THREE

Three and a half months after he'd left Indigo Beach, Beau got a call from Susan while he was at Pete's Chop Suey House on a date with a beautiful, smart, sexy woman his age who happened to be a well-known actress, too.

"Take the call," she said with a saucy grin. She'd only just gotten off the phone herself with her mother first, and then her dog-sitter in New York.

He sent her a lazy smile, put down his chopsticks, and said hello to Susan. "What's up?"

"The premiere for *Flowers from the Heart*. You still haven't answered the invite, and your publicist is being deluged with questions, Mike Carter is calling me, and I'd like to know if you're going."

"I don't want to."

"That's obvious."

"But I will. Since Mike called."

"Did you think he wouldn't? You might not have been the leading man, but your role was substantial. Directors like their actors to show up. Of course, if I need to invent an emergency for you, I will."

"No." He looked at the actress eating her noodles. She had a very kissable mouth. He could have her in bed tonight if he wanted. They'd actually be a pretty awesome couple.

"Are you showing up solo or with a date?" Susan wanted to know. So would the publicist.

He should bring someone. Show Lacey they were completely over, once and for all. But something in him caused him to utter, "The former."

He didn't want to say *solo* or *alone* out loud. The actress would want to know what the conversation had been about. She might feel dissed that he didn't ask her to the premiere. Not that she had a right to be. This was only a first date, and she'd asked *him*.

But egos were big in Hollywood.

"Got it," said Susan. "I can tell you're with someone."

"Uh-huh."

"Okay-bye," she said fast.

Susan had already been probing the past month to find out more about what was going on with him. She'd said she sensed a difference in him—a subdued quality—that appeared separate from the professional evolution he was making. But he hadn't shared with anyone, not even his basketball and gym buddies, all of whom had noticed how much he'd slowed down the few times he'd made it out to LA on his breaks from the movie in Canada with Danvers.

"You're a great person," he told the actress an hour later at her door, and kissed her on the cheek.

"I get it," she said sadly.

"I'm sorry," he said. "It's definitely not you. You're awesome. I'm just not in a dating frame of mind right now."

"And why should you be?" she said brightly. "You're Beau Wilder." She grabbed his hand. "We can be friends with benefits. I swear, no strings attached. That's actually better for me now, too."

Friends with benefits.

There was only one person he could do that with, and

hell, who was he kidding? With Lacey, he'd have to call it *best friends and soul mates with benefits*. Anything less wouldn't work for him. Any woman besides Lacey wouldn't work, either.

He was stuck, dammit.

In love.

He squeezed the actress's hand and let go. "Can't do it," he said, "but I'm incredibly flattered."

He got out of there quick.

There was a limo waiting outside his gated house. The driver hopped out and opened a rear door. Out stepped Walker, his mother's new husband.

Beau's heart lurched. Was Mom okay? He rolled down his window.

"She's fine," Walker barked in his elegant Virginia drawl, reading his mind. "I'm gonna ride in with you."

The man was obviously used to getting his way.

"What's this about?" Beau asked as soon as Walker settled into the low leather seat of his Porsche Spyder.

"Hello to you, too." Walker's tone was practical. Not cold. Not warm, either.

"I suppose it's nice to see you," Beau said, "although this doesn't feel like your typical friendly surprise visit."

"You get enough friendly surprise visits to know what a typical one is? And how do they happen when you got a damned gate in front of your home?"

The man didn't back down. "Okay, you got me. I don't get *any* friendly surprise visits."

"Sounds like you want some. Must get pretty lonely out here."

Beau pulled the car into a cavernous garage that held two other what he called *fine automobiles*. That's what his father used to say on the front porch—"*That's a fine automobile!*"— when an exceptional design cruised by the Battery house.

"I suppose it does get a little quiet," Beau said, opening a door for his unexpected guest. "I stay busy. But I'd love to see Mom out here—"

"Oh, we both know that would be the visit from hell." Walker waved his hand at him as he trudged past him in his beige linen jacket, crisp white shirt, and red silk bow tie. "At least the way things stand now. Let's get a drink, shall we? And maybe a couple of steaks."

Two hours later, Beau was done cooking, done eating, and he had a little bit of a buzz. If Walker did, he didn't show it.

"Let me explain why I'm here," Walker said.

In the South, you always fed and watered someone first before business was discussed.

"Go ahead." Beau felt the old wall come up.

"You know how many royals have married through the ages for political reasons?"

"Yes, sir."

"That's how it is with a lot of Southern couples from old families. I'm not saying it's right, or smart. But your mother and father ran in the same high-society circles, and to keep their power and prestige—and to honor their heritage— that crowd tends to marry one another, even now."

"I know that. Which is one reason I left."

"I don't blame you. Your parents tried very hard to make their marriage work. In the end, they truly did love each other, as friends. *Good* friends. But your father couldn't resist the siren call of love. He used to say that Tula was only 'his woman on the side,' but everyone who knew about their relationship knew it was a love match. Neither he nor your mother wanted to hurt you. They wished you'd never found out. But as much as what happened hurt your mother, she understood, you see, because she loved *me*."

Well, hell.

Beau poured himself another drink. "This isn't making me feel any better about either of my parents."

"Let me finish before you pass judgment," Walker said. "I had the social pedigree your grandparents expected your mother's suitors to have, but I wasn't wealthy. Your grandparents said they'd cut Julia off if she married me—"

"Sweet old Nana and Pops? Damn."

"People live within their own culture until someone comes along and shows them something else. They thought they were doing the right thing, standing for tradition and family."

"This is all way too old-fashioned and ignorant for me."

"I'm not saying it's not." Walker's tone was dry. "There's a new freedom that the generations before you never had. The point is, I was a product of the culture, too. It would have been dishonorable for me to go against your grandparents' wishes. So I purposely stayed away to give your mother no choice but to forget me."

"I'm still not impressed," said Beau. "They should have divorced and married the people they loved, not continued such a farce." He shook his head once. "I hate to say this aloud. But my parents were shallow. They had no gumption. I don't respect them, and I'm ashamed of them."

"Now, you hold on." Walker pointed at him, his voice steely. "They didn't want you to come from a broken home. They made their sacrifices for *you*."

Beau gave a hollow laugh. "So I'm to blame? I kept them from their true loves? Although, wait—Dad saw his every weekend."

He knew he was acting like an angry, sarcastic teenager, but he didn't care.

"No." Walker stared him down. "You're not to blame for anything. Not *one* thing."

Beau's throat tightened hearing that. He thought about

how nice he'd been to Tula and Ricky, how he'd looked forward to seeing them, how he'd almost wanted them as his real family. And then how he'd go home and rave about his weekend adventures with his father to his mother at the supper table. "Sure, I'm to blame. For at least some of it."

"No, you are *not*." Walker's rebuke was sharp. "Being a man is letting go of those illogical feelings we had as children. Own 'em, and let them go. Otherwise, you'll use them as an excuse your whole life to justify your own bad choices. Your parents' flaws and regrets are theirs. They've already lived them. Live *your* life."

"It's not fair to Mom that she bore Dad's unfaithfulness alone. And I never told him—"

"She's strong as an ox, and she's sorted through it. Who are you to tell me or her that she can't handle her own life? And your father didn't need to hear that you loved him and forgave him before he died. He already knew you loved him. And about not getting forgiveness? Your father understood why you didn't. He wasn't stupid. And it wasn't even on his radar. His role was to love *you*. And he did with his whole being. I know he did. We talked about it often."

Beau stared straight ahead at the wall where his multiple awards were framed next to photos of him at charity golf tournaments, premieres, biking and running in triathlons. No family pictures. Nothing but professional stuff.

"I know it doesn't seem right to you," Walker said, "but when your parents were with you, they felt the power of being a family. Don't you see? They needed you as much as you needed them. You made them better people than they were without you. They both believed that. Maybe they were weak, shallow, prideful, arrogant, in their way. But they loved you, son. So you can either let your mother die not feeling connected to the one miracle that came from her union with your father. Or you can allow her to celebrate the single facet of their relationship that was shining and whole. *You*."

Beau stood and turned away, trying hard to compose himself. But he couldn't. He couldn't speak.

Walker said nothing, either. Beau heard him get up, put his glass in the bar sink. "I've given you a lot to think about."

Beau inhaled a sharp breath and turned around. "Thank you for coming."

It was almost midnight.

"I'm going back," Walker said.

"Tonight?"

"Did you see me with any luggage?" His mother's new husband grinned.

Beau's mouth inched up. "No. You old bastard."

"I have a private plane waiting. Just like you celebrities do." Walker pulled out his phone and spoke to his limo driver. Beau had no idea the driver had never left.

"You're a helluva guy, I must say." Beau walked him to the front door. "I can see why Mom fell for you."

Walker shrugged. "I've got a certain charm. It's finally made me rich, in more ways than one." He stuck out his hand, and Beau shook it hard.

Then as if by mutual agreement, they wound up in a strong embrace.

"You're a good kid," Walker said.

"Thanks. I really appreciate your talking to me."

"Show it by going home to see your mother."

"Does she know you're here?"

"Yes. She was worried about it. But I told her that sometimes it helps to get someone else involved. And she wants to be close to you, son. She was willing to do anything but come out here herself. She was afraid you might see her at the door and shut it in her face."

"I'd never do that." Beau felt horrible that she'd even imagined he would.

"I know. But no mother wants to be estranged from her child. Your mother would rather live in limbo forever than risk losing you. I reminded her that there was a third alternative: y'all connecting again."

Beau told him about the premiere.

"We got the invitation. She was hoping you'd come home for it." Walker stepped over the threshold and onto the front porch. One of Beau's security guys was waiting to escort him to the street. "Don't tell Julia I told you, but she already bought her dress."

Aw, Mom. That touched Beau's heart. He had to admit it. The split-second look he shared with Walker confirmed their mutual love for a woman who'd been alone for too long.

"What took you so long to come back?" Beau asked him. "It's been almost ten years since Dad died."

"Oh, I've been courting her," Walker said with a chuckle. "I was always there, waiting for her to decide she was ready, giving her little hints that she deserves happiness. But we all have to decide for ourselves, don't we?"

"When did she decide she was ready?"

"When she stopped beating herself up about you."

"When did that happen?"

"Just recently. When you came home for this movie, and she heard about you kissing a woman on Fort Sumter. Lawd, boy, the whole town heard how you took her out there on a boat and served her dinner. Your mother finally realized you must be in love. And that meant she hadn't damaged you as much as she thought she had."

But Beau was a grown man. It was his responsibility to get past childhood issues, not his mother's. "She never should have beaten herself up. It's my fault she's been doing that. You're right. I've been an ass. I wish I could take it all back."

"She's your mother. And stop blaming yourself for the natural feelings you had. All you needed was some perspective. No one was stepping up to the plate to give it. You're a big movie star. It's kind of intimidating."

"Thanks, Walker, for being that guy."

"My pleasure, son. So is it true? Are you in love?"

"Yes," he said, his whole world stopping and restarting in that moment.

Walker finally got a twinkle in his eye. "That's good."

And it was.

Walker turned toward the security guard waiting ahead on the sidewalk. "Follow you?" His back was slightly bowed. His neck above his jacket was frail, his silver hair thinning on top.

Dammit, he was an old man, and he'd come all the way out to California to talk some sense into Beau's head, and now he was turning right back around.

Beau felt a huge surge of affection for the guy. "Wait up." He dismissed his employee and accompanied Walker to the limo himself. All he did was open the door for him. But he wanted it to be so much more. He had a lot of catching up to do with his mom. With his life back home. And now with Walker.

"It's not too late," Walker said, reading his mind again.

He winked, and the limo took off.

CHAPTER THIRTY-FOUR

Nancy Brenner gave Lacey a job. "We're practically family," she said. "And I need someone to run my new design showroom. I'll train you."

Lacey had made gains in her housekeeping business, but now she was salaried. Now she didn't have to kowtow to Biddy and her friends. Now she got to play with wonderful accessories and furniture and fabrics. She had so much to learn. But she loved it. Every time a customer came in, she was able to wrap them up in a story about how that couch could possibly work for them, or what that lamp suggested about life, love, and happiness in its own humble way.

And none of it was bogus sales talk. Nancy told her friends that where Lacey went, an aura of possibility followed—stories of what could be for that customer, or what already was that should be celebrated or had heretofore been underappreciated or forgotten.

She and Henry were still in the RV. Sheena and Walt were happily puttering about at Devra's waiting for the baby to be born. But in a few more months, after they'd helped Devra through her first month with the baby, they were coming back to get the RV and head out on the road again.

Lacey's friend Patrick was coming next week to take

back the trusty ambulance. Nancy said she'd loan them her spare car until Lacey had enough money to buy an old used one, which would be within a couple of months, she hoped.

"Mom," Henry said now, "when are you going to finish that cool story?"

"Soon."

"I hope so."

They'd recently seen two almost identical white vans in the grocery store parking lot. So that night, she'd told Henry a story about a mom and a son in a white van who were stopped at a red light. And on the other side of the intersection was a van that looked just the same. No big deal, until the light turned green and they passed each other. That's when the mom and the boy saw *themselves* in the other van. It was like a mirror image, except the boy in that van was holding up a sign that said, HELP ME!

"How could they be in two vans at once?" Henry had asked excitedly that night.

"I don't know. They didn't know, either. So they turned the van around to find out. But the other van sped off!"

Henry was avid to hear more. But for some reason, Lacey couldn't spin the story right off the top of her head. It was too complicated and exciting. Something big was there, bigger than her usual stories. She started writing down ideas, possible scenarios to explain the weirdness of that scene. And it became so thrilling, she kept a notebook with her.

Another scene came to her, and another. The next thing she knew, she was writing a book called *Two White Vans*. It was the only title she could think of at the moment. But she was excited even by that. She made up a Photoshop stock cover and glued it onto the front of a spiral notebook.

She bought a fancy purple pen and gave herself a pen name, too: Brenner Clark.

She felt almost as if she were having a secret affair. But it was with *herself.*

"Mom, hurry up and finish that book!" Henry said every night. He refused to listen to any other stories she made up until she was done. He took to reading library books. They went there a lot. It reminded her so much of how she'd read all the time as a kid.

She'd loved reading.

She'd always loved stories.

She wished she could tell someone besides Henry . . . an adult. She wanted to know if she was maybe a little crazy to be carrying around that notebook. But she was afraid to tell Nancy. What if Nancy thought it was silly? Here Lacey was her new store manager! She was supposed to be thinking about inventory and turnover.

One night, she could hold it in no longer.

She called Sheena. Their relationship had shifted even more in a positive direction since Sheena had learned that the handprint of Timothy Brenner in the concrete had belonged to her own first love, Lacey's father.

"This might be a little crazy," Lacey said, "but I like telling stories."

"I know," said Sheena. "You always have. From the time you were little."

"I did?"

"You made them up and sat and told yourself, and then Devra."

"Wow."

"It's because of you that I'm Sheena."

"It *is*?"

"Yes. You loved this little comic book I'd picked up about a jungle girl named Sheena. I had to read it to you every day. And one day you called me that. You were no more than two. Your father and I thought it was cute when you kept doing it. So I let you continue. It made me feel special. Like I was an exotic mother with superpowers."

"It did?" Lacey got tears in her eyes. "Why didn't you ever tell me?"

"I was embarrassed." Sheena still wasn't a big talker, especially when it came to emotional topics.

"Oh, my," said Lacey. So maybe she wasn't, either.

A beat of silence went by.

"So I'm writing a book," she decided to share. "A book for kids in middle school, but I'm telling the story to Henry, meanwhile."

"I'm not surprised," Sheena replied. "You came to this naturally. Appalachian folk are storytellers. I tell my own, you know."

"You do?"

"Every quilt."

Lacey's heart lurched. "Of course, that's true." How could she have missed so much about her own mother? What stories had she dreamed as she'd sewn those quilts so lovingly by hand?

From that day on, Lacey felt a rightness about what she was doing. She still loved her design showroom job. But her true passion—apart from being Henry's mom—was getting her stories out. When she finished the one about the two white vans and the people inside them, she had a list of ten others she wanted to write, too.

So a few days later, when she and Henry received their invitation to the premiere of *Flowers from the Heart*, to be followed by a reception at the Indigo Beach fishing pier, she was busy and happy—

And then she wasn't.

Like that.

It pissed her off.

Beneath everything—as much as it was wrong to be dissatisfied when she had a happy, healthy child and her new passion for writing—she was profoundly sad.

Beau was gone. Beau was the guy she'd love to talk to about stories. She'd made up a few for him to get him through that script. He'd get it. He'd been Dudley, after all, so he'd understand more than most that she longed to create stories for children. One of the first reasons she'd been attracted to him was because he was Dudley. That should have clued her in.

And now he was coming back.

She was terrified to see him. What if he was over her completely? She was afraid she'd break down and weep when she saw him.

Maybe she shouldn't go.

She laid her head down on the galley table in the RV—it was where she wrote when Henry was asleep—and closed her eyes.

She had to go.

So did Henry.

They had to support Mike, see their friends . . .

She had to face Beau.

CHAPTER THIRTY-FIVE

The fun park was relatively quiet again. Beau purposely chose this time to visit. Rick—as he forced himself to think of his childhood frenemy now—was lying sideways on the putt-putt course, repairing something in the mouth of a huge plastic shark with its jaws wide open.

"Hey," Beau said quietly from behind him.

Rick jerked up and back, twisted himself around, a wrench still in his hand. "You're back?" He looked a lot like Dad: same strong jaw that Beau had. Same straight nose and wide mouth. But there was Tula in there, too, around the eyes. She'd always been funny. He had her laugh lines.

Beau shoved his hands in his jeans. "Yeah. I was a jerk last time I saw you. I wanted to apologize."

Rick shoved himself up from the ground with an audible groan. He probably weighed thirty more pounds than Beau, and a lot of it seemed to be muscle. When he stood, Beau remembered what a formidable opponent he'd been in the parking lot they'd fought in that long-ago day.

Brothers, whispered through his brain. And this time he didn't shove the thought away.

"I understand," Rick said simply. He stood there, the wrench dangling from his hand.

Beau was massively uncomfortable. But he couldn't go—yet. "Hey, that day you followed me down Broad Street and I threw a punch before you could get a word out, why did you come anyway? Was it to fight? Or something else?"

Rick shrugged. "I was mad at you for ignoring me all those years. We'd been such good friends. So part of me wanted to taunt you. If that led to fighting, so be it. But there was the other side, too. I hoped that maybe we'd pick up where we left off and be friends again. As if none of that other stuff ever happened."

Beau nodded. "We *were* good friends." He felt his mouth tighten to keep in the emotion. "When I found out what was happening with my dad and your mom—and then to find out you were—"

He couldn't get the words out.

"I know," Rick said in a raspy-hoarse voice. "I felt terrible for hiding it. I wanted you to know. Hell, I wanted to go home with you guys every time you came over. You'd go off in that pickup truck, and I'd go back inside the cabin with Mom." He swallowed hard.

Beau shook his head. "It was tough for both of us."

"Yeah." Rick looked at him a second, then down at the ground.

Beau shifted his stance. "Maybe we can talk again sometime."

Rick nodded slowly. "I'd like that."

"I'd like to hear how your mom is doing. I'll never forget those ranger cookies."

Rick laughed. "Oh, yeah. Those cookies bulked me up pretty good during wrestling season."

"It was surreal coming here and seeing you."

Rick rubbed his forearm across his chin. "Yep. I always liked this place."

"I'm glad it's still going strong."

Rick looked around. "Thanks to your dad. He loved taking us here."

"That he did."

"I'm real grateful to him," Rick said softly.

"Well, he was your dad, too." Once the words were out, it didn't sound so bad. "Don't feel guilty about anything. Truth is, you got rooked."

"So did you."

Their eyes finally met and held.

"Well, all right," said Beau. "Dad would be happy to know we're talking."

"He sure would." Rick held out his hand.

Beau clasped it.

"Good to see you, man." Rick's gaze was serious, sincere.

"You, too." Beau couldn't even describe the emotions he felt knocking around inside him. It was one of those moments in life where something old was healed and something new had begun. It was raw. Uncomfortable. But he didn't want to be anywhere else at that moment. It was plain right. "I'll come again soon."

"Gonna bring that little boy?" Rick asked, then squinted off at the sun lowering in the sky.

Yep, it was one of those questions that was loaded.

"I'd like to," Beau said. "We'll see."

"Uh-huh." Rick grinned. "I'll be looking for y'all."

"One more thing." Beau felt kind of embarrassed telling him. "I've got a movie premiere happening tonight at the American Theater." Maybe Rick had never seen one of his other movies. What if he saw *Flowers from the Heart* and thought all his work was hypersensitive and quote-unquote, important? "You're welcome to come. Bring company. The party afterward is on the Indigo Beach pier."

"Sounds interesting," said Rick as his phone started ringing. "Maybe I'll see you there."

"All right."

Rick raised a hand in farewell and started talking into his receiver.

Who was it? His wife? Did he have kids? Beau wanted to know.

He walked out of the park, past the batting cages, and through the concession area and the maze of pinball machines. He remembered one time he'd smoked his father in the batting cage. He'd been about nine or ten. No doubt Dad had faked being such a lame hitter.

The edge of Beau's mouth turned up. He and Ricky had been rooked, yes. But they'd also been lucky to have Dad at all. A lightning flash of love struck deep into his heart, cauterizing the wound there that had lingered raw and angry for too long. His childhood was what it was, and it was his. Beau wouldn't trade anymore. He wanted his memories. And he loved his father.

Miss you, Dad, he allowed himself to think for the first time since his father died. And when he crossed the bridge onto Indigo and saw the wide expanse of sea, he could swear the world had become bigger and brighter.

CHAPTER THIRTY-SIX

Lacey would make it through the premiere night. She'd see Beau and be happy for him, happy for all the cast and crew. Then she'd go home and continue the life she'd begun with Henry on Indigo Beach.

That was her plan. All she had to do was look at Henry and know it was the right one. He loved it here. He loved his new friends. Indigo Beach, Lacey knew with certainty, was good for him.

Tonight he was dressed like a little man in a cute tuxedo. He looked so dapper in it, the retailer asked him to model in their next fashion show and rented it to them half price.

Lacey was wearing a great dress she found at T.J. Maxx: a lavender halter-style in shot silk, simple and chic, with neutral platform pumps. She wore her makeup these days the more natural way Simone had taught her, and since she was back in the South she'd curled her hair to give it a little extra bounce down her back.

But she forgot everything—all her worries and excitement about the people she'd see at the premiere, even Beau—when she saw the actual movie.

She was blown away. Mike's vision had really paid off.

Adam and Simone were excellent. The story was well paced and thought provoking. But Beau stole the show. He was spectacular as Evan. She totally forgot the man she'd made love to as she watched sensitive, foolish Evan, who didn't get the girl. In fact, she bought in to Evan so hard, she cried when he died.

It wasn't until the lights went up in the theater that she remembered that Evan was still alive. It was hard to believe he was Beau, who'd been so hot walking down the red carpet outside the theater on King Street in Charleston that girls everywhere shrieked his name and waved posters that said, WE <3 BEAU.

He'd lost himself completely in the role.

She had to congratulate him. There was no room for awkwardness about their personal life. She was in love with the man, but tonight she was a fan of the star. He deserved kudos, and she wanted to provide them.

She'd grabbed Henry, Bob, and Carol from the theater babysitter and told Simone and Dickey they'd meet up at the party in front of the cat display, where George would be hanging out with his other cat friends from the movie.

It was nighttime, and the pier looked beautiful dressed up in festive lanterns. A band played classic beach music on a small stage. In the distance, the lighthouse stood tall and proud, the outside railing lit and a spotlight shining up its side. Memories flooded back, all good ones. The happiest days of her life had been spent there, with her, Beau, and Henry sitting at the table with those funny shellfish place mats, eating breakfast, running outside to the breaking surf, watching movies in the living room.

"Lacey!" crowed Biddy from nearby with three of her friends, two of whom had been clients of Lacey's as well. "Fancy seeing you here!"

For a second Lacey's spirits faltered, and she turned to

the three kids. "See there?" She pointed to a nearby table full of sweet and savory snacks. "Grab a plate and put four things on it. One of them has to be a vegetable. I'll be there in a jiffy. No elbowing anyone out of the way, either. Promise?"

"Promise!" the three of them said together, and ran directly there.

She turned back to Biddy. "Why wouldn't I be here?" she asked lightly.

"You know, being that jinx and all." Biddy gave her the eye. It was supposed to be funny—Southern girl funny—which is why her friends tittered with her.

Lacey remembered all the times her quiet mother let women at the craft fairs walk over her, and she decided, once and for all, to let Greta Gildensturm wake up from her long slumber once and for all.

Why had she ever let her sleep?

She held her head high, her neck straight, and threw back her shoulders. "I wonder why you're so jealous of a jinx," she told Biddy. "Since day one, you've not liked me. It makes me think I got something you want. What is it, you think?"

She looked at all the women in turn, skewering them with an unrepentant stare.

"She was only teasing," one of her other housecleaning clients said, her cheeks red.

"What would she have cause to be jealous about?" muttered a third. "You used to wash her toilets."

"And if it weren't for you taking advantage of poor naive Nancy Brenner, you still would be," said Biddy.

Lacey arched a brow. "Nancy's not naive." In fact, Nancy had told Lacey that Biddy was slicker than chicken guts on a doorknob, so Nancy always made her pay ninety percent of her custom order purchases up front rather than the usual fifty percent. "But I'll be happy to tell her you think she is."

"Now, don't go doing that." Biddy made a face. "She's got my sofa to re-cover."

"And my two lamps on order," said a cohort.

"I think I know what it is." Lacey put her hands on her hips and gazed boldly at her island nemesis. "At first, I thought you were annoyed that I'm happy despite not being married or rich like you. Then I thought you might be jealous because I've had adventures that most women stuck in a rut can only dream about. But now I think I know. Every jab you take at me only confirms what I suspected—you kinda dig me, Biddy."

"I do *not*." Biddy's face turned pale.

Lacey moved closer. Biddy and her crew took a step back. "Are you sure you don't have a girl crush on me right now? I don't mean lesbian—although I won't rule that out; you wouldn't be the first—but I think you must be dying to go to lunch with me. Be my BFF."

She kept a straight face.

"You're out of your *mind*." Biddy sounded a little out of breath.

"See?" Lacey chuckled. "It's really kind of cute how my low-class ways send you into a tizzy. And guess what, you're in luck. I'm going to have a little Greta Gildensturm in me forever, whether I'm married, rich, poor, or single. She's along for the ride, no matter what, and since I call Indigo Beach home now, I guess you'll just have to get used to that fact." She opened her purse, pulled out her new business card from the furniture store, and tucked it in Biddy's plunging neckline. "Call me. I'm not sure I'll go to lunch yet. You'll have to pay, of course, and I expect champagne. But you've intrigued me enough that I'll consider being your friend, Biddy."

And she walked away without looking back. She could feel their shock. She'd stunned them with her Greta blast, and it felt good . . .

The kids, their mouths full of cookies and their mini carrots uneaten on their paper plates, were dying to get to the cats. And they'd been so patient. So she steadfastly ignored all stares her way—maybe she was channeling Greta better than she thought—and found the kitties in a portable adoption trailer, lounging in cages in fleece-lined beds and separated from the public by a glass window. The side of the trailer was open, and the trainer was there, keeping an eye on activity around the feline stars.

"George!" the kids all yelled together.

He looked imperiously down at them from his perch, his tail whipping slowly around his body.

"Can we see him up close?" Henry asked the trainer. "Please? I miss him!"

"Sure." The trainer grinned. "You took such good care of him during the movie." He took them into the trailer, and Lacey couldn't help being excited, too. She missed George and what he reminded her of—their special time at the lighthouse.

The trainer got him out and crouched low so the kids could pet him.

"George." Henry's voice cracked as he petted the cat's head gently.

Bob and Carol did, too, murmuring sweet nothings to him.

George patiently allowed them their due.

A huge crack of sound from one of the band members' electric guitars, followed by earsplitting reverb, jolted everyone on the pier from the speakers wired above the crowd, including George. He leapt from the trainer's arms and raced between Lacey's legs straight out of the trailer and into the crowd.

"*George!*" Lacey and the children yelled.

Carol burst into tears.

"Stay here," Lacey told the kids. "I'll find him."

"I have to stay," the trainer said, his face stricken. "I'm so sorry. I shouldn't have taken him out."

"It's my fault," Henry said, his chin wobbling.

Bob was mute, but his eyes were big.

"It's not anyone's fault." Lacey spoke calmly, although her stomach was in knots. They couldn't lose their favorite cat in the world. "He probably hasn't gone far."

But it was dark, and there was so much noise and movement. No cat wanted to be around that. She wished she could find Beau. Mike was on the stage now, giving a nice speech, but she could barely listen, she was so frantic in her search for George.

Once she made a full circle, she returned to the trailer to see if he'd somehow come back.

"No," said the trainer.

The kids were crying.

"I'm going back out." Her tone was still calm. Being a mom required a lot of good acting skills sometimes. She'd never realized until she'd become one. "Have faith. George isn't stupid. He's probably hiding until the party's over."

What a night.

Only three minutes later, she got a big shock: "Lacey and Henry Clark, report to the cat trailer" came over the pier loudspeakers.

What could that mean? Surely, Henry wasn't out looking for George, too, in this crowd.

When she got back, she saw a security guard with the trainer, Bob, and Carol.

But there was no Henry.

"Where's Henry?" she asked the trainer, her heart in her throat.

"He ran off before I could stop him." His expression

was miserable. "I left the cats and went after him, too. But he disappeared so fast."

"We yelled at him to come back." Carol wrung her hands.

"I held on to him," said Bob, "but he was mad."

"I've already alerted the entire security staff to look out for him," the security guard said. "He's here somewhere, so don't be alarmed."

"Of course, I'm alarmed." Lacey's voice shook. "Call for him again on the loudspeaker."

The guard radioed someone to do just that. But after one minute, when Henry still hadn't shown up, Lacey ran back out into the crowd.

"Henry!" she called, terrified.

Why was the party still going on? Didn't people realize what was happening? Apparently, security did and wanted to spread the word. Another loudspeaker message was broadcast: "Will all partygoers look around them for a small boy, age five, Henry Clark, in a tuxedo. He has curly brown hair, is of medium-brown complexion, and is in search of a cat missing from the animal trailer . . ."

Oh, God. This was Lacey's worst nightmare.

But at least everyone was looking. Well, not everyone. There were pockets of people laughing and drinking as if they hadn't heard the announcement. The party hadn't stopped. The band kept playing.

She'd been so worried about George, but that was nothing compared with this. What if someone had walked off with her boy? Was there any way he could have lifted himself up on the pier railing and fallen over?

The fear was so deep, she could barely see. *Don't panic*, she told herself. Henry wasn't stupid. He had a good head on his shoulders. He wouldn't go over the railing. He wouldn't go off with a stranger.

But would he disobey her and leave the pier on his own to look for George?

If he had, how come he hadn't been found yet?

She was about to burst from fear when someone grabbed her arm.

It was Beau.

Her rock, she realized.

CHAPTER THIRTY-SEVEN

"We'll find him," he said. "They've already found George, and he's back in his cage."

"Thank God for that," she said, but her arm was knocking so hard against his side that she worried she was going to fall down. Her knees were gone. Absolutely gone. "He's not here anymore. He's left the pier. I can feel it. I've already searched the length of it five times, and no one reported seeing him when his description came over the loudspeaker."

Beau felt her fear, and his own, too, moving slowly through him, like an ice floe traveling across an Arctic bay.

It was a pitch-black night, but the beach around them was softly illuminated by the pier itself and the nearby lights of the town. No one was in sight on the beach. The yawning blackness on either side of the light field didn't bode well.

"A lot of people are looking," he said, "Mom and Walker included. The police have already been notified. We're going to find him, okay? Believe me. And in case you're wondering why they're not stopping the party, the last thing we need is a mass exodus of cars."

She couldn't speak.

Ricky came up then, the man from the fun park—Beau's half brother. "Here's a flashlight from one of the security guards. I've got a portable LED spotlight in my van. It's battery-powered and charged. I'll be right back."

"We can't wait that long," Beau said. "Get it and start walking toward the lighthouse. That's where we're headed right now. We've already got people fanning out in the opposite direction on the beach, just in case he went that way. And the police are setting up a checkpoint to screen all cars leaving the vicinity. They're also driving to the lighthouse right now and walking from there toward the pier. We'll get him somewhere in the middle."

Lacey gave a little cry.

"We're going to find him," Beau assured her.

"Without a doubt," Ricky said, and took off.

"Of course he's headed to the lighthouse," she said. "But look how far away it is."

"I know," Beau said grimly. "But if you were Henry looking for George, how would you think?"

"I'd think that George went home. Home to his couch."

"Exactly."

He sensed renewed hope in her. As scary as that blackness ahead was, at least there was a target at the end of it, one that even a little boy could see alone on the vast expanse of sand . . .

The lighthouse.

Together they stumbled down the sand dunes onto the hard, flat beach. The tide was out. Henry could be anywhere on either side of them for a hundred yards each way.

Away from the pier lights, the moon glow was more evident, although it was only a sickle in the sky, floating amid a vast expanse of stars.

"Henry!" Beau called with all his might, and sprayed the flashlight over the beach in a constant back-and-forth motion.

Lacey called her son's name, too, over and over.

But the roar of the ocean muffled their voices.

It broke Beau's heart that Lacey was crying softly, but still she trudged ahead, her steps unflagging.

"We're gonna get him," Beau said. "Never fear."

"I'm glad you're here," she said, her voice throaty, almost unrecognizable.

"Me, too," he said. "I was looking for y'all all night. I was besieged with reporters and well-wishers, but I just wanted you and Henry."

Still they moved forward, calling Henry's name, but with no luck. And then they heard a shout behind them, saw a light wobbling back and forth. It was Ricky, running with the portable spotlight.

He caught up with them, and boy, did the power of that spotlight make it easier to search. Another two long agonizing minutes went by when Lacey saw a shadow. *Two* shadows.

"There's something over there!" she said, pointing far ahead, closer to the water than the dunes. "Shine it that way!"

Ricky did, and sure enough, there was a small figure, still unrecognizable as Henry but moving forward—toward the lighthouse. And next to him was a larger, taller figure. In the distance, Beau could see wobbly lights heading their way. The police were already on the beach.

"Keep the light on them." Beau immediately took off. Behind him he heard Lacey running after him. Ricky, too, must have been jogging, because the light illuminating the boy and what looked like an adult got brighter and brighter.

"Henry!" Beau cried. "It's Mr. Wilder and your mother. We've got George!"

The small figure stopped moving and turned. Beau could see a splash of white on his chest—Henry's tuxedo shirt. The taller figure was stooped and thin.

Dickey.

"Stay there, Henry! Dickey, don't move!" Beau's heart surged with a desire to protect that boy, to put him in time-out, to hug him close, and chew him out for scaring them so. And he wanted to do just about the same thing to Dickey.

Thank God the old man was with Henry. Not that he was much protection—hell, he might have been the one who got the kid into the mess in the first place.

Beau would withhold judgment until he knew more.

"Henry!" Lacey cried. "Henry, stay right there!"

Finally, Beau was upon them. Henry grabbed on to him and held tighter than a barnacle.

Lacey gave one wild sob, and then she was on Henry, too, hugging him close. "George is okay. You shouldn't have run off like that. You should have waited for me."

Beau stepped back and let her hold Henry tight. Her voice was shaky, but she was in control. He could tell she didn't want to freak Henry out too much.

"Don't cry, Mom," Henry said, crying a little himself. "I was only going home to the lighthouse. I knew George was, too. I was going to pick him up there and wait for you to get us. Dickey came with me, so I was okay."

Beau looked at Dickey, who was nervous as hell, shaking his head. "I saw him scoot out from under a rope on the pier to look for that cat and told him there were bad guys in the dark. But he wouldn't believe me. So I went with him. He was going to go alone, and I didn't have time to let anyone know."

"Don't you have a cell phone?" Beau asked him.

There was silence for a moment.

"Aw, hell." Dickey shook his head again.

"He forgets about it," Lacey told Beau. "Only Junior

Earnhardt calls him." She looked up at him. "Thank you, Dickey. I know you meant well. And if you could stop telling lies—I don't know if you can, but I hope you try—maybe next time Henry will believe you when you tell him there are bad guys in the dark."

"I'll try," said Dickey. "I'll more than try. I'll outright stop."

"You have every reason to," Lacey reminded him. "Look how many people love you. If you want to make up stories, do it on paper like me."

Beau was dying to ask what she meant by that.

She shook Henry's shoulders. "You should never go off on your own. Dickey was telling you the truth."

"Yes, Mom." Henry's eyes, even in the dark, were visibly wide.

Rick came up, shut down the light, called someone. "We found him," he said. "Yeah. he's fine. Got an old man with him. A friend. Right. Turning around now."

He put the flashlight back on, and they walked down the beach, back to the pier. Lacey held Henry's hand the whole way, and they talked softly about normal things, like what songs they were playing at the party and whether Henry could have some food from one of the tables. He asked Beau what he'd been doing since they saw him last, and Beau was glad to tell him about Canada and Los Angeles. Dickey didn't say a word. Neither did Rick, but Beau was extremely grateful to him for his quiet support.

"Do they have stars like this in Canada and Los Angeles?" Henry asked him.

Beau looked up. "No. I've never seen a place with shinier stars than Indigo Beach. I think they cut them out of tinfoil here and throw them up into the sky."

Henry giggled. So did Dickey. Lacey did, too, surprisingly.

There was a lot to celebrate.

Beau could breathe a sigh of relief. Mother, son, and Dickey were okay. Hell, even the cat was.

He was the one in trouble now.

CHAPTER THIRTY-EIGHT

The party was still in full swing when they got back to the pier. Before Lacey could thank him for his help, Beau was accosted by several reporters. Lacey was left to get Dickey back to Simone, Bob, Carol, and Mike.

Mike and Simone were totally freaked out by what had happened, and as jittery as Lacey still was, it touched her to see how much they cared about both Dickey and Henry. Mike hugged the two wanderers close, his eyes filled with tears. "How could you do this in the middle of the party?"

"George," Henry explained.

"George was fine," Mike said. "Dickey—" He stared at his father-in-law with such despair and worry.

"I already got an earful from Lacey," Dickey said. "I'm gonna beat my own ass if I lie to anyone again. And someone is going to have to teach me how to use my phone."

Simone quietly handed Mike a tissue, then got down on her haunches and held Henry's hands. "I'm so glad you're back," she said. "Will you come out to California for our wedding?"

"Whose wedding?" Henry's little face still registered some anxiety from his ordeal.

"Mine and Mr. Carter's." Simone grinned at him.

Henry smiled back. "Really?"

"Uh-huh." She stood and looked at Lacey, her expression as droll as ever, but her eyes shining.

"Wow." Lacey hugged her tight. "I'm so happy for you two! When did this happen?"

Simone made a feeble fight to get away. "When we got back to California, I hung around the family a lot. And . . . we clicked."

"Big-time." Mike pulled Simone away from Lacey and kissed her.

Simone—would miracles never cease?—went along with the fervent PDA, and when it was over actually sighed happily. "Dickey's the best man. I want you to be my maid of honor, Lacey."

"Of course."

They fist-bumped.

"I always thought I wanted a gothic wedding." Simone chuckled. "But we're doing motorcycles instead. You'll get to ride one again. Won't that be cool? Henry can be in the sidecar."

"I can't wait." Lacey laughed. She couldn't escape Greta if she tried.

Henry, Bob, and Carol were yelling, "Wedding! Wedding!" and jumping up and down.

But then Henry abruptly stopped. "I want to check on George. I'm hungry. And I want to go to bed."

So the evening ended soon thereafter. Lacey never got to catch up with Beau. She had no idea if she'd see him again before he left, either. What if he had a plane waiting for him at the airport?

Of course he did. Either that, or he was going to stay with his mom.

Maybe if she found his mom, she could pass on a message . . .

But apparently, Mrs. Wilder and her escort had already left the party.

She was so tempted to call him. His number was still in her phone. But if she did, he'd get the wrong message.

"We need to write Mr. Wilder a thank-you note," she told Henry when she tucked him into bed. "And his friend Rick, too. For helping us."

"Okay," he said, and grabbed her hand. "Mom, did you ever finish that story?"

With his little hand in hers, she tortured herself with the thought that she had nearly lost him that evening. Thank God she hadn't. "I'm almost done," she assured him. "And when I do, you're the first person I'm going to read it to." More than ever, she was burning to finish *Two White Vans* for her boy.

"Okay, I hope it's soon," Henry murmured. "I want to know how I can be in two cars at the same time. And why am I holding up a sign that says, HELP ME?"

"You're going to have to be patient and find out," she said pertly. She kissed his forehead and turned out the light.

The next morning, a knock came at the RV door, bright and early. Lacey sat up in bed. For all she knew, it could be Sheena and Walt. Or even Patrick from California, here to pick up the ambulance.

She peeked out between two curtains, and her heart jangled like a fire alarm when she saw it was Beau.

Her rock.

Her man.

She wanted to tell him—*so badly*.

Greta would. Greta would grab him by the lapels and lay a fat kiss on him, then say what she had to say, come what may.

But it was too early in the morning for that.

Wasn't it?

She wrapped herself up in a polyester silk kimono robe and pushed the door open.

"Hey," she said, and couldn't help a big smile. He looked so good.

"Look at you." He squinted up at her. "Early-morning sunshine. I wake ya?"

"Yes." She kept grinning.

"I wish I'd been there with you."

"Me, too." She held out her hand and pulled.

He walked inside.

And before they could say anything else, he wrapped her whole body in his and kissed her.

It was just right.

And simple, too. Everything could be so damned easy if she let go and let it.

He pulled back. "I love you."

It was as natural to hear that from him as it was to breathe, she thought. "I love you, too," she said back, the words as inevitable as the tide washing up and over the beach each day, scrubbing it clean of footprints and sand castles, seaweed and shells, and making it new.

His eyes were full of mischief. "I came to take you two to breakfast."

"You did?"

He grinned. "Yep. You're not cooking this time."

"My, my."

He opened her robe and stared at her Donald Duck T-shirt and scarlet boxers. "Damn."

"You're making me blush."

"You'd better go get Henry before I take you outside to that ambulance and have my way with you in the back."

"Not a bad idea."

Thirty minutes later, after Henry finally got a move

on, they were bumping along the sandy drive to the light-house.

"Breakfast is *here*?" Henry sat between them, his legs poking out straight for some reason, instead of dangling over the side of the seat.

"Breakfast, lunch, and dinner, as a matter of fact," said Beau. He pulled the ambulance to the back.

What? Lacey stared at him. But his expression was impassive.

"Hurry up, Mom." But Henry couldn't wait. He leapt over her lap to get out and ran straight to Timothy Brenner's old handprint in the concrete and put his hand inside. "That's the secret signal to my superpower friends," he said when Lacey and Beau joined him. "Now they know I'm back."

"Great," said Beau. "What are you going to do when your hand gets bigger?"

Henry scratched his chin. "I don't know."

Beau laced his hand with hers, and Lacey was so happy, she could barely feel herself walk over the scrubby grass and sand to the front door, which was now painted red. Smelled pretty darned fresh, too.

"Don't touch it," Beau warned them.

Pink geraniums—in blue pots, no less—waited on either side.

"What's happening?" Lacey asked, her pulse thrumming in her wrists, her temples.

"I told you," said Beau. "Breakfast." Carefully, he grasped the knob and pushed the door wide open. "Come on in."

They let Henry go first, but Lacey was right behind.

"George!" Henry cried.

There he was, sitting on his couch, looking like he'd never left it. And on the coffee table in front of the cat were a bunch of framed pictures of family: Beau's mom and Walker; Sheena and Walt at Fort Sumter; Henry in the surf with Lacey; Beau and Lacey and Henry on the sailboat in Charleston Harbor; even one of the trailer gang from the studio. They were family, too.

Lacey swallowed a lump in her throat. "This is amazing," she said with wonder, then turned and looked at the kitchen, where the table was set for three. Coffee had been brewed, the oven registered that it was on, keeping something buttery-smelling—and maybe something hickory-smoked—warm inside. Three glasses of orange juice waited on the counter.

"Take a seat," Beau said.

Henry yanked out his chair. Lacey sat down carefully, her wrists a little trembly. She was so overwhelmed with surprise and love, she could barely speak. Beau went to the oven, pulled out a tray of biscuits, a bowl of scrambled eggs, and some fine, crispy bacon, and put them on the table.

"I love Bojangles," he said, when he added a big spoon to the eggs.

Lacey laughed.

They took turns passing everything around.

"Just like the old days," said Henry, chomping on a piece of bacon.

"Don't talk with your mouth full," Lacey reminded him for the umpteenth time.

"I think I'm gonna run today," Beau said. "It's fine weather. And then maybe go surfing. You wanna go with me, Henry?"

"Sure," Henry said. "But we have to leave, don't we? And Mom sold my surfboard."

"I got it back." Beau acted like they were discussing the weather. "Your mom's, too."

"You did?" Lacey put her hand over her heart. "How'd you know I pawned them?"

Beau looked at Henry, then pointed at his head. "Dudley. He knows everything."

"Yeah, Mom," Henry said with a grin.

Lacey put her fork down. "Uh, what else did you know about us while you were gone?"

Beau looked innocent. "Nothing. Except you stayed in your RV. I have to wonder about that."

"Why, pray tell?" She cast a sideways glance at him.

He shrugged. "There was this cool beach house to stay in where the kids got surfing lessons and the moms got great private apartments. All you had to do was *apply*."

Lacey's stomach dropped. "That huge ad about the home for single mothers in the *Indigo Beach Times* was *you*?"

"Not me. My foundation."

Lacey dropped her chin on her hand. "You're a piece of work. I didn't *need* your help, Beau. Henry and I did just fine, didn't we, Henry?"

"Sure, we did," he said. "But I wish I'd known about those surfing lessons."

"You don't need 'em," Beau said. "T'll be giving them to you—that is, if your mother agrees."

Lacey pushed back her chair and stood. "Please make yourself clear, Beau Wilder. Because you can't charm me into losing my girl power, okay? I need full consent to whatever's going on here. Or . . . or—"

He stood up, too. "Or you'll go," he said simply.

"*Mom*." Henry looked between them both.

"I-I don't want to," said Lacey. "But I can't live being second fiddle to a movie star. I need to be the star of my own life, and if that sounds selfish, I'm sorry. But it's time I pay attention to what I have inside me, too. Or it'll all go to waste."

Beau came to her and wrapped his arms around her

waist. "I agree completely. Which is why I'm asking you, not telling you: Will you stay here all day today for breakfast, lunch, and dinner? And will you go surfing with me? You'd make me so happy if you would. George would like you to stay, too."

Her eyes stung. "Yes. I'll do that." It wasn't too much to ask. "Henry, too."

Beau smiled. "All right," he said, as if he'd just achieved a huge victory.

It made Lacey feel kinda important. She grinned.

"Yes!" Henry jumped from his chair. "George, we're staying *all day*!"

George really didn't give a hoot, but he pretended to when Henry came over and scratched his ears.

Lacey grabbed Beau's hand. "I'm still a little confused. Why is George here? How can we stay all day?"

His face went from light and happy to ultra-serious in less than a split second.

Very gently, he pulled a tendril of hair from her face. "If I have to ask you every day for the rest of my life whether you'll stay for breakfast, lunch, and dinner, I will. I want you with me."

He took both her hands. "But I never want to take you for granted. I can't promise, my darling, that we will have breakfast, lunch, and dinner in the same place every day. You know I want it to be here at the lighthouse. Nancy said she's only too happy to turn it over to us if we want it. And George's trainer said we can try to own him, too."

"Really?"

Beau nodded. "But life has a way of getting crazy. You think you got it all figured out, and then wham—something new hits."

"Don't I know it," she murmured, thinking about last

night, about their first night together in the lighthouse, and everything that had happened in between.

"But whatever happens and wherever we are," he said deliberately, "I want to be with you and Henry. You're both my life. Last night made that very clear. You come first, no matter what."

She held up their laced hands and kissed his knuckles. "Home is where you are," she said. "As long as you're with us, we are *fine*."

"Ain't that the truth," he said, his eyes filled with love and hope.

Everything good.

He kissed her, and she was whole.

"You guys!" Henry protested. "Stop!"

George narrowed his eyes in their direction.

Lacey laughed and pulled Beau over to the couch. She patted it. "Take a seat, sweetheart."

"I don't know," Beau said, eyeing George askance.

But he sat down, and Lacey was positive it was because he was lured by her charm—and wasn't that awesome! She put George in his lap—and tried not to think too hard of what those jeans were shielding from her gaze—and Henry crawled onto hers.

She took in all the family pictures—such a treasure trove of them—and wrapped her arm through Beau's. "Do you own a *Waltons* DVD?"

"Yes. I like the end where they all say good night. And that Grandma—she's a firecracker."

"Dang." Lacey considered him a moment. "I caught me a good one, didn't I, Henry?"

"Yes," he shouted in glee.

Beau high-fived him. "You said it, not me, Miz Clark. Remember that."

"I'm never gonna forget." Lacey laughed. "Ready, guys?"

"Yep," said Henry, swinging his legs.

"As I'll ever be." Beau felt George's slow, steady breathing under his palm.

They leaned back into the cushions, gazed at the sunbeam falling on the table from the kitchen window, and listened to the waves and the gulls welcoming them home.

Read on for an excerpt from Kieran Kramer's next book

Trouble

WHEN YOU WALKED IN

Coming soon from St. Martin's Paperbacks

CHAPTER ONE

Cissie Rogers was back in large print fiction with Mrs. Hattlebury when she heard the front door of the Kettle Knob library open and a woman's laughter fill the air.

A woman's *fake* laughter, which trailed off on an artificial sigh.

Cissie's skin prickled. There was only one person in western North Carolina who laughed like that: Janelle Montgomery. As a kid, she'd been just as smart as she was pretty, but starting in seventh grade, she'd given up trying to win the spelling bee and the science fair. Cheerleading became her thing, that and wrapping boys around her little finger.

Now Janelle had wrapped a whole town around her little finger. She was mayor of Campbell, the neighboring town.

"Boone Braddock," Cissie heard Janelle say, "Stop it. Stop it right this instant."

Cissie stopped breathing. *Boone Braddock was in the library?* Her palms instantly dampened. And her lower belly—contrary to her wishes—began a slow tingling burn of awareness.

What did Janelle want Boone to stop? Kissing her? Being too hot for his own good?

"Where's the librarian?" Boone's whiskey-and-gravel voice made Cissie's heart race, and not because he was too loud for the library, which he was.

"Rumor has it those two were caught doing it like rabbits up near Frazier Lake in broad daylight last week," Mrs. Hattlebury whispered loudly in Cissie's ear. "But Deputy Scotty let 'em off the hook. He has to, don't you know."

"I hate mayors," Cissie said. Sexual frustration made her ornery. "They think the rules don't apply to them."

She wished *she* could have sex by Frazier Lake—but not with Boone. He couldn't even remember her name. With Mr. Darcy. Too bad he wasn't real. Maybe if she dressed up Boone like Darcy—

No. They were nothing alike.

"All politicians are that way," Mrs. Hattlebury reminded her.

"Especially mayors," Cissie declared. She knew she was making no sense, but she didn't care. When it came to Boone and Janelle, she was a mass of petty insecurities, and she indulged them freely, the way she couldn't stop herself from eating freshly popped popcorn, no matter how full she was.

"You don't really hate all mayors, do you, dear?" Mrs. Hattlebury asked too politely, which meant she thought Cissie might be a tad touched, as they said around here—like Cissie's maternal grandfather Pappy.

"No." She made a comic face and tried to chuckle. "Of course not. I-I need some caffeine. The library coffee pot broke."

She needed a man, too, but surely her bitterness was all about temporary chemical withdrawal.

"Maybe it's just Janelle who gets on your nerves," Mrs. Hattlebury said thoughtfully. "She's a bit full of herself. But not Boone. He's the best man in this town three hundred sixty-four days of the year. He does have his moments on that other day. But we love him, don't we?"

Cissie turned red. "He's an, um, adequate public servant." But she was thinking of him in those jeans of his and that indescribable place where his faded zipper flap rode like a roller coaster over some pretty impressive terrain. He was more than adequate in that department. She was evil for having noticed, but she had sunglasses on at the time, so it was okay.

"Adequate?" Mrs. Hattlebury drew in her chin. "Why, Boone's smile lights up every room he enters! Don't forget his great-great-great-great-granddaddy—"

"I *know*," Cissie interrupted rudely, but how many times in her lifetime was she going to hear about Silas Braddock leading a ragtag unit from Kettle Knob down to King's Mountain during the Revolutionary War and springing a surprise attack on an isolated British outpost and soundly defeating them?

The Revolutionary-era Rogers clan had been reading books, writing letters, and analyzing poetry at the time of the raid in the privacy of their home in Kettle Knob. No one had knocked on *their* door to ask for help at King's Mountain. But avid scholars that they were, they made sure to record the event after interviewing every man who'd gone. And they'd dutifully given the account to the library for safekeeping.

Mrs. Hattlebury pressed on. "Sandra Lee and Frank, God love 'em, bought the high school brand-new band instruments last week."

Boone's father Frank was loud as a tuba. His mother

Sandra Lee was shrill as an off-key trumpet. Not only did they never shut up, they couldn't sit still. They were the Tasmanian devils of western North Carolina. Wherever they spun their influence, dirt clods went flying—usually at the groundbreaking of one of their mountain golf resorts—and they made lots of money.

"They've never contributed a dime to the Friends of the Library fund." Cissie couldn't believe she said that out loud. You weren't supposed to talk bad about that family.

"But, honey." Mrs. Hattlebury's eyes softened in pity. "They're Braddocks. You're a Rogers. And ne'er the twain shall meet. Surely you understand. We've all learned to appreciate the distinction. You each bring your own special gifts to Kettle Knob and live in harmony." She paused. "Don't you?"

If totally ignoring each other was harmony, then yes.

Mrs. Hattlebury kissed her good-bye, and Cissie sighed herself, a real sigh. She was tired all of a sudden—tired from staying up late with Pappy last night and tired of the way everyone in this town was slapped with a label like a bunch of canning jars lined up on a shelf from the time they left the womb. She didn't know why she'd ever come back—except of course she knew why.

She loved the smell of pine sap in the morning. The call of a mama bear to its cubs from far off. The way the mountains rolled like giant waves toward the Rogers home, humble as it was. And she loved the people here. There were damned few phonies. They looked out for each other, yet they were also fiercely independent.

Mountain stock.

There was nothing like it.

"Well, hello, Miss Librarian," gushed Janelle in her tight pink sweater, fluffy silk scarf, white jeans, and heels—you know what kind.

And then there was Boone in those inappropriate jeans

of his and brown boots. A serious mayor didn't wear Levis and Carhartts—and then have the temerity to look like an Abercrombie and Fitch model! Nor did he have dimples when he grinned. And he most certainly didn't spend half his time on a football field exhorting boys with perfectly good brains to smash into each other and risk getting concussions.

Inside, Cissie's heart thumped madly. Her petty insecurities were so bad right now, she tilted her head and smiled her best librarian's smile ever—close-lipped, helpful—to suppress thoughts like, *Why, oh, why don't I ever pluck my eyebrows?* And *Maybe I should shop at someplace other than the SPCA thrift shop.*

She wasn't much into beauty tricks. Or fashion.

But she *was* into books. She could go on *Jeopardy!* and win the Daily Double if it was about books. She could literally kick anyone's ass in a book take-down. She didn't know what that was—yet—but it sounded kind of fun. Something involving a boxing ring, a roped boundary she could bounce off, and an opponent to shout down in the middle of the ring when the ref asked questions about the top ten hardcovers on *The New York Times* list.

"How can I help you?" she asked.

If Boone hadn't been so lucky all his life, his gaze these days should have turned slightly stupid, even cross-eyed, considering all the tackles he'd endured in high school.

But no.

When she looked into his eyes, she was brought back all the way to fourth grade, when he'd given her an apple from his lunchbox with a tiny heart carved into it with his thumbnail. He'd liked her for about five minutes. And then he'd moved on to some other girl—literally—by the time she'd finished eating that apple.

Maybe she shouldn't have eaten it. Maybe he'd wanted

her to save it until the skin grew wrinkled and the tiny heart yellowed.

What did she know about romance? Nothing!

"We've got some interesting news," he informed her.

His lethal levels of testosterone, combined with a shockingly clear-eyed confidence and his scarily ambiguous use of the word *interesting,* made Cissie's temples thrum.

Do you know my name? she wondered. *How could you have you forgotten that apple? And why are you here with news of any sort when you don't even have a library card?*

"It's good news," said Janelle, her glossy pink mouth bowed up.

Uh-oh. If Janelle thought it was good, Cissie would probably hate it. And the fact that they were here at all . . .

Something wasn't right.

But Boone was here. Boone, in her library! It was worth noting in her geeky girl journal that night. She was on her fifty-fifth black-and-white marble composition book. She'd started them in sixth grade.

Cissie tilted her head the other way, like an excruciatingly slow metronome, because she had no idea how to stand, how to project confidence, how to *wow* the way Janine and Boone did. "And what news is this, may I ask?"

Ugh. She sounded like a prissy schoolmarm, or a spinster librarian, which she was—but she wasn't a fossil. She refused to be a fossil. That happened when you had no lusty thoughts left. She had lusty thoughts. She had them all the time—

About this guy, who was currently skewering her with the most compelling look she'd ever seen in her life: powerful, calm, and somehow penetrating to her very soul—

As if he got her.

There was no way he got her. But it felt like it. Probably because she was desperate and imagining things.

"For budget reasons," he said, "the county wants Kettle Knob and Campbell to merge libraries."

Cissie's heart froze. Then a panicky thought galloped through her head like Paul Revere on his horse: *The legend of the library will end with me. The legend of the library will end with me!*

No more librarians would find their true loves here.

Sally Jo Moore even hoped the legend applied to library volunteers. "'Cause my heart's in the right place," she said on a regular basis, eyeing the front door hopefully through heavily mascaraed lashes. "I'da been a librarian if I hadn't met Satan's spawn at the Dollar Tree. But I got my angel Hank Davis as a result, so I never regret it. No, I don't."

Wait until Sally Jo came in with Hank Davis later and heard the news! She might even drop to the ground, she'd be so devastated. And how would she and Hank Davis get to the other place? They'd need a car.

Cissie's jaw locked like an anaconda.

"We'd use the storefront next to Harris Teeter," Boone went on, "halfway between the two towns, so everyone can stop by when they pick up their groceries." His dimples came out—as if *that* show of charm would make his statements less shocking and egregious.

Cissie's face heated up like a hot plate. The legend didn't matter. It was only a silly story, built on a fluke of fate. She'd explain to Sally Jo that it wasn't worth losing sleep over. What mattered was the preservation of Kettle Knob's historic library.

Yes, that was what mattered!

"But that place used to be a tattoo parlor," she croaked, "and before that, a bar."

Her ancestors would roll over in their graves if their precious historical documents were housed in a place that lacked dignity and decorum.

"Think how many more book customers you'll get," Boone said. "Plus, your inventory will increase when you team up with Campbell. The budget for new books will go down ten percent, I'm sorry to say, but that's okay. Because if we stay here, we'll lose fifty percent of it. The rest would have to go to upkeep of this old house, and the county thinks that's not an efficient use of funds."

Blah blah blah. Too much information, way too fast. But Cissie was a Rogers. She could think on her feet. . . .

Too bad she couldn't think. It was that damned legend her heart was hammering about. Sally Jo would lose hope of finding the right man. Pappy would go to his grave without dancing at Cissie's wedding. And she'd never meet her soul mate.

Not that the legend was *real*.

But books were. Books and historical documents. And Sally Jo's lack of car.

"I-I can get the Friends of the Library to help with the upkeep," Cissie said. "They already do help a great deal, but we can raise more money. If everyone chips in, we should be fine. This building is on the historic register. It's worth saving." She looked pointedly at Boone, whose family could save the library by writing a single check, but his handsome, brown-eyed gaze merely flickered with mayoral impatience and sex static, which was always humming within him, like an old transistor radio left on by accident.

"This building could see other uses." Janelle tossed off the library's long history with ease, the same way she flung her shiny curls over her shoulder. "It's time we have a place where the communities of Campbell and Kettle Knob can interact and share resources." She sounded so phony. *Like that's a big surprise*, thought Cissie. "We'll have the opportunity to read, research"—Janelle cast a meaningful look at Boone—"and enjoy our archival documents. Together."

Only Janelle could make going to the library sound like a sex act.

Cissie was about to sneeze. She always did when she was unduly agitated. She turned away, held her breath, and by some miracle got the sneeze under control. But the tiny break was enough to remind herself that a Rogers always sounded reasonable. They won things with their heads.

"Those were Rogers papers," she reminded Janelle, "bequeathed to the town of Kettle Knob. Campbell didn't send anyone to King's Mountain, nor are they represented in any of our archival documents, except in passing reference as a neighboring town."

Campbell thought it was hot stuff because the Grey Poupon man from the legendary 1980s commercial came from there.

"He ugly," Sally Jo always said.

And a super famous female pop star with current hits went to grade school in Campbell.

"She's a beeyotch," Sally Jo insisted only yesterday. "She didn't contribute to UNICEF. I sent her agent uh onvolope with all these pretty children on it, and he musta thrown it away."

And a lot of rich people lived there, too, in Boone's parents' original fancy golf resort, which was now old enough that it was described in the newspaper's crime column as an "established high-end neighborhood" every time someone got their leaf blower stolen or their Mercedes keyed. Most Campbell residents commuted to their doctor and attorney jobs in Asheville and only came to places like Kettle Knob to feel like they'd gone backwards a hundred years for a few minutes.

And now Campbell had attracted a high-tech research facility with international connections.

But apart from that, Campbell was boring.

"Campbell don't even have a good scenic overlook for

couples to make out at," Sally said every Valentine's Day, which was when the Campbell Country Club held its annual two-hundred-fifty-bucks-a-ticket black-tie gala to benefit heart research. "Every mountain town should have at least one."

"That King's Mountain raid was definitely a Kettle Knob thing," Boone agreed with Cissie now. "But. . . ."

But?

His family had led the local charge in the historic battle. Cissie's family had documented it.

There were no buts!

She told him all that with her eyes. But he didn't appear to be able to read her anymore, if he ever had. Probably because Janelle crossed her arms so that her breasts nearly spilled out of the top of her sweater. Boone didn't exactly look at them, but they were like the elephant in the room—two DDD-sized elephants.

"Campbell never bothered to save journals from the Civil War, either," Cissie went on doggedly. "We have nine leather-bound Civil War–era journals in our collection."

All donated by the Rogers family.

Janelle's mouth soured. "Campbell was too busy to record anything."

It was too busy being high on itself, like you, Cissie wanted to say. But she was a coward. And maybe she was wrong about Janelle being a narcissist. After all, everyone had been wrong about Cissie in high school. She wasn't nerdy. Much.

"Listen." Janelle dropped her arms. With her boobs back into place, tension eased a tad. "It's time to put old rivalries behind us. Think of it this way: *Buncombe County* sent a regiment to King's Mountain. We're not going to get nitpicky about where those citizens lived, are we?"

Okay, so Cissie was on the right track about Janelle, and surely, Boone wasn't okay with this plan.

"You gotta admit, it's hard to find this place," he said.

He'd never found it, that was for sure. "It hasn't changed location in almost two hundred years," Cissie snapped.

He shrugged his square, manly shoulders. "You're tucked away behind Main Street. But if we move right off the interstate? The library will be hopping. Kettle Knob's history will be more accessible than ever to more people. It's a win all around."

Cissie's ears burned, and her tummy flopped around like a fish. Something was happening to her fingernails, too. She'd never felt them before, but now they were all tingly and buzzy, and the sensation was going up her arms.

"I know what this is about," she said.

Getting into Janelle's pants. Spreading the Braddock glory. That was Boone's win-win.

"Better resources for Kettle Knob and Campbell," he replied like it was a no-brainer. "Progress despite trying times."

Cissie's tongue felt thick and stupid. She turned to Janelle, hoping she'd have better luck addressing her. *Don't think sleeping with our mayor means you're going to get your hands on our precious Kettle Knob documents*, she wanted to say. *Don't think that Campbell can boss us around. And don't you dare think you can ruin our stupid legend.*

But she couldn't get the words out.

The truth was, some part of her must have really believed in fate. Deep inside, beneath her logical brain and her tendency to bluster, she'd thought she'd find true love *here*, at the library, with a stranger who walked across the threshold and swept her off her feet.

She was such a schmuck.

Mama had been the Kettle Knob librarian, working on her Ph.D. part-time, when Daddy came to a writers' retreat at nearby Appalachian State and ventured to Kettle

Knob to check out the historic library, only to fall in love instead.

They might be in Cambridge, England, now, researching esoteric subjects and lecturing for three years, but they wanted grandchildren. She knew this because last week her mother had called and said, "I'm writing a thesis on A.A. Milne's *Winnie the Pooh*. Did you know he went to Cambridge?" which surely was a broad hint.

And if Cissie had to sleep alone the rest of her life because karma boomeranged on her for not keeping the legend going, she'd be unhappy, to put it mildly. She imagined she'd start muttering under her breath and yelling at children. She might even die behind her desk at the old tattoo parlor-turned-library.

"Start preparing," said Janelle. "It's gonna happen."

"Over my dead body," Cissie eked out in a trembling whisper. In her head she said it the way a scary, possessed person would have, in a voice that came from the depths of hell.

But no. She couldn't manage that. A Rogers stayed calm and logical. Except for Pappy. He was a throwback to some earlier rabble-rousing generation, probably from medieval times.

"Suzie—" Boone said.

"*Cissie.*"

"I meant Cissie—"

Too late. He was the mayor. And he'd given her that apple. He should be ashamed of himself. How many were in their high school graduating class? A hundred twenty? And they'd been together for twelve years, most of them?

On shaking legs she stalked past him and Janelle to her desk, where she sat down with a plonk and stared stonily at the front door. She felt very alone.

If ever her soul mate was to show up, now would be a really good time. Especially as time was about to run out